PRAISE FOR DONNA DECKER AND *DANCING IN RED SHOES WILL KILL YOU*

"It took me ten years to understand that the story of the Polytechnique massacre did not belong only to me, but belonged to all those who wanted to bear witness, to understand. My private story, however, does belong to me. And the Polytechnique massacre story is built on thousands of private stories of victims and their families, of the Polytechnique students, teachers, employees, and of all those whose life was transformed on that day. In *Dancing In Red Shoes Will Kill You*, Donna Decker re-imagines private stories to transcend December 6th and bring back to life the memory of my classmates."
—NATHALIE PROVOST, P. Eng., wounded on December 6th, 1989

"December 6, 1989 – a seemingly ordinary winter night – fourteen people are dead at l'École Polytechnique de l'Université de Montréal. Amongst these, my sister: Maud. Possibly, before this date, as important as it was, the phenomena of violence against women still seemed abstract, without face, without soul, of no importance. This 'problem' in our society is all too often summarized as a few editorial lines in a judiciary chronicle or revealed in dark photos of an anonymous body found in a squalid alley.... Until now – Donna Decker's novel offers us the most comprehensive accounting to date of the crime that continues to engage the conscience of a country."
—SYLVIE HAVIERNICK, sister of one of the fourteen victims of the Montreal Massacre

"A beautiful elegy. Decker's debut novel builds bridges through her life-affirming prose. *Dancing in Red Shoes Will Kill You* broke my heart."
—MAUREEN BRADLEY, Associate Professor, Department of Writing, University of Victoria

"From the very first words of her prologue, Donna Decker draws you into the story. You are 'there' before you are fully aware that her beautifully crafted novel is tackling profound issues. I believe that caring about a problem, emotion, without taking action to solve it,

is irrelevant. *Dancing in Red Shoes Will Kill You* is the marriage of emotion and action. Decker's novel underscores the myriad ways in which women's lives are shaped — and too often destroyed — by the inequality that often leads to violence. Her book offers us the chance to delve deeper into conversations about gender inequity and violence against women that must be confronted to ultimately enrich the lives of us all — women and men."
—JODY WILLIAMS, Nobel Peace Prize Laureate (1997), Chair, Nobel Women's Initiative

"This novel, based on the tragic events of December 6th 1989, is an important commemoration of victims of the Montreal Massacre. With convincing characters and meticulous reconstruction of details, Donna Decker shows us that the killer was not a lunatic, but that his actions were a direct consequence of the negative attitude towards women in society. This is a very important point because once you proclaim someone like him a monster, it means he is an exception, and therefore society is not to be blamed for his actions. On the other hand, if you make a reader aware of the atmosphere of hatred towards women, the whole society becomes responsible for his heinous crime. This book is also a strong condemnation of society's negative attitudes towards women's emancipation. I am grateful that Donna Decker, with this book, has made me aware that in modern times, in a civilized country, women were killed just because they were women."
—SLAVENKA DRAKULIĆ, author of *Holograms of Fear, Marble Skin*, and *S. A Novel About the Balkans*

"Each December 6th since 1989, I gather with women working against male violence from Vancouver, Montreal, Moscow, London or Paris to acknowledge the importance of the Montreal Massacre but also to organize a better future for women. Still, Donna Decker, in her novel *Dancing in Red Shoes Will Kill You,* through excellent journalistic research, reveals and conveys some social and political realities that I didn't know. She links historical facts with the story-telling techniques of fiction to help us imagine how other men and women lived those days. Most importantly, she commits to women

and to honesty about this specific group of women. Time, unearthed details, and her feminist sensibility holds out for us a perspective on the truth of those public and private events. Sparked by both the murders and the responses of our institutions, thousands of women took over Canadian streets protesting murderous male rage. After twenty-five years, extreme events of male violence worldwide again illuminate the rape culture that spawns them. Reading this book puts us in good company while we consider when and where to run for shelter from men's violence against women and when and why to defy it."
—LEE LAKEMAN, author of *Obsession, with Intent*

"This historical novel could not be more timely. Anchored in the events of the Montreal Massacre, the book imagines in rich and carefully researched detail the possible lives of the women engineers attacked by the shooter on December 6, 1989, and the lives of their friends, family members, and others affected by the shooting, including engineers, feminists, and even feminist engineers on other campuses. In doing so, the novel does a justice to the women the world lost on that day. In addition to humanizing those affected by the Montreal Massacre, the book expertly contextualizes the misogynist school shooting in the broader settings of sexism in engineering, violence against women on college campuses and gender-based violence more broadly. A must read for anyone seeking to make sense of the all too real connections between gender-based violence and barriers to advancement of women."
—DONNA RILEY, Professor, Department of Engineering Education, Virginia Polytechnic Institute and State University

"This book is immaculately researched, and the characters empathetically imagined. Given the recent media scrutiny of gendered crime on college campuses, it is a must read!"
—KEVIN O'HARA, author of *Last of the Donkey Pilgrims*

# DANCING IN RED SHOES WILL KILL YOU

# DANCING IN RED SHOES WILL KILL YOU

## DONNA DECKER

*Inanna poetry & fiction series*

INANNA PUBLICATIONS AND EDUCATION INC.
TORONTO, CANADA

We gratefully acknowledge the support of the Canada Council for the Arts and the Ontario Arts Council for our publishing program. We also acknowledge the financial support of the Department of Canadian Heritage through the Canada Book Fund.

*Dancing in Red Shoes Will Kill You* is a work of fiction. All the characters and situations portrayed in this book are fictitious and any resemblance to persons living or dead is purely coincidental.

The poem that opens the book, "A Red Shirt" is from *Selected Poems 1966-1984*, by Margaret Atwood, Oxford University Press ©1990. Used with permission by the author.

*Note from the publisher:* Care has been taken to trace the ownership of copyright material used in this book. The author and the publisher welcome any information enabling them to rectify any references or credits in subsequent editions.

Cover design: Val Fullard

Library and Archives Canada Cataloguing in Publication

Decker, Donna, 1956–, author
          Dancing in red shoes will kill you / Donna Decker.

(Inanna poetry and fiction series)
Issued in print and electronic formats.
ISBN 978-1-77133-201-9 (pbk.). — ISBN  978-1-77133-202-6 (epub). —
ISBN 978-1-77133-204-0 (pdf)

          I. Title.  II. Series: Inanna poetry and fiction series

PS3604.E243D35 2015          813'.6          C2015-901837-4
                                                              C2015-901838-2

Printed and bound in Canada

Inanna Publications and Education Inc.
210 Founders College, York University
4700 Keele Street, Toronto, Ontario, Canada M3J 1P3
Telephone: (416) 736-5356 Fax: (416) 736-5765
Email: inanna.publications@inanna.ca Website: www.inanna.ca

MIX
Paper from
responsible sources
FSC® C004071

*To Mary Lou and Ralph Decker who gave me this one life.*
*To Caitlin and Allie and Kellan who gave me a thousand more.*

(for Ruth)

My sister and I are sewing
a red shirt for my daughter.
She pins, I hem, we pass scissors
back & forth across the table.

Children should not wear red,
a man once told me.
Young girls should not wear red.

In some countries it is the colour
of death; in others passion,
in others war, in others anger,
in others sacrifice

of shed blood. A girl should be
a veil, a white shadow, bloodless
as the moon on water; not
dangerous; she should

keep silent and avoid
red shoes, red stockings, dancing.
Dancing in red shoes will kill you.

—Margaret Atwood (from "A Red Shirt")

*One alien is a curiosity, two are an invasion.*
—Ursula K. LeGuin, *The Left Hand of Darkness*

# PROLOGUE

## DECEMBER 6, 1989

SNOW PELTED THE WINDSHIELD of the rented Chevy Corsica. He turned off the engine, sat in the frigid cold, in the dead quiet, alone in the university parking lot.

He zipped his anorak, ran his hands through his hair. His short hair. Four days ago, he had sheared his unruly curls right after visiting his mother. She was delirious with her birthday present, some lame journal covered in satin. Said "Mom" on it. She would not shut up about getting it early. "*Mais oui!* I love it. So beautiful. You picked it out yourself?" She kissed him then, and he let her. Normally, he hated her touch, anyone's touch.

*Focus,* he told himself, but his mind wandered back to that scene just days earlier in his mother's kitchen. He had purchased the journal on the same day he purchased his weaponage, as he liked to call it, waxing lyrical to himself about the irony of birthdays for mothers and death days for daughters.

He pulled on his cap and black gloves. Checked to be sure the radio was turned off and the lights, though he knew they were already off. Habit. Be sure everything is in order. Just like an engineer. Ironic. He took the letter from his breast pocket. Opened it. Read it. It was perfect. Folded it. Returned it to his pocket. Got out of the car.

He shouldered the front door closed, opened the back, and grabbed the green plastic bag that held the semi-automatic. Six hundred dollars worth of Sturm-Ruger. A Mini-14 hunting rifle, little brother to the M14 the U.S. Forces used. Nothing mini about this guy. He patted his pocket with his left hand. Hunting knife where it should be. Banana clips tucked into his belt at his lower back. He slammed the back door. December 6: D-Day.

He walked up the slippery hill, taking the most vertical route to the engineering building, the back staircases, famous among students, he had been told, for pre-exam stress relief. They ran them, up and down, during finals and mid-terms. They panted and recited mathematical formulas on the way up, physics equations on the way down. The stairs were steep, cutting into a hillside that rose nearly straight up, zigzagging to the main building. Janitors salted, but thick ice limned them still. They looked treacherous. He was up for treachery.

His uncle's words came back to him from summers long ago when they would hunt: *Focus. Aim. Squeeze.* He recited this mantra: *Focus. Aim. Squeeze.* His uncle was said to have trained with Delta Force, the elite U.S. Special Forces. His teaching brought his young nephew to this crossroads, where he would face his victims, and prepare for war. He and his mini were ready. He had learned from the best. He knew the hunt. It was up to him. The Canadian army could bite his ass. He would show them how to take down the enemy with speed and acumen. They had sorely missed their chance to recruit him. They would rue the day. At the top of the stairs, he paused to catch his breath, to scan the façade of the building directly in front of him. Yellow brick. Six stories. He gripped his green garbage bag and marched to the entrance. Two students flew out the door, nearly knocking him over, mumbling apologies. He closed his eyes and swallowed his rage. Not now. Pace. Pace. Timing is everything. Maximize numbers. *Focus. Aim. Squeeze.*

Inside, he jerked back his hood, adjusted his cap, trekked through the immense lobby, past the security guard, into the central corridor of the building. He took the escalator to the second floor. He turned right at the café, the aroma of coffee heavy in the air. He walked the few steps to the Registrar's office, entered into the open door, and sat down in one of the chairs. He unzipped his coat, sat back. Four women on high stools behind windows looked like tellers in a bank. Students took a number as they came into the office, and they lined up to see these women. Each teller dealt with one student. This continued for half an hour. He waited. He watched. He had been here before, in this very office to apply to this very engineering school two years ago. He had been rejected. His life plans had fallen to shit. He had applied again this past March, nine months ago. Nine months was enough time to grow a human being. Enough time to gestate a determination. His was a fulminating determination. A final solution.

And why? The answer was right there in front of him. Two of the four students at the teller's windows were women. What the hell were they doing here, where engineers were made, the best of the best. They did not belong. Damned entitled. He had told the admissions officer. Spoken the truth. Women were taking over the job market. It was wrong. This was 1989. They assumed they had the right to be here because the Canadian government did not have the gonads to tell them they were not fit to be engineers or cops or firemen. What was wrong with being a mother or a wife? The admissions officer had said he would be in touch. The women were everywhere he looked. The two at the window. The one he passed in the foyer. The old hag serving coffee. *Get the fuck to a nunnery*, he shrieked inside his head. But he sat still, cradling his garbage bag, adjusting his cap.

"May I help you?"

He startled. How had she gotten so close without his noticing? He was freaked out but would not show it. He stood, and she was his height exactly, 5', 9". Had he turned he would have looked her directly in the eye. He did not turn but strode out of the office, pretended he had not heard her.

He snapped to. *Focus. Focus. You have done this before. Tracked these halls, stared into these classrooms. You own the place. Seven visits since October, seven pre-missions within eight weeks. Remember, this is the real deal. So be a man. Do it.*

# 1.

IF ANYONE WERE THE ODD DUCK of the CanTech sisterhood, it was Marin. While most of the female students at the school of engineering wore nondescript clothing, Marin had long ago cultivated her own style, a hint of bohemian, a whisper of exotic, all stemming, perhaps, from her lifelong dream to create scenery for the theatre or opera. More artist than engineer, Marin's naturally straight hair was always carefully arranged, often hot-curled into a mass of bobbing ringlets. Her makeup was always striking, particularly around her eyes. They were *yeux pers*, a mix of light brown and green, hazel, just like her father's. It was universally accepted that they were her best feature, but her smile was a close second. It was a family trait, also inherited from her father. His Slovakian ancestry deeded to the Hazeur siblings a no-holds-barred, winsome smile.

Of the five Hazeur children, she was the one with brio, a vivacity that drew others to her like sunlight. It could not be quelled. Even when she was disenchanted, Marin was alive with possibility and always moving. Marin's was a face people contemplated. If she was a petite woman, just over five feet, Marin defied it with high heels, shimmering necklaces, and a mélange of wild colours. She would wear a red cardigan over a purple T-shirt over a black lace skirt that fell to her shins. Argyle knee socks and red Converse sneakers would complete the ensemble. Often, she wore textured and vibrant scarves around her hair or neck or waist. Marin painted and primped, artistically representing herself. She was a young woman who turned heads, and she liked that, especially when the compliments came.

Still and all, Marin had tamed her fashion exuberance sometime after her first semester at CanTech. Displays of femininity were noticed, drawing unwelcome attention. Marin had not wanted to explain herself, so she fell back on the bland comfort of turtlenecks, sweaters, and khaki pants, stealthily adding a contraband silk scarf or bejewelled bauble on occasion. If there was any consensus about the stereotypical female engineer, Marin was not it. She was a Pisces, for one thing. Though she was endowed with an impressive memory, she disliked discipline and confinement, tending toward the beauty of art and nature. The diligence required of engineering students wrenched her spirit, but she had adapted by now. She was, after all, nearly thirty, and after this academic year, she would be in her final year of study.

"The purpose of school is to challenge your mind, MoMo," her brother Hilaire told her. He had graduated from CanTech two years earlier, and there was no question, the engineering school was the most prestigious, and that was saying something, given that Montreal, an island fifty by sixteen kilometres, the second largest French speaking city in the world, was also the second city in North America, after Boston, with the highest concentration of university students.

To say the function of CanTech was to challenge her mind was the understatement of the century. God knows Marin had discovered this to be the undeniable truth. That first year, everything had been new, and the challenge, if tough, was not crushing. The second year, she and everyone else in her class had asked themselves, more than once, why they were there. The third year, despair had set in. The challenge Hilaire had talked about pushed Marin and the others to the breaking point. There would be progress by the fourth year – at least, that is what everyone who had gone before promised Marin, though there would continue to be scant sleep, minimal social life, engineering problems that seemed unsolvable, and the monotonous schedule. Marin had friends who vomited and sobbed before their heat transfer exam and who popped entire bottles of antacids trying to solve the Hamilton cycle problem. It had been brutal, but it was never boring. She had made it this far, into her third year. She had grown the armour, acquiesced to the turtleneck, weathered the intensity. No matter the skirmish, she would soldier on.

When Marin was eighteen, the prestigious École Nationale de théâtre du Canada in Montreal had promised to make her dream come true. If she had had her way about it, she would have learned to build sets for film and opera, for Broadway maybe. This had been a dream since her parents had taken her and her sister Sybille to a Christmas performance of *The Sound of Music* when Marin was ten and Sybille twelve. The convent gates, the Von Trapp mansion, the frightening nighttime cemetery, the *Auf Wiedersehen* song – she had fallen in love with all of it. Though École Nationale accepted only sixteen production students a year, eight French and eight English, Marin had been confident she would be one of those. It had seemed, in the moment, within reach, though Marin had also applied to the Université Sainte-Catherine's Environmental Arts Design program as a backup. She had purchased a navy blue beret, sent off her portfolio to École Nationale, and imagined herself a Canadian version of Mary Cassatt who lived among the pigeon cotes, high above Paris, with a bevy of young female artists surrounded by warm, flaky croissants, watercolours and fine cream-coloured shawls. When she was not admitted, Marin had donated her beret to the Salvation Army. She had then registered for classes at Université Sainte-Catherine to get her Design d'Environnement degree. She would become a scenic designer and fabricator one way or another.

With her pack of friends at Université Sainte-Catherine,

Marin had studied and spent countless hours in studio. Most of her friends had been working toward degrees in the arts. Any excuse for an adventure was a good excuse. They had quested after treasures in consignment shops, hosted costume parties and keggers, wore hats and pajamas to class. Theirs had been a silly, whimsical edginess that the undergraduate art world embraced. They had consulted each other on hairstyles, karaoke song selections, and recipes. Their friendships and social life had made up for any strain brought on by their studies.

At CanTech, where academics claimed every waking hour of a student's life, however, she had only three people she could really call friends. Marin relied on these for her daily dose of sanity in the hyper-competitive world of engineering. Chantal and Renee were part of her Materials study group, but Noelle, a mechanical engineering student, was an honourary member with whom they ate lunch most days. The study group became family in engineering school, became your lifeline. Since the hallmark of engineering education was the team approach to problem solving, for eight hours a day, you took classes with your group, you ate with them, you did homework projects with them, and when you were not with them, you talked to them on the phone. You did all but sleep with them. As if there were time for sleep. There were always those rare few who joined the engineering bowling league or played guitar in a band. Some played video or strategy games all night long, but the invigorating social life as Marin had known it at Université Sainte-Catherine ended when she entered CanTech.

The study group had to suffice and sustain since there was no easing up in a demanding curriculum designed to weed out all but the most resilient. Its own sort of social phenomenon, perpetually switched on intellectually, the study group meant, for example, listening for longer bouts than Marin would have preferred about Noelle's plans for her heating and ventilation systems. Noelle thought of herself as a straight shooter, inflicting Marin with the "truth" about her wardrobe and on her tendency to get hurt or stumble. Noelle pointed out Marin's occasional flawed analyses of roofs, trusses, or bridges, and, in particular, her wrong-headed understanding of the Challenger explosion in 1986. Marin blamed the officials at NASA for allowing the launch to proceed despite warnings from engineers. Noelle took a more utilitarian view, placing blame squarely and solely on the failure of the "O-ring" seal in the solid-fuel rocket on the Challenger's right side. They would never agree on how best to ascribe responsibility, but the debate inspired lengthy lunch-time talk whenever George was absent.

Marin learned tolerance from guys like George. Testing her mettle every day at lunch, he never stopped talking. Ever. No matter how many others were at the table, it was George who kept up a running monologue that could not be ignored and could only be countered by a louder voice or a fist pummelling a table to get attention. Pisces were known for despising know-it-alls. George was Marin's thorn.

"Professor Henson did not have that ODE right," George pontificated. "I went to his office before class this morning, and good thing I did. I solved it at two a.m., went to sleep for three hours, then got up and finished the problem sets for the rest of the week. Henson was happy for my coming around, I'll tell you. I really got him out of a bind. Imagine if he had come into the classroom with that...."

"George, did you actually get all of the ordinary differential equations and the vector differential problem sets done already? For the entire week?" asked Renee, who was staring George down, as if daring him to confess a tall tale.

"Indeed I did. And I read the *Royal Society Proceedings* articles. And you all? Not finished yet? Hmmm..." he said, offering them a wide-eyed challenge.

This went on obnoxiously, every day, through the salads and grilled cheese sandwiches, and interminably through brownies and coffee, if anyone could bear to stick it out. While some students unearthed solution manuals from alumni or older students, George was the first to boast that he was a living solution manual and would never risk getting caught cheating.

George wanted to create linear logic alarm systems for use in hospitals and prisons. He would go on about the customized sub-features he would incorporate that would allow a programmed voice to announce "Evacuate the building" or "Fire" to a few portions of a structure at a time in order to enable evacuation in an orderly manner from one zone to another. His prison systems got him really amped. He sketched out alarms that could not only notify people in a building of dangers like fire and smoke, but could also control door locks, ventilation, and even pressurize areas in order to stop a fire from moving. The systems were sophisticated and innovative, and no one doubted George would be a top-notch engineer, if his personality did not tsunami potential employers.

Renee was far quieter. She had told Marin she began reading *Popular Science* magazine when she was six. She had loved to build things from household doodads. Her father was an engineer, and she could still recall how he had beamed when his daughter won the rocket competition in fourth grade, and how he had called her "daddy's little engineer." Her dream was to get a job in the medical device industry and to eradicate colon cancer. Renee's mother had died when she was nine, the same year she won the trophy for her rocket. She carried a photo of her mother, a physical therapist with a quiet smile and glossy black hair, everywhere she went. Renee was determined to invent a way to insert a miniature video camera with lights into the entire small intestine using ultra-thin tubing that the patient could swallow. Where an endoscope could only go partway, Renee's device would allow photos of the entire intestine. It was a mission of love that she had committed to as a child and recommitted to every time the going got tough.

Chantal was the lynchpin of their study group. In her fourth year in metallurgy, she was one of the top students in the class, male or female. She was twenty-two, with a full head of red hair. Seven years younger than Marin, she had the same flair for presenting a confident face to the world. When Marin discovered that Chantal had acted in plays in high school, she relaxed into their instant theatrical bond that found them reminiscing dialogue from *South Pacific* and *My Fair Lady*.

Within their small group, Chantal was nicknamed Geber, thanks to Marin. Unable to study late one night, Marin had discovered an article about Abu Musa Jabir ibn Hayyan, known in Europe as Geber, who lived from 721–815 AD, and was an Arabian alchemist from the country now known as Iraq. Geber popularized the idea of the Philosopher's Stone, which said that mercury and sulfur combined to make gold. The word "gibberish" is derived from his name. Chantal became Geber when the three friends rejected "Gibber" as too stupid and "Gerber" as evoking baby food. Geber, pronounced *gee-ber*, stuck. While Chantal did not love the nickname, she had to admit that she had long been fascinated by the concept of the Philosopher's Stone, and so the name was sanctioned.

There was no clearer authority on materials for Marin or Renee. Whenever they had a question about the physical or chemical behaviours of aluminum, chromium, copper, iron, magnesium, nickel, titanium, or zinc, Geber was their woman. She knew them all, knew their cellular structures, knew their inter-metallic compounds and their alloys. She knew the technology of these metals, and the way science is applied to their practical use. Chantal had become mesmerized as a child when an engineer at a science museum demonstration took a piece of wire called shape-memory alloy, crumpled it into a ball, heated it with a lighter, and then formed it, magically, into a perfect coil. That coil was Geber's *Sound of Music*, and she and Marin often compared notes about how they had found their vocations at an age when most girls were finding Barbie.

Marin loved Chantal, Renee, and Noelle. Far quirkier than her artist friends at Université Sainte-Catherine, they were the kids in secondary school who got straight As, and ran the school newspaper and the science club. Not an artist among them. In the crucible of engineering school, they were becoming her people. They developed their own sort of sisterhood among the bevy of brothers. Marin alone had an actual brother. Tall and slim, with a froth of the straight, glossy hair that each family member claimed, Hilaire carried himself with a confidence that Marin slowly absorbed, one engineering course at a time. Not only was he her mentor and tutor, he was her life coach. Even when they were younger, Hilaire had never failed to find Marin's lost keys, her missing wallet, the sunglasses that disappeared from her dresser. Unlike the others in the family, Hilaire had never teased Marin about her forgetfulness or her clumsiness. He had simply gone into the kitchen to get a towel when Marin spilled her milk or broke a vase. She could count on Hilaire for telling the truth. He had read somewhere that only 42 percent of women in engineering completed their degrees compared to the 62 percent of men who competed theirs. The reality was, Hilaire had told Marin, that most of the students were male, and all of the professors were male. Engineering school would demand all of her best energies, would co-opt her mind for four years. It would make her a stronger person, a high-ly-skilled person, but she would pay a price. Her intellectual life would need to be privileged above all. Her days would be circumscribed, focused on problem solving and equations. It was not a bad life, but it was not the artistic, fun-loving life she had led at Université Sainte-Catherine.

Even with the gift of her brother, Marin needed her alliance with her female friends, and their sisterhood was as much a stabilizing force as was Hilaire. Geber had been the sisterhood's best cheerleader, assuring the other three through their first and second years. It was horrible, she had agreed, but it could be managed. Year three, she had announced, was the worst. She had been right. After Marin, Renee, and Noelle finished their portfolios in their second year, demonstrating that they had learned the basics of engineering, they were free to choose their specialties. Marin embraced Materials, a bit of a change from the structural engineering track she had always assumed she would pursue. Materials gripped her, and though she had not given up on designing and creating for theatre, she could not learn enough about how materials could be changed, enhanced, and maximized. Renee was opting for the same in order to create materials miniature enough to detect colon tumours. Noelle decided on mechanical engineering, something that surprised no one, given that she had grown up on a dairy farm with a father who invented agricultural machinery. The good news about third year was that it came with a dose of hard-earned confidence. If they felt stupid, even idiotic, the first two years, they had at least survived the plebian phase. Besides, they were all driven. It came with the territory of being a woman in engineering.

At full-tilt consciousness, they were always exerting their intellectual muscle. Marin missed her old world where students, male and female, mixed casually, not always hell-bent on solving equations, or competing with each other to get the right answer the fastest way. For all the laughter and ribbing this semester, the study group kept their eyes on the final presentation in their Electromechanical Processing of Materials class. Four of them would present on Thermodynamic and Transport Properties of Electrolytes – Aqueous and Molten. Even though the presentation was months away, Marin, Geber, Renee, and Stephan, a student all of the women agreed pulled his weight in the group but who did not need to run the show, had been strategizing to stun the professor, to bring the wow factor. That day, December 6, would be a day to remember.

# 2.

D EIRDRE COULD NOT QUELL the memories. As she packed her trunk, her four high school years at Renfrew Collegiate Institute were firebombing her mind. Tomorrow, she was leaving for university three hours away. Tonight, the past was grasping at her. To distract herself, she tried arranging her hair into two braids, like she used to do when she was nine, but her hair was so thick that two black ropes seemed to emerge from the backs of her ears, a look that was clearly unbecoming. Besides, her face was no longer round and pink. She had grown cheekbones somewhere between Girl Guides and braces, and what her mother used to call her "jelly belly" had grown slim and toned from years on the track team. Indeed, she had sprouted to 5', 5", taller than her mother, before her fourteenth birthday. Once the braces had come off, her sister Camille declared that Deirdre's teeth had grown "massive and white," but her girlfriends assured her that Camille was a little brat and that Deirdre looked perfectly pretty and considerably less awkward.

"The Ayatollah Khomeni has not read the book," Deirdre remembered her English teacher Mr. Marche telling the class as he held up his copy of *The Satanic Verses*. "This is literary news, my friends. Literary news. This book so inflamed Iran's Ayatollah Ruhollah Khomeini that on Valentine's Day he issued a death threat called a *fatwa* for Rushdie. The classroom was quiet. "What do you make of that? How can we make judgments about things we do not know?" Mr. Marche walked across the front of the classroom and looked into the eyes of the students. "In what world is that responsible, adult behaviour? Remember, folks, this is 1989. This happened not five months ago."

Deirdre ran her fingers through one of the loosening braids, realizing she had been swept up again in high-school memories. They were tenacious. She would miss her English teacher most of all because he had asked the best questions. Everyone teased her that she loved Mr. Marche, but Deirdre knew it was not love, not even a crush really. Mr. Marche was the kind of person she could imagine talking to for hours without ever once being bored. It was not that he was a handsome man. Ironically, he looked like a bulkier version of the author Salman Rushdie himself, with a dark beard and wire-rimmed eyeglasses, though Marche had longer hair than Rushdie, and he was not balding. In fact, several dozen times per class, the teacher had had to sweep his hair back from his face where it constantly fell across his eyes.

When a man burned copies of *The Satanic Verses* at two bookstores owned by the University of Ontario in January of her last year, Mr. Marche had urged the class to keep an eye out for news about the book. This is going to explode, he had told them. Explode it did, and Deirdre had followed the details of the war on Rushdie, not quite sure why she could not get enough of this story, but it had something to do with prejudice and the way people hated one another for no reason. When Gerard Le Chance got shoved into the school lockers two years before because he wore hearing aids, the guys bullying him had said he was "retarded" and a "freak." Deirdre tried to find the logic in things, tried to see how something made sense from each person's point of view, but far too often there seemed no sense to be found, and she felt stymied. In the case of poor Gerard, she was full out angry and had told the bullies so. It seemed the older she got, the harder it was to find the rationality in the world's daft events.

When Mr. Marche began the class with calls for updates on any literary news, most students had ignored him and used the time to find their homework in their backpacks or to volley whispered *Rain Man* lines:

"*I get my boxer shorts at K-Mart in Cincinnati.*"

"*We're not going back to Cincinnati, Ray, so don't even start with that.*"

"*Boxer shorts. K-Mart!*"

Against this banal din, Deirdre and Mr. Marche had discussed whatever tidbit of literary news she had brought with her that day. Bookstores bombed in Berkeley and Bombay. Rushdie given twenty-four hour police protection. Crowds in Bombay carrying banners reading: "I am Ready to Kill Rushdie" and "Rushdie = Rush + Die." One or two others had joined the discussion, usually to ask questions, but they swiftly drifted off.

"I was a super nerd wide receiver," Mr. Marche had told them on their first day of class in their final school year. "I was on the school quiz team because I never got a literature question wrong, but I had a hard time getting a date for prom. Go figure." It had been his ability to poke fun at himself that made Mr. Marche popular among the students in Deirdre's school. He had worked them hard, and he talked about those places on the other side of the world, something that aggravated Deirdre's mother at the dinner table. He was the smartest man Deirdre knew. *The Satanic Verses* warned against the "absolutism of the pure," Mr. Marche had said. It is a novel," he said, "that forces its readers to consider the value of 'hybridity'." Deirdre had not cared that she did not understand what Mr. Marche meant. She had agreed to read the book anyway, challenge herself to grow. Maybe some of the insanity she had been seeing in the world would get clearer.

As she zipped her last sweater into her mother's worn tweed suitcase, Deirdre decided to abandon *The Satanic Verses*. She had only fifty more pages to read, but it was slow going, and it was long overdue at the library anyway. Mr. Marche had offered the class this challenge just after the infamous *fatwa* was issued: anyone who read Salman Rushdie's novel and did a class presentation on both the novel and the controversy surrounding it would not only receive extra credit, but he or she would have the start of an extraordinary essay for a college composition course. Deirdre and one other student had taken him up on the challenge. She and Leonard, a tall skinny tuba player who read four newspapers a day, did the presentation on the very last day of classes. Mr. Marche had been ecstatic. Deirdre had, admittedly, skimmed the book, but had gone to the library to read every newspaper article on the Ayatollah's *fatwa* and Rushdie's going underground. She had tried to imagine the kind of fear the author was living with every day, knowing he was hunted. Leonard had filled in with serious helpings of information about Sunnis and Shiites. Their classmates had been intrigued that there could be so much fervour over a book.

It was in Deirdre's nature to finish what she started, but she figured she had done enough in this case. She would leave the book for her sister Camille to return to the library. Deirdre wondered, sometimes, why she cared about things that happened so far away. Why she cared at all, really. Her friends and classmates did not. They could tell you that Geraldo Rivera's nose was broken in some TV brawl with skinheads. They could sing every lyric to "Love Bites" by Def Leppard and recite the number of goals Wayne Gretzky had scored that season. But did they know that after forty-one years of apartheid in South Africa, and while serving more than two decades in jail, Nelson Mandela met with white-supremacist President F. W. de Klerk in July? No and no. So why was it that she could? Was she a freak of nature? Why was she not obsessed by the usual teenage girl things like dances and makeup? Where did this curiosity about the wider world come from?

Certainly not from her parents. Deirdre Sevier grew up in a house where the men talked incessantly and the women served the green bean casserole. Earlier that evening, Deirdre and her family had had their goodbye dinner together in the dining room. Her mom had cooked her favourite: homemade poutine, or French fries covered in cheese curds and smothered with brown gravy. She even had a heaping bowl of ketchup chips on the table, something only Deirdre liked.

Tonight's dinner was exactly the kind of normal Deirdre needed for her last meal. So many nights had gotten charged, particularly when she had mentioned what she was doing in Mr. Marche's class. Deirdre's father knew little more than what was on the nightly news about Rushdie or the *fatwa*, and she was certain her mother would chalk it all up to the devil's work, as the novel's title surely indicated. Mr. and Mrs. Sevier were not thrilled with Mr. Marche. They could not understand why he talked so much about things like Tibet and the Dalai Lama and South Africa.

"What do these things, interesting as they may be, have to do with literature?" her father asked.

"It's about writing and working to change the world, Dad," she replied.

"Why must it change again?" he asked every time.

And, as if dancing a well-choreographed routine, Deirdre responded: "So suffering can stop and people can live in freedom."

It went on like this sometimes for the entire supper period, with Deirdre defending Mr. Marche as a man who was teaching them about the world they were heading into after high school and college, while her father waved his hand at her explanations, *pishawing* her defences.

"If people would just do their job, the world would be a better place. Then there'd be peace," he would conclude.

"Your father is right you know, Dierdre. Why get involved in all of this fuss and bother in places on the other side of the world? We have enough to do right here in Canada. Now eat your dinner. Isn't this corn buttery, so yellow. I got a dozen from Mr. Bruse...."

No such chaffing went on tonight. The glow of the candles her mother had placed in the centre of the table centred the family's energy somehow. Maybe it was the void of Deirdre's imminent departure they were all feeling. Whatever it was, the meal was exactly what Deirdre had hoped for. She would miss her parents, and she would miss her sister. But she was ready to go, ready to get on with her life.

Aunts, uncles, and cousins rang the doorbell, as the Seviers were finishing. Only a few of them lived in Renfrew, but the others made the trip because Deirdre was a family favourite. Not only was she the oldest, but she was the first in the family to go to a university. Mom had invited the aunts and uncles and cousins for cake and ice cream and farewells. They were proud and quizzical, and they pelted her with questions about her roommate, her major, what colour comforter and sheets she had purchased. Would she be homesick? Would she write letters? They promised care packages.

Soon enough, they all headed to the living room. Dierdre's grandfather and two of her uncles were with the RCMP, or the Royal Canadian Mounted Police, and at family gatherings they out-boasted each other, relating perpetrator and police antics. Her father was the only civilian among the group, an Operations Team Manager at E.T.M. Industries Inc. about a mile down the road in Renfrew, but he loved the stories. Often the uncles and Grandpa became so entertaining that the entire family listened to them go on this way for hours. Tonight was no different. Meanwhile, Deirdre's mother, a nurse at Renfrew Victoria Hospital on the maternity wing, and both of her aunts, former elementary teachers who were stay-at-home moms with new babies and several older children, huddled around the kitchen table analyzing the merits of the NordicTrack Uncle Henry just ordered or the new VCR Aunt Cheryl just learned how to program. Eventually, at the least conspicuous moment, Deirdre slipped away and up to the bedroom she shared with her sister Camille to finish her packing.

# 3.

MONTREAL IN SEPTEMBER should be a huge love fest of wind and colour, but today was unseasonably cold, and Jenean rolled over to grab another few minutes of softness and warmth, as she ran through the loose agenda for the weekend. She wished she could be more like Bart, who snored away at her side, and who could not muster a thought, let alone a word, before his third cup of coffee. He eased into the day like a Buddhist monk, sitting perfectly still on the sofa, mug in both hands, staring out the window. He did not do agendas on weekdays or weekends. She had timed him once without him knowing. He had sat with a hot cup of coffee on a Tuesday morning while she had made tuna salad sandwiches and packed hers into her backpack next to an apple and two cheese sticks. She had ironed her white blouse, dried and styled her hair, applied make up, dressed, wrote a thank-you note to her mother for the birthday gift she had sent from Holt Renfrew, gave Gertrude her breakfast, and walked her around the block before starting her car in the garage. She had done all of this before he stood to refill his mug.

If Bart sauntered into a day, Jenean fast-forwarded. They were perfect for each other, really, even if they were opposites in so many ways. She was petite; he inches over six feet. While he had a fullness to his cheeks that imbued his face with a sense of authority, Jenean had chiselled cheekbones that were no less potent for her slight frame. After several years together, they had come to a wordless accord. She worked every day from dawn to dusk in downtown Montreal, though there were times she worked from home, writing a weekly column on politics and society for the Sunday magazine *Mot du Jour*, Montreal's largest French newspaper. Bart worked for the province of Quebec as a supervisor of an environmental technician crew. Her job required her brain to be marinating through the night, plotting out the next story, the next angle. His required old-fashioned sleep. She the brains, he the brawn, they joked. But it was no joke. They endured, they agreed, because they had the weekends to go antiquing and open-air marketing. Other people's old stuff and vegetables cinched them together as no careers or political ideologies or religion could.

On most Saturday mornings, they got up at six and headed for Annabelle's Petit Déjeuner on the corner. It was the one day a week Jenean did not blow-dry and style her short hair, and Bart did not shave. They would read the papers, eat bacon and eggs and fruit, power up on Annabelle's strong coffee. Jenean had learned to bring a book during their first year together, so she could keep busy while Bart finished reading the paper cover to cover and downed his requisite fourth cup of coffee. He did, indeed, move incrementally faster on the weekend, so Jenean never brought a big book to Annabelle's, usually a collection of poetry or short stories. Also, she made out her to-do list.

Bart worked eighty hours a week making sure snow was plowed and ice was chopped from frozen manhole covers in winter. The rest of the year, he oversaw the repairing and cleaning of roads, the cutting of wayward tree limbs that encroached on city streets, and the preparations for the travails that came with another northern winter. No matter what the season, he was the walking weary when he got home at night, leaving little time or energy for errands, buying gifts, repairing leaky faucets. Bart caught up on the weekends, after he and Jenean traipsed their route of antique shops in Old Montreal and the Marche Jean Talon.

This morning, they arrived at Annabelle's nearing noon. Jenean felt bold and rested, having slept in and taken a long hot shower, leaving her short hair to air dry. When Annabelle poured their coffees and took their order, Jenean breathed in the bitter aroma and felt a deep peace she could never seem to make happen by sheer willpower. These moments just presented themselves at the most unusual times, and she revelled in them, relaxing her shoulders and stretching her neck to relieve the perennial tension that lived there. Annabelle's was exactly where she needed to be.

"How's the new column coming? You were at Western University this week, right?" Bart asked, interrupting her bliss. The newspaper had been read, cup number four was at hand.

"I was at Western," she said, feeling her shoulders tighten. She consciously lowered them, brought her hand to her neck. "I was also on the phone with the University of Ontario, and far too many more universities to even tell you about."

"What is it? What are you writing about this week?" Bart asked, folding the paper in half, then half again, headlines out.

"Well," Jenean said, taking a deep breath, "where should I start? Here's the deal: I'm researching Canadian universities and women's experiences in them. Are they inherently sexist or not, is the basic question. What I'm finding – and other scholars with new studies are onto this case too – is that sexism is rampant. I have a slew of examples...."

"Let's hear them," Bart said, his eyes trained on hers.

Jenean sighed. "Okay. Do you want to hear about the strippers at the engineering stag parties during graduation ceremonies? The university that calls its engineering mascot, which is a giant wrench, the Rigid Tool? Or shall we start with what happened with the blow-up doll at U. of Ontario two years ago?" As if something important suddenly occurred to her, Jenean put her mug down, unearthed her notebook from her purse, and jotted down a note before looking up at Bart.

Though he tried to stop himself, he laughed out loud. "The

Rigid Tool? No offense, but that is kind of funny, don't you think?'

Jenean looked at Bart, chewed her toast slowly, then replied, "No."

They remained quiet for a moment, listening to the chatter of customers around them and the whir of fans over the giant cook stove at the back of the diner.

"On its own," said Jenean, finally, "maybe it is not the worst nickname for a mascot, but given all of the other heinous behaviour I've heard about this week, it is one more example of the banal and the barbaric."

"Hmm," Bart murmered. "Alrighty then."

Jenean sighed again, leaned forward in her seat. "Let me ask you a question, Bart. You're a man. What is it about the male anatomy that makes it such a compelling object of scrutiny, especially for university-aged men. Why can't it remain – flaccidly – inside their pants?"

Bart picked up his mug, held it in front of him, and met Jenean's eyes. He shook his head. "I do not know the answer to that, Jenean. It's just a guy thing, I guess." Bart took a long time to drink from his coffee, putting his mug back onto the table without looking at her.

Jenean reached out and placed her hand on Bart's. "Bart, seriously, that was a rhetorical question. I don't want to argue about this. This writing is hard enough. Can't we just have some peace this morning? I can get back to it later tomorrow."

"Perfect idea," he said. "Let's get out of here anyway." He gently tapped Jenean's open hand adding, "We get only one day a weekend to get errands done, and you want to see that movie later, right?" He helped her into her coat and smiled a peace offering. Bart eschewed conflict whenever he could, and her ruminations were not worth an ongoing battle. He would listen. He would read her columns, tell her she did a professional and thoughtful job, but he would not get into it with her. "I can never win, Jenean," had been his reasoning whenever she had quizzed him on this score. Women's issues were fraught, he believed. She had best discuss these with her former colleagues at the magazine *La Vision et La Voix* or with her friend Clara. He was all about equality, he maintained, but he would leave the details to her and her friends. When they needed a strong-arm, he would be there for them. In the meantime, he would go about his business, and she could go about hers.

Jenean stood, shoved her arms into her coat, and put her small notebook and pen into her purse. She drew her scarf around her neck and tucked it into the front of her coat. She was still reeling under the heaviness of the notes she had taken this week. There was so much more to say, but for now, she would have to put it aside to enjoy the market, later a movie, and Bart. She moved her disquieted brain into low gear, placed her hand in Bart's, and felt the ease that came with resigning herself to the habits of a weekend.

*

Bart snored steadily while Jenean typed, fiercely, into the dawn of Monday morning. *Mot du Jour* would be reluctant to publish this next weekend, she knew. There was a public impatience with women's fight for equality, but she had to write it before it ate her up. Besides, they had given her free reign on her column topics, and the editors had never balked in the past. She poured another mug of coffee, her fourth, and she wrote.

> Boys will be boys until the girls want to play. What better way to jettison girls from the field than to make the game unbearable.
>
> A university campus is generally, though falsely, thought to be a bastion of equality. The sexist climate and practices on today's Canadian campuses, in fact, cause a massive roadblock to women's full participation in the life of a university. Yet, campus leaders, all too

often, respond with silence or denial.

Contrary to what many believe, women's lower status is not part of some natural order. It is, in fact, part of a system of discrimination called sexism. Here is how it works, in word and deed (all of these, sadly, are true stories that happened at Canadian universities): In a physics class, a student wrote a stellar paper. The professor handed it back and said, "Good girl." She had three teenage sons.

A male college professor was offered a striptease as a holiday gift by his students.

"Tubbing" is where male engineering students in ski masks and gloves drag women from their dorm rooms and throw them into bathtubs of cold water.

A male medical doctor training clinicians, five men and one woman, began each day with this: "Gentlemen, shall we begin." One day, one of the men said that one of the clinical students was a woman. The professor replied, "You could have fooled me – she has no tits."

On being told by a female engineering student that she had won a scholarship, a male professor said, "Congratulations, my dear. You may now proceed to purchase yourself a husband."

Not long ago, two dozen engineering students passed from one to the other a life-sized inflated female doll, shoving a beer bottle in and out between its legs. Several of the young men threw the doll to the ground, jumped on it, and simulated rape. On the same campus that same week, one woman was sexually attacked, and another was physically attacked by a group of male students. Both women were treated at hospital emergency wards.

An ad in one student newspaper read: "Show your enthusiasm, get out there and belt your spouse." At this same university, it was reported that women's dorms were raided while they slept. Women woke to their underwear stolen then plastered on the dining-hall walls decorated with ketchup and and mud to represent blood and feces. Degrading labels were adhered to the undergarments such as, "Do you take Visa?"

Lamentably, there are hundreds more stories like this that could be told. What is there to be silent about? What is there to deny? Women are here to stay. Universities should refuse to allow sexist behaviours on their properties. They should recognize the obvious: that this sort of sexism affects the quality of life for its female community members whose freedom is mitigated by such callow behaviour.

They should hire more women faculty. Sources tell me that only one percent of all female faculty are in engineering and applied sciences. Something like seven percent of full professors are women. Where are the professors with whom students can identify? Where are the role models for women in the professions?

Whatever fear, insecurity and vulnerability are driving this male malevolence needs to be excised and/or healed. A focus on gender equilibrium — the condition within a system in which all competing influences are balanced – should be sought. Dare I suggest the powerful tools of self-reflection and compassion for all humanity? Boys will be boys when long ago the time to grow up and be men has passed – unless they are challenged to man up.

The sky was still black when Jenean crawled into bed, her brain spent. She had said what she had to say, and no matter how envious she was of how deeply and serenely Bart had been sleeping for hours, she knew that she could only earn her peace at the cost of laying out in words what troubled her soul.

# 4.

DEIRDRE FLOPPED ONTO HER BED and looked around her room. So much had happened here, but for the next four years, all of her life would be lived from the base camp of a dormitory room in Meese Hall at Aquitaine University. Her bedroom at home was so familiar, so safe. She had picked out the paint herself when she turned sixteen. "Outrageous Green." Her mother had had serious misgivings, particularly when Deirdre had begged to paint her built-in bookshelves in high-gloss "Impatient Pink." "We are not a tropical island, Deirdre. We live in Canada," she had said, as they checked out with two gallons of each. "Impatient Pink" would have to do for her little sister's room across the hall. Mrs. Sevier was not one to waste, and if they had to buy two gallons, they would make those gallons count.

Posters covered all four of Deirdre's walls. There were even a couple on the ceiling. Hands down, her favourite was Jimmy Cauty's "Gandalf With Hobbits," an atmospheric poster in greys and blues showing Gandalf, Sam, and Frodo with stacks of dead Orcs. Deirdre had stared at this poster for hours, imagining herself in the mist and moisture of Tolkien's world. She had decided not to take it with her to college only last night. It was a time to start fresh, she thought. She would acquire new posters along with her new life. Likewise, she was leaving behind the "Canada Calls You" travel poster, "Hello. My Name is Luka" poster, and an oldie but goodie from her best friend Lea, the "And There Won't Be Snow in Africa this Christmastime" poster. The other poster on her ceiling was of Princess Buttercup and Westley holding hands at an open gate, trees and mountains rising in the distance. She and her friends watched *The Princess Bride* twelve times at twelve different sleepovers, and they pinky swore, after their debut viewing in the theatre, that no other movie would replace it as their all-time favourite.

As for the half-dozen handmade friendship bracelets, she would leave these in her top drawer along with all of the letters she and Lea had ever written to each other. She tied them up with a ribbon after she learned that Emily Dickinson had done the same with her poems. She would leave the ring Ethan had given her for their one-year anniversary last year. It was an opal in a heart-shaped setting. She had worn it constantly until Lea had told her she had seen Ethan's car parked at Chrissy Beringer's house one Friday night this summer when he was supposed to be visiting his uncle in the hospital in Ottawa. Deirdre had called Chrissy and asked to speak to Ethan. Chrissy had sputtered, feigned ignorance, then put Ethan on. "Deirdre? Is everything okay?" he had asked, his voice rising to a near squeal.

"I would have to answer that question with a NO, Ethan. Everything is not okay at all, but there is this, Ethan. We are over. O-V-E-R. Never speak to me again." She had hung up, cried for two hours, stared at Gandalf and Sam and Frodo and longed to enter another space and time. When Ethan had called back, she did not answer. She told her mother she had a headache and was going to sleep early. The next morning, there was a bouquet of colourful daisies and a letter on her front stoop. Deirdre had brought them inside, dumped the letter and flowers into the kitchen trash, and vowed never to give her heart to another boy to maim and disparage. The opal ring, however, was simply too pretty to get rid of. She would keep it in her drawer and figure out what to do with it another day.

Deirdre opened the Rushdie novel that perched on her bed-side table then closed it again. She had to let it go. She had read enough of it. Deirdre's idea of escape had always been books, and she had contemplated getting her degree in English literature at university until her math teacher had nudged her to "the road not taken," as she called it. Mrs. Longre had an engineering degree from Aquitaine University, and she said she knew an engineering student when she saw one. This was not a complete surprise, of course. Deirdre had aced all of her math and science classes. The moment she got home from school, she took a Coke and a bag of potato chips up to her room to do two hours of calculus homework. Time vanished. Being presented with a problem for which there was a definite solution that had to be discovered, that enticed Deirdre. She would rework problems over and over until she got them right.

Mrs. Longre had recognized this, but it was something else she had told Deirdre that stayed with her.

"Engineering is hard, Deirdre," she said one day after class when the other students had filed out. "It takes guts to be a woman in an engineering school. Let me tell you a story." Mrs. Longre sat on the edge of her desk, spreading her plaid skirt over her legs with her palms. Deirdre held her books to her chest and waited.

"When I was a bit older than you, I had a physics professor who told our class that physics was not for girls. Abstract mathematical and scientific concepts were better suited for male brains, he said. From that moment on, Deirdre, I was deter-mined to get the highest degree possible, higher than whatever he had. Anger drove me to finish my degree at Aquitaine, and I began my graduate work the very next year."

Mrs. Longre had stopped there, glancing toward the window facing the quad festooned with students drinking chocolate milk and eating bagels.

"Mrs. Longre," Deirdre began.

"Oh, I am sorry, my dear," the teacher responded, as if aware once more that Deirdre was there. "This is the hard part of the story, and I want to tell it to you just right. You see, I left graduate school before I finished my degree, despite my best intentions. To this day, I believe it was one professor who triggered my downward spiral. I was in my second year, in a chemistry and materials course. I was one of two women in the class. The professor said to me, as casually as if he were commenting on the phases of the moon, 'What is it with you? Do you want to be a man? Get an engineering husband? Why are you here?'"

"Oh my God," Deirdre had said. "How awful...."

"It was awful. It was thoughtless and stupid, and it still makes me furious. The real problem, however, is that it got to me. His words got under my skin, stayed with me. I tried to shut them out, but I would wake in the night with them in my ears." Mrs. Longre's grasped handfuls of her plaid pleats.

"I am so sorry, Mrs. Longre," said Deirdre. "Didn't any of the others in the class say something to him? Challenge him?"

"No. No one challenged any professor in that school. We were all just so happy to be there. No one took an unnecessary risk and certainly not on behalf of a girl. They probably wondered the same things. Why *was* I there?"

"So what happened next?"

"After that semester, I went home for the winter break, and I cried every day."

"Did you talk to your parents?" Deirdre asked.

"No. I never said a word. The first person I told about that professor's words was my husband, years after we were married. Something about my own self-doubts connected in a perfect storm with that professor's words. I simply could not get past them," Mrs. Longre said, gazing again out the window. "But, you my dear, are so sweet to let me go on like this. And I'm not even getting to my main point. I'm telling you this story because I want you to know two things: engineering *is* still hard for young women like you. Those prejudices are still out there, and most engineering professors are men. But, and this is the second thing, *you* can handle it. You are strong."

"I am?"

"You are, indeed," said Mrs. Longre. "I've had you in class a number of times, and I've watched you among your classmates for years now. You are a natural leader. Other students respect you and come to you for advice. I've noticed you helping your male classmates much more often than they've helped you with calculus problems. The times are changing. We need women in engineering and the sciences. We've lived with male designs for too long. It's time to see engineering from a female perspective. If I had had your grit when I was your age, I would not be teaching high school right now; I might have been in Ottawa designing the National Gallery of Canada. But here I am, and here you are, yet your future is ahead of you, Deirdre."

Mrs. Longre then placed her hand on Deirdre's head, as if to give her a blessing. "May the force be with you, my dear young engineer, "she said, laughing and shooing Deirdre off to her next class.

Deirdre had to admit that Mrs. Longre might not be wrong about her future. That very same night, when Deirdre told her parents about the idea of studying to be an engineer, she saw them light up in a way they certainly had not done when she had announced her plans to be an English major several months earlier; they thought studying English literature was a pie-in-the-sky idea with no practical value. "A waste of money," her father had said. "What will you do with a degree in English? Do you want to be a teacher, Deirdre? Is that really what you want?"

She had not been sure what she wanted, then. She had not been sure she would ever be sure. Having a job teaching literature like Mr. Marche had seemed like a cool idea. Yet, she was intrigued by the things Mrs. Longre had told her about her experience at Aquitaine. In some ways, it seemed so backwards. Surely things had changed? And Deirdre did love a good math problem. Engineers could do so much. She had been reading about how they worked on solving problems and tackling issues all over the world like pollution and even human rights. Her view of what engineers did had expanded since Mrs. Longre's talk. They worked to cure cancer, to make animated movies, to create an über-food that could end world hunger. Engineers seemed like her people. They cared about the world enough to try to help it. Such a nerd, she could hear Lea say, whenever she thought about math. Such a good soul, she could hear Mr. Marche say, whenever she thought about the world's poor.

And now it was now. Here she was, in her childhood bedroom, with a view of the Bonnechere River outside her windows, for the last time. Tomorrow, she was leaving for university. She would enter her first year at Aquitaine University as an engineering student. Mrs. Longre had written her a brilliant letter of recommendation. Mr. Marche had done so too, suggesting she take as many English courses as possible for her electives. She had not had the heart to tell him that electives were scarce for engineers.

The party downstairs was for her, yet she remained in the quiet, trying to memorize her room, her family's voices, her small town. What would it be like on a campus with 14,000 other students from all over the world? She supposed if it got loud enough or too crowded, she could take the ten-minute walk to the shore of Lake Ontario that Aquitaine's brochure boasted, or the twenty-minute walk to downtown Kingston. Still, it would all be so different. No more family meals every night. No more daily phone calls to her girlfriends. No more Mr. Marche. Her life as she had known it was about to change, and Deirdre was terrified.

At least her friends would be arriving soon to join the party. All but two of them had gone off to university already. Emma and Lea would be leaving tomorrow as well, but they had promised to stop by to say goodbye, though they have been saying goodbye for weeks now, practising.

Lea and Deirdre had been best friends since they met as toddlers when their mothers had attended the same Bible study at Our Lady of Fatima Church. While the mothers sipped coffee and read passages from St. Paul's epistles, the girls romped in the playroom that had been overseen by the elderly and dear Mrs. Plumbere. Mrs. Plumbere had baked the best peanut butter cookies, and she read Lea and Deirdre all of the princess stories they requested. When the little boys had gotten rambunctious, Mrs. Plumbere calmed them down without raising her voice. She was magic, Lea and Deirdre had maintained. She was their secret fairy godmother, and whenever they were in trouble, the girls had known, somehow, that Mrs. Plumbere would be there to save the day.

When Mrs. Plumbere had died three years ago, Lea and Deirdre wept at her funeral. Shortly after, they had written her letters on soft linen stationery that they then burned in a tiny bonfire they made one night. Death would not keep Mrs. Plumbere from showing up at the absolute perfect moment, they had decided. She was their angel.

"Every time we smell a peanut butter cookie, every time our eyes light upon a princess, there she will be," the girls had chanted whenever they felt down.

The noise downstairs was getting louder. Deirdre's uncles must be telling their badass stories about criminals and high-speed chases. Deirdre nestled into her old quilt and imagined Lea's reaction when she got Deirdre's going-away gift, to be opened only when she got into bed on her first night in her college dorm at the University of Ontario. It was a tiny silver frame encrusted with pearls, Lea's favourite stone, with a cameo-sized photo of Lea and Deirdre and Mrs. Plumbere when the girls were no more than four years old. In the photo, Mrs. Plumbere was wearing her grey hair in a loose bun with ivory combs holding it up in back, and the girls were in tiny Osh-

Kosh B'gosh overalls, each holding a cookie up to the camera. Deirdre had discovered the photo in the attic when she was packing for college. She had never seen it before, and she was quite certain Lea had not either. If she had been searching for a gift for her best friend that would be guaranteed to make her cry and feel nostalgic all at the same time, this miniature photo was it.

The doorbell rang. Deirdre heard the voices of her mother and aunts ushering the "university girls" into the house. It was time for goodbyes. Deirdre rose and checked her hair in the mirror, brushed a tube of clear gloss across her lips. She tucked *The Satanic Verses* under her pillow, pushed aside the bright blue milk crate that held the books, journals, and notebooks she would take to universiy. She was packed, as ready as ever for tomorrow, which would bring hellos and new friends.

# 5.

OFTEN, IN HER THIRD YEAR, Marin contemplated that she had never intended to become an engineer, or planned to fall in love with a professor. Yet both had come to pass. If Monsieur Toissolle had not taken her aside all those years ago at her parents' annual Christmas fest, she would never have applied to CanTech. "My dear Marin," Monsieur Toissolle had said to her as she seated herself next to him on the sofa to eat her dessert. "Do you still long to become a scenic designer, to create on a grand scale?" Monsieur was a retired chemical engineer who had grown up with her father in France. He had come to Montreal with his family as a boy the year after Marin's own father had arrived on the island. He had never missed a Christmas yet. The confirmed bachelor delighted in the career aspirations of all five of his friend's children.

"Ahhh, Tolley," Marin had said, patting his hand and calling him by the name all the Hazeur children used for this beloved man, "I still do want to create the biggest, most realistic archways, verdant gardens, pristine and sparkling skies. Most of all, what I want is to bang nails into wood and to paint and to weld metal to metal. I want to get into the grittiest birthing of theatrical worlds." Marin had breathed deeply, taken a bite of pumpkin pie. She had seldom spoken with such passion about her dreams unless it was to Tolley. She had trusted him, felt he understood her more than others did. He was the sagest old man she knew.

"Marin, here is what you must do," Monsieur Toissolle had said. "You must enroll in CanTech and take a degree in engineering."

"CanTech? The engineering school? But that is…" Marin had said.

"Marin, my Marin, if you want to create industrial-sized sets in Montreal, you need credentials. If you want to be taken seriously, to be awarded contracts, you must be an engineer, my dear. You have come this far, why not persevere?"

Marin would not be accepted at CanTech without work in math, physics, and science, so she went back to to take the requisite courses. She had known Tolley was right. He had simply confirmed that her road to success would be longer and more arduous. Determined to be accepted, Marin had studied constantly. Those long afternoons with black coffee at Université Sainte-Catherine had disciplined her concentration. But math had not come as easily at first, particularly when the variables started to move, as they did in calculus. So, Marin had rewarded herself after each hour of study with a Mounds bar or M&Ms, whatever the vending machine had to offer.

It had been her brother who coached her through. She and Hilaire spoke the same language when it came to hockey, and she had figured correctly that this would translate into her baby brother supporting her through math and physics. Marin and Hilaire were Montreal Canadiens fanatics. They had barbed each other incessantly when they were teenagers with team stats, and Marin had held her own against Hilaire's expertise. On the spot, she could recite the team motto, "*Nos bras meurtris vous tendent le flambeau, à vous toujours de le porter bien haut,*" or, "To you from failing hands we throw the torch. Be yours to hold it high." The motto had come from the 1915 war poem, "In Flanders Fields," by John McCrae, which also happened to be the first year the Canadiens won the Stanley Cup, a fact she announced proudly whenever Hilaire tried to catch her off guard. When it came to Le Bleu-Blanc-Rouge, she knew her stuff, and Hilaire granted her the same respect he did his buddies. Often, in fact, Marin had been in tow when Hilaire headed for the stadium. They had been a team, and he skated her through the goalposts of engineering school. She would love him always for this, though when it came to Canadiens' history, she would whip his butt every time, and he knew it.

*

Whenever the crisp harvest smells of autumn returned, as they did now, Marin recalled in exact detail how she had met Trey in October 1979. Marin was the darling bartender of Le Tap then, ten years ago, the bistro-bar sandwiched between Mexican and Indian restaurants on St. Denis, the busiest street in the Université Sainte-Catherine neighborhood. Le Tap approximated upscale but missed by half a kilometre. It was in the details, Marin maintained. The bar top itself was made of a thick slab of black cherry. Its lineaments were sage and steady, but its patina was weary. Three coats of polyurethane and a vigorous sanding between each coat would have resuscitated the cherry's soul, but Jack, the owner, was too busy bringing in as many blonde, buxom coeds on Thirsty Thursday as Le Tap could hold. His business plan: let the young males in heat follow them to the bar, purchase a mother lode of pitchers all night long, and make Jack rich.

Le Tap was a good thing. Jack knew it. Not one DUI linked to his bar. These kids walked home to residence halls around the corner, to apartments just blocks away. Or they puked on the Metro. No skin off his back. So long as they bought and boozed on Thursdays, returned Fridays and Saturdays, he met his mortgage and child support obligations, and he was free the rest of the week now that he had Marin. Marin was the most dependable bartender he had ever hired, and he had hired a few in his day. They had all done him dirt. The first and last stole from him, the ones in-between screwed with his inventory, his alarm system, and, finally, his wife. Jack hated bartenders. He had once dreamed of a female bartender, a Marin: pretty, smart, organized, reliable. Jack had nearly forsaken that dream until she walked in that late August afternoon. He was sipping an iced Chambord at the bar, scratching at his account book. She wore a loose khaki blazer over a white, long-sleeved shirt and a red tie, a power tie like those worn by the businessmen who stopped in during the weekdays for a beer and a Reuben. Despite the tie, there was nothing masculine about this woman. She walked with confidence, she held herself with poise, but she smiled the smile of the girl you wanted to know. The girl to whom you would be willing to confess that your dad hid his empty Tia Maria bottles in the laundry room and your sister had a baby when she was only thirteen. Those bright eyes, that welcoming face. She was stunning. Better yet, she was charismatic and clearly spontaneous, walking in off the street to claim a job for herself. She was a woman who was used to getting her way without imposing on others. Le Tap would love the shit out of Marin. Jack loved her already. Instantly.

"Mr. LaPrade, I am Marin, and I would like to be your new bartender. *Ca va?*"

Her gaze never wavered. She held Jack's eyes. He nodded. It was settled. "Tomorrow at four. Can you begin then?" he asked.

She shook his hand, smiled, and said, "Thank you. I will be here."

It was only as Marin walked out of the bar that Jack noticed she was a tiny woman, about 5' 2". Her robust presence defied such a small frame. She remained at Le Tap the entire four years it took to complete her degree at Université Sainte-Catherine, and she continued on while she took the prerequisites she needed to be accepted at CanTech. Bless the starry heavens that she was there, or Jack could not have kept the whole enterprise afloat.

In her sketchbook, in stolen moments, Marin re-designed Le Tap from the time she punched in until the time the "kids" arrived in droves from Thursday through Saturday. She kept the black leather sketchbook beneath the bar for those rare moments when she could charcoal her ideas for transforming Le Tap from dingy pub to alluring café, something one might find in Le Plateau proper. Marin drafted a new logo for the street edifice to replace the lacquered painting of a keg that swayed above the front door, all garish and abject. Marin envisioned a glazed terracotta fresco of potted ferns, baskets of French loaves, and slim bottles of olive oil. She created a Mediterranean ensemble for the booths that lined the walls of Le Tap. Each bench seat would be upholstered with damask, hued in magentas and patterned after grape vines. Crenellated drapes would mimic sea breezes. The entire design a medley of the French Riviera with Sicily. Jack gazed at her sketches as if upon a mirage, envisioning a sumptuous future outside of his ken.

One Saturday night when the crowd was thick with university students and a handful of professors laying claim to Le Tap's roomiest booth in the front corner of the bar, visiting for a nightcap after a retirement party, Marin discovered her sketchbook on the bar. She never left it out. One of the staff who had come behind the bar to replenish olives and lemons must have moved it to get at the ice chests. Her book was opened to the pages with her most recent drawings, her plans for redoing the cherry bar top with a layer of hammered bronze. Marin had painstakingly penciled in the tiny bronze nails that would secure the large sheet of bronze to the cherry, spaced exactly two inches apart. She had shaded the metal such that the indignities of the hammering were visible in all their weathered pride. Bronze had been Marin's favourite metal since she was ten years old, when her father took her to visit Gaetan Trottier, artist and sculptor, best known for his bronze sculptures, in Old Montreal. Not even Jack had seen this page. The cost, Marin estimated, would be steep, and installation and craftsmanship would require Le Tap to close for several days, and that could never happen until the height of summer when classes were in recess, so she took her time working on this idea.

Marin watched from behind the bar as a man picked up her sketchbook and sat with one leg on the floor, the other on the crossbars of the stool. He held a glass of Chateauneuf-du-Pape, Le Tap's higher end red wine, in one hand and her sketchbook in the other. Marin had poured several glasses of the Papa, as she and the waiters called it, for the table of Université Sainte-Catherine professors a half hour earlier. Seldom did Le Tap clients order such fine wine. The young professor who was among that group had caught Marin's eye because he was profoundly striking. And here he stood holding her sketchbook, seemingly studying her newest bronze bar sketch.

Her oldest sister Sybille would not have found him appealing. Neither would her friends at Université Sainte-Catherine. He was not exactly handsome, not six-pack and glistening handsome. His face was all cheekbones and straight nose, his dark eyes intensely focused. His hair was dark and cut short on the back and sides, left longer on the top where it lay in waves, not unlike Rob Lowe's. He wore a manicured beard, no moustache, and looked more European than Canadian. On second thought, Marin considered him rather arresting, the sort of man you took time to consider well, before you were sure it was attraction that gave you pause. Even now, as Marin perched behind the bar, she found herself drawn to the man studying her sketchbook. Strangers typically put her on guard long before she was comfortable enough to let them catch her fancy.

"*Bon soir*," she said, smiling at the man from across the bar, gesturing toward her sketchbook. "Do you like my drawing?"

"*Bon soir*," he returned, nodding, and passing the book back to her, as if embarrassed to be caught with her sketchbook. "You have talent. Your attention to detail is ... these miniscule nails, bronze, eh? Such perfection. You're a student at Université Sainte-Catherine in the Design Arts program, *oui*?"

"I am. How do you know this?" Marin wiped up the bar top next to the man, removing an empty pitcher and a half dozen beer glasses, placing them into the plastic tub behind the bar.

He leaned forward, offered her his hand. "I'm Trey Dentreau, a professor in the Design Arts program. I've seen you many times on campus, in the coffee shop in the afternoon." Marin shook Trey Dentreau's hand.

"You've been watching me?" she asked, wary, or charmed perhaps, casting a glance to her left to spot where Sean, the rugby-playing waiter was stationed.

"I'm sorry to say, I have been watching you. I don't mean to scare you. I admit ... I was admiring your, your work ethic. You study so hard. You drink your coffee black in the afternoons, and you use a Sharpie highlighter in your texts, and you take notes in a notebook whose spiral is at top instead of at the side. You must forgive me, I'm no danger to you. I simply think you are ... lovely." Trey Dentreau stopped here, looked at Marin, picked up his glass of red wine, and turned as if to go.

"You go so soon?" Marin asked, wishing Trey to stay, yet bewildered by her precipitous comfort with this stranger who observed so much.

"I'm such a fool. I've presented myself as some kind of dunce. You'll forgive me if I vanish into the professorial pack in the corner." He stood now, removing his leg from the barstool. He leaned in a little, not quite onto the bar, but closer.

They looked at each other over the bar, Trey preparing a last word before going, Marin unsure if she wanted him to go. "But you do like my drawing?" she asked.

"*C'est bon.* Yes. I like everything," he said. He reached out, laid his hand on hers lightly for a second. Then he walked to the roomiest booth in the bar and wedged back into his colleagues' party.

Marin wiped up the bar, preoccupied, wondering about this Trey and feeling sick to her stomach.

So many years later, Marin could laugh at that initial sick

feeling, comforted by the history she and Trey had long been forging. Engineering school demanded so much of her time and her spirit that sometimes Trey took a back seat. Remembering how they began, the tentative and sweet nature of their barroom acquaintance, held Marin together when engineering school messed with her equilibrium.

# 6.

AFTER SHE FILED HER COLUMN every week, Jenean had a sacred tradition. She took a long, steaming bath in lavender bath salts and rose petals. The air in her tiny bathroom became misty, and the scent quelled her racing brain. On filing day, it was the one peace-filled hour she could count on before she started the writing process all over again. Bart was off to work. She was not expected at the paper until this afternoon. The phone was unplugged. This was her time.

She settled her white terrycloth robe onto the hook of the bathroom door, placed two thick towels on the vanity, and set her notebook, pen, and eyeglasses on the tiny wrought-iron table by the window. When she stripped off her sweatpants and sweatshirt and stepped into the tub, she breathed deeply, easing gently into the hot water.

This room was the one place where she could think clearly. It was as if the lavender eased all of the tension and cramped muscles of her mind. As if air more easily played about, loosening up calcified thoughts, setting ideas free. Without this weekly ritual, Jenean knew she could not survive. It was where she became human again after living life as a disembodied brain for a full week.

In this very same steaming hothouse, Jenean had conceived of *La Vision et La Voix*. How many years ago now? The monthly had been launched in 1980, and ultimately, the darned thing hit a circulation of forty thousand before it crashed and burned three years ago. God, how she had loved that magazine. It was everything she had wanted. Who would have thought that four young women could start a feminist magazine in Montreal and make a professional go of it for six years? And only forty years after women got the right to vote in Quebec – the last bloody province in the country to "allow" women the vote.

Jenean eased deeper into the water, focused on her breath, observed that when she thought about the magazine, about its demise, her breathing became shallow, the muscles in her shoulders and neck tightened. She had to let all that go. It was over. She had a new life now. She was a journalist, a columnist for a premiere Sunday magazine.

Still, why did she feel sometimes cursed with this commitment, this intrepid commitment to writing the truth. Writing the whole truth, not just one of the well-trod paths of the status quo that so many readers wanted to hear. She would certainly be more popular if she could just lighten up. Aughhh ... how many times had she heard that in her thirty-four years? *Just lighten up, Jenean. Life is not so hard, not so difficiles, ardu, compliquer. You think too much. You over-analyze. Take it easy, girl.*

Jenean sat up fully in the tub and shook her head. She had to shimmy off the past that sometimes felt intrepid enough to infiltrate her precious bath time. Those words and voices from her past knew when she was vulnerable, and they hid behind clouds of misty lavender and pounced on her when she was at her most lax. "Not today," she said out loud, "*n'est pas aujourd'hui,*" as she turned on the tap to top off the tub with hot water. She reached for the jar of lavender salts and spooned another tablespoon beneath the gushing stream. "Out, out..." she shouted to the voices that soon vanished from her weary mind.

For all her feistiness, Jenean had to concede that she was a measured liberal. That may have been what had sealed the deal at the magazine. She was not "feminist" enough, some had said. Where Jenean had aimed at humour and a more holistic sensibility, incorporating, for example, writings by men into the magazine, – creating, goddess forbid, the 1983 special issue in which male writers shared their thoughts on feminism – her former friends, the radical wing of the provincial feminist movement, had taken issue. Nah, that was too polite. They had been fucking incensed. They had demanded that the magazine be tougher, and not align itself with patriarchal, fascist pigs who played nice until they could coerce the naïve editors, including Jenean, into flushing the entire enterprise down the toilet.

"My goal is to reach a broad spectrum of readers," Jenean remembered having told a reporter during that embattled time, "a public who may not have considered themselves feminists but are a bit more open-minded." She could recall her own words verbatim because they had been thrown in her face so often after that. She had simply wanted a good magazine filled with phenomenal writing. She had known a monthly tirade was not a business-savvy route to take. As feminists, they could achieve their ends with thought-provoking, well-written, well-researched articles. Was this not the goal of feminism at large: to make social change? To engender equality for women? Had they really expected to do that if they clobbered readers over the head with raging diatribes?

But she had been shouted down time and again, and the magazine folded. It had been her proudest brainchild, but it was gone, and her grief was put to rest one day at a time, one Sunday column at a time. She could not abide by Emily Dickinson's warning: "Tell all the truth but tell it slant." Dickinson was right, of course. The world could not handle the raw truth. It preferred a prettified version. People preferred their truth lavendered up, wrapped in scented towels, offered gently over chamomile tea. Jenean Belisle could not coddle her public such. She would not. If feminism had taught her nothing else, it was that the truth was worth questing after.

Jenean rested into the warmth of the water, shooing the parading memories aside. This had been a long week. Sometimes, the truths she had to share with the world were truths she wished she did not know herself, but in the end, she could always lay it all down and get into the tub to embrace the simple life if but for a delicious moment.

# 7.

THE LETTER FROM LEA was just what Deirdre needed. She found it stuffed into her mailbox with a package of Hermit cookies from her mother and flyers from the campus theatre and judo clubs. She shoved them all into her backpack and ran to her dormitory. Lea was three hours away at the University of Ontario studying psychology, and Deirdre missed her more than anyone else back home. The girls still told each other everything. Deirdre opened the letter, sampled a cookie, and relaxed into this brief interlude with her dearest friend. According to the letter, Lea was loving university. She was earning spending money by participating in psychology department experiments about colour blindness and memory. She had gained eight pounds and could no longer fit into her favourite jeans. She was thinking of pledging a sorority. This gave Deirdre a slow ache in her stomach. She closed her eyes and settled into her bed for a while until the feeling passed.

Lea loved the photo of Mrs. Plumbere, of course, and she reassured Deirdre that it sat on her desk in her dorm room. For the first week of school, she had cried every time she looked at it. Lea had given Deirdre a handmade book that must have taken her weeks to research and compose. Deirdre had wondered what Lea had been working on so diligently at the Renfrew Public Library for all of August, but Lea had explained that she was working on her summer reading program, a requirement at UO. When Lea handed over her goodbye gift that last night in Renfrew, with Deirdre's relatives all around, Deirdre had fought back tears. *What Women Engineers Do and Why They Do It,* the title read. Lea had bound the book with a spiral wire at the local print shop. She had stitched a cover made from tiny pieces she had cut from Deirdre and Lea's prom dresses and graduation gowns and scraps from their old T-shirts and flannel nightgowns. Each page told the story of a different woman engineer. Deirdre had hugged the book to her chest and pulled her best friend out the back door to the enormous tire swing Mr. Sevier had hung from the old maple when Deirdre was just six. They still fit two at a time, inside the tire tube.

"You are the best, Lea. I can't imagine life at university without you, without your red curls."

"I know. Me too," Lea had said. "I cried all afternoon, and, oh my God, when I handed that book over to the printer for the binding, right in the shop I burst into tears. I was mortified, D. Do you think we'll stop crying when we get used to university?"

"God, I hope so."

Lea and Deirdre had become quiet then, swinging gently from the tire swing.

Lea had spoken first, into the dark night. "Let's promise, D. No matter how awesome our new friends are at university, no matter if we meet the men of our dreams or get the careers of our lives, we'll always stay friends."

"I promise," Deirdre had said, tears in her voice.

The two friends had sat twirling until all of the relatives had come to kiss goodbye and all of the stars had positioned themselves in the Canadian sky. When they hugged a final farewell, with hearts broken open, it had been, technically, their first day of university.

After she folded Lea's letter back into its envelope and tucked it into the shoebox where she stored keepsakes, Deirdre sat at her desk, turned back her calendar, and counted. This was her thirty sixth day at Aquitaine. The homesickness was over. She had made friends, and she actually liked the food in the cafeteria, especially the corn bread they served on Thursdays with beef stew. How had time moved so quickly?

The first day she had not been sure she would make it though, and she had contemplated calling her parents to whisk her back to Renfrew. Her seminar in engineering had begun when a small man with dark hair and a beard breezed into the room, introduced himself, and never stopped talking or moving for the full ninety minutes. "I am Dr. Sanjani," he said. "In this first-year engineering seminar, we will be exploring biomimetics and biomimetic research." No small talk, right to business. Without saying a word, he handed a bulk of syllabi to a student who sat in the front. The professor simply looked at the student, then lifted his chin, indicating the rest of the class, about a dozen students. Translation: Pass these syllabi around.

He turned to draw a rudimentary tree on the blackboard. "This course will explore how engineers mimic or copy shapes found in nature. We will be investigating why similar shapes occur in so many natural things and how physics changes the shape of nature. Why do trees and birds and plants look the way they do? Why can't trees grow taller than they are? Why is grass skinny and hollow?"

As he paced the front of the classroom, positing question after question, Deirdre looked at the syllabus that was finally passed her way. She would be reading articles like "The Mechanical Design of Trees," and "On the Mechanics of Balsa Wood and Other Woods." Most of the articles were from something called *Proceedings of the Royal Society of London*. She had never heard of this, nor had she heard of the *Journal of Materials Science*. Suddenly, Deirdre realized the professor had stopped speaking and from the way his head was inclined to the side, she knew he had asked a question. He was looking at them. No one spoke.

"Allow me to rephrase the question," he said, raising his voice half a decibel. "How tall can a tree grow? Does anyone want to take a stab at that?"

From the row behind her, Deirdre felt the air move in the silent and still room, as a brave student raised his hand. The professor nodded at the student.

"I am not sure how tall a tree can grow, but there is a limit, and that has to do with how far up the trunk a tree can pull water ... I think."

"Do not say 'think.' Be confident. You are quite right. Cells called tracheids move water from one cell to the next. As you ascend a tree, the diameter of these cells shrinks, and water transportation becomes compromised. Eventually water flow stops, and we get what is called 'drought stress.'" The professor turned and wrote "drought stress" on the board. "Branches and leaves at the top become, essentially, dehydrated, and they die. This makes for a limitation, a maximum height for that tree, if you will."

Deirdre wrote "tracheids" and "drought stress" into her notebook, but the professor was speaking so rapidly that she knew she would have to review her notes and fill in gaps as soon as class was over. Otherwise she would forget everything. The only saving grace was that Professor Sanjani wrote all terms on the board and tended to muse a bit, giving the students a chance to catch up.

Immediately after her seminar, Deirdre's Principles of Engineering Practice course met once a week for lecture and once for lab. The syllabus said to expect six hours of homework a week. She soon learned it would be more like ten. There were four lab experiments to do, four case studies, one final synthesis, and one final project. The case studies had to be done in teams, and each team had to present just one solution in a fifteen minute presentation. All members had to speak. Her team members included Jon Chen, a student from China, and Steve and Allain, both from Ottawa. The four of them worked together, almost daily, for the entire semester. Their first lab was on the invention of the transistor as an example of a creative failure methodology. It was not her favourite lab. That would have to be either Speed of Light or one of the solar topics, Solar Cell Performance or Simulation of Solar Cells. She was surprised how much she loved the sun and how much joy she took from "The Solar Cell" lecture her professor had given the third week of class. Into that night, Deirdre had pondered how relatively few years ago, people had relied solely on the sun for energy. How in such a short time the world had come to rely on traditional energy sources that would be depleted, possibly within her lifetime. None of the girls in the dorm were interested when she had tried to explain to them about the possibilities of renewable energies like wind and hydro power, but Deirdre knew she had found her people in engineering, people who thought about topics like the sun as much as she did.

The real surprise of the semester turned out to be PHIL400, Feminist Philosophical Thought. Because it was a year-long course, this meant Deirdre would have no other elective that year. Of the twenty-four students, only two were male and only one was a first year, and that was Deirdre. Feminist Philosophical Thought had not been her first choice. She was not even really sure what feminism was. But the class was offered twice a week from 10:00 to 11:15 a.m., the only slot that worked with her lab schedule. Professor Oliver was her best shot, so she showed up at her office on registration day and asked her permission to join, though the class was recommended only for third and fourth year students.

"Have you done any feminist reading?" Oliver had asked, peering over her tortoise-shell glasses to look at Deirdre who stood up straight on the other side of the expansive desk, staring at the professor's crystal blue earrings that dangled and caught the light of her green desk lamp

"I haven't, but I did check out the class reading list at the bookstore, and I already started to read Adrienne Rich's poetry, hoping you would say yes, and..."

"What is your major again?" the professor had asked. She had stopped rearranging sheets of paper on her desk and was giving her full attention to Deirdre now.

"Engineering," Deirdre had replied.

"Really? It is the rare engineering student who is interested in philosophy, never mind feminism."

"Honestly, Professor, I love to read. I love a challenge, and this class fits perfectly into my schedule." Deirdre had kept the professor's eye contact, but she felt her shoulders raise a bit, uncertain that this last snippet of honesty indicated a winning rationale. The professor had laughed, reached out for the form Deirdre held in her hand, and signed the waiver that allowed Deirdre into the upper-level course as a first-year student.

"We meet tomorrow at 10:00 a.m., Deirdre. I look forward to having you in my class," Professor Oliver had said, smiling quickly, and returning to the papers on her desk. Deirdre had thanked her and dashed across the quad to the registrar's office before the professor could change her mind. She had gotten in, and that was good for her schedule, but what was she in for?

*

Aquitaine was getting media attention and lots of it. Right off the bat, the Feminist Philosophical Thought classroom was abuzz. The university was a hotbed of unrest, according to one newspaper. The No Means No campaign had started in September with a thorough pamphleting of the campus, students going dorm to dorm to share information and raise awareness about sexual assault at the university. This seemed simple enough to Deirdre, but that was before things went ballistic, and Feminist Philosophical Thought really heated up.

Deirdre had not been ready to call herself a "feminist" when she first arrived at the university, but she had to admit that some of the reading made sense, and the happenings on campus had her considering the world in a different way. The No Means No Campaign was the talk of the campus

After one student's rape, one too many for the Canadian Federation of Students, they launched the No Means No campaign just this September. The CFS representatives wanted to do something positive after the rape victim had dropped out of school. "No recourse," she had kept saying, after the university's judicial system failed to remove her attacker and after a protective order had failed to keep him out of her fourth-year seminar. She saw him every day. He whispered when he walked by. She could not take it. A few angry students had wanted to kidnap the jackass, tie him up, and stick him in the middle of the quad after writing "Rapist" in Sharpie all over his body. Cooler heads had prevailed, and the No Means No campaign was adopted.

Commissioner House, a first-year male residence, responded with venom to the No Means No campaign, posting vulgar signs in their dorm windows, which faced out into the quad, directly across from Deirdre's dorm. In enormous masking-tape letters, the signs read: "No Means Kick Her in the Teeth"; "No Means Down on Your Knees, Bitch"; "No Means More Beer"; "No Means Yes and Yes Means Anal"; "No Means Dyke"; "No Means Tie Me Up."

A group of women students in Deirdre's class, known for putting stop signs in places on campus where women had been sexually assaulted, were not standing for the likes of Commissioner House. They got busy. They spoke to every campus administrator, insisting the Commissioner boys take the signs down. No one helped. They wrote letters to the boys' mothers telling them what their sons had been up to. They called the boys in the middle of the night and told them to take the signs down. Deirdre listened to all of this with horror and amazement. Back home in Renfrew, things like this did not happen. At least she had never heard of them. Truth be told, she could not wait to get to class each week to catch up on what the activist women were up to. This was real-life problem solving, and she had a front row seat.

But Feminist Philosophical Thought was a bit of a vexation to her friends in Meese Hall. The only other person she could talk to about this class was Rosalie, a second-year who lived down the hall from her and who was also in the class. The girls in her dorm, she learned, were not "girls" at all but "women." Any human who had reached the age of eighteen, her professor said, could be rightfully called a "man" or a "woman." Deirdre knew she would always be a "girl" at home, but she decided to practise at school, and her friends noticed when she called to them, "Women of Meese Hall. Let's go to dinner."

"Are you serious, Deirdre? You're going all feminist on us? Should we call you Gloria Steinem, get you a *Playboy* bunny outfit for Halloween? She is the one who did the undercover *Playboy* stint, right?" The sniping was playful, and her friends yanked on her ponytail to make that clear. They were not hostile, simply puzzled.

"Aren't there radical lesbians in that class, Deirdre? Aren't you afraid? I have seen some of those butches, and they could kick the crap out of you and me and the football team."

The fact was that Deirdre had been afraid of some of the students at first. They had strong opinions, and they were loud and angry a lot of the time. The first week, Ellen, a tiny woman with a shaved head and the most muscular arms and legs Deirdre had ever seen, had stormed to the front of the class and drew a map of the world she envisioned, a world where no men existed, and where women lived in peace. "Death to Patriarchy," she had written on the board beneath the sprawling map. "Long live Charlotte Perkins Gilman and *Herland*."

Professor Oliver had assigned the novel *Herland* the week before. Deirdre had told her roommate Jenna about it. "The novel is about a utopia written in 1915, and it's actually really cool. There's this expedition party, three guys who go in search of this uncharted land where only women live. Two thousand years earlier, all the men were killed when a volcano erupted and sealed off the only passage out of *Herland*. The women set up this ideal society. You know, no war, no domination. Then these men come, and they mess with things, and one of them rapes one of the women."

"Wait," said Jenna, bouncing up and down on her bed, where she sat crossed-legged. She did this when she got energized. "So, these women live alone with no men for two thousand years? Why don't they die out? They can't have sex, so there are no babies...."

"There are lots of babies. It is so cool. They...."

"How, Deirdre? How are there babies when...."

"Parthenogenesis. Asexual reproduction. It occurs naturally in some plants and some species of bees and scorpions..." Deirdre had explained, recalling what Professor Oliver had told them about the science of Gilman's novel in class.

"No way," Jenna had said, sitting very still on her bed now, but twisting her blue hair elastic into knots.

"Way," Deirdre had responded, laughing. "So, these women live in harmony, but things gets messed up when the men come along and try to have power over the women."

"Can you actually imagine that, Deirdre? You and me and Sam and Lisa and Rosalie and all the girls here living alone without boys? No boys? How could that be a good thing? Lisa would drive me crazy with her constant Boy George albums. Wait, there would be no Boy George! Oh, my God, but Sam would have to have electricity for her electric curlers...do they have electricity there? Wait, wait.... D, this isn't real, right? This partheno thing can't really happen? Are you sure you should be in this class?"

After Ellen had written "Death to Patriarchy" on the board in the classroom and returned to her seat, Professor Oliver had thanked her, then added, "Separatist politics are an important topic for us to consider, but let's think about this: how practical it is to create a separate 'colony' in which women exist separate from men. Are we quite sure Charlotte Perkins Gilman meant for her utopia to be taken literally so much as a metaphor for an alternative power structure, one we might imagine if we were able to look beyond the way the world is organized today?"

Ellen and Roberta were part of the activist group that called themselves FRRF (Fucking Radical Rogue Feminists), the ones fighting hardest against the Commissioner House signs. They had explained at the beginning of the semester how they got the name. One day, their friends Cheryl and Jen had been walking past an engineering party when they saw effigies of nurses hung from trees and smeared with ketchup. Furious, Cheryl and Jen had torn the effigies down, put them in the trash, and set them on fire. One of the drunken partygoers saw them and chased them, screaming "Fucking Radical Rogue Feminists!" The term stuck, and the women who hung out at the campus Women's Centre, including Roberta and Ellen, co-opted the name.

Roberta was a big woman in every sense of the word, and her voice boomed whenever she spoke. Her strawberry blond hair had a mussed-up look, as though she had run her fingers through it still wet and got on with her day. Nodding, she had turned to Ellen and put her hand on her back. "What you write is nothing but the truth, but Professor O. is right: we have to change the system from within. We don't have a *Herland* to head out to. All we've got is this." Roberta had opened her arms wide and swiveled around to demonstrate the entirety of the classroom and the campus outside the windows. "*This* is what we have, Ellen. Patriarchy screws it up for women every day, but we have to keep fighting to save it."

They were no longer scary to Deirdre. She had spent the entire month of September and the early days of October with Roberta and Ellen and the other women whose confidence and rage sent out force fields ahead of them, proclaiming their politics. When exactly she stopped being afraid, she was not sure. Maybe it was when individual students told their stories about their lives, maybe it was when they shared what they called their "feminist click" moments, but one event did stand out. It was when Roberta asked about Mary Daly, a professor who taught at Boston College in the States. "Is it true," Roberta asked, "that she does not allow men into her Women's Studies classes?"

"It is true," said Professor Oliver. "Dr. Daly is a feminist theologian. She has two doctorates. She doesn't allow men into her advanced Women's Studies courses, only into her introductory Women's Studies courses. She does, however, privately tutor any men who want to get into her advanced classes."

"Why does she refuse to let them in?" asked Ben, one of two male students in the class.

"Well, according to Dr. Daly, their presence inhibits the class discussion, she said. Her intention is to create a *Herland* of sorts where the female students can speak freely, challenge patriarchal concepts in a safe zone, without having men in the class who might get defensive," the professor explained.

"Have you ever thought about doing that?" Ellen asked the professor, glancing at Ben and Whit who always sat together near the window.

Professor Oliver nodded and raised her eyebrows. "Yes. Many times, in fact. But I won't. The bottom line is this: men *need* to be here. They need to understand how they have been privileged and how power works. They need to hear from women themselves how oppression has hurt them, continues to hurt them. They need us."

Ellen looked thoughtful, then asked, "Have you ever had any trouble from men in one of your classes?"

"Never. I think it's because I meet with every enrolled male student in my office before the course begins. Right, Ben and Whit?"

Ben and Whit nodded. "She does," said Ben, leaning his elbow on his desk and holding his chin in one hand. "When

I went in, Professor Oliver explained that this class would be different from any other I had taken, and she was right." Whit patted Ben on the shoulder and took over the telling of the story. Deirdre could not get over how much Whit looked like the young Westley in *The Princess Bride,* all muscular with a sweet face (before Westley grew that silly moustache), thick blond hair, and "eyes the colour of the sea after a storm," as Princess Buttercup would say.

"Professor Oliver said that the Number One goal was to create a safe space so that each of our voices could be heard," Whit said. "She gave us these studies to read. They explained how in 'regular' classrooms, men dominated class discussions, got called on more often than women, and basically, how gender politics played out. She said her aim was to reverse this trend and that our job, as guys, was to cooperate with this new way of being...."

"Yeah," interrupted Ben. "She has a few rules. We have to wait until at least one woman student has spoken before sharing. If we have our hands up and she does not call on us, it is because she is waiting for the women to have a chance to share first. Then she will call on us."

"Were you pissed?" asked Roberta.

Ben and Whit looked at each other and shrugged. Ben twisted his mouth to the left, a sign he was thinking hard. Ben was always thinking hard. In fact, Deirdre had determined after the very first class that he looked like a professor in the making. No matter the weather, Ben wore a brown tweed jacket with huge flap pockets and a velvet collar, something he surely found at a thrift shop. Even on those early humid September days when he wore shorts and a T-shirt, Ben donned the tweed.

Whit laughed. "No," he said. "Not mad. More like sort of stunned. It had never occurred to me that there had been studies about guys and girls in a classroom. This was all new, but I wanted to learn this stuff, so I sucked it up, I guess."

Ben crossed his arms and sat back in his seat. "Me too," he said. "What he said."

"Don't take this the wrong way," said Sarah in a voice a bit too loud. "But my boyfriend says any guy who takes a feminist course is gay. I bet you get that a lot, right?"

"Yep," said Whit. "A lot."

Ben shook his head, sat up straight in his chair. "No disrespect, Sarah, but I'm so tired of that. Seriously. The world is that simple? Feminism equals gay? There can't be other reasons?"

"Well," retorted Sarah, as if channelling her boyfriend, "what other reasons are there? I'm just asking." Deirdre wondered why Sarah was taking this class, why she was so provocative.

"You're just insulting us, Sarah, that's what you're doing," Ben barked. The room was quiet for a long time, waiting to see what would happen. Then Ben added, almost in a whisper, "There was this girl in Mali. I was in seventh grade. Her name was Amaya. My mom and I sent money to support her education each month, not much, but something to help. She sent us letters and a photo. She had these long black curls and the darkest eyes and a huge space between her front teeth. We put her picture on the fridge, and we talked about her like she was my sister. At Christmas, we sent her photos of us and invited her to stay with us if she ever got to Canada. We sent her a blouse my mom made out of this pale blue cotton. It had white rick-rack around the bottom and the collar. We never heard from Amaya. We don't know if she got our gift. A few months later, we got a letter from the agency that helped distribute funds to Malian children. It said she had died from complications from female circumcision, that they were very sorry. Amaya was seven years old." Tears appeared in the corners of Ben's eyes. The room was still.

Ellen stood up. Deirdre recalled another student telling her that Ellen had been sexually assaulted when someone broke into her apartment a year or so before. She had fought him off. Neighbours had called police. The man had never been found.

Ellen got a giant dog after that and shaved her head. She did this huge art installation about the attempted rape, called it "Blood and Hate." Not much made Ellen cry, the student had said, but kindness got to her in a big way. She stayed by her seat for several moments then walked slowly over to Ben and stood in front of him. They looked at each other, Ben's eyes glinting with tears. Neither looked away. Professor Oliver sat on her desk and waited.

"Will you help us with the No Means No fight?" she asked Ben.

"Yes," he said, softly, looking into Ellen's face.

"May I hug you?" Ellen asked. Ben nodded. She hugged. He hugged back. That was all. Ellen returned to her seat. Professor Oliver smiled. She, too, had tears in her eyes. Sarah looked at her hands folded on her desk. Deirdre could not explain the feeling she had in her chest, the pressure behind her eyes, but she knew something very big had just happened.

# 8.

*

SYBILLE'S PSYCHIC CONNECTION to her sister Marin baffled the scientist in her. A biomedical researcher, she relied on empirical evidence, yet her sister seemed hard-wired into her subconscious in some inscrutable way. Now that Marin's life was more settled, Sybille had the recurring dream about her sister far less frequently. When she had it, however, it was always the exact same, a reliving of that horrible, very real moment at the bus stop from years ago.

Marin was seventeen and working as a cashier at one of the shops at Montreal's Mirabel International Airport, the same job that Sybille had once had, in the summers and at night after school. That particular Sunday, she had finished her shift for the night and walked to the bus stop. The air was cool, and Marin buttoned her coat up tight. She sat on the bench beneath the open-air kiosk. She was about to fish out her book from her bag, when she felt someone behind her. She stiffened. Before she could turn to look around, Marin felt one hand on her shoulder, the other brushing her hair from her face. Marin began to scream when a moist hand clamped onto her mouth. She jerked forward to get away, but the hand held tight, the one over her mouth, another on her neck.

He spoke into her ear. "Keep very quiet, and you will be okay. Stop screaming. Now." His voice was deep and wavering, as if his vocal cords were damaged or frozen. Marin became very still, but her mind was racing. *What to do? What to do?* She kept thinking as hard as her brain would allow. Terrified, she tried to look around. She knew no one would be there. Sundays were always quiet. She was often alone at this bus stop. And she had never been afraid before. Again, she jerked her torso away from this man. She had to get away.

He smelled of wet wool and dank skin. His breath was heavy with smoke. He kept speaking, leaning his head against hers. She could barely hear him, so rigid was she with fright, but he was repeating something. What was it? "Pretty girl. All alone. Too bad...." Was that it?

Marin braced herself. Then, without a hint, she shoved the entire weight of her body back with all of her strength. She slammed into his chest, shook his hands from her neck and head. She screamed the instant his hand left her mouth. She tried to get up off the bench and run.

He pulled her down. Slapped her on the side of the head. Drove a knee into her back. She arched. Tears came to her eyes.

"No," he screamed into her ear, yanking her head so far back that she looked into his face. He wore a wool watch cap. Tufts of dark hair escaped from its edges. He had a short beard, and his eyes shone with light from the street lamps across the road. He stared into her face, pulled her back hard, even further, her head nearly touching the ground. He kept jerking her down and shoving her back up in a frenzy of movement. Marin felt herself blacking out and tried to shake her head to stay awake. This made him furious.

"You bitch," he bellowed. She felt his hands on her neck again. He shoved them down deeply into the neck of her coat. The buttons she had just done up popped off, landed on the concrete beneath the kiosk. He was squeezing. Marin strained against him, trying to use her feet to no avail. He was so strong. She felt herself going under. At one point, she did not care. No use fighting. He would kill her. *Maman...*

Marin came to. She realized she had gone blank. What had happened. She tried to move, but he was still there, in front of her now. Her coat was undone, her pants....

Suddenly, she woke with a fury. She lunged off the bench. She could stand. His hands were no longer on her. He was no longer in front of her. Was he gone? No. She smelled him before she saw him. He was outside the kiosk, his pants undone. He was looking down. Without thinking, Marin bolted. She ran toward the airport. The gates to the employees' entrance were open. The security guards would be there. She had to get there. She ran and ran and ran....

Meanwhile, Sybille had jumped out of bed, trying to catch her breath. She must have dozed off. Something was wrong with Marin. Sybille felt herself suffocating. Standing in the middle of the bedroom, she felt a heaviness she had never known. And the heaviness was pure bad. The clock said 8:34 p.m. She must have dreamed. She could not shake the feeling. She sat back down onto the bed. *Marin,* she thought. It was Marin. She knew it. She always knew it when something happened with Marin. She would be getting out of work, taking the bus. She should be home any minute. Sybille mentally reviewed Marin's weekly protocol, setting it side by side with her dream, the feeling of her throat closing. *Marin. What had happened?*

Just then, she heard the front door open and Marin come in quietly. Marin was never quiet. On any given Sunday night, Marin was a flurry of stories from the airport store. She would keep her parents and Sybille in hoots imitating the customers' requests.

"May I please to have a ... a container of ... aching head..." one man had asked, working his best English to explain what he needed.

"Do you have a headache?" Marin had asked, holding her head in her hands and grimacing, as if in acute pain. The customer had nodded without stopping, holding his own head in imitation of Marin, the two of them looking like some lame vaudeville act mirroring each other.

"Yes, yes. Headache. Very bad. Pills?"

Marin had made a grand display of handing over the miracle aspirin to the customer, and her family laughed. Marin was a comedian. She was a bright light, as their mother always said. Sybille knew her parents looked forward to Marin's return each Sunday night. She was better than any television sitcom they could tune into.

Sybille listened as Marin said hello to her parents. They asked how her night was. She said it was fine, that she was tired and wanted to go to bed. Every Sunday, Sybille had dinner with her parents while Marin worked. At the end of Marin's work day, the sisters sat up for hours talking before Sybille returned to her apartment. Sometimes, if it got too late, Sybille spent the night. Fully awake and sitting once again on her childhood bed, waiting for Marin to come in, Sybille tried to will away the dream, the fear that kept her shoulders tightly bunched near her ears. Was it a dream or was it a premonition? It certainly had happened before. When Marin had fallen off her bike and had to get stitches in her knee, Sybille had known something was wrong before anybody had told her. She had been at the roller rink, skating with her friends, when her knees suddenly gave out, and she had sprawled onto the floor in the middle of the group skate. Left and right, skaters had swerved to avoid her. She never fell. What had happened? Why had she fallen now with nothing in her path? When she had gotten home that day, she heard the entire story of Marin's emergency department visit, saw the row of neat black stitches that held the skin of her sister's knee together.

"When did that happen?" she had asked Marin who was perched on the sofa with her leg propped up.

"Right after lunch," she had said. "I was going to Elise's house, and I got onto my bike, pedalled down to Court Street, and all of a sudden I was on the ground. I think I hit a stone. It hurt wicked bad."

That Sunday night, Marin opened the door and came into the bedroom. She was silent. Sybille found this bizarre.

"What happened?" Sybille asked. "I had a dream..."

Marin stood up straight. She looked at Sybille then turned to the door. "I am so tired, Sybille. I just want to shower and go to sleep."

"Marin, honey, did something happen at work? Will you please talk...?"

Marin stood stone still, shaking her head side to side slowly and holding her coat close to her chest, up near her neck, as if warding off a cold breeze. When Marin left to take a shower, Sybille got ready for bed. She would stay the night. She needed to be near her sister. Something was up. Long after, as she lay quietly beneath the covers, she heard the shower water running and running. She knew Marin would not talk as surely as she knew she had to stay exactly where she was, just in case.

The next day, Marin was gone off to school before Sybille left for work in the morning. Sybille returned to her parents' home that night, knowing they were out visiting friends. Marin was at the kitchen table with books covering the expanse. She looked up when Sybille came in.

"Hi," she said, putting down her pencil and shifting to look Sybille directly in the face.

"Hi," Sybille said. "Are you okay?"

Marin nodded. "You had a dream about me last night?"

Sybille hung her coat in the hall closet, poured herself a glass of chardonnay in the kitchen, and came to sit across from Marin at the table.

"I had a dream I was suffocating. I could not breathe. I was terrified. When I woke up, I instantly thought of you, as if you were in some kind of trouble. It was really awful."

Marin looked at Sybille. Her eyes were filled with tears, and she blew her nose.

"What happened, Marin?" Sybille asked, reaching across the table, laying her hand on her sister's.

"What happened," said Marin, "was that I was attacked. At the bus stop." Marin told the story in stops and starts, staring at the wall behind Sybille's head. "He strangled me. He was so angry. Said he would kill me. He almost did. I blacked out. I don't know. I do not know, Sybille, why I came to consciousness again before he killed me. When I did, I ran. I just ran. I fell. I screamed. I ran...." Marin's shoulders heaved and she sobbed. Sybille went around the table and held her.

"Oh, my God, Marin. Are you okay? What should we do? Did you call the police? Should we go to the hospital?"

Marin could not speak. She cried and leaned heavily into Sybille. "Mo Mo, you saved yourself. Honey, you are safe now. It is over. You are safe."

When Marin grew calmer, Sybille led her to the sofa. She lit Marin's favourite vanilla candle, and she wrapped them both in the patchwork quilt their mother had made. Marin seemed to doze for brief moments, her hand resting on Sybille's shoulder. Then she would jounce to life, sit up straight, and stare into space.

Sybille begged Marin to call the police, to tell their parents. She shook her head. She would not call the police. It was over. Then she remained still for a long while. Maybe she would call the police tomorrow. They should know. Other women could be hurt. She would tell her parents, yes. In time. They should know, she agreed, but Marin wanted to work it through for herself first.

She worked hard to adjust to life after near death. There were the small things – she never waited for the bus alone again, always enlisting a male friend or one of the airport security guards to wait with her. She carried mace in her purse. She looked around her constantly. During the next year, when the family was playing cards and telling goofy stories, Marin's laugh was not as full. The loose laugh she was known for growing up, that was missing. Maybe only Sybille noticed, but it was true. Marin was less Marin by some microscopic measure only a sister would notice. That man at the bus stop had not killed Marin, and that was a mercy. But he had squeezed from her something primal, something of her life force. A stranger in the night had taken that from her. From her family. But she was alive. And that – for sure – was a mercy.

*

Lying in bed one crisp October night two years later, relaxing into sleep, Sybille believed that the bad dream was behind them for good. Marin had started her classes at the Université Sainte-Catherine and it seemed that all was good. When the phone rang, she knew it would be Marin, calling on her break from her new job at Le Tap.

"I'm shaking, Sybille," Marin said as soon as Sybille croaked out a hello. "It's like my heart and my head are pounding. Not like a headache, more like when Papa took us ice-skating that time at the pond, and I saw Eddie Verlaine there. Remember how much I liked him, Syb? Well, I have this same feeling, and I am so freaked out. I need to talk. You weren't sleeping, were you?"

This was big. Sybille had not heard Marin talk about a man in a very long time. Men used to tell Marin she was beautiful nearly every day, and Marin enjoyed the attention. She was comfortable around men, found an easy rapport with them. That one night at the bus stop had put an end to that. Sybille was sure that men still noticed Marin and still complimented her. The way Marin looked had not changed. She was still stunning. On the inside, however, she was altered. Less buoyant. More guarded. Sybille understood that her sister needed to talk now, so she sat up in bed and pulled her robe around her shoulders, searched in the dark for her glasses.

"Who are you kidding? Me sleeping when I can be listening to my baby sister talk about men at midnight? Marin, it is midnight," Sybille said, offering a lighthearted jab before settling into the pillows she propped against her headboard. "Okay, MoMo, spill it all. I'm listening."

Though Sybille was older than Marin by two years, they were twins in all the important ways. While most people spotted the family resemblance, particularly that signature family smile, few would mistake Sybille and Marin for actual twins. Sybille's hair was several shades darker than Marin's, and though Sybille was only a few inches taller than Marin, she was not as wiry. She was solid and compact and Marin was lithe and springy. Their eyes were the same, and their smiles set everyone at ease. "Those Hazeur girls," their family friend Tolley was wont to say, "make a rainy day abound with sunshine."

If Marin was the homebody, Sybille was the daredevil in the family, never one to refuse a strenuous hike or swim. When she was in university, Sybille spent nearly three months in Nepal climbing Katmandu and Annapurna and travelling by foot eight hours a day. After that, she had ventured to Gabon, on the equator in central West Africa, teaching biology to high-school students for two years. Though she had no money in the bank, she had borrowed $500 from her mother, and left for that first job in a country dense with rainforest where people spoke more than fifty separate languages and where tropical diseases such as malaria and filariasis were deadly. Once back in Montreal, her wayfaring fantasies had continued. She had missed Africa and longed to someday get to Madagascar. Work and family had provided fulfillment in the meantime, until she could hatch plans to get to those remote places.

Sybille and Marin were the kind of sisters who did not need to articulate every feeling or thought. Excepting Sybille's exotic adventures in dangerous places, so much of their experience had a shared history, down to the toothpaste they preferred and the aunts they secretly abhorred. Sybille knew when her sister needed comfort. So much of their past and present was synchronous that they could cut to the chase in important matters. Sybille heard the panic in Marin's voice and met it with her silliest.

"Get to it, Toots. Tell me. Some guy..."

"A customer," Marin explained.

"Fraternizing? Is that legal?" Sybille asked, turning on the bedside light.

"Ughh, Sybille. He seems like someone I could like, someone I could go on a date with. I...." She got quiet, thinking.

"You should go on a date," Sybille said. "It is time, Marin. Go on a date if it feels right," Sybille urged.

Marin was quiet again. Sybille listened to her breathing for a time, before she spoke tenderly. "It has been two years, Marin. You are nineteen years old and a university student. You can live your life. It's okay. Really." She imagined Marin holding the phone to her ear, clenching the cord with her right hand.

"I believe I will," she said, seeming to try out the words before hanging up.

Sybille stayed awake for a long while after. Marin deserved to meet a good man, a kind man who could love her with all of her quirks. She could not cook. She did not care for cleaning or laundry. If an accident were going to happen, it would happen to Marin. Flat tires, broken windshield wipers, spilled milk, spoiled leftovers. "She lacks common sense," Papa had always told Sybille, and Sybille had always countered in the same way, "but, Papa, you must admit, she is the life of the party, and she is true blue, like a faithful mutt, as Hilaire always says. She is our Marin, and she is her own woman, Papa. No one in our family can disco dance like her. Admit it now. She is a funky-town girl." This last had always made Sybille and Marin's father laugh. He was not sure what it meant, but the sound of it made him almost giggle.

"Of course, you're right, Sybille. I just worry about her. She is a clown, our little clown, but she is a stubborn-headed girlie. You, you are the level-headed one. Sure, you go off and do crazy things like living out in the woods for two weeks, but you pack the sleeping bag and utensils and flashlight. Marin – can you imagine Marin in the woods for two weeks? What would she pack? The hairspray, the lipstick, the shoes that cripple? When you two were little I took you to Parc National de Grands-Jardins. Do you remember? You ran and ran, and little Marin, she was so fragile, so sweet and tiny, but she did not have your temerity."

She knew well why her parents worried about Marin. Sybille herself worried about Marin, but she had been observing a change in her younger sister these past years. The tide was turning. Marin was coming into her own, learning to trust again. All would be well. Sybille felt a flutter of warmth, a grace she supposed, and she took it as a sign that things would go well for her *twin* sister.

# 9.

## DEIRDRE ~ OCTOBER 1989

"**P**ROFESSOR, LOOK, WE MADE PAGE B4 of the *Kingston Eagle*." Ellen was standing tall, as she always did when she had something urgent to say. "Our letter to the Commissioner parents? You know, the mothers of the guys who put up the repugnant signs in the dorm? It got printed." Ellen had unfolded the newspaper, and was holding it up for display. Deirdre could see that the headline read: "Campus Pranks Turning Nasty."

"Most of you have heard this before," Ellen was chirping, gleeful. "We wrote the letters on October 12, but let me read it again for the sheer pleasure of hearing the brazen language with which we have taken back justice."

She recited from the paper:

To whom it may concern,
As a group of concerned women, we are writing to you about your son at Aquitaine University. Your son has participated in a ritual that is fostering dangerous attitudes towards women. By posting a sign in his window at Commissioner House suggesting he would not take "no" for an answer from a woman, he is contributing to the number of sexual assaults against women in society and in particular on our university campus.
We hope that you may be able to convince your son that "NO MEANS NO."
Sincerely yours, *A Group of Concerned Women*

Ellen lowered the paper and looked around the class. "Isn't this amazing?" she asked. She yanked the newspaper up again. "Listen to this: 'Aquitaine, which produces some of Canada's most influential lawyers, has put itself on the notoriety map this week when male students pasted up signs trumpeting violent and obscene responses to the university's No Means No rape awareness campaign. The mocking messages included statements such as No Means Harder, No Means Dyke, and No Means More Beer.'"

Deirdre's head was spinning. The Commissioner guys were not letting up. Deirdre knew that the FRRF had sent the letters, hoping that the mothers, in particular, would talk some sense and civility into their sons, but she had not read a newspaper in days. Her study group had been consumed with work on their Solar project for Principles of Engineering Practice. They had just learned that she and the guys, Jon, Steve, and Allain, were accepted to present at the Student Engineers Solar Conference at CanTech in Montreal on December 7. Theirs was the only group from the class to be selected for this prestigious conference, and they were scrambling to create their overheads and charts. They would drive to Montreal on December 6 and attend a dinner and plenary session that evening. Deirdre was feeling the workload pressure. The Solar Conference at CanTech was big, but Ellen's announcement about *The Kingston Eagle* story reminded Deirdre about the class debate based on the Commissioner House debacle. It was next week. Her stomach clenched. There was simply too much to do.

She had to admit that the Commissioner signs seemed sort of benign at first, but every day they were becoming more obnoxious, as if the guys were having a competition about who could be the grossest. The women in her dorm faced the signs head on whenever they looked out their windows. Deirdre knew the women of FRRF had used all the official channels. They had talked to security, administrators, professors, and

several deans. All claimed their hands were tied, that disci-
plinary action took place at the level of the judicial process.
Without further recourse, a frantic FRRF sent those letters to
the mothers.

Though the in-class debate meant loads more work, Deirdre
was happy that she was on the feminist side of the Campus
Sexual Assault argument. She would be taking the position
of one who thought men and women should have the same
rights. Students' names had been pulled from a hat by Professor Oliver. When Roberta had discovered she would have
to argue against her own cherished and fervent position, she
was vocal about it.

"Why should I argue for something that is heinous to
me? Why be on the side of patriarchy for even one minute?
In what god-awful world does that make sense, Professor?
Especially on this campus where sexism is a team sport."
Roberta had not wanted to let this one go, though she had
known for some time that the debate teams would be drawn
randomly from a hat.

Professor Oliver had nodded as Roberta spoke. Deirdre
loved how she always looked at you when you spoke, clearly
listening and thinking about what each student said, as if each
one mattered. She had come around to the front of her desk
and perched on its corner. This was her way. When she was
pondering a question or when she wanted to share a story or
explain a theory, she sometimes even got right up onto the
desk and sat cross-legged in the middle of it. If Deirdre did
not hold the professor in such awe, she might have acknowledged that she found her adorable. Professor Oliver was a
petite woman with short chestnut hair in the style her own
mother had loved of a skating star named Dorothy Hamill.
Her professor's outfits were unpredictable. This was a treat
for Deirdre. Her engineering professors were anti-stylish. All
but one was a man, and they wore either white button-down
shirts with khaki pants or T-shirts under crew-neck sweaters.

No variation. No colours, only tan, white and grey. The one female engineering professor wore a navy-blue pantsuit every day. Deirdre did not know if it was the same suit or if she had a collection of them in the same colour. She wore matching leather shoes, pumps with a chunky heel, eminently practical for a woman who was on her feet all day long.

Given the vacuum of vogue in the engineering department, Deirdre found Professor Oliver's wardrobe enthralling. She was quite hip for a woman older than her own mother. This professor loved colour. Deirdre's absolute favourite thing she wore was this bright turquoise jacket, all puffy with down. On occasion, Professor Oliver could be spotted in the distance, all the way across campus, so bright was her jacket. Equally intriguing were her diaphanous skirts worn with black leather boots and her oversized turtleneck sweaters with long silver and turquoise chains and matching earrings. On some days, she wore plaid jumpers with white blouses underneath, like a Catholic schoolgirl. On others, she looked like she was heading to luncheon on a yacht, donning a navy-blue blazer over a crisp white shirt, khaki slacks and penny loafers. She fit no mold. It was refreshing. On this particular day, Professor Oliver wore loose black pants and a black leotard shirt, topped with a flowing purple sarong that acted more like a cape than a wraparound sweater. She had drawn the sarong snugly around her torso, as she adjusted herself on the desk.

"You raise an important question, Roberta," she had said, slowly and rather quietly. On any given day, Professor Oliver had more energy than all of Deirdre's engineering professors combined. She was a tiny dynamo, and her voice was exuberant and penetrating. Seldom did the class strain to hear this woman. On this day, as she sat on the desk responding to Roberta, she had seemed particularly and deeply thoughtful.

"Why should we put ourselves in the shoes of our enemies? Why should we not only consider their points of view but actually go one step further to inhabit their points of view, to speak as if *we* are *they* in a debate?"

She had looked out at the class now from her perch at the front of the room. Had she expected someone to answer, to counter Roberta who leaned forward in her seat, elbows on the desk, fists holding up her face? The room had been quiet.

"Professor, are you suggesting, somehow, in some crazy way, that doing this is good for us, like, like eating broccoli?" Ellen had asked. She was sitting in front of Roberta, jerking her hands out in front of her, palms up, incredulous at what this woman might well be saying.

Professor Oliver had remained placid on the desk, the purple in the sarong picking up the deep blue in her eyes, as a slant of sun crossed directly in front of her in a perfectly straight beam. She had moved her head slightly to the left, as if breathing in Ellen's words.

"You know, Ellen, I may indeed be suggesting that." The professor had pursed her lips together and shrugged them to the side, suggesting she was giving this one serious contemplation.

Before Ellen or Roberta could respond, Deirdre had raised her hand. Her hand was in the air, in fact, before she even realized it. Good God, what was she doing? While she had compassion for Roberta and Ellen and the rest of FRRF who filled the two rows of seats near the window, she was also tenuous, spoke little in the class, and felt sometimes out of her depth. The Robertas and Ellens were activists. They had the biological female symbol tattooed on their biceps. They were in their final year at Aquitaine. They had taken sixteen thousand more Women's Studies classes than Deirdre. Had they not been part of the group of students from campus who drove to Ottawa to hear Parliament deliberate over Bill C-43, that restrictive new abortion law? Had they not chained themselves to the railings of the Public Gallery in the House of Commons and showered pro-choice leaflets onto the heads of the Parliamentarians? Good God, these women had sparked a national debate about the mistreatment of women on university campuses.

With her hand in the air and the professor turning to face her, Deirdre had swallowed then taken a deep breath. "Well," she had begun, glancing over her shoulder at Roberta. "Roberta makes a good point, and I think we should consider it carefully." The class had stayed quiet, and Deirdre noticed that Roberta's fists were now resting on her desk instead of supporting her weary head. Deirdre had taken this as a good sign and willed herself on.

"It is very hard to even consider the view of another when we know that the other would never, in a million years, consider *our* point of view, when we know that there are men in power like those we have read about in our books, like those on our own campus, who do not care one iota what we think or feel." Deirdre had paused, noticed some of her classmates nodding. Ellen had given one deliberate nod. Roberta had sat very still, listening. Ben and Whit had leaned forward in their seats, their arms hanging over the fronts of their desks. Professor Oliver had smiled at Deirdre, asked her to continue.

"However, if we don't examine, I mean really examine and understand the perspectives of those who disagree with us, especially those who have power over us, how will we ever be able to convince them they are wrong? How will we be able to talk to them?"

Professor Oliver had held Deirdre's gaze for a long time, and Deirdre wondered if she had stepped out of line. The professor had continued to look at her, as if taking her in for the first time.

"Nice work, Deirdre," she had said. "Let me remind the class that Deirdre is a first year engineering student. Impressive indeed." Deirdre had been embarrassed and thanked Professor Oliver silently. Inside, she was jubilant.

# 10.

CRAIG BERSEAUX POUNDED a beat onto the Aquitaine crest that covered his notebook and silently repeated the words printed beneath the large X in the middle of the university seal, *Emollit Mores Nec Sinit Esse Feros.* He neither knew nor cared what this meant, especially today. He was, yet again, waiting for his calculus professor. Always late and breathless upon entry, the professor arrived at the moment Craig had had enough. Craig was tired and brooking no fools. The guys had laid waste to Sunday night, and Craig's last clear memory was of lying prostrate on the roof of Commissioner House with Jack and Kevin. His buddies had been screaming at the blue moon. Craig had smiled, passed the bottle to Kevin, and then it was morning, and he made his way to calculus.

Professor Hansveldt was an untidy jumble. Though he had the requisite garb, it was all sorts of akimbo. His lavender print tie was tucked into his crumpled white shirt front. His tweed jacket was tufted with the fluff of Mr. Infinity, Hansveldt's cat. Craig knew about the cat. Everyone in Advanced Calculus 380 knew about the damned cat because it is what made the loopy professor late every day. Every day, a new Mr. I. tale got told before X approached infinity or velocity was squared.

Craig could have clocked the guy. "No Hansveldt on a hangover," Kevin had grumbled before he rolled over on the roof that morning, going back to sleep. "Fuck Mr. Infinity." Craig was always the more devoted student of the two anyway. He hated missing class when his mother was tutoring after teaching all day at Herold High School in Bancroft, Ontario, just to send him spending money. If she could sacrifice, so could he. He could nap later. He tossed on his Aquitaine sweatshirt and new jeans and headed out, just as Kevin had crawled through the window of their room and headed to bed.

"Craigster, man, gonna get some ass tonight or what?" Craig ignored him. Kevin was the guy in the house who came from money. His father was an engineer for General Electric in Mississauga, and his mother was the daughter of some French ambassador to Egypt, or was it Jordan? But he was scum. Craig had known this the instant his mother was unwrapping his new sheets to put on his bed last semester and Kevin was staring at her ass. Creep. Craig put this out of his mind, pretending he did not witness his roommate's crass voyeurism. He had to survive, and survive in Commissioner House he must.

Commissioner House was an institution. Not exactly a frater-nity. More like a rumpus room for nearly-grown-up men. The week-long summer initiation had separated the Commissioners from the geeks. What had started out as mindless, stale stuff, became barbarous. Most plebs could not hack it. They left mid-course. The dozen who had remained had earned their place in Commissioner. By the end of initiation week, Craig had sat on the wide hallway steps, nauseated, sweating and not exactly proud, but a Commissioner after all.

Sport Humping was his expertise. Craig got away with things because he was blessed with good looks. Trim and tanned, he had broad shoulders from rowing during summers on his cousin's lake. He had penetrating blue eyes and hair that fell below his ears in dark swaths. He had earned the nickname "SpoHo," during his first year, when it reached 30 degrees Celcius and rained like a bludgeon every night. Rain or shine, Craig sport-humped his way through the girls' soccer and field hockey teams and the dons in the residences. It had come naturally after years of athletic training, doing a series of push-ups with a woman beneath you on the ground. Taking the coin from her mouth with your teeth was the trickier part, but Craig had mastered this after his second try, explaining to the women he encountered – when he had to – that if he did more push-ups than the other guys, he would win enough money to finally buy his mother the short version of the *Oxford English Dictionary*, the one she had always longed for, the one with the tiny magnifying glass in the little drawer. Most girls had been so stunned by his confidence that they did not ask what he was doing or why, but when they did, Craig was ready with his OED story. His burgeoning collection of coins still held campus rank. No one had seen the likes of SpoHo.

Jack, president of Commissioner House, a senior chemical engineering major from Kingston itself, was proud of his recruit that year, and Jack had never wavered in both his admiration and in his hatching of new schemes to test Craig's loyalty to Commissioner.

Craig admitted only to himself that he was weary of Jack's incessant tournamenting of his "man among men," as he called Craig. "This here is my man. The SpoHo Craigster."

"Enough said, there, Jack. I do appreciate it, but you're making me blush," Craig had said at the last house meeting, the kickoff meeting for fall semester, his third at Aquitaine University. With Commissioner House on probation, Craig had wanted to low-ball Commissioner's infamous antics for fall semester. The head of the Student Housing Council, last spring, made clear that Commissioner House was not a sacred cow, despite its prestigious alumni, many of them engineers, who donated potently and consistently to the university coffers.

Perhaps Flawless Freshling was a mistake, Craig had thought as he sat among the guys last week listening to Jack drone on about plans for this year's black-tie Engineer's Ball. Flawless Freshling had always been a first-year girl held up to incoming students as the paragon, the Queen of Queens, the unattainable one guys fantasized about in their dorm rooms. Jack had been resurrecting this old tradition since his father urged Flawless Freshling on Jack in a fret of single-malt nostalgia the night before his son left for the university. "She is the one you bring home to mother. She is the one like no other..." his father sang into the night from his porch rocker, ice cubes tumbling, voice baritoning the wonders of quintessential femininity to the neighbourhood. And so Jack had proposed Flawless Freshling during his orientation week, and the 1970s tradition lived again. Craig had predicted it would not survive this resurrection, but he went along with it to shut Jack up.

Not much would survive, thought Craig, as Professor Hansveldt scratched away at the board, if those ridiculous feminists did not shut the hell up. Already, not even two months into the semester, he had heard one of his housemates was being taken out of school by his parents. They had received the same letter his mother got from some women's group. *Tattling bitches.* Thank God his mother had not mentioned it. He would have to find a way to bring it up, and soon. The newspapers were rife with this stuff. It was so blown out of proportion, some small, vocal minority was twisting things, making something minor like masking tape signs in dorm-room windows into national news. To most people on campus, the entire thing was a joke. But no, not to these oversensitive freaks. God, he was so sick of them. It was just a joke, a stupid joke. *Try laughing, why don't you?*

Craig put his head on his desk. He was worn out by the bullshit. Seconds later, he let all of that go when the professor's chalk screeched on the board, and he said, "Well, kids, let that be it for today." Just two more classes after this, Craig mused, and he was home free for the weekend.

# 11.

S ARAH, THE STUDENT whose boyfriend maintained guys who took a Women's Studies class were gay, was a third-year political science major. She made the opening remarks for the feminist side of the Campus Sexual Assault debate team. Sarah wore her long hair pinned up with a long stick that looked to Deirdre like a skewer. The mechanics of that lone, slim device holding such a brimful of hair preoccupied Deirdre far too intently.

"One in four female college students can expect to experience rape or attempted rape during their college careers according to a study done by Mary Koss of Kent State University in 1985. Rape and sexual assault is the only violent crime against students more likely to be committed by a person the victim knows. Alcohol and drugs are implicated in 55-74 percent of sexual assaults on campuses according to another study by Muehlenhard and Linton in 1987. And many studies show that more than 90 percent of sexual assaults never get reported to the police. We must take action today to change our campus."

Speaking out of turn, sitting with his team in a row of seats facing the opposing team, doing his best to play the role of an anti-feminist, Whit taunted: "Where did you get those wild statistics, Sarah? Yank them out of your...?"

"Whit, please hold your questions until both teams have presented their opening arguments," Professor Oliver interjected, looking Whit in the eyes a long time, seemingly torn between putting him on warning and allowing the heckling to serve some pedagogical function. The class had already engaged in an extended conversation about the role of heckling in a debate. Some had felt it was unprofessional and should not be allowed. Others had felt it would be more "real-world" and would help the class work through strategies for coping with heckling.

"Roberta and Jen, your team is up. Opening arguments, please," Professor Oliver said.

"Thank you, Professor. Good morning, class," Jen began. Jen was pre-law. This was her venue. She would shine, despite having drawn the short straw and representing the patriarchal position for the day, a position she maintained she did not understand at all. Jen was the tiniest woman in the class, but the one with the deepest voice.

"Ladies and gentlemen, I ask you to consider these alleged statistics offered by Sarah. One in four women is raped on her university campus. Can this be so? If it were so dangerous for a young woman to go to university, would Canada's parents actually send their daughters so readily? These statistics are, quite frankly, fabricated. It takes the politically incorrect person, the brave person, to say so. Today, I will be that person because so much is at stake."

As the class shuffled in seats, readying for fireworks, Sarah consulted with her team: Deirdre listened in along with Ben and Audrey, an English major from Boston, Massachusetts who wore Red Sox earrings every day. Sarah was highly piqued over Jen's provocative statement, but she cautioned her team to be calm.

Jen continued. "What we have here is a simple abuse of statistics, as I have already said. Sarah, our team insists you offer your sources publicly."

Sarah gave the go-ahead to Ben, and he stood and passed a sheaf of papers to his mother, who was seated on his left. She was his invited guest for the day, given Professor Oliver's open-door policy for special class events. "Please pass these around the room. You will find all of our team's sources indicated here. One of the things we knew coming into this debate is that a feminist position on sexual assault is always countered on the basis of fraudulent statistics, and we anticipated correctly that your team would go for the obvious kill right out of the gate."

"So yours is the feminist position, Ben?" Jen countered, in a voice that jolted Deirdre. "Please define this term 'feminist' for us who are not, perhaps, so well-educated in this terminology." Jen's derisive tone was noted by Ben and his team, though he did not acknowledge it explicitly in his response. The class had discussed previous to the debate the tone people often use when speaking about feminist issues, a tone that is at once dismissive and hostile. While the group had concluded that the best approach to such a tone was to ignore it and to respond, simply, to the question being asked, most of the class members found this the biggest challenge of all. Ben modeled the non-confrontational strategy to the best of his ability.

"Happily, Jen, I will define 'feminist.' A feminist is a person, man or woman, who supports the political, economic, and social equality of women. It is really that simple."

"Might I add something?" asked Ben's teammate Audrey, playing with one of her dangling red earrings. "These statistics we have offered are not 'feminist' statistics. Rather, they are statistics compiled by federal agencies and universities including the Canadian Centre for Justice Statistics, Canadian Advisory Council on the Status of Women, Statistics Canada, Canadian sexual assault centres, and many more.

Camille, a fourth-year physics major from Vancouver, spoke next for Jen's team, her voice unusually loud in the crowded room. "Let's face the facts, shall we? What we know is this: girls on a campus get drunk, sleep with a guy they meet at a party, wake up to regret it, do the walk of shame, then cry rape. It is simply true.... And wait, did you check out those first-year chicks at the football game this weekend? The ones wearing those orientation khaki overalls. Did you see them? They had signs written on their butts that read: 'Lick it, slap it, suck it' and 'Slip inside and ride.' What do they expect?"

Before the professor could intervene, Deirdre said, "Camille, statistics indicate that rape victims are no more likely to fraudulently report rape than are victims of other crimes, including robbery. Susan Brownmiller's *Against Our Will* estimates that only about two percent of reported sexual assaults are fraudulent reports."

Camille stood up and banged her fist on her desk. "That is pure crap, Deirdre," she shouted, pointing at her with her right hand. "Girls do this all the time. They say yes to sex then feel skanky and claim the guy raped them to save their reputation. You know this. We all know this. Does your team have anything good at all to say about guys?" Camille sat with a *thwack*. She looked at her teammates, who nodded more at her intimidating tone than her clarity of position.

Sarah stood now, mirroring Camille's stance. "Frankly, no. Not here, not this semester. Look at the Commissioner signs. Look at the administration's non-response, the nurse effigies. Look at the risks FRRF is taking to counter this because the people with power won't use it. *Wink, wink, nudge, nudge,* mob mentality reigns."

The room shifted again, releasing some of the pent up energy into the atmosphere.

"But that's not what I wanted to say. I want to address your 'skank' comment," continued Sarah. "This is an old stereotype that really needs to be laid to rest. It does not hold up, as my team has already indicated with the two percent statistic about fraudulent reporting. A far more troubling discovery has been made in the past few decades in large psychological studies in Canada and the United States. According to psychological research made over the course of the last twenty years, a high percentage of men, in university, admit that they would, if they had insurance they would not be caught, commit rape."

Sarah held Camille's gaze. The room was dead quiet. Sarah was waiting for a response from her opponents. Finding none, she sat down.

"Jen, your team can respond to Sarah's comments, please," said the professor.

Roberta spoke, standing and leaning toward Sarah's table. She had remained surprisingly quiet throughout. On any given day, Roberta was the one to jump-start the class with some report on current events. Today, she had remained in the background, until now.

"I think what Camille is saying is that we are tired of being bombarded by statistics. It sounds like you're saying all men are violent and dangerous. They rape women. They beat women. They stalk them. Why in God's name are women still marrying men when they're such monsters?" Roberta sat down again. Deirdre noted the strain in her face. She hated the role she was forced to play. Roberta was doing her best to represent a counter-feminist position, but it was playing on her last nerve.

The emotional air in the room was electric. Professor Oliver stood. "Let's do this. Our time for our panels is nearing its end. Why don't we postpone final arguments until next class and open the class, now, for deliberation. Our ground rules are simple: listen to others with respect."

Ben's mother raised her hand gingerly. Professor Oliver nodded to her. Deirdre noticed that she had the same deep green eyes Ben had, but her hair was much lighter than his, a muted auburn. She turned to face the majority of the class, placed her palms together and brought her pointer fingers to her lips for a few contemplative seconds. She lowered them to say, "I am Nora, Ben's mom. I, for one, believe what the feminist panelists are saying. I am quite a bit older than you, so I speak from experience. Being a woman is an every-day challenge. It is frightening walking in the dark, going to a dimly-lit parking garage at night, being alone in your own home sometimes.

Every woman here, no matter how old, knows what it is like to be constantly on guard. It is socialized into us. That is not so for men and boys. Also, I did not hear *any* statistics from the other panel. What is it *you* believe. And Camille, this is a Women's Studies class. It is a place where the subject is women and their lives. Saying good things about men is not a requirement."

Deirdre felt that warm flush in her chest that accompanies a bold truth.

Roberta cleared her throat, placed her palms face down on the desk in front of her. "I learned something today, and Nora has just pointed it out. The anti-feminist position does not offer significant studies of its own. Rather, it tears down studies that conflict with its view of men being superior. It is a reactionary position, and it relies on making the same few points repeatedly and with increasing noise and threats."

"I've noticed that too," said Audrey. "It's as if reasonable dialogue is impossible. Why is that?"

"Good question. Why is that? Can we get some thoughts on this, on why dialogue is so difficult around the issues of violence against women?" the professor asked the group at large.

"The topic is threatening, I think, to men," said Ben. "They see themselves as targeted, as the bad guys, and they get defensive. In order to keep the peace, I think we avoid this sort of topic – on our campus anyway," he said, looking at the professor rather than at the full classroom. "Unless it comes at us like a Commissioner House storm."

"Exactly, Ben," said Professor Oliver. "Men see themselves as targeted. But why is this? Why aren't men angry, outraged even, at the men who *hurt* women, the men who make a bad name for men?"

Ben nodded. "I don't know. This is not a zero-sum game. It's not a competition between men and women. If women are mistreated by men, it is up to men to speak up to stop it."

"Exactly," said Nora, smiling at her son. "Surely there are

some students in Commissioner who do not approve of those signs. Where are their voices?"

Professor Oliver thanked the class for playing their roles so well. They would debrief the next time they met. Deirdre put on her coat, grabbed her backpack, and headed out the door. Ping-ponging thoughts colonized her mind. She headed to the cafeteria to eat a sandwich and to clear her head.

# 12.

IN EARLY AUTUMN, the colours at Montreal's Botanical Garden were still lustrous, the smells earthy and the air crisp. Jenean and Clara preferred it here when the crowds were minimal, when summer tourists had gone off to their real lives. The humidity had faded. Yet, even after the summer, with its blaze of blossoms and cool streams and Spanish moss, the botanical gardeners coiffed the wildness of nature's beauty into pristine glory throughout October, and both women believed that was the best time to visit. It was just last year that they had committed to an annual Botanical Garden outing after having their hearts stolen by a family of red foxes with four red-coated kits who romped at the woods' edge near the rose garden with its famous ten thousand rose bushes.

Clara and Jenean held fast to the few traditions that they had launched since becoming dearest friends about ten years ago while walking their dogs along the waterfront in Old Montreal. Gertrude and Zoe had become gal pals even before Jenean and Clara got to introduce themselves to each other. The two dogs had sniffed and scampered and followed each other all around the park, feeling the freedom of being off leash in the springtime sunshine. Jenean and Clara had sat on a bench in the shade watching them, and what had begun as an awkward conversation with a stranger led to daily phone calls, shared interests in social issues, and strikingly similar family backgrounds. Each was the eldest of two children with a younger sister. Each had an alcoholic father, now in recovery, and a mother whose legacy as a 1950s housewife neither had wanted to emulate. Clara was married with no children. Jenean had not yet met Bart, and was too busy with the *Sturm und Drang* of journalism to think about marriage or children.

Clara taught in an elementary school, and she was the most centered person Jenean knew. That had not always been the case, Clara had told Jenean. In the early 1970s, she had been searching for her soul. She studied Transcendental Meditation and watched film clips of Maharishi Mahesh Yogi. She had travelled across Europe with one backpack and a dope-dealing boyfriend. When she had returned home, she started working as a cocktail waitress in a tony golf club, but the patrons kept making lewd comments under their breath, so she quit and enrolled in college to study education. She proclaimed feminism as her religion when she read her first issue of *Ms. Magazine*.

"Gloria Steinmen's article, 'If Men Could Menstruate,' changed my life," she had told Jenean shortly after they met.

"You have got to be kidding me," Jenean had crowed. "That is my all-time favourite article in the world."

Suddenly, right there in the park, with Gertrude and Zoe sniffing every doggie rump they could find, Jenean and Clara bantered lines from Steinem's *Ms.* Article, imagining a world in which men had the same monthly cycle women did.

"Men would brag about how long and how much," Clara quoted, applauding herself and Steinem after.

"'Gifts, religious ceremonies, family dinners, and stag parties would mark the event'," Jenean added. Both women raised their eyebrows and gave exaggerated nods.

"Okay, here is my favourite line of all," Clara said. "'Sanitary supplies would be federally funded and free!'"

"Amen, sister," Jenean shouted. "Don't you love her quip about guys bragging on the street about being 'a three pad man'?"

"But wait," said Clara, standing now, and striking a rhetorician's pose. "Men would convince women that sex was *more* pleasurable at 'that time of month.'"

The women had burst out laughing, and onlookers stared. Gertrude and Zoe had returned to their bench to check out the hilarity. And that was that. Their friendship was sealed with the blood of a sassy Gloria Steinem riff. Thereafter, they were inseparable, talking at least once a day by phone and always seeking out ways to spend time together.

They were opposites in significant ways. Clara practiced Buddhist meditation daily. She considered all viewpoints carefully, and she came to judgments, if at all, exceedingly slowly. For every birthday or holiday, she wrapped up books by Buddhist monks and nuns, explaining that these would change Jenean's life. It was true that Jenean yearned for the tranquility Clara exuded, but she had a phobia about wasting time. Until she met Clara, she had never done nothing. She made to-do lists at red lights, and her "monkey mind," as Clara called it, was particularly frenzied. Jenean's inner life, Clara told her, was like Faulkner's *The Sound and the Fury* with its paragraph-long sentences that required unflagging attention to decipher. Her beloved Jenean was brilliant but *busy busy busy* inside her mind. As for Clara, Jenean maintained she was a walking William Wordsworth poem, "The World is Too Much With Us; Late and Soon," a poem that eschewed the world's vapid and pointless hustle and bustle.

Jenean would tease her mercilessly. "In 1806, Wordsworth knew these things, but for our time, we have Clara Doody. Twins separated by nearly two hundred years, Doody and good old William Wordsworth are sentinels charged with warning us about what ails a world spinning out of control."

That they could jest, even mock each other, lovingly was a gift. For all of the meditation materials Clara offered Jenean, she was drawn to Jenean's zest and curiosity, her fearlessness. Jenean put herself out there, in front of Canada's reading public, with an uncanny mix of vulnerability and bravado. Clara knew what this cost Jenean: the sleepless nights, the addictive research, the confrontational interviews. Still, she admired her dearest friend for her selflessness. Calling a spade a spade brought on winning and wrathful responses from all over Canada and even from the United States, yet Jenean took them all in stride.

The friends argued too, fine-tuning their disagreements over the years. Most often, they went round about the differences in the English and Francophone cultures, in particular the differences in feminist cultures, in Quebec. Clara, who was born in Ontario, found her strongest links to Francophone culture in Montreal where her husband Frank and Jenean had both been born. Each had been clear with her that Quebec was the homeland to all Canadian Francophones and that nationalism was crucial to their sense of identity, certainly since the Quiet Revolution when Quebec was given "a new lease on life," as Jenean had put it, "and freed from the Dark Ages."

"I see that. Think of it, Jenean, we're freed from the Dark Ages still. You are the only woman writing editorials for *the* country's premier Sunday magazine of *the* premier French newspaper. That is big. Bodaciously, enormously, stupendously huge."

"Does it even matter?" Jenean had asked.

"Of course it does. *You* can really, really make a difference. And you are. But you've got to cut yourself some slack. That column on the bullshit happening to women at the universities was brilliant. You can't solve all of Canada's problems with your column, and you can't deliver feminism on a platter to readers who want to see it decapitated. You can only do your best, girl."

This sunny day, they were headed to the Japanese garden, created in partnership between Japan and Canada, premiering just the year before. They walked slowly, taking in the magnificent loping Lespedeza Gibraltar, the waterfall flowers, in full, pink dramatic bloom. They detoured when they spotted a patch of Jack-in-the-Pulpit nested in a shady grove. Discovering these tiny ministers was a treat. Though they visited the gardens regularly and seldom needed to read the brochure, they checked it now and were reminded that there were 21,000 types of plants, flowers and trees on the grounds, and two hundred different bird species. And the fox family, of course.

It was the contemplative minimalism that appealed to Jenean and Clara. Lily pads floated languorously atop the central pond. Sizzling orange Koi swam to and fro. These, the sign said, represented friendship. The tiny wriggling bodies could be observed from the many wooden walkways built over the pond. Standing tall around the perimeter of the pond were stalks bursting with red berries and yellow florets. Shade gardens replete with colourful blooms framed the flagstone walkway on the pond's perimeter.

"Everything must lie in harmony in a Japanese garden," Clara read from the guide book she had purchased the previous year. "Nothing is left to chance."

"Not a thing," was all Jenean added.

The Stone Garden and Tea Garden were spaces of such simplicity that Jenean felt her blood pressure actually drop when she entered. The clean, minimal lines, the dashes of coloured petals against grey rock, and the open air whisked all cares away on contact. From inside, the friends could hear water spilling over rocks outside the open-air doorways. Greenery clung to the rocks, cheery and bright at the water's edge, and Japanese maples hovered overhead.

The friends made their way to the bamboo huts and stretched out on the wooden pallets there, designed for the comfort of resting patrons. The huts allowed them to get out of the hot sun and to share their lunch. Clara had made chicken salad sandwiches on multi-grain baguettes, and Jenean had brought celery, carrots and hummus along with slices of gourmet carrot cake from the bakery down the street from her home. Clara loved carrot cake, and Jenean surprised her whenever possible with a sweet treat, knowing that left to her own devices, Clara seldom indulged in desserts. Jenean felt it was her mission to contribute to the sugary happiness of her friend.

"I think this may be the only place in the world where I feel entirely at peace," said Jenean. "When I'm here with you, that is."

"Ditto. Ahhh ... the trickling water, those rich smells. The birds and breezes and tall grasses. My problems melt when I walk through these gates, I swear," said Clara.

"Let's toast to peace," offered Jenean, pulling out the carrot cake and handing Clara her slice.

"Vixen!" shouted Clara, taking her cake in both hands and holding it up like a burnt offering.

"Let us eat," Jenean said, "and let us just be. Canadian politics and university bad boys be gone. Out, out! This is a day to indulge in nature and cakes made of vegetables."

"Here, here," said Clara.

The friends stayed beneath those huts for hours considering colour – ochre and yellow and purple – before rising to take in the bonsai garden with its tiny, well-manicured trees. It was hard to believe that some were over three hundred years old. A large part of the collection had been recently donated by Japan's Nippon Bonsai Association, Clara read. They followed the perimeter road to the gate of the gardens. Clara asked after Bart. Jenean asked after Frank. The October sunlight held out until closing time and as they made their way home on the train.

# 13.

"**A**FTER THAT INTENSE DEBATE in Feminist Philosophical Thought, Deirdre Sevier, you need a party," Rosalie implored.

"It wasn't so bad, was it?" Deirdre asked.

"Have you even been to one party since you came to Aquitaine, D?" wailed Jenna. "Come on. It's Friday. I'll do your makeup. We need to do this Commissioner-Bennett House party as a team. We're all wearing leggings and shoulder-duster earrings. You should totally wear that turquoise top with the shoulder pads. Come on, let's bounce."

Deirdre had been warned about Commissioner House parties, of course, but this one was at the adjoining dorm, Bennett. It was a small detail, and she knew it. Everyone knew about those Commissioner parties. Even CNTV television and newspapers knew about Commissioner. Their orientation leader had been explicit: "When it comes to Commissioner House, just say no! Go with friends. Stay with friends. Those guys are the kings of schmooze, knaves. Talk you into anything." Rosalie and Jenna and the others did not seem to remember this or to care, but Jenna was right, she had not gone to one single university party yet, and she had been a university student for how many weeks now? What could one party hurt?

She felt guilty, like she was betraying her classmates in Professor Oliver's class. After all, these were the guys with the disgusting posters they claimed were a joke. Sometimes, to be quite honest, she felt like Roberta and Ellen could get a little zealous. Still, Deirdre felt she should be above these kinds of parties, but she also felt she owed her friends something. She was always doing homework, always tired. She could give up one night, a few hours. Part of university life was a party or two, right?

Jenna cranked up Bon Jovi's "Livin' on a Prayer," handed out tiny nips of peppermint schnapps she had brought from home, and the girls ran back and forth between dorm rooms to borrow eye shadow and hairspray. As each girl was ready, she modelled her outfit by vamping in the hall as if on a runway. They cheered each other on. "That is so clutch, D," Rosalie shouted when Deirdre showed off her turquoise outfit and tee-tered down the hall in the five-inch suede pumps Jenna insisted she wear. "You are bad to the bone, girl," Jenna screamed, as Rosalie sported her pearl grey sweatshirt, cut at the neck, so her purple tank top was visible. By the time they were ready to leave their dorm to walk across the quad to Bennett, it was dark and cold, the sky awash in brittle clouds, with a sliver of a moon beginning to glow. They were a stylish squadron, singing and zig-zagging to "Walk Like an Egyptian" all the way there.

A young man named Craig greeted Deirdre and her friends at the door. He was dressed in a navy pinstriped suit, a creamy-white shirt, and a maroon-and-gold striped tie. Bennett and Commissioner men always wore suits to their parties. It was part of their ethos, they said. Duran Duran's "Hungry Like the Wolf" pounded in the background.

"Good evening, Miss Deirdre Sevier, Miss Rosalie Raina, other lovely girls," he said, smiling at them all. "It's a pleasure to meet you. I'm Craig Berseaux, designated greeter for tonight's festivities. Welcome to Bennett-Commissioner Houses."

Rosalie and Deirdre stared at each other and then at Craig.

"How do you know our names?" demanded Rosalie, hands on her hips.

"First things first, Rosalie," he said. "Please introduce me to your friends. Rosalie introduced Jenna, Sam, and Lisa, but she continued to look Craig in the eye, awaiting an explanation. "Don't be unnerved. I don't have ESP or anything. The truth is, I noticed Deirdre one day as I was walking across the quad, and I asked a friend who she was. You were with her, Rosalie. My friend gave me your names. His name is Matt Johnson. He lives in Commissioner with me."

Rosalie checked in with Deirdre with her eyes to see if Craig's explanation passed muster. Deirdre shrugged, not sure yet whether to feel complimented or wary, but she and the others followed Craig into the party's din.

"Might I get you ladies a cocktail?" Craig offered. They all nodded and spied an upholstered plaid loveseat in the corner of the room to settle into. Jenna had teased Deirdre's hair into a wild mane, and Deirdre felt like her head were twice its size. She usually wore it simply, in a thick braid that fell loosely over one shoulder, but tonight she felt a fright. She was not alone, however. Every female in the room had enormous hair and eyes outlined in kohl. Craig returned with three red plastic cups. A young man he introduced as Kevin held three more.

"Cheers," said Craig, handing out drinks and foisting his cup into the middle of the group, urging everyone to toast. "To your first Bennett-Commissioner house party. May it be the first of many more." They all nudged their plastic cups together and drank.

Deirdre was not fond of beer, but it seemed a necessary evil in high school and university. She and Lea had resisted the pressure to drink until the summer before their senior year when they decided to have it out on their own terms. Lea's older sister's boyfriend Todd had gotten them a six-pack of the cheapest beer he could find. They pooled their allowances and gave Todd the money for the beer and another couple of bucks for the trouble of delivering the beer to St. Kendrick's cemetery one Friday night in July. Deirdre and Lea had been there waiting for him beneath an enormous weeping willow whose branches touched the ground in a circle wide enough to allow space for a dozen friends.

They had forced down the beer, some kind of Labatt budget lager. In no time they were confessing their secrets, pinky swearing each other to never tell a soul. Deirdre admitted being a little in love with Mr. Marche but hating the singer Phil Collins. Lea confessed to loving Phil Collins, hating *A Fish Called Wanda*, and most-definitely-secretly playing with the three Special Blessings dolls her mother had had ordered from the States for her each Christmas for the last three years.

"Are you kidding?" Deirdre had shouted, as Lea forced a palm over her open mouth.

"I am not, and don't be mean. I love my little angels," Lea had whined.

"They are so ... but, Lea, how can you even play with them? Aren't their hands glued together so they can pray all the time?"

"You can move their hands, Deirdre. Don't be a dope. They can even kneel."

"Does your mom still make those tiny nightgowns for them, with the angel wings on the back?" Deirdre had burst out laughing then, unable to pretend she did not find this hilarious.

"Stop. You are a bad best friend," Lea screamed and then rolled onto the ground laughing. "I never told you this, D, and if you ever breathe a word of it to anyone I will deny it and then kill you. Mom made me a nightgown with wings last Christmas...."

"Last Christmas, like when you were seventeen years old?" Deirdre asked.

"Mmm hmm," nodded Lea.

They had both been very quiet for a few seconds, and then they laughed until their sides ached.

Deirdre drank from her red cup, which had been refilled, and barely heard Craig talking to her. She was distracted by her memories of Lea and by a combination of Richard Marx's anguished lyrics and the incessant chatter of students crammed into small rooms all along the hallway. White lights hung from three fake palm trees in the corner of the room, opposite a massive TV, shedding just enough light for Deirdre to see the outline of people's faces. When Rosalie and the others were suddenly walking away, following Kevin to the next room where a buffet of junk food was set up, Deirdre heard Craig whispering in her ear before she even realized he was there. She startled, but he calmed her with a sure palm to her shoulder. "This past summer," he said, softly, as if they were sharing a secret, "there were dozens of white roses on the bushes right outside the window in my room. The air was like perfume, even in early fall. I took my coffee into that little garden every morning, beneath that trellis. I'm not sure if you can see where it is." Craig stood up and pulled Deirdre gently by the hand. They stood at the window. "I also love morning glories, don't you? They were beautiful this year. My mother grows them back home."

She turned fully to face him and stepped back a quarter pace. "Just who are you?"

"What do you mean?" Craig asked.

"You talk like a Disney prince or something. Are you an English major?" She could feel the beer going to her head, but she was not drunk, not like the night with Lea in the cemetery. She felt warm and relaxed. She would have to pace herself with the beer though. She found herself curious about Craig in a way she had not been curious about any other boys at Aquitaine.

"Oh, shit, no. I'm studying to be an engineer. My mother, now she is an English teacher."

"I'm an engineering major, too," Deirdre said. "Wait, let me guess, chemical engineering, right?"

Craig took her hand again and led her back to the loveseat where they discovered a boy with thick black glasses and a Van Halen T-shirt who appeared to be sound asleep sitting up. They both nudged in next to him. "Love Shack" was vibrating the end table near the sofa, and girls in heels as high as Deirdre's were dancing as best they could in the close quarters.

"How did you know that?" Craig said. "Don't even tell me you see me in the future surrounded by test tubes wearing thick safety glasses."

"Not at all. I just know chemical engineering is popular. I'm thinking about materials science and engineering, at least I think I am for now. Tell me about your mom. Was she ever your teacher in high school?" Deirdre asked.

Before he could answer, Jenna returned briefly, handed Deirdre another beer, and fled into the crowd to meet up with some classmates from Psych 100. "Just checking in. Buddy system and all," she yelled over The B-52s, as she ran off.

"I have an idea. Let's turn this sofa around, and we can look at the stars outside," said Craig. "It might be quieter that way."

He and Deirdre got up. Craig shook the student asleep on the sofa. He grunted, stood up, and walked away. Craig moved the little sofa around to face the window, creating a more private space for the two of them. They sat down again.

"My mother is really smart, and she has enough patience to fill Lake Ontario. She made me read all the time when I was growing up," Craig told her.

"What did she make you read?" Deirdre asked.

"*Catcher in the Rye, To Kill a Mockingbird, Chronicles of Narnia, Lord of the Rings, Hobbit...*" Craig said.

"You are such a poser," Deirdre yelled, sitting back to look directly into his face. "You do not love Tolkien and Narnia and..."

"Damned if I don't, Deirdre Sevier. Who doesn't?" Craig shouted back.

"Not one single boy in my high school, unless you count Leonard. I'm sorry. I just thought..."

"That I was trying to impress you, right?" Craig asked, touching her cheek lightly with the back of his hand then taking it away.

"Actually, yeah," Deirdre admitted.

"I am trying like hell to impress you. But I did read those books. Trust me, Deirdre." Craig moved his arm to the back of the sofa, just above her shoulders. His look, or was it his voice, was a lodestone that pulled Deirdre's gaze to his face, which was closer to hers than she might have imagined. He smiled. He looked calm, and he looked smart. She almost laughed to herself. *How can he look smart,* she thought? *You're either smart or not smart, but to look smart?* She determined it must be his hair, dark and long and raked back from his forehead, very Westley. Lea would have called him a "Dexter": smart, preppy, but not overly nerdy. His eyes were nothing if not perilously blue. They were not a little-boyish blue, like her cousin's. They were not quite the murky blue of her ancient biology teacher in high school. This blue was the blue of aristocrats, of men born to power who eschewed it in favour of goodness, the kind of blue eyes the Buddha would have had, were he born in the west.

"You look smart," she said, before she thought out her words. This was not like her. Deirdre was one to weigh every utterance. She had learned decorum from her church-going mother. Surely it was the beer talking, but she'd only had two, and she was taking tiny sips of this third. Craig certainly did not seem to be paying the sort of attention to her that her mother called the "nefarious intent of university rogues."

Boys had pulled her hair and stolen her mittens in grade school because she was "pretty," according to the teachers to whom she had complained. This had been confusing. Boys who had pushed her or pulled her hair did so, by all accounts, because they liked her? But pushing and pulling were things you did to someone you did not like. So, what was the advantage of having a boy like you if he treated you as if he did not like you? For the remainder of grade school and much of high school, Deirdre had ignored boys. They had not made any sense, and she certainly had not wanted one to like her and bring on all sorts of "nefarious intent" and pain. Deirdre had stuck with the girls until she met Ethan. And then just as she began to understand some of the reasons her friends all wanted boyfriends, Ethan had been unveiled as a cheater, and Deirdre committed to taking a hiatus from boys for a while.

Very quietly, so close his head was leaning against hers, Craig told her she smelled like lemons. She liked that. He was drinking a clear liquid from a red cup like hers.

"It's vodka. Stoli," he told her. "Would you like some?"

Deirdre took a sip from Craig's cup and quickly handed it back to him. A sharp steel liquid made its way down her throat. When Craig got up to refill his cup, Deirdre realized the sound of the crowd seemed dulled. She leaned her head back against the sofa, feeling heavy and tired and something else she had not felt for a long time. Craig looked good, smelled good, said all the right things, yet Deirdre felt like she could curl up and go to sleep. She would have to find Rosalie and the others, so they could walk back to the dorm together. It must be late.

As she was about to rouse herself from the warm spot, Craig returned and handed her the big red cup again. He sat down next to her and put his arm around the back of the sofa, this time touching her shoulder lightly. He stared into her eyes, and suddenly, yet slowly, moved toward her and kissed her on the lips. It was a long and quiet and gentle kiss. It was the kind of kiss that left you wanting another just like it, the kind of kiss that erased so much. Deirdre wedged back into the sofa and looked into Craig's eyes. Was he for real? Could a boy be this nice at a house with a reputation like Commissioner's? Her internal struggle melted in the warmth of the series of kisses that followed. She relaxed a bit. *What could kissing hurt*, she asked herself. *And he is so nice.*

Craig sat up after a few minutes and looked at her. "Tell me all about you, Deirdre," Craig said, rolling long strands of her hair around his index finger.

"I love Tolkien," she whispered, putting her hand into Craig's.

"And ... I think I hate Salman Rushdie."

"That *fatwa* really sucks," Craig said, rubbing her hand with his fingers. "The Ayatollah...."

Deirdre leaned into Craig and kissed him before he could finish. She had never done that, but it felt good. It felt right. Maybe she would stay at Commissioner House a little longer.

# 14.

RUE SAINT-DENIS was their stomping grounds. Ever since they met at Le Tap, whenever Marin and Trey could manage to eke out a free evening, they meandered the busy street taking in its crazy-quilt façade. Each city block was home to dozens of petite houses, all wedged together, no walkways between them, no yards. Brick houses butted up against stone houses painted bright pink. Some were left a rough-hewn milky grey. Next door might be an electric blue house with green shutters. Some were cottage-like with mansard roofs and pretty windows that jutted out, overlooking the street. Most of the four-storey buildings had balconies replete with eclectic smatterings of personal possessions: plants, haggard Christmas wreaths, sagging beach chairs. Anything but uniform, the street was alive with variety and colour and noise. Tiny lights glowed from restaurants. Bicyclists wove among traffic and parked cars. Families and college students roved from shop to shop, enjoying ice cream cones and whispering secrets.

Once Marin was in engineering school, their leisurely nights out were infrequent. Marin missed the pace of those early days and mused on them often. Saint-Denis was where Marin and Trey grew to know one another deeply and dearly. Their first date had been at Bistro à JoJo on St. Florian, two weeks after they met, a smoky, worn blues bar that earned the title "Blues Temple of Montreal" when the Johnny Blue Band began performing every Monday night for two years in a row. This, according to Marin and Trey, had launched a musical tradition in the Quartier Latin. French and English blues and rock bands took turns performing in this place so tiny the audience could see the band members sweat. Old church benches surrounded the perimeter with small round tables propped in front. A cramped mezzanine opened out onto Saint-Denis when the weather was warm, waning sunlight spiking into the dingy interior. Though Marin and Trey had spent several nights a week at Bistro à JoJo for nearly a year, drinking Sleeman's from tall glasses and listening well into the morning to guitars straining heartache, they maintained they had fallen in love at the Jazz Festival on the first of July in 1980, Canada Day.

Whenever anyone asked how they met, they responded as a team. Among the mimes on stilts who appeared to float among the crowds, playing accordions and pretending to sing into small megaphones that looked like tubas, amidst the bawdy, carnival atmosphere and the beer tents and the dozens of stages, Trey claimed he only had eyes for Marin. Marin would pick the routine up from here, adding that on that Canada Day, while toddlers bounced on grassy patches and grey-haired men smoked a joint and a bald man in a leather jacket danced with a woman with platinum hair and sparkling earrings that hung to her neck, she fell in love with Trey. An Ethiopian grandma nearby swirled a tiny grandchild in her arms like a windmill, tiny braids poking out from her head, her skin the smoothest, blackest Marin had ever seen. Another woman with long grey hair and a flowered sundress waved her hands in the air near one of the stages. On a happy, joy-filled summer day, while a young man carried a tray with dozens of cups of beer high above his head to sell to the masses lounging on concrete steps and ragged quilts, while the lead singer of a band from France crooned, wearing a maroon silk shirt with enormous sweat stains on the sides, a black bow tie at the neck and a fedora on his head, while women in head scarves and babies in strollers with sippy cups and women in cocktail dresses and dangerously high heels strolled, while there, Trey and Marin, best friends, fell in love.

Five years after she met Trey, Marin told Sybille one night at dinner, "I'm moving tomorrow morning. I'm moving in with Trey." She took another bite of her lasagna before looking at Sybille.

Sybille and Marin shared a third-floor apartment about an hour from Saint-Eustache where their parents and other three siblings lived. The apartment was in Mile-End, the French and immigrant neighbourhood near the Italian section of town and their favourite haunt, the open-air market Marche Jean-Talon. Their parents had lived there long before they married and then after Sybille and Marin and the others were born. Mile-End, the largely working-class neighbourhood, was one of the oldest in Montreal and one of the most diverse. Mile-End homes held a special place in the sisters' hearts. They had a distinct style that had come to define "neighbourhood" for them. Rectangular with flat roofs, the Mile-End houses were made of brick, and each two-to-three storey building housed two to five residences. While they were soberly designed, the wrought-iron staircases and balconies saved them from the prosaic, offering, rather, a sturdy hint of Europe.

From their open window, Sybille and Marin could hear neighbours shouting in French, Italian, Arabic, and Spanish. Outside the ground-floor apartments, tiny gardens burst with daffodils and purple hyacinths in early spring while mid-summer brought clematis, dahlias, and gladioli. They knew the neighbours by name, gave the children who came to greet them at the end of the day little treats: a cookie, a lollipop, a whistle. Mealtime scents were varied and mouth-watering. Italian mothers simmered sauces plumped with ripe tomatoes and entire garlic cloves. The scent of freshly-baked bread and rolls was on every street corner in the warm weather. Everyone in Mile-End visited Schwartz's Hebrew Deli, the oldest in Canada, founded in 1928, for their steak spices. Backyard grills barbecued steaks all through the summer, and the sharp tang of Schwartz's secret hot-peppers was omnipresent. All other noise and aromas left the room after Marin spoke that night.

"*Comment?* Marin, you are telling me this the night before?" Sybille quizzed. Marin was many things, beautiful and dynamic, but she was rash and intense. One had to tread lightly.

"I only made up my mind last night. Why wait?" Marin responded, staring at Sybille.

Sybille put down her fork. "Well, it would have been nice to have some time to get used to the idea. We *have* lived together for five years, Marin, and I think…."

"Sybille. For God's sake. Trey and I have been together forever, it seems. Do you expect us to live apart for all time? I believe it's time. I'm sorry if this is a shock." Marin took a sip of her wine.

Sybille was quiet for a time, moving bits of hamburger and tomato about her plate. Finally, she spoke. "It's not a shock, Marin. I'm happy for you. I just didn't expect it without warning. Look, it's all okay. We love Trey. You will be happier there."

"Thanks, Sybille. I love you," Marin said, tossing her plate and fork into the sink, grabbing her coat, and rushing out to meet her friends. "I will be home late," she shouted, half out the door. Before the door slammed shut, Marin rushed back in and hugged her sister tightly, for far longer than usual. Then she was gone again. Sybille sighed, finished her dinner, and tarried at the dining-room table until after the sun had set.

*

Two months later, Trey came to visit Sybille. He was very serious, wearing a poker face.

"I need to talk to you, Sybille. You are the older sister. I need your advice." Trey sat on the edge of the sofa.

"What is it, Trey?" Sybille asked, already guessing what would come next.

"The last eight weeks have been, well, something else. Marin has had two car accidents. She got burned when she was cooking on the gas stove. Her long sleeves caught on fire. She was bit by the neighbour's dog…"

"She is something special, Trey," said Sybille, laughing.

"But Sybille, I went to bed before Marin got home from class last night, and when I woke to noise at three a.m., there were ten people in the tiny living room. They were dancing. There were papers with math problems on them everywhere. There were bags of chips and bottles of wine…."

While Trey clearly had a longer list, Sybille stopped him. She knew all about it. She had lived with Marin since she had started at Université Sainte-Catherine five years earlier. If she weren't so adorable, Sybille could have pummeled her many times over. Marin was like no one else. She was confident, funny, happy, but she was a force to be reckoned with.

"You're going to have a funny life, Trey. She is a wonder and a woe. I must confess, I am happy I will not be the one to spend so much time in the emergency department." Sybille patted his shoulder and laughed. She had not expected to feel such relief when Marin moved in with Trey. She felt guilty about it, yet she had to face it. She missed her terribly. They were partners, twins, like Abbott and Costello, they always said. Marin was her alter ego. Bound by more than family ties alone. Best friends. This did not change when Marin left the apartment in Mile-End, but secretly Sybille felt a weight was removed from her shoulders. Marin would be safe with Trey. He would learn to cope with her kerfuffles, patch her up when she got bruised and burned. It was the price of love.

*

Sybille had faith in Trey. She knew that Marin had weathered their first date like a trooper, overcoming her fear in his nurturing presence. He was a gentle man, and when Marin eventually, much later on, told him about the night at the bus stop, he cried and held her and cried. Marin had shared that story with Sybille.

When they had fallen asleep after the talk about the bus stop, later that night, Marin woke to the sound of Trey in the living room, crying quietly, not wanting to wake her.

"Are you okay?" she asked, pulling on her robe, and sitting next to him.

"You did not deserve that, Marin. You did not," he said before he could no longer go on.

Marin rubbed his back. He pulled her to him and held her as they sat there with moonlight flooding the floorboards at their feet. Morning arrived in hues of magenta. Trey took her hands before she was fully awake. He was kneeling on the floor in front of her. He looked calm.

"Did you sleep, Trey?" she asked, quietly, sitting up.

He shook his head, his eyes never leaving hers.

"I feel stupidly protective. Even of the past. I want to keep you safe and happy. I'm so sorry that happened to you," he said.

"I know. I do know this. Trey, I'm okay. There are times when it is hard, very hard, and I get afraid all over again. For today, I want to move on. I told you about that night because I wanted you to know, so it won't stand in the way of us."

"When it's hard, how can I help?" he asked, rubbing the backs of her hands with his fingers, softly.

"Be here. Hold my hand, like this. Be my friend."

He nodded. They smiled nearly imperceptible smiles and sat for a while longer.

When Sybille was at her loneliest in the Mile-End apartment, missing her sister, this was the story she dug out and replayed. Trey was the healing that Marin needed, and the peace that this brought Sybille outweighed all else. Marin opened up the world, and Sybille remained contentedly in her shadow. She knew Trey felt the same way

# 15.

H ER SILENCE UNNERVED her friends. She would not speak about it. Mostly she slept or lay staring at the ceiling. Rosalie brought her food from the cafeteria, though she ate little of it. On Sunday, two days after they party, Jenna took her into the shower saying it would make her feel better. Then Jenna stayed with Deirdre all evening, brushing Deirdre's hair and painting her fingernails a soft pink.

Deirdre had been unconscious and naked when the girls found her that night at the party in one of the bedrooms. When they had searched every room in Commissioner and Bennett Houses to no avail, Rosalie and Jenna sought out Craig. He was standing with a group of guys around a keg. He had pointed to the last door on the right at the end of the hall. "Taking a nap," he had said, then looked away.

She had not responded when they tried to wake her, and they panicked. Jenna had poured the cup of beer she was carrying onto her head, and Deirdre woke with a start. She was groggy and limp, did not remember what happened. The girls had asked over and over.

"Did he hurt you, D? Was it that guy Craig? Are you okay?"
Deirdre just looked at them and closed her eyes again.

"Oh, god, Rosalie. I think he drugged her, the bastard," Jenna had cried.

"No ... maybe she just had too much to drink?" Rosalie had asked.

"No. She never drinks that much. You know that, Ro," Jenna had said, pulling Deirdre up into a sitting position on the bed. "Jesus Christ, why the hell did we leave her alone with him? Oh, shit. Let's get her the hell out of here right now." Rosalie was trembling, but she managed to find Deirdre's clothes and dress her quickly. The girls had helped her stand up. When it was clear she could not walk by herself, they had propped her between them and left Commissioner House by a side door.

Back in their own dorm, the girls had tried to sit Deirdre up in her bed and get her to talk. But Deirdre kept leaning into her pillows. "Just want to sleep," she had mumbled. Suddenly, Deirdre had bolted upright, looked at the girls and said, "Gonna be sick." Rosalie grabbed the small trash can from beneath Deirdre's desk just as Deirdre vomited into it. Jenna had held back her hair, and Rosalie felt her forehead after she lay back down on her pillow. She was sweating and feverish.

"What do we do?" Jenna had asked. "Do we call the police? A doctor? Will she be okay?"

"I'll get my comforter and sleep in here tonight. We'll watch her. We need to see what she remembers, what happened." Rosalie had returned almost immediately, and the girls set up their comforters like sleeping bags on the floor next to Deirdre's bed.

"If that asshole raped her, Jenna, I'm going to kill him," Rosalie had whispered before falling asleep.

"Me too," Jenna had quietly responded.

*

Deirdre's dreams were chaotic and vague. There were only brief moments of lucidity. She kept saying "No." Loudly. Firmly. She could feel her arms straining, pushing against something. Phrases on a repeating loop: "You're beautiful. Just trust me." Though her friends asked her a million questions, she could remember nothing. Hours were lost, it seemed. The last thing she remembered was kissing Craig, sitting on that plaid loveseat, hearing three guys in suits standing on chairs singing "Stand" by R.E.M. Now she felt exhausted, dizzy all the time, as if she might faint. She woke in the night shaking and panicked. There was one other thing. It kept coming and coming at her. She fought it. Shards of pain shot through the very centre of her body. She had flashes, images of being held down, something heavy on top of her, talking non-stop, telling her to be quiet. Her arms were bruised, but the bruises had faded to a yellow by the time she noticed them in the shower days later. She did not know if Jenna had noticed them too.

Deirdre felt hungover, though she had only ever felt that way once, the day after she drank the beer with Lea in the cemetery. The only thing Deirdre could concentrate on when she woke in the dark of the night was the book Lea had made for her. *What Women Engineers Do and Why They Do It.* She began to read it constantly, reading it aloud to Rosalie when she had the energy. By Friday, a week after the party, she could not stop.

"Julia Brainerd Hall (born 1859 – died 1925) helped her brother Charles to research and develop aluminum. She arranged the financial funding and ran the business which became an international success. Charles went on to become wealthy and famous. He gave no credit to his sister at all, nothing for her dedication and genius." She paused.

"Do you believe that, Ro?" she asked. Before Rosalie could answer, Deirdre went on. "G. Jean Hoppert (born 1949) worked for M&M and created a machine that churned out six-foot slabs of uncut granola bars without harming a single grain. Kudos bars she made."

"How are you, D?" Rosalie asked, brushing Deirdre's hair out of her eyes and stuffing another pillow behind her back. "We're worried...."

"Listen to this," said Deirdre, never looking up from the book. "Jane H. Rider (born 1889 – died 1981) lived to be almost a hundred years. She got the dairy industry to pasteurize milk.

Saved all those babies from infant death in the early 1900s. Julie Morgan was an architect *and* a civil engineer who was refused admission to the École des Beaux Arts in Paris because she was a woman. She fought it and graduated in 1902. When she retired in the 1950s, she had built over seven hundred structures, including churches, schools, hospitals, university buildings, you name it..."

"Deirdre," Rosalie shouted. Deirdre looked up, raised her eyebrows.

"What?" she asked.

"Are you okay, D? Are you well enough to go to the infirmary?"

"Fine, fine. Just a flu or something," Deirdre said, reading again. "Roberta Nichols (born 1931) developed a car that could run on ethanol, methanol or gasoline and got it to reach one hundred and ninety miles an hour, and did you know...."

"Deirdre, let's put the book down for a minute," Rosalie said, taking the book gently from Deirdre's hands. "I have to tell you something."

Deirdre looked at Rosalie quickly, then looked away. She waited.

"Professor Oliver wants to come to see you," Rosalie said. "She asked about you in class today."

"Oh God, I missed class. Oh, God." Deirdre leapt out of bed and rummaged through her drawers. Rosalie grabbed her hands and pulled her slowly back to the bed.

"It's all right. I told her you were sick. I talked to her, Deirdre. She asked if she could visit. I hope it's okay."

"Here? Professor Oliver is coming here?" Deirdre asked, her eyes wide.

Rosalie assured Deirdre she had time to rest. The professor would be another hour or two. Deirdre rested back into her pillows, closed her eyes, and sighed. Rosalie stared out the window and waited.

After an hour a quiet knock awakened Deirdre. "May I come in, Deirdre?" the professor's voice called from the hallway.

Rosalie went to the door, and Deirdre pulled the covers up to her chin.

Rosalie pulled up a chair from Deirdre's desk, and offered it to the professor.

"Thank you, Rosalie. You're a good friend. If it's okay with Deirdre, I'd like to speak to her alone. Is that okay, Deirdre?"

Deirdre looked at Rosalie. Rosalie came over to the bed and kissed Deirdre on the head. "I'll be back with some supper in an hour or so. Love you," she said and closed the door as she left the room.

*

Not quite two weeks after the Commissioner-Bennett party, on the same night that the Berlin Wall came down, ending communist and Soviet rule, FRRF took over the Aquitaine Principal's office for twenty-four hours. Roberta and Ellen had tried to arrange an earlier protest on the field outside Commissioner House when a group of about twenty males showed up to play baseball, each carrying a bat. The women left, fearing the worst. The Commissioner guys knew FRRF had tracked down their names and home addresses, knew they had sent letters to their mothers, had sent press releases to the media. The first-year guys in Commissioner who taped the signs to their windows knew what was going on, knew they had triggered rage in the women on campus. Still, weeks later, the university administration and the Student Housing Council were silent on the issue.

The idea for the sit-in was Roberta's, but everyone in the class was on board to support FRRF What recourse did they have? Escalating activism to get the administration to hold the Commissioner students accountable had failed. They were not being listened to. So, at 9:00 a.m. on November 9, about thirty women, from FRRF, from Professor Oliver's class, and from the Women's Centre, entered the Principal's office with a list of demands. They met with Principal Elias Plumber for an hour. He heard them out. Still, he maintained he had no control, that the Student Housing Council and those in charge of judicial proceedings were the people to address such issues. When the women explained that the actions of the Commissioner students had broader, more dangerous, implications for women, Plumber merely nodded. "These actions pain me," he said, "but it is out of my control."

It was a slap in the face.

So the women stayed, settling into the well-appointed office for the long haul. The word spread fast across campus. Those crazy feminists had stormed Principal Plumber's office and were holding a sit-in, like in the late 1960s, going all Vietnam and Kent State on the Number-One man on Aquitaine's campus. By late afternoon, at the beginning of the coldest November anyone could remember, about one hundred female students were spilling out of Principal Plumber's office, into the hallways, and onto the outside steps of the administrative building. Fearing backlash, they wore head scarves covering their faces when they entered the building, in order to protect their identities. They had drafted a list of demands that did not call for the expulsion of the men of Commissioner House. Rather, they demanded that Plumber make an immediate public statement denouncing the behaviour of the Commissioner men; that the men of Commissioner House sponsor, organize, and implement a campus-wide educational campaign on sexual assault for men; further, that the Commissioner men raise $5,000 in donations for an organization that helps women who are victims of male violence with the stipulation that the money be raised by men from men; and, lastly, that the Sexual Assault Centre in town be funded by the university since it did not have a sexual assault crisis centre itself.

Inside the Principal's plush office, about half of the women sat along the perimeter of the capacious office and allowed the scarves to drape along their shoulders. The rest of the women sat cross-legged or were prone on the dense oriental carpet in the middle of the office. Male supporters waited outside and supplied the women with hot coffee and snacks. The women held steaming coffee cups and munched on graham crackers and cheese wedges, glancing at the clock from time to time.

That evening, Deirdre leaned against a barrister's bookcase in a corner of the office. She had not wanted to come. Rosalie insisted. She told Deirdre their entire class was going to be there, that it was their duty as students to stand up for what was right. The sit-in was a last resort. It was all so crazy, but Deirdre dressed in her warmest turtleneck sweater and corduroy pants and walked with Rosalie to the Principal's office. It was dark. FRRF had sent word that the Principal had long gone. A press conference was held on the administrative building steps at five p.m. Ben and Whit and some other guys were camping outside the huge window in Principal Plumber's office, and every few hours or so, new women entered to relieve those who had been there for some time.

Now Deirdre sat close to Rosalie and took a sip of the coffee someone handed her. She watched the snow fall outside, straight down, shimmering in the glow of the streetlights. It was the exact kind of snow her grandmother used to gather into bowls for Deirdre and her sister, when they were little, thick and fluffy. Grandma would drizzle it with maple syrup. For one moment Deirdre was back home, a little girl again. Then it was gone. The world had stopped thirteen days ago. She could not think clearly. Going to that party at Commissioner House had been a mistake. She had known better. That was the only clear thought that persisted. Every time she thought of it, she felt sick. Ashamed.

Suddenly, Deirdre snapped to attention. Ellen was standing in the middle of the room, her voice raised. Roberta and Ellen had refused to wear head scarves. "Bring it on," they had said. "Let them come after us with their baseball bats and their hate. I'm ready to kick some ass." They were on fire.

"We need to stick together," Ellen said. "They get away with anything they want at Commissioner. They are flagrant, refusing to take the signs down. Principal Plumber and senior staff are cowardly. Commissioner House acts with bold impunity. And the administration does not say boo. It is up to us. No more fear. Look, this is war. We met with every dean we could find. Professor Oliver is an ally, but she is not tenured, so she is at risk. The Principal says he's powerless over his own administrative system. Who the hell can make these boys behave like human beings but us?"

Roberta stood up and joined her in the middle of the room. "You have to admit," she said, "we scared the shit out of those rich boys out there at Commissioner. Letters to their mamas, phone calls, all that press. We're national news, and yet, their apology was bullshit. After the media hunted them down, all of them said their names were 'Donald,' and that it was all a joke. What bullshit. Good God, one of them grew up down the street from me in Ottawa, Arthur Brown, their spokesman."

Deirdre must have dozed off, for when she came around, she heard a woman named Susan Carson from the Sexual Assault Centre speaking. She had a head of wild grey curls, and her wrists jangled with silver bracelets. Deirdre heard her lilting voice as if from under water. She kept being pulled away from the words by dozens of tiny candle flames that were glowing upon the office mantel. She heard everything Roberta and Ellen said, saw their gesticulations, understood they were furious, but somehow it all played out at a nebulous distance.

Susan Carson looked around the room. "Does anyone have anything she would like to share with the group. It's only ten p.m. and we'll be here through the night. The personal, as you well know, is political. We may as well use this time to talk to each other. "

The women were silent for a long time after Susan spoke. The wind pounded the paned windows of the principal's office. The lights flickered. From the depths of the room, where she was nestled far into one corner, a young woman blurted, "I was raped at Commissioner House." Deirdre jolted, raised her head, stretched to see who was speaking. The girl wore her hair in a loose ponytail, and she pulled the edges of a blue cardigan sweater tightly across her chest.

"It happened last semester. I went to a party because a boy in my English class invited me and my roommates. Some of the second- and third-year girls told us about Commissioner, warned us not to ever go there. But this boy in my class always talked to me. I thought he was cute and polite, and my roommates were going with me, so I ignored the warning."

She began to cry in muffled sobs, and someone next to her leaned in and said, "It's okay. Take your time."

Susan said, "Thank you for sharing. What's your first name?"

"Jill," said the student, still crying, but attempting to continue. The room was warm though the wind fumed in the trees outside the windows. The snow was no longer coming straight down but blowing at an angle. Deirdre sat upright, pulling her knees into her chest, listening.

Slowly, methodically, two women nearest the massive fireplace began to quietly crumple paper and arrange kindling from a pewter bucket, to light a small fire. Birch logs were meticulously arranged in a brass holder, and the women blew the fire into warmth and brightness. By the time Jill spoke again, the fire cast a golden hue over the office.

"I had to go really bad, and the downstairs bathroom was being used. This boy in the hall saw me, said I could use the bathroom at the top of the stairs. I told my friends I would be right back. I set my cup on a tall table in the hallway, outside the bathroom. When I came out of the bathroom, the boy in my English class was there. He said, 'Hi. It's great you're here,' and he handed me my drink. 'This yours?' he asked. Then he said, 'Come with me a minute.' I did." She began crying again. Soothing voices came from around the room: "Take your time, Jill."

"Why the hell did I go with him? What was I thinking? Where were my friends? I'm not even sure how long I was upstairs ... with him." Jill sobbed into her open palms. Her shoulders shook, and in the fire-light, Deirdre could see the fine russet strands that had pulled away from her ponytail.

"Will someone get Jill a cup of coffee?" asked Susan. "This isn't an easy story to tell, Jill. You're doing so well."

Jill continued. "I followed him – of my own stupid will – down the hallway. I didn't know where I was or where I was going, but I trusted him." Jill laughed, one arid and quick laugh. "Why? Tell me why did I trust some boy in some class who was cute and wore a suit? Commissioner boys always wear suits to their parties. It's their trademark or something. Oh God..." she sighed.

The only sound was the crackling of the fire. No one moved. Deirdre leaned forward over her knees. She was perfectly alert, listening to every word. Rosalie placed her hand on the small of Deirdre's back.

"We went into a room, his room, I think. There were three desks and three beds. I drank from my cup, only a sip. Something told me not to drink from that cup. He gulped his down. I looked around at the posters of women ... then the lights were off. Suddenly. The door closed behind me. I felt him come close and put his arms around me. I could smell beer when he whispered in my ear, in this slow-motion voice, 'You are so beautiful.'" Against the wall, Jill shifted, sat up tall. Her voice became clearer, louder, as she came to the end of her story.

"I turned toward the door to leave. I felt uncomfortable, but he held onto me so tight, kept saying I was so beautiful."

Deirdre felt a sharp pain in her head.

Someone in the crowd moaned softly. Jill sobbed.

Susan comforted, "It's okay, Jill. This is not your fault. You did nothing wrong. You're not alone." Other voices echoed Susan's words, "Not alone, Jill."

Jill took a deep breath, blew her nose, continued. "He pulled me toward a bed. He sat down next to me, put his arm around me. 'You look amazing, Jill,' he said. How the hell could he know that? It was so dark in that room. He asked me if I had a new blouse and ran his fingers low along my neckline, as if tracing a necklace. And ... and here's the thing. It felt nice. He smelled so nice. His voice was quiet, not that whispering thing he was doing before, just calm and nice." Jill took the coffee someone held out to her.

"Drink this, honey. Take a sip."

Jill took a drink and went on. "I thought he liked me. The way he was talking. I'm an idiot, I know. But I didn't run. I stayed. I wanted to be there sitting next to him, talking to him. It was weird, and I felt so tired. I just wanted to be there listening to the things he was saying. I feel so stupid...."

Susan spoke, "You're not stupid, Jill. Believe me."

Suddenly, the rest of the story spewed out of Jill. "And then he was on top of me. Pulling at my clothes. I couldn't stop him. He wouldn't listen. It's like I wasn't there. He kept saying, 'Trust me.' It hurt like crazy. Then, it was over. He got up. I thought he was still there, and I was terrified he would do it again, so I stayed completely still for a while. But he was gone. I got dressed. I had to pull my blouse low to cover my skirt. He had ripped it. I wanted to go to the bathroom. I knew I was bleeding. Bastard. He hurt me so much ... I just wanted to get out of there...."

"Jesus, Jill. You must have been so afraid," Sarah said from across the room. "I'm Sarah. I'm in that same English class. Who is this creep?"

Jill seemed not to have heard her.

"I ran. I stood at the top of the stairs and looked at all the people partying downstairs. I saw my roommates in the corner, near the bar. I saw so many people. And then I saw him. In his navy pin-striped suit. His baby blue tie. He had one leg up on a low windowsill, and he was talking with a group of Commissioners, other boys in suits and ties. And they were smacking him on the back. I ran out the front door. Into the dark. All the way back to my dorm."

While Jill cried quietly, while the fire snapped and spit, Deirdre held her head in her hands. Then, suddenly, she forced herself to her feet, though she was wedged against the bookcase and several female bodies in the overcrowded principal's office. Finally, she stood straight. She looked around her, as if seeing the dozens of women surrounding her for the first time. "Oh, my God. That's what happened to me. Exactly what you said. I was raped. At Commissioner House," Deirdre shouted, staring at Jill.

Jill's eyes widened.

The room was still.

"What is his name? Jill. What is his name?" Her eyes never left Jill's, begging for an answer.

Jill nodded several times, understanding. "His name is Craig."

Deirdre closed her eyes and exhaled loudly. Her shoulders slumped, and she sat back down next to Rosalie. The tears came, wracking her entire body. Rosalie held her. Time dissolved, became internal and raw and clanging. Susan was talking to Rosalie, handing her a piece of paper with her phone number on it. Jill did the same, after she came to sit by Deirdre for a while. Deirdre did not speak again. All of her words were gone. A deep ache remained.

Later, she and Rosalie and their housemates walked home. Sometime after midnight, there were still women in the principal's office, spilling out into the street. A few TV cameramen sat on the outside steps drinking coffee. The snow had stopped. The moon slit the black, still sky with a crescent of light.

# 16.

MARIN HAD NEVER FELT more like a girl than she did in engineering school. In her largest class, there were sixty students, nine of them women, only fifteen percent. In her other classes, there were far fewer. Women stood out as a distinct minority. On the whole, this was not a good thing. They wanted to blend in among the other engineering students, but there were engineering stereotypes and traditions that either put women under a microscope or ignored them entirely.

There were the jokes. *What's the difference between a woman engineering student and garbage? Garbage gets taken out once a week.* There were also the flyers that got passed around surreptitiously, like the one Marin found in her bookbag one night when she made a pot of coffee and settled in to do problems.

HAZARDOUS MATERIALS DATA SHEET
The Chemical Properties of a Woman:
Reacts well to gold, platinum, and all precious stones.
Explodes spontaneously without reason or warning.
The most powerful money-reducing agent known to man.
Very effective cleaning agent.
Hazards:
Turns green when placed alongside a superior specimen.

Marin crumpled up the sheet before she finished reading it all. Hilaire had warned her about this sort of thing when she started, but she had grown tired of the persistent stereotypes after her first two weeks at CanTech. They were as ubiquitous as they were invalid: women engineers were ugly nerds who loved *Star Trek*. They wore no makeup, and did not shave their legs or underarms. They wore unisex clothes and had either aggressively short hair or long hair wrestled into taut pony-tails. Most were lesbians. If an engineering student happened to be an attractive female she was clearly being flirtatious and looking for a husband. She could not be serious about her career. Regardless, a woman's chances of making it into the professional world of engineering were slim.

Sadly, Marin saw that this latter statistic bore out. After her first year, her cohort group of women had shrunk by forty percent. The students who left gave a variety of reasons, but Marin had seen through all of them. It had not been because of grades. Half of the women who left had "A" or a "B" averages in their engineering courses. On the record, they told CanTech they were leaving because of the heavy workload and the pace of the curriculum. Privately, they had told Marin and others they felt discouraged by male faculty and peers. They had not felt supported. It was true that the engineering faculty was predominantly white males who were fifty years or older and who had tenure. The climate clearly favoured male students: professors called on them more, gave them more detailed feedback, asked them more complex questions than they asked the women students. There was no denying this.

"But it's changing," Marin had argued with Nicole, one of the group partners she was closest to in her first year. "We are changing it. We have to tough it out." Those were Hilaire's words, but they had become Marin's own. She would tough it out, and Nicole should too.

"My confidence is shot, Marin," Nicole had answered, gazing off into the hallway, as they sat at a small table in the cafeteria, away from the Georges of their class. "I just can't keep propping myself up. I'm tired of it all. I tape stupid mantras up on my mirror and read them every day, and I feel like an idiot. 'I am good. I am smart. I am an engineer,'" she repeated in a sing-song voice. "Am I an engineer? Am I really? If I am, then where are the engineers who look like me, Marin?"

Nicole had wanted to design roller coasters and theme-park rides. She had wanted to bring a female view to a field that had long been the sole domain of men and to see how this might change the kinds of rides offered to the public.

"Nicole, there are women engineers, and you know it. Look at Dr. Rajiv and Dr. Moss and ... who is that one with the ... Dr. Bonnet."

"Three of them in the *entire* university. Seriously, Marin? The odds are against us. Besides, we spend all of our waking hours doing problem sets and labs. We have no social life. When was the last time we had a beer at the pub?"

"Oh, God. I can't remember what beer tastes like, but we've come so far. We're so close to finishing our first year. If we can do this, we can do next year. Then, then we get to specialize and that's when it will all make sense. And there are women engineers in mechanical...."

"I can't do it, Marin. I already submitted my letter to the Dean. This is a hellish boot camp. I know these things seem small to some students, but I can't take it. Every time a professor hands back an exam, some guy nearly pretzels himself looking over my shoulder to see what I got, or someone shouts, 'What did the girl get? Did I beat the girl?' But you know what the worst thing is, Marin? Seriously? It's the feeling of being observed. You know, constantly scrutinized. Do you know this feeling? Like you're being watched covertly, as if the men in the room are waiting for you to do something wrong, or quirky, or female."

"I know," Marin had nodded. "I do know."

They had both been quiet for a time, then Nicole hugged Marin and said, "I'll miss you. I'll miss Renee. I might even, for one miniscule of a second, miss George and all of his pompous, blowhard hogwash, but I will not miss the way I feel so small here. I won't miss that at all."

Marin had thought of this conversation often the next year, when she, herself, wanted to give up. When a woman left engineering school, it was felt by all the other women because their numbers were so small. Each one who remained asked herself, even if subconsciously, "Can I really make it?"

This was the one topic that threatened to splinter the sisterhood in Marin's third year. Chantal would not acknowledge the palpable hostility Renee and Marin had felt on occasion from their male classmates and even some of the professors. Whenever they discussed it, Chantal remained quiet, focused on her homework. When they asked her directly about it, she said she had not noticed. When they pushed her, she said, simply, it does not pay to go there.

"We're lucky at CanTech," she said soberly, one day when Renee insisted Chantal share her thoughts. "It's a wonderful school. The sexist jokes, and sexist traditions like Lady Godiva, do not go on here anymore. There were some pretty disgusting things that happened a long time ago, but those days are over. It is only at the English schools. This is a French school. We work together here." Chantal looked them both in the eye for a long time. Then she resumed working problems in her notebook.

Renee looked at Marin who looked stricken. Marin mouthed, "We'll talk later," and she held up her thumb and pinky finger to simulate a telephone. There would need to be debriefing, but it could not happen now in front of Chantal. The topic was closed for good. Chantal had made that clear. But Marin and Renee could not deny their own experiences or Nicole's, which had driven her to drop out. They would need to lean more heavily on each other than ever before. Later that day, before leaving school, Renee met Marin near the coffee shop.

"Who the hell is Lady Godiva?" Renee asked. "I was too intimidated by Chantal's imperial self to ask. Do you know?"

"I do. I heard about her from my brother. She is legendary in engineering schools," said Marin.

"For God's sake, who is she, Marin?"

"Well, she is some female, usually a fabulous-looking student, who rides naked on a horse around campus during engineering week. She is a big hit among the men, and she...."

"Totally naked?" Renee screamed.

"She wears a blanket around her, but her legs are bare, and the blanket is sometimes tugged from her shoulders by rowdy engineers...."

"Wait, wait, you mean *the* Lady Godiva who was the wife of Leofric III, Lord of Coventry?" Renee asked, deadly serious.

"How in God's name do you know that?"

"My dad loves history, you know, so I'm a bit of a history buff. I like to know things."

"Impressive," said Marin, giving Renee's shoulder a pretend punch. "You are something else, girl."

Renee sat up straight, struck a professional pose, and lectured, "So, Lady Godiva famously begs her husband to remove the unbearable taxes he's laid on his people. The woman hounds him. He says, okay, I'll get rid of them if you ride naked through the streets of the town. Some pervert, eh? But, she agrees, and sends out a big fat proclamation that all of the people in the town must shut their windows and not look out. So, she gets onto this horse and rides with only her very long hair to cover her. One guy – there's always one – the original Peeping Tom, he bore a hole in his shutters to check out Lady Godiva, and guess what? Our Tom was struck blind. The jerk of a husband kept his word and abolished the taxes."

Marin clapped when Renee was done. "Brava! Well told."

"Thank you, thank you," Renee said, standing to take a bow. "But, Marin, what in the world does Lady Godiva and taxes and nakedness have to do with engineering?"

"She's the patron saint of engineering. Apparently, as the story goes, she captures the essence of selfless dedication to making the world a better place, which all engineers are bound to do. There is even a song...."

"No way, a song?

"There's a song. It goes like this, I think: *We are, we are, we are, we are, we are the Engineers/ We can, we can, we can, we can, we can demolish forty beers....* Anyway, U. Ontario even has a band, the Lady Godiva Memorial Band!"

"An engineering band?"

"Yep. A marching band that doesn't march. They meander and spell band 'bnad' – you know, because engineers aren't supposed to be able to spell. They play drinking songs, offensive crap..."

"The usual."

"But, they have albums. I listened to one called *Band With the Runs*. My brother and I found it in that used record store downtown."

"How is it?"

"Pathetic."

*

The stupid-ass antics of some engineers was not a huge concern for Marin, though Chantal's denial of any problem whatsoever seemed odd. Frankly, Marin did not have time to be distracted by the boys. She saw it all, and she chose to forge ahead with her work because tackling these issues seemed too daunting. Maybe that was how Chantal felt too.

In her second year, Marin had developed the strongest arms in the family by toting the 1,000-page tome, *Advanced Engineering Mathematics,* everywhere she went. Her brother Hilaire had teased her constantly about "dating" Erwin Kreyszig, the author of the book, famous among engineering students for having loved both art history and math when he was a youth in Pirna, Germany. The story goes that he sold his artwork to fund his university studies where he eschewed art and made a lifelong commitment to mathematics.

"He is your soul-mate, MoMo," Hilaire had teased. "The man loved art, but he had to walk the scalar fields through numerical linear algebra working ODEs into the wee hours in order to become the man he was, the man who wrote that enormous book you get to sleep with every night!"

Hilaire had loved to toss engineering lingo at Marin, especially when she was in her first year, nearly drowning under the weight of terms like "vector differential calculus." It had taken her a full week to figure out that "ODE" meant "ordinary differential equations." It would take her a lifetime to forget them. They were braided into her brain so tightly after two years that her scalp ached chronically.

Marin had to admit that what she really loved about school was Materials Engineering, the concentration she chose upon entering this third year. The two hellish years she spent at CanTech before diving deeply into the continuum of stress and strain, truss forces, torsion and bending, was all in the past. Every tortuous minute of the last two years became crystallized in her Mechanics of Materials courses. Though this third year was proving the most gruelling yet, there was wisdom for a lifetime here.

If her goal was success as an engineer, she had to understand how elasticity and equilibrium worked. She had to fully embrace bending and stress-strain curves and kinematics. This last, kinematics, was the geometry of motion, the consideration of bodies or objects and groups of objects without consideration of the forces that cause their motion. Some days are just like that, kinematic: people were there, simply there, and she did not have the wherewithal to consider why they were there or how they got there.

The mechanical properties of ceramics, metals, and polymers – their strength, stiffness, their ductility – all of this Marin found fascinating. She loved exploring the relationships between structure and properties in all classes of materials including metals, ceramics, electronic materials, and biomaterials. Her professors emphasized the role of processing and microstructure in controlling these properties. Lecture topics included torsion of a circular shaft and beam bending. Marin's goal of designing structures, that dream born of her first encounter with *The Sound of Music* as a child, was in sight, even if she was not sure how it would all come together. She knew artists and designers manipulated materials and space to make an audience believe it was inside a European country at war, but how she would merge her design creativity with her passion for materials was not clear yet. It all boiled down to the practicality of the thing, learning, for example, what new materials could make an amusement park ride faster; what new materials could be used for hip replacements or to repair and preserve objects of cultural heritage in museums; what new materials could repel malaria-carrying mosquitoes and repair nano-sized bones. Materials science and engineering simply made practical sense in a world that needed help. And a world that needed art and theatre and opera.

There was much to do, but paying too much attention to the engineering machismo that had brought Nicole to her knees was not going to benefit Marin. This may be "a man's world," as her mother had once told her, but Marin was in it, and finally, after two hard years, she had earned her place in her concentration. She was focused and serious, all the boyish games be damned.

# 17.

D EAN GRIME'S ENVOY showed up on an afternoon seventeen days after the party. Commissioner House was in sluggish, après-weekend mode when Associate Dean Philippe and his administrative assistant knocked on the don's apartment door. Jack happened to be at the vending machines and overheard them asking for Craig Berseaux.

Bounding into their room, Jack jumped on Craig's bed and pounded on his shoulders to wake him from his weekly afternoon nap. "Dude, you are so fucked. The Dean's lackey is here. What did you do, man? Get up. Get down there now, dickweed."

"Bite me, Jack," said Craig, rolling over and yanking a handful of blanket over his head.

"I kid you not, you asshole. They are here now, with the don – what's his name – Jim, I think. Anyway, Jim is on his way up to escort you downstairs. They do not look like they are giving us House of the Year award."

Outside his window, snow squalled. A flimsy covering crested the rooftops across the quad and the walkways below. When he had gone for a nap, the sky was still at rest. Craig breathed deeply and got up. He put on khakis, a blue button-down shirt, and a navy polka-dot tie. He brushed his teeth and whisked back his hair with water before rushing down the stairs, nearly crashing into Kevin at mid-flight.

"Craig, man. What the...?"

"No time, Kevin," he said, slapping his housemate on the arm and continuing on to the don's apartment. Outside the closed door, he straightened his tie, ran his fingers through his hair, then knocked and entered.

Jim stepped aside, as Craig walked into the small living room. "Dr. Philippe, how nice to see you. And is this the new administrative assistant in Dickens Hall? I'm Craig." Craig extended his hand.

The assistant introduced himself as "Jean Charles" and shook Craig's hand firmly.

"Craig, sit down," said Dr. Philippe. "We have a serious matter to discuss. Surely you know why we are here." The associate dean's curtness caused Craig to sit up straight in his seat. He noticed the associate dean nod to Jim, who left the room quietly.

"Indeed, sir. I'm sure it's about the window signs. My mom got a letter. I imagine...." His eyes roved between the two men, inquiring if he had surmised the reason for their visit.

"It is not about the signs. This is difficult, Craig. Dean Grimes has insisted on this visit. We have had a complaint about you ... about a party here two and a half weeks ago. A young woman, a first-year student. You were seen kissing her, providing her with alcohol. She maintains that she was ... she was raped. By you."

The room was hushed. The snow outside fell, quietly, persistently now. Rare for November. Craig stared at the men, moved his eyes continuously from one to the other. He shook himself, stood up, walked to the door, returned. He did this several times, as if working out what he had just heard.

"Rape? She said I raped her? Wait. Who is she? That was two weeks ago, you say? Oh. My. God. She said that?" His voice punctured each word with a voluble beat. Craig returned to the chair, looked at the men, held his hands to the side of his head, and ran his fingers through the tangles in his hair. "Is this a joke?" he asked Dr. Philippe, glaring at the man.

"This is by no means a joke, Craig. This is a very serious issue, and we..."

"Preposterous. Pure lunacy."

"Nevertheless," began Dr. Philippe.

Craig stood, pointed his finger in the direction of the campus center. "They've been railing against Commissioner House since the freakin' middle ages.... Trumped-up charges! Jesus, we eat those for breakfast, Dr. Philippe. You know this. You ... you were, you are, a Commissioner man. Weren't you?"

"That is beside the point, Craig. Were you with a young woman, a first year, at the party? Did things, maybe, get out of hand, too much to drink? I need you to come clean about this, Craig. Before the police...."

"Police? Police!" Craig was shouting now, pacing the room. "When have we ever had police?" He stopped in the middle of the room, as if to compose himself. He took a deep breath and returned to face the associate dean. "You have known me a long time, sir. Am I the kind of man who would do such a thing? Who would *need* to do such a thing?"

Jean Charles raised his head now, no longer peering at some innocuous spot on the carpet. "Did you really just say..." he began, but he was cut off by his superior.

"Craig, the girl's philosophy professor has been to see the dean and the girl has spoken to the authorities. You must..."

"What? What can I do?" Craig implored. "I have never raped anyone in my life."

"Fix this thing, Craig," Dr. Philippe said, placing his hand on Craig's and looking directly into his eyes. "Fix it now, before it gets out of hand."

Jean Charles made a huffing sound, but when the associate dean fixed his gaze on him, he became silent.

"Fix it? Some lame ass ... first-year girl yells rape, and my good name is crap. And *I* need to fix it?"

"You, yes. Only you can fix it, Craig."

All three men remained completely silent. Then Dr. Philippe

patted him on the back, and they left.

Craig remained in Jim's apartment for a long time, sat in a deep and worn leather chair facing the windows, watching the snow. His mind ricocheted around a triangle of thoughts: *police, party, parents.*

It was true. Seldom had the police been called in on a Commissioner House matter. Aquitaine University liked to deal with its student disputes internally, but little Deirdre had taken it a step too far, or her professor did. Police mucked up everything, asked too many questions, acted all threatening. Craig had to avoid the police at all costs. And his parents could *not* find out about this "claim." *Goddamn women. What the hell?*

Craig reviewed the party; he knew who she was. That Deirdre had come of her own free will. *He* had not even invited her. Christ, he had not even known her until that night. *And, man oh man, who in the world looks that hot and does not want to be noticed?* For one asinine second he thought she could be Flawless Freshling, but Christ, that girl was totally third base. *This is bullshit.* He had seen it a million times. Girls come to a guy's house, drink his beer, flirt their asses off with him, then, when things go their natural course, they cry "rape," or even date fucking rape. *What the hell is that? Just pure regret, that's what.*

Who in his right mind would believe any woman who wears come-fuck-me shoes like that and visits Commissioner House? *Don't we have the worst reputation of any single house in all of fucking Canada? God, this sucks.* Craig pulled himself up in the leather chair and thought about his mother. She could not know about this. But if his father found out, it was all over. He would lord it over his wife like a laurel wreath. "Good son gone bad, Lee Ann. Always told you. Little lemming – eh – no different from the rest. Boys will be boys, just want a little action. Pure and simple, Lee Ann: it's nature."

Craig was different from the rest. His mother told him so. He was a smart, complex, kind young man who would make a solid future for himself at Aquitaine. He was well read. He cared about others. He loved classical music, played the piano in high school until his father....

"No," Craig said aloud, jumping out of the chair and rushing back up to his room. She cannot know about this. Craig would fix it. How? Oh, God, he had to think. Maybe, maybe he should just tell his mother. Back in his room, Craig sank into his bed and pulled up the blankets.

After a sharp rap at the door, Jack entered. "Hey, man. You okay?"

"I'm screwed," said Craig.

"This Dean Grimes on your ass, Craigster?" Jack asked, sitting on the edge of Craig's bed.

"Yep. And the associate dean. And some professor. And, quite possibly, the police."

"Holy fuck," said Jack, slamming his left hand down on Craig's bed.

The Commissioner brothers sat quietly for a while, pondering. Jack broke the silence. "What are you going to do, Craig?"

"I don't know, Jack. I'm going to fix things, I guess."

# 18.

"**T**HIS AQUITAINE DEBACLE is getting stupider by the minute," Jenean called to Bart, who was shaving in the bathroom.

"What Aquitaine debacle?" he shouted back. "Didn't you go there to write about those engineers who hung the Volkswagen Beetle frame off that bridge? "

Jenean got up, walked to the bathroom door, and stared at Bart. "That was in *Vancouver*, Bart. Did you not just read the paper verbatim? The Aquitaine University story, the No Means No campaign gone awry?"

"The thing about the signs in the windows, in the men's dorm?" Bart asked, looking at Jenean. "Seriously? Isn't that old news by now?" He returned to shaving, peering at himself in the steamy mirror.

Jenean took a deep breath, leaned forward in the doorway. "Four weeks ago. But the Principal at Aquitaine finally took some respectable action just yesterday, so I interviewed Dean Grimes and Plumber himself. Since I had to drive almost three hundred kilometres, I tried to interview some students...."

"Hmmm. I guess I thought you went to Aquitaine for..."

"For God sake's, Bart, listen to me. I told you all of this. Remember? Aquitaine University sponsored the anti-date-rape campaign called "No Means No," and guys in a first year male residence plastered their windows with despicable signs that said things like: "No means kick her in the teeth" and

"No means 'down on your knees, bitch.'" You seriously do not recall this?"

Bart stared into the mirror. Jenean stood up straight, turned as if to go. She was peeved that he did not remember. Bart reached out and touched her shoulder. She turned back to face him.

"I do remember. I do. Frankly, I just ... I guess I didn't see it as big a deal as you did," he said, his hand still on her shoulder. She took a step backward. "No?" she asked. "You don't see violent, hateful signs as a big deal, Bart?" She removed his hand from her shoulder, placed it back on the vanity edge.

"Guys are jerks in university, Jenean. Who doesn't know that? That's the way it is...."

"Aughhh..." Jenean howled. "Enough, Bart. I have a column to write. If I can't convince you, I will have to try to convince the rest of Canada." Jenean closed the bathroom door and returned to her desk. She closed her eyes and breathed deeply, trying to shake off her fury at Bart. Why did she even try to talk to him about this? So maddening. Jenean worked to centre herself, and when Bart came in to kiss her goodbye, she did not look up, just accepted his kiss on her cheek, and kept on typing.

We expect boys to behave badly, and so we turn a blind eye when they do. We cop a resigned attitude. We trivialize, excuse, normalize their conduct rather than confront it, as if badly behaving boys were inevitable, genetic, biological, a force of nature.

This is permission of the worst kind. And it is being vaunted at Aquitaine University. The administration's four-week silence, *ipso facto,* condoned the actions of the men of Commissioner House who hung vile signs in their windows to protest and mock the student-led No Means No campaign. Canadian media has been awash with the vulgar wording of those posters these past weeks. The boys have had their fifteen minutes of fame.

Let's focus on the extremes to which Aquitaine's women students had to go in order to get the offensive signs removed. Their rage turned active when, for the first time in Aquitaine's history, thirty women walked into the Principal's office in Dickens Hall, and asked for a meeting. Proclaiming he was powerless, Elias Plumber ignored the obvious – that women have a fundamental right to pursue their interests with dignity and without harassment. The women refused to leave for twenty-four hours. They were joined by a hundred others throughout the day and night. They wore scarves across their faces to protect their identities and presented a basic list of demands. While only women occupied Plumber's office, supportive male friends gathered outside the building, sending up food in baskets and handling communication on the ground.

Earlier, a group called FRRF (#&&&@## Radical Rogue Feminists) was planting stop signs around campus to mark the places where, it was rumoured, women had been sexually assaulted. They left chalk notes near Commissioner House that read "We Are Watching You." Aquitaine's women were fed up with the boys. The boys were bound to retaliate. Everyone waited.

Then came the sit-in, a throwing down of the gauntlet to the one man who could make the boys toe the line. With a reputation for its drunken excesses on homecoming weekends and first-year orientation rituals – all of this passed off as "Aquitaine spirit" over the years – Aquitaine has piqued the curiosity of the media who began asking, "Is Aquitaine a haven of Canadian misogyny?" When CNTV arrived on campus, the university took notice. Principal Plumber remained quiet. Perhaps Plumber was feeling in over his head. He could handle the Ascension Street parties and the engineers and their phallic initiation vulgarity; they were traditions.

Plumber had handled all of it, but these women and their demands were vexing, particularly when CNTV took notice. He did not need his alumni loyalty to wane. He had doctors, lawyers, and engineers to keep happy. They loved their old school, loved it, more than any Harvard or Yale alums loved their alma maters in the States. He had 14,000 current students to keep happy, the best of the best. The students had the highest entrance grades in Canada. Aquitaine had the highest retention rate in the country, for God's sake. There were no empty beds.

If this were a first, a freak incident at Aquitaine, perhaps it could be chalked up to developmental immaturity. But Aquitaine prides itself on its "muscular" educational traditions. Parents dropping off their children in early September were greeted with signs on several student residence halls lining the side streets of the august university: "Bring Your Virgins Here" and "Why Beer is Better than Women: Beer Doesn't Run to Tell the Police When You Rape It."

Aquitaine's on-campus Sexual Assault Centre closed this year when funding was withdrawn. When the campus' Women's Centre posted signs showing the locations of sexual assaults on campus, one senior faculty member said he had never heard of a sexual assault on campus and ordered campus security to take them down. When the women students met with Principal Plumber this week and indicated these and other facts, he said he had not known about the closing of the campus Sexual Assault Centre. Meanwhile, the Kingston Sexual Assault Centre reports a doubling of crisis calls from 1988 to 1989. Half of the calls came from Aquitaine students.

Only after media attention resulted in letters of protest and threats to withhold fundraising contributions from alumni concerned about the safety of their daughters did Principal Plumber, after four weeks, issue a statement condemning the actions of the male students who reacted with vulgarity to the No Means No campaign. The signs came down.

The boys, every one of them identifying himself as "Donald," issued an apology – of sorts. They had failed to realize their signs were offending people. Their spokesman told the *Kingston Eagle*, "We now realize our humour was in bad taste. As for the feminists, it saddens one to see that a small vocal minority can twist things and make something very minor into international news."

The "shenanigans"at Aquitaine University gnaw at the soul. Even for a feminist plenty used to the game-playing of sexism, this is different somehow, foreboding. Maybe it is because the players are so young. Commissioner House residents are just eighteen, barely out of boyhood. What made them so hateful, so aggrieved, so entitled to their sexual needs being met on demand? What is the problem with hearing "no" and respecting that "no"? One young man who passed the sit-in at Dickens Hall that night pointed to the protest, "This whole sit-in makes me feel like date-raping someone." He meant it as a joke, he later said. Will the jokers never grow up?

Let's get at a real answer to this real problem of entitlement and privilege rather than settling for the circular and reductive adage that boys will be boys. Only the privileged can joke, can take advantage of their position as men to laugh at those who are harmed by sexist behaviour. Sharing power does not come easily or willingly for the powerful. It may take time for the boys to come around, but a few stiff consequences from Principals with principles can make time fly.

# 19.

L EE ANN WORKED her counted cross-stitch by the fire, waiting for Craig to get home. He had called that morning, before she left for school, said he would be home after his last class. She had his favourite French apple pie in the oven, and she had let Brill, their ancient Golden Retriever, out into the yard to greet Craig. Once or twice, she got up to check the pie, toss another white birch log onto the fire, and look out at Brill, who had settled in beneath her weary old car. Craig would remind her that she deserved a new one, a sporty Jetta or one of those tiny KIA SUVs. Something nice for a change. But they both knew she would not get a newer car until he was finished with school. He was her project for now. So she would make do with the bangs and dents of the Chevy until her son became an engineer.

It was unusual for Craig to come home on a Thursday, to come home at all until near Christmas really, but she was becoming all too used to the unusual. The letter she had received some two weeks ago – from those Aquitaine women – was vulgar. Craig had put up a sign in his dorm window that somehow contributed to sexual assault, the letter had claimed. Daniel had not seen the letter because Lee Ann burned it in the fireplace as soon as she had read it. The letter had also said that Craig was caught up in "dangerous attitudes towards women," had implied that he was dangerous to women. It had urged her to speak to her son immediately, to ask him to take the sign down and to apologize.

She had done nothing. Craig had called her and told her some of the guys' parents got letters and asked if she got one. He had told her it was a bad joke and that the Commissioner guys were reporting it to the administration. Lee Ann had pretended the letter had never come. Tried to will herself to believe it was some obnoxious joke, as Craig had claimed. Because she only spoke to Craig once a week, on Sunday nights, she had not wanted to talk about it on the phone, during the precious time they had when he told her stories about school and his friends and his classes. She had not wanted to muddy up their phone call by talking about the letter. He got so angry when confronted, like his father. But it haunted her – that letter. Try as she might, she could not imagine her son writing those foul words. She could not.

And now Craig was coming home. She would refuse to worry until she had to, but it seemed Craig wanted to talk to her alone. He knew his father would be at Gil's Bar and Grill around the corner until midnight, his pickup truck parked in its spot, under a swaying weeping willow, where it was nearly hidden from view by the long-armed, arching branches. He never walked to Gil's, though even poor old Brill could limp the distance along with him in ten minutes. Daniel liked to say of himself, "I work hard and I play hard," as if to ward off complaints from Lee Ann about a nightly bar tab. Of course, there was no such tab since Daniel bartended, and while imbibing on the job was frowned upon, it was not forbidden. Daniel went from his shift at Feinder Lumber Company straight to Gil's, ate a pulled-pork sandwich, and hung with the mates every night but Sunday. Mostly, he went straight to sleep when he got home, but sometimes he tried to get a rise out of Lee Ann by tackling the only topic that got to her: her son. Daniel pulled out this big gun on only two occasions: whenever he drank straight vodka and whenever Lee Ann made the mistake of mentioning something good about Craig. The first she could not control – they had told her this at that Al-Anon meeting she had gone to years ago. The second, she could control. She kept quiet about Craig, though she longed to share her concerns about her son. Her prayer chain would have to do, and Craig was one for whom the chain chronically prayed. Lee Ann kept it vague – *Dear Lord, let Craig do well on his exams, let Craig be a kind young man, let Craig work well with authority* – but she kept it going, worrying lest a lapse in the chain's supplications allow for a mishap that got by God's watchful grace.

Waiting now for Craig to get home, she considered calling the prayer chain, to ask for generic prayers for a boy in trouble, but she thought better of it and resumed her cross-stitch.

Where Lee Ann taught English and Latin at the high school in town, she was beloved. She was not one of these dramatic types who recited Hamlet's "To be or not to be" monologue with arms wide open in the middle of the cafeteria, like Mr. Foster. Not vain like Mrs. Bouble with her plus-sized designer suits and ostentatious matching shoes. Lee Ann was reserved, professional, and kind. She was the teacher who kept apples and foil-wrapped cheese wedges in a tiny fridge in the front of her classroom in case a student got hungry. She was the one who always went to the funerals of her students' parents, who slipped a Mass card into the basket at the front of the funeral parlor, a quiet affirmation of a celestial future for the dead.

Lee Ann did not feel a need to announce her Catholicism in any more obtrusive way than the occasional Mass card or prayer chain request. She felt no need to mention that she attended Mass twice on weekends because she liked the guitars and folk music on Saturday evenings and the more formal organ's drone on Sunday mornings. The rosary sodality welcomed her as its youngest member, and her peach pie was the new favourite at their monthly meetings. When Lee Ann bemoaned the fact that in off seasons she would have to make the pie with canned cling peaches, the kind that made the pie all drippy with juice, the sodality smiled. "We love it that way, dear. However you make it, it's charmed." So, she made peach pie all year round. Betty Meriette, a widow who lived one street over from Lee Ann, brought the vanilla ice cream, and Suzette, a retired R.N., a plastic bag of crushed walnuts, to add a touch of protein.

Lee Ann had not always been so devout. As a teenager, she had asked the usual questions: if there is a God, why does he let the people he loves suffer? If there is a God, why was he so unavailable for biblical characters like Job and Eve? She had watched her grandmother die of breast cancer, her own mother staying after Mass to light candles to Saint Peregrine, the patron saint of cancer patients. So many times had she heard it, Lee Ann could recite word for word the novena to the saint: "O great St. Peregrine, you have been called 'The Mighty,' 'The Wonder-Worker,' because of the numerous miracles which you have obtained from God for those who have had recourse to you. For so many years you bore in your own flesh this cancerous disease ... *da dum, da dum, da dum* ... His great goodness and mercy. Amen"

And for all this, still Grandma died in agony. No morphine pump like today. No helping hand from the saint or from Jesus himself. "It is God's will," her mother had said. It was God's will that a sweet and loving grandmother die wracked with pain? Why is it, she had wondered as a teenager as she walked into the town centre to her volunteer job at the nursing home, that St. Peregrine got cured by Jesus? That her cranky neighbour got cured of gout? But a woman who had loved the Lord every minute of every day got hell on earth and no outstretched hand?

Lee Ann had spent many a youthful year hating the Lord with as much vigour as her grandmother had loved him. She had hated him right into university, up until she met Daniel in her university writing class. Daniel had replaced her enmity for God with something newer and more plaguing than she could ever have imagined.

*

Though he was failing his university composition course, Daniel did not look unduly burdened. Still, Lee Ann offered to tutor him, upon the recommendation of their professor. They met in the commuter cafeteria twice a week to brainstorm Daniel's essays. Alone in her room at night, Lee Ann tried to figure out what it was about Daniel that she liked. It was not easy to put her finger on. He was a big guy, not so much tall – though he had to be six feet – but solid. A force. His hair was long and unmanaged. She could not imagine him taking a comb to those dark locks, could not conceive of him caring one whit how he appeared. Nevertheless, he was confident. He wore patched jeans and pale flannel shirts with his sleeves rolled up, and when he leaned his forearms on the cafeteria table, listening to her explain how a thesis statement worked, Lee Ann could not concentrate. The corded muscles in his arms distracted her. Could she really like a boy because of his arms? Surely arms were not an erogenous zone. Even *Cosmopolitan* magazine did not discuss arms.

Maybe it was his eyes, though she seldom dared look into them. They had power over her, she swore. She could not look away, so she chose not to look, focusing on the paper in front of her or on her sandwich or – on his arms. The truth is, she had looked into his eyes, early on, before their power had taken hold. Daniel's eyes were hyacinth blue. "Aquamarine," her mother would have called them. Sometimes almost navy in the late afternoon, as they were the day she agreed to tutor him. When Lee Ann dared to look right at Daniel, he was always looking right back. Even when she was avoiding his eyes, pretending to be concentrating on their work together, she could feel him looking at her, taking her in, studying her.

It felt good, in a bad way. She had no words for this feeling. She liked it, sort of. She wished he would take her hand sometimes. She wished he would ask her out to a movie. But she would be unable to look him full in the face to answer him without turning shades of red. And would she answer "Yes?" When she thought about him before falling asleep at night, she imagined looking deeply into his eyes and being unafraid. She played out long scenarios in which he said, "Lee Ann, you are so beautiful."

He would then ask, "Can I kiss you, Lee Ann?"

She would blush, look him square in the eye and nod. She imagined that kiss all kinds of ways: sweet and tender was her favourite, but she had a fondness for firm and passionate, or small pecks that built to one long kiss. She fantasized about Daniel scooping her up into his arms, whisking her outside to some imaginary shoreline, laying her beside him in the sand, and kissing the dickens out of her, like the lovers in *From Here to Eternity*. These fantasies made tutoring especially difficult since Lee Ann had no indication Daniel liked her. He simply looked at her all the time, not enough evidence to conclude movie-calibre kissing would ensue.

In the light of day, Daniel had less confidence about his writing than he had in her dream the night before about his kissing. He thought he had no good ideas for paper topics.

Lee Ann told him he did. "How about a process paper on changing oil in a car?" she asked.

"Yeah. That's a good one, Lee Ann. That will rock the professor's world, shake his little red bow tie right off his shirt, won't it? Who on God's green earth does not know how to change oil?" He stared at her, head cocked to the right.

"I am serious, Daniel," she said, cocking her head to mirror his inquiry. "Not everyone knows how to change oil. I don't."

"By everyone, Lee Ann, I mean guys," he said, stating the obvious.

"Right," she said. "Right." And then and there, Lee Ann heard what Daniel said another way.

This hearing another way was, of course, a decision, but it was a decision made with such alacrity that it barely rose to consciousness. If she had gone with her gut, she might have blurted out something like, "What are you saying, Daniel? All your readers are not guys. Not all guys can change oil. It is not a skill you are born with." But she did not blurt it out. Rather, she ignored the queasy feeling in her stomach but did allow herself to think that this did not bode well, not in terms of a potential romantic relationship with him. Not that she was thinking of a relationship with him, but if she were, it would be over now because he was, well, kind of dumb and prejudiced. *But wait, oh wait.* She could see this another way. What he meant by "everyone" was everyone who would be interested in car stuff. He was not making an ideological point at all. Rather, he was assuming female readers would not, by and large, be interested in changing oil. Was that so bad? Was it not, in fact, mostly true?

It was not until years later that Lee Ann stopped to analyze this shift in her hearing. The analysis came unbidden, on nights such as this, when she was focused on stitching tiny mauve "x"s into fine linen and waiting for her only child to come home to talk to her. Nights like this were for the kind of reckoning that could not have come any sooner than it had come. She was not ready before. She was not really ready now, but the reality of her life insisted upon being heard as the raw truth.

Lee Ann had not stopped to analyze after she and Daniel were married or after Craig was born or after she had taken up her lapsed Catholicism with an ardour she had wished she still felt for her husband. She reconciled with the Church as had Saint Peregrine in his early years. A political opponent to the papacy in the thirteenth century, Peregrine had been forgiven, became a priest, was cured of his cancer, and was canonized almost four hundred years after his death in 1345. Not that Saint Peregrine was a role model. Lee Ann's resentment toward the saint had never quite expired. But he was a person to consider when she tried to make sense of her own return to the institution whose politics were confounding. Hers was a desperate faith.

Over the years, Lee Ann fine-tuned her hearing. She was capable of "ignoring" Daniel's most cockamamie ideas. She held onto the potential in Daniel. Though he dropped out of university the semester after their tutoring sessions, having failed to turn in all but one of the assignments in University Writing and having drunkenly damaged an emergency call box at a weekend party, he had potential. He had once been a good and gentle and loving boy, a boy whose soul imploded before it grew up. It broke her heart, from the day he had told her about it until now. The only loyalty she could offer him was a perpetual belief that he had the potential to be a good man. Someone she and her son could love.

The physical infatuation had popped like a fat balloon long ago. Though, for the record, Daniel was a fine kisser. A bit rough, even clumsy. But their early intimate life had not been unlike her earlier fantasy life. Idyllic really, romantic and tender. It vitalized Lee Ann, was part of what sustained her years later when she sought consolation in Daniel's potential. At her most gut honest, she could not reconcile herself to the man he had become. He was vain, angry, and mean, especially when he drank a lot, without ever being truly sorry. Even when he apologized, it felt like it was all her fault.

Truth be told, Lee Ann seldom got to gut honesty. One of the few times she had, all hell broke loose. Once, Daniel found her reading the pamphlet someone had left in her mailbox at school without a note or a name. Just an anonymous pamphlet outlining the services at the local domestic abuse shelter. "An abusive partner," it read, "wants to deny your experience. He wants to pluck your view of reality out of your head and replace it with his." The only reason she did not rocket the thing into the trash can, then and there, was because of one line: "Boys learn controlling and coercive behaviour from the central male role models in their lives." Her stomach had jerked about in spasms. She had shoved the pamphlet into her grade book, and rushed back to her cubicle in the English office. She was sweating. She was mortified. Who could have left the brochure? Who could have guessed Daniel was sometimes rough to deal with? She never, ever talked about Daniel or her marriage, only about Craig. Always about Craig.

And it was Craig's image she could not shake, as she sat in her cubicle and prayed no one would come in. She had to think. It was hard enough enduring Daniel at his worst, but to think Craig could be anything like his father was inconceivable. Why had this thought never crossed her mind? Lee Ann felt deeply stupid in her small cubicle with the world's greatest literature – all there in front of her, next to her. Books by Shakespeare, Dickinson, Thoreau, Cather, the Brontës. And there she sat, clearly an imposter teaching kids about life. What the hell did she know? Not even as much, evidently, as a colleague who wanted to help. Had she never given serious thought to how Daniel might affect Craig's behaviour? She was certain, always so certain, that Craig would be like her, sensitive, kind, long-suffering. But like his father? Lee Ann had to resist the urge to faint. She was dizzy, sick to her stomach. She did not take the rest of the day off *only* because she wanted to draw no more attention to herself – clearly, someone had been watching – but she was in no shape for teaching Poe's "The Black Cat" to twenty-four sixteen-year-olds.

Lee Ann plunged through the day with fortitude born of habit. Back at home, she made herself a turkey sandwich and pulled out the pamphlet again. "The abusive partner devalues his partner's work." *Oh God.* "He thrives on creating confusion. He escalates arguments. He insists on sex when she does not want it. He makes pronouncements." *Oh good God.* "He does favours his wife does not want." Lee Ann had more lingerie she had never worn in her very bottom dresser drawer. She had stiletto heels in leopard print, in black patent leather, in blood red. She never wore them. Daniel had insisted on buying her an enormous jewellery box lined with mirrors for her last birthday. She owned just enough jewellery to fit into the very smallest of its drawers. The ornate box sat prominently atop her dresser, where she would have liked to keep her books and the stained glass lamp she had made, but the afternoon she had taken the jewellery box down to move it to her closet shelf, Daniel had appeared like a force in the bedroom.

"What are you doing with that?" he had asked too loudly.

"Putting it on the shelf in the closet. I think it will fit better there," she had said quietly.

"I knew you didn't like it, Lee Ann. Why didn't you just tell me? I could have saved myself a paycheque instead of buying my wife something she hates."

"I don't hate it, Daniel. I quite like it. It's just that...."

"No need to explain," he had said very calmly. "I see it all. No problem." He had turned to leave the room.

"What do you see, Dan? What is the all you see?" She had been exasperated with his opaque insinuations.

"Nothing, Lee Ann. Let's drop it. From now on, how about this. I just hand over a wad of cash for your birthday. Forget the hours I put into looking for the perfect gift. It's just like the shoes – the goddamn shoes you never wear because they make your feet hurt. Huh. Thousands of women all over the planet wear those exact kind of shoes. Can't pick up a magazine without seeing high heels, but my wife? No, oh no. They hurt...." Daniel trailed off, his voice getting quieter though his temper was clearly piquing.

"Listen. I'll put the jewellery box back," she had said, moving to pick it up from the closet shelf.

"Leave it, Lee Ann," Daniel had growled, taking a step toward her. "Just forget it." He surged out of the room and down the stairs. She had listened to him close the front door, get into his truck, and hurtle out of the driveway.

So engrossed in this memory was Lee Ann that she did not hear Daniel enter the room that night. He stood over her shoulder reading the pamphlet. His huge hand plucked it from her before she realized he was there.

"What is this? Are you kidding me? Domestic fucking violence?"

Lee Ann stood to face him. "Daniel. At school ... someone...."

"Are you kidding me?"

"Listen to me, Dan..." she said, grasping his shoulder.

He shook himself away from her. "Do ... not ... touch ... me," he said, slowly, calmly. He stared at her hard.

"Daniel..."

"Aughhh ... Lee Ann." He threw the brochure onto the floor and went up the stairs to their room. She heard the door close. He did not slam it. She wished he did. His quiet rage was a bad thing. It appeared to go away, but it sprang unawares after a time. It might wake her in the night when Daniel insisted she explain exactly how he was an abuser. Daniel never raised his voice. He remained consistently measured, logical, just a guy looking for some answers. Beneath the surface brewed trouble.

Too afraid to go upstairs to bed, Lee Ann found her rosary and lay down on the sofa, pulling the afghan her grandmother made her over herself. *Dear God, let him calm down. Let him listen to me, so I can explain. I can explain.*

Drifting off, she dreamed about the letter she had just received from her sister. Had she told her sister she might visit her in Chicago next month? Yes, she had, and Janice was ecstatic in her response. He would be furious. He hated her sister. Janice was divorced. Daniel did not approve of divorce, thought Janice bilked her husband Mitch out of alimony just to stick it to him for having an affair with their neighbour. If Janice had not gained so much weight, he had argued, Mitch would not have strayed.

Janice was ten pounds overweight, by her own admission. And she walked five miles every day. Mitch's affair had nearly crushed her. Mitch had moved into the neighbour's house before Janice had even had a chance to hire a lawyer. She had to see him leave that house every morning wearing the dark grey striped suit she bought him last Christmas, or the J. Crew trench coat she got him when she and Lee Ann had shopped last September.

In her dream, Lee Ann wrote to Janice telling her she was beautiful, her hero, no matter what happened to her marriage. She was writing the word "marriage" when she heard Daniel's voice. "Marriage is like this, honey, about complete and open communication and honesty. No secrets." She awoke with a start when Daniel sat down on the edge of the sofa and looked at her. He took her hand, the one wrapped in the rosary. She could tell he was thinking.

"Honey, husbands and wives don't have secrets from each other. They don't talk about each other to outsiders. People who interfere are troublemakers. You need to tell me when something like this happens, right away...."

"You weren't home. I would...."

"Shhh," he said, smoothing her hand with his right hand, still gripping it with his left. She could feel his wedding band digging into her knuckles. "It's all right now. Everything is all right." Daniel stroked her hair, laid his head next to hers, nuzzled her neck. She could hear his breathing, rapid. *Jesus God, he wants sex. God, no. Please....*

"Come to bed, honey," Daniel said, pulling her off the sofa, taking her hand, drawing her to the stairs. "We'll put this behind us, the way God intended." This was code for the "sacramental marriage bed," a term Daniel picked up from one of his proselytizing co-workers. Sex in the bed of a married couple was holy, was God's work, according to Hugh, the holy co-worker. When a husband turned to his wife in intimacy – in their bed – it was blessed, holier than anyone else's sex, in fact. It healed everything. It purified. Daniel was not a believer. He hated that crap, he told her all the time. The sacramental marriage bed, however, was one thing he latched onto. After every fight they had, into the bed they went. Daniel needed his wife, the love of his life, he told her. He needed her healing love.

Lee Ann followed Daniel up the stairs. She tried to control her breathing, to remain calm. Were she able to teleport to the Congo, she would have. Lee Ann did not hate much in the world, but she did hate the sacramental bed. She was still confused, upset, afraid. She could not say no, not now that things were calmer. She could not risk his rage again. Rebuffing Daniel meant she did not love him. This had been made plain, on the few occasions she tried to explain she was not feeling well, not in the mood, nine months pregnant with Craig. There was no refusing a husband, Daniel explained. She might as well ask for a divorce, so deep was the pain of her sexual rejection. How could she not crave his love, as he craved hers?

She submitted. Silently. Shrivelling inside. Crying quietly through the night next to him. He snored, draped his satiated body across hers. *If I could die right now,* she thought, *it would be a mercy.*

Lee Ann snapped out of her reverie when she felt the needle prick her finger. She was all right. She was alone. Craig was on his way.

# 20.

"YOU DON'T GET IT, Trey," Marin shouted from the bathroom in the apartment. Shaking her wet hair and clasping a mint-green towel around her, Marin came into the living room where Trey was staring at a drawing on his drafting table. "This public garden is a symbolic space, symbolic of Canada," she said, tilting his chin up with her fingers, so he would look at her. Marin had agreed to help Trey with his submission for the contest to design a garden for downtown Ottawa. Entries were due in less than a week, and Trey had been brainstorming around the clock all weekend.

"I know. I know about the symbolic space, Marin. I know all about it. How could I forget when you are on about it so much?"

"I can't help it when you are not really hearing me...."

He looked at her and sighed. "I hear you loud and clear. We need to employ a national symbol. We have three, no four. Think about it. We've got hockey, the beaver, the RCMP, and the old maple leaf...."

She placed her palm on top of Trey's head to slow him down. "Seriously, Trey. I know I keep saying it, but the beaver is the only symbol that makes sense, even if it is plain ridiculous. How you are going to make a public garden look like a beaver, I don't know, but if anyone...."

"Hold on a second. What about hockey? We could have a flower bed shaped like a rink, with..."

156

"Hockey? No way. No hockey. No Royal Mounted Canadian Police. Hockey is violent, Trey, and the Mounties, with those tight riding pants and shiny black boots – Canada is not a polo field, for God's sake."

"The Mounties are a revered institution...."

"I know, but they don't represent the Canadian people. They represent the law, and hockey, well, hockey represents lawlessness."

"Whoa there, Marin. You know how I feel about the game."

Marin placed her hands squarely on her hips. He had thrown down the gauntlet, and he knew she knew about hockey. Hockey certainly would not do for a garden motif, but it sent Marin down memory lane: Hilaire talking his sisters through televised games like a commentator every weekend when they were growing up. "Oh, I absolutely know how you feel about the NHL, Trey. But can I just say three words to you? Good Friday Massacre, 1984."

"That was four words, Marin. And just stop. One brawl does not...."

"One brawl? One mother of a bench-clearing brawl. How many minutes in penalty time? Ten players ejected?"

"Two hundred and fifty two penalty minutes, but what is your point?"

"My point?" Marin shouted. "Jean Hamel was unconscious. *La bataille du Vendredi Saint* ended his career, Trey. Hockey cannot equal Canada, and if it does, we are barbarians. Especially when your job is to create a contemplative garden...."

Marin's voice trailed off. She paced the five square feet of floor space in the living room, her arms crossed tightly in front of her. Trey pushed his chair away from the table slowly then stood up, as if preparing an elaborate defence.

Marin beat him to the punch. "And what about that Richard Riot on St. Patrick's Day. One hundred arrests. Maurice Richard suspended for the season. He knocked someone out or something...."

"Cliff Thompson, Bruin's linesman. He was only…"

"Who gives a damn, Trey?"

"Oh, for God's sake. Stop yelling, Marin. The Richard Riot – now that is not fair. That was 1955, and Richard was tossed because he was French Canadian, and you know it."

"Seriously. That is what you have to say about the Richard Riot? Well here's what I have to say: hockey, long may it live. There is no bigger fan than I, but it is savage and not a good symbol. Amen."

Trey wrinkled his brow and appeared to be in deep thought. Marin waited, running her fingers through her wet hair.

"That's why we also have the beaver," Trey said, perfectly seriously, standing and counting off on his fingers. "First, the beaver is a critter who toils diligently, building elaborate nests of mud and twigs."

Marin did not want to laugh. She wanted to win the argument, and Trey seemed to be coming around, but this was too funny. She managed to swallow down a snicker, as Trey continued.

"Second, he triumphs over the seasons. Third, he is non-predatory and humble. At his core, he is the truest symbol of Canada yet. I … I believe you may be right. Forget hockey. The beaver is our boy!"

Marin hooted, but Trey was on a roll and paid her no attention. "The beaver, *Castor canadensis*, is the largest rodent in Canada, in all of North America for that matter. He's called "amik" in the Algonquin language…."

Marin burst out laughing, and Trey stopped immediately.

"What? Why are you laughing at me?" He looked hurt.

"I am not really laughing at you. It's just that I have been trying to get you to consider the beaver…."

"I know. You think I don't listen to you, but I do. I've been going bat-shit crazy studying the beaver all week, and I think you are on to something, much as it pains me to toss you this bone."

Marin went to him and laid her head on his chest, hugging

him tightly. He resisted at first, then hugged her back. After a few minutes of quiet and warmth, they pulled apart, and Marin sat down at the table, stretching out her arms and folding her hands. Trey sat down across from her.

"Okay, give me everything you got. Beavers – go!"

Trey sat up straight, pretended to adjust a tie at his neck, cleared his throat and began.

"The beaver received the highest honour ever bestowed on a rodent on March 24, 1975, becoming an emblem of Canada on that very day. The beaver is an herbivore, eats aquatic plants and the soft tissue of bark. However, he is preyed upon by foxes, coyotes, wolves, eagles, and others. He has appeared seven times on the postage stamp. Beavers exhibit what is called 'Dear Enemy Phenomenon,' at least the Eurasian beaver does, where the beaver who inhabits a territory will become familiar with the scents of its beaver neighbours and respond less aggressively to said neighbours than it would to strangers."

Marin folded her hands in a triangle and rested her chin on her pointer fingers. She smiled at Trey. He was perfectly serious, the consummate professor in lecture mode. She nodded, indicating he should continue.

"The amazing thing about the beaver, if what I've told you is not enough, is that it is a keystone species, which means it has a disproportionately large effect on the environment relative to its population. It creates wetlands used by many other species, thereby shaping the very environment it inhabits. This is good. Oh, Marin, this is good because I'm a Quebec designer, and Quebec does more to shape Canada.... Oh, symbolically, this is ... sorry, I'm off track." He took a deep breath, continued gently. "In conclusion, the beaver plays a critical role in maintaining the structure of an ecological community ... oh, wait, wait, one more thing. He has a lifespan of twenty-four years and mates for life. He is monogamous. The couple raises its offspring together; a typical couple will live with their kits, about two to four of them, in one pond."

Trey folded his hands and rested his chin on them, mirroring Marin. They looked at each other, remaining perfectly still.

Without moving, Trey whispered, "One little pond."

Without moving, Marin said, "Never have you been more attractive to me. I want you badly."

Trey smiled. "Canada is known for its national politeness," he said, "its cooperation, industriousness, patience, its concern for order and stability, so yes, the beaver sums it up quite nicely. You were right."

Marin stood up, walked over to Trey, took his hand, and led him into the bedroom. "We shall discuss this no further," she said. "We shall put the beaver to bed."

# 21.

JENEAN ~ NOVEMBER 1989

THEY WERE ALWAYS LATE for yoga class. Clara and Jenean met at the gym every Thursday evening and then went for wine and omelettes in Le Plateau after. Once a month, on Saturdays, they went shopping in the underground on Rue Sainte-Catherine, and the last time they went, Clara got new sneakers.

"These are supposed to cushion your feet, so they're protected when you pound on them," Clara said to Jenean, as she rushed into the locker room that Thursday. She held out her left foot and wiggled it around, showing off her turquoise-and-silver shoes.

"Well pound away, baby. We are – once again – late. Close your locker up. Get a move on," said Jenean, heading for the door to the yoga room with her bottle of water and mat.

"Wait for me," shouted Clara, shoving her coat and purse into a locker and slamming the door. "You cannot even begin to know what kind of day I had, Miss Jenean bossy pants...."

"Oh, my God, Clara, come on!"

Yoga kept Jenean sane. She felt more space in her body and mind after the class each week. She even felt taller. Sometimes she tried to get there on a Tuesday evening as well, but more often than not, her deadline interfered, or she had to finish reading a book in order to file a review by midnight. Thursdays, no matter what, were a commitment.

The friends peered out onto the soft night from their wicker chairs and chrome table at Le Café Cherrier, peeking through the vines that clung to their last dregs of life along the exterior walls. Soothed after yoga, they sat at the same table they claimed every week. Le Café Cherrier was a light and airy restaurant on Rue Saint-Denis in the Quartier Latin, the part of Montreal that attracted artists and writers and musicians. The streets were always busy.

When Jenean turned back to the table, Clara was looking at her.

Jenean raised an eyebrow, took a sip of Chardonnay, and said, "what's happening?"

Clara leaned back into her chair. "You are not okay, my friend. I can see it in your face."

"You're right. I'm not okay. I am, in fact, miserable, even after yoga. Good grief." Jenean brought her glass to her lips but did not drink. "The thing is, I think my job is killing me. The Aquitaine story is just so nasty."

Clara sighed. "Jenean, this is not new. You, of all people, should know this. The Aquitaine kids are just that, kids. Stupid kids. You can't let it get to you."

"Are you kidding me, Clara," said Jenean. "Seriously. Is this the Clara I know telling me not to let it get to me? She who...."

"Stop. Okay. I'm sorry. I know this is important to you. I really don't mean to be a prig. It's just that I watch you anguish over these stories, and I worry."

"And you don't anguish over them? Where do you put these stories, Clara? What do you do with them at night when they creep out of the shadows and grip at your conscience?"

"I don't know. I guess...."

"It's Frank, isn't it? You can talk to Frank."

"Well, Frank is...."

"Frank is a guy who gets it, Clara. You are so stinking lucky you can't even see it. I am alone."

"But Bart is...."

"Bart cannot hear me. I am beginning to wonder if anyone

can hear me. Oh, he listens. He looks me in the eye. He pats my knee. He flings me a platitude now and again. But he simply cannot understand. How can he be so casual about things that make me wild with fury?"

"He's a guy, Jenean. I know that sounds stupid and simple, but that's really all it is," Clara said, reaching for her hand. "Listen to me, Jenean. Look at me. I am *not* arguing that men are biologically different, not blaming what you see as cavalier on hormones or brain chemistry. What I'm saying is that these issues don't cut to the core of his being like they do for you. He doesn't have to *live* them every day."

"But I do, so why can't he show some empathy?"

"That is a good question. He might work on that a bit."

"Why can't Frank come over and coach him?"

"Mmm ... that's not such a good idea. Can you just imagine Frank trying to talk to Bart during a football game about the social construction of gender and masculine privilege? He'd get drop-kicked out the door."

Jenean had to laugh at this. It was true. Even if Frank was the rare husband who "got it," he was not in the business of selling it to other guys.

"I don't know, Clara. I'm just so pissed off half the time. What's the sense?"

"It's hard, Jenean," Clara said softly, leaning forward. "You've been frustrated with this relationship for a long time now. Do you ever think it might be time for a change?"

"Change? Break up with Bart? I think about it, but then I remember the good times, or he does something sweet."

Jenean rested her head back against her seat, closed her eyes and sighed.

"It's not even about Bart. It's about me. Me. The way I see the world is so – so completely not like the way others see it. It's like ninety-nine percent of the time, I see what other people do not, or I see something as a huge issue and they see it as a rough patch in the road. Alone is how I feel."

"Now there, my dear, that's not fair. You are far from alone."

"I know. But you said it yourself, Clara. I can't let it get to me. So what, some university boys write odious words on their dorm windows? So what?

"In some ways, Jenean, yeah. So what? You can't fix it all. It is too big."

"It is too big. Absolutely. But If I don't do something about it, I can't live with myself. The reality is, though, I can't live with myself now. The hatred I see, especially in young university men, boys really, when it's not infuriating me, it's grinding down my will."

"And Bart?" Clara asked.

"Bart? Bart's world is unscathed. He sleeps at night. All night ... and you do, too, Clara. My best friend. How can *we* be that different? What is wrong with me?'

"Not a thing. You just care more than other people. Nothing that a little sleep or another glass of wine won't cure tonight. Which will it be?"

Jenean admitted she was exhausted, apologized to Clara, and walked home from the café, saying she needed to feel the autumn air and to just breathe. Clara hugged her goodbye, and Jenean felt the tears quicken immediately. She felt alone and angry and bone-tired and she could not imagine how to fix it.

# 22.

A T HER WEAKEST, Lee Ann held on to one story. Daniel had told it to her when they were in university brainstorming ideas for his composition process paper, long before they were married.

"Didn't you have any hobbies when you were young? Did you go camping?" she asked, coaxing him to think about paper topics, wanting to get to know him better.

"Hobbies?" He puffed air through barely parted lips, shook his head side to side.

"Yeah, you know, like fixing up old bicycles, fishing...."

"I know what a hobby is, Lee Ann," he said, cutting her off, and gazing out the tall cafeteria windows to the stand of poplars lining the perimeter of the patio. "I had a hobby once."

Lee Ann sat back in her chair, crossed her legs at the ankle, and listened to Daniel talk. Her memories of that day came in morsels. She could see the way Daniel held his coffee cup in two hands, his fingers fanned out, masking the white Styrofoam. She could hear his voice, hesitant to tell the story, yet aching to share it. She could smell his shampoo, fresh and herbal, as he pulled his seat closer to her.

Going to Mass every Sunday with his parents and younger brothers, Daniel learned to love the scent of burning candles. He saved and saved his allowance when he was twelve until he had enough to go to the craft shop downtown. He bought pastilles of bees wax, six-sided blocks that looked like faded gold soap. He bought a double boiler and wicks and molds. At home, he made a tiny candle for his parents and each of his younger brothers, then took a pen and etched each one's name into the side of the candle face in thick block letters. His mom had tears in her eyes when he presented them.

He got more serious about candle making the summer before his first year in high school. He bought tiny bottles of scent to drip into the melted wax before pouring it into molds. He especially loved one small fluted tart mold that made flat disk candles, the kind you put on a plate or float in a bowl. He made his own molds too by pounding scraps of metal he found in the garage into rectangles and cylinders. Lee Ann revisited this story so often over the years that she could no longer tell if what she remembered were the real story or a story enhanced by her emotional reaction to Daniel's telling. She loved that boy who made the candles, loved the way Daniel's voice hushed when he spoke about his younger, softer self, as if he were a distant cousin.

Daniel grew animated when he described the candles he made in shapes of pyramids and tiny cottages with little chimneys and tiny windows he had carved. Lee Ann watched him put down his Styrofoam cup and form the shapes of a pyramid and a cottage with his hands, indicating the intricate details as if the candles were actually in front of him. Neither before nor since had she experienced Daniel engaged in such a beautiful memory of himself.

One Mother's Day, he made a pumpkin spice cottage candle for his mother and a lemon eucalyptus one for his grandma. Sometimes he made them for the girls at school, not girlfriends really, but girls he nodded to at lunch. He was shy, barely able to talk to them. But they heard he made candles, and they begged him to make them pink ones and lime-green ones, so he made them candles that smelled like vanilla cookies and Christmas trees and tangerine and spice. He gave his favourite teachers candles at Christmas.

"It was completely nerdy, Lee Ann," he said. "But I loved it – the process – it was so damned peaceful up in my room, watching the wax turn to liquid, warm and smooth, almost milky, and then re-forming into other shapes."

One summer day when his mother asked him to move a small wooden bookcase from her bedroom to the basement, Daniel asked if he could put it in his room. On it, he arranged all of his candle-making accessories, dug out a label maker from the junk drawer and made labels for each category: wicks, fragrance oils, molds, pastilles of wax. He wedged cardboard between each section, creating the effect of cubbyholes. Everything he needed was right there, no longer stuffed into plastic bags and shoeboxes in his closet.

Daniel's father had never been a fan of this candle making. His busting never ceased. "What the hell, Dan. There are tiny little punks out there who would kill to be on their high school football team, and here you are, this strapping guy, sitting at home making perfumed candles? What is wrong with this picture? You tell me. Tell me, Dan?'"

Daniel told him, "I don't want to play football."

"Really? Really now? Since when is it about what you want? It's what's good for you. I want you to talk to the coach this week, son. Go to that pre-season practice, and talk to him. Do you hear me?"

There was no arguing with Daniel's father.

"Forget this candle crap. Be a man, Daniel, for God's sake."

The coach suited Daniel up and sent him out to practice with the team the very first day. Daniel was 6'1" and 185 pounds. They needed an inside linebacker. Done deal. He was too tired at night to make candles. He missed looking into a candle flame and zoning out, especially on cold autumn nights when the sky outside was black as ink or in the middle of winter when snow was falling softly. He felt in sync with himself then, the world okay, but there was no time for any peace with football.

During the fourth game of the season, Daniel scored a touchdown. It was a complete accident. The ball fumbled out of the hands of the intended receiver and right into his. *Oh shit*, he thought, saw a clear path, and ran like hell to the goalpost. No one could catch him. The crowd roared. He could actually hear his father screaming, "Run, son, run!" Under the goalpost, he slammed the ball into the ground and jumped up and down like he had seen the other guys do. His teammates hog piled him. They won the game, 7-0. His father could not stop talking about it, told the story over and over at dinner, told his brothers that he had always known Dan would be a superstar on the field.

At this point in the story, Daniel stood up, cleared his throat, and went to pour himself more coffee. When he sat back down next to Lee Ann, he spoke slowly. One day shortly after that, when they sat down to dinner, his mother asked his father if he had gone to Salvation Army that morning.

"All set, dear," he said. Daniel never forgot those words. "All set, dear."

Daniel's mother speared a green bean and smiled at him. He never forgot that green bean either, wondered why in the hell he remembered that bean. "I sure will miss those sweet candles, Dan," she said.

"What do you mean?" he asked her.

His father kept talking then, about the Stanley Cup, about the damn salaries, and about some player wearing a damned mask because of his asthma, but Daniel interrupted him. "Mom, what do you mean?"

His father coughed and cut his meat into tiny pieces.

"All your candle-making equipment, the boxes of beeswax and wicks, all of it went to Salvation Army this morning," she said. "Your father felt it was time to put aside the hobby, with sports and school and all, and I...."

Daniel knew it was true, but he was praying it was some stupid idea of a joke. His chest hurt. He put down his fork, pushed his chair back from the table, stared at his father, and waited for him to say something. When he finally looked up, his father, too, shoved his chair back, and looked his son in the eye. "It was time. You've moved onto bigger things. Time to put away childish things."

"You got rid of all of my candle stuff?" he asked. He had to hear him say it.

"Yes," he said, never looking away. They sat like this, staring at each other for a long time. His mom was talking in the background, but it sounded like garbled chatter. When he finally could understand what she was saying, he heard: "Daniel, we thought you wouldn't mind now that you're in high school."

Daniel stood up, began to say something, but swallowed it down. He walked out of the room, grabbed his backpack in the kitchen, and stomped up to his bedroom.

The bookcase was gone. The labels he had made were clumped together in the wastebasket, along with the cardboard sheets he had made to create the cubbies for supplies. Everything was gone, even the block candle he kept by his bedside. No more molds, wicks, blocks of bees wax. Even the tiny tin of matches he kept on his desk was gone. Daniel turned on the overhead light. The flat white plate covering the shining bulb cast shadows into his closet and a surgical glare onto his bed.

He lay down, pulled up the blankets. In the middle of the night, he woke crying so hard that he could barely breathe. His mom had come in earlier in the night, tried to explain that his father had thought it best. "It wasn't your fault," he told her. But it was her fault. He did not expect his father to get it, but his mother knew him, knew what he loved. Why could she never stand up to the guy? When it mattered, when it mattered to Daniel. He was tired of making candles anyway, he told her. They never talked about it again. When his brothers or grandma asked him about making candles, he just shrugged, like it was all in the past. But the pain stayed, as if he had swallowed a hard, dark walnut whole, and it just sat there in his gut.

One month later, home from school earlier than usual, Daniel was in his room doing homework when he heard his father on the telephone in the downstairs hallway. He must have been speaking quietly because Daniel did not even know he was home until he heard him laugh. Moving quietly to his bedroom door, Daniel listened. His father was never home during the day. What was he doing?

"I miss you too. I'll be there Sunday night. Don't forget ... what?"

Who was he talking to? And in a voice Daniel had never heard before, all soft.

"Oh, he did? I'm glad. I knew Sammy would love that candle shit. Now he can make them till the cows come home. Did you give him everything I sent to you, all three boxes?"

Daniel numbed, stood stock-still, straining his ears to hear, willing himself not to hear.

He heard his father laugh again. "Oh, you'll get it, baby...."

Daniel gripped his door handle, stepped back into the room, and slammed the door with all the force he could muster. He wanted to open it and slam it again. And again. And again. His father must have thought it was the wind blowing the doors closed because he never came upstairs. The walnut inside Daniel metastasized.

Lee Ann had spent the mother lode of her marriage in mid-wifery to that candle-making boy, believing she could crack the walnut shell, heal the raw and meaty innards and deliver Daniel to the softer man he was meant to be. Was she wrong? So very wrong?

*

Lee Ann heard Brill's barking and a car door slamming just as the oven timer buzzed. The synchronicity jarred her. Whatever Craig had to say about any signs in windows was meant to be. At least he was coming home to talk to her about it. She breathed deeply, offered a quick prayer for her son, and greeted him at the door. "Hey, Mom," he said, hugging her while Brill wedged between them, wagging his tail frenetically.

"Craig, honey, how are you? How is school?" she asked, holding him at arm's length to take him in. So handsome. Aquitaine T-shirt. Baggy shorts, sneakers unlaced.

"Why in heaven's name are you wearing shorts, Craig? It's almost winter?"

"Long story, Mom. What is that smell?"

"Your favourite...."

"Don't even tell me you made me apple pie, and do not even think of telling me you got the vanilla bean ice cream to go on top?" He feigned awe.

"You bet. Only the best for my son, the engineer," she said proudly. "I'll get that pie out of the oven. You grab the ice cream from the freezer, and we'll sit in front of the fire. Sound good?" Lee Ann turned to look at Craig again. He was staring off into the night outside the kitchen window. He seemed distracted.

"Dad home?" he asked quietly.

"Dad. Home? At eight-thirty at night? Where do you live, Craig Jean Berseaux?"

"Just checking. Things can change, Mom, you know."

"Oh, no, no, no. Things ... do not change, my love." Lee Ann clicked off the oven timer, removed a perfect apple pie from the oven. The scent of hot apples and cinnamon drove all other thoughts away. Mother and son gazed upon it together and smiled.

*

Craig sat by the fire, holding his plate in front of him, looking at Lee Ann. "Thanks, Mom," he said, "for making my favourite."

"You're welcome, honey," she said, savouring this moment. She knew how to do this, to savour moments of calm before storms. Instinct warned her that what was coming was not good. Sure, she had gotten the letter, but this was something else, some atavistic knell that warned her to stay alert. Was it habit? Was it that Lee Ann was put on guard every time her daily pattern was altered in the slightest? She waited. No need to invite pain in before it was fully ripened.

"Mom," he began.

She smiled at him, placed her plate on the coffee table, picked up her mug of tea. The mug said "Canada's Best Mom," a present from Craig when he was nine and in the fourth grade. The mug she chose each time she made Earl Grey de la Crème, the tea her sister had brought from the States when she visited, the tea she prepared when she needed to see its soothing blue corn flowers and to taste its velvety dusk. She waited for her son to speak.

"Mom. At school, there's been an incident," he began again.

She nodded, holding her mug with both hands. Looking at him, she raised her eyebrows indicating she was ready to hear more.

"There is this ... a girl ... from first year ... she has ... she has reported that ... she was raped...."

He looked to the window, out into the blackness of the night. Lee Ann's eyes never left his face. Her shoulders wedged into taut formation. This was something new, not the letter. Craig's head jerked back and forth several times, as if to will himself to finish the telling. He wrenched himself back to face her.

"She says I did it. I raped her."

Tiny lights flashed before Lee Ann's eyes. She took a deep breath and steadied herself against the vertigo that lurched. Her mind roared. She felt all of her defences rise up to deny what she had just heard, but the words kept repeating on a loop. *I raped her. I raped her. She says I raped her.*

On the last two words, Craig's voice scratched into a higher note, as if the speaking of those words, "raped her," needed to be forced out into the air, into their home in the presence of his mother. He shook his head side to side for the longest time. His eyes were wild, raised upward, as if looking to the ceiling, to the sky, for an answer to a puzzle. He kneaded his outstretched hands, one with the other, over and over. Finally, he stopped moving. He took in a long breath. He faced her and then raised his eyes to hers. She held his gaze, her head tilted to one side. Her "Canada's Best Mom" mug in both hands.

"Say something, Mom. Please, just say something," he said.

She looked at him. He was her son. He was someone she wanted to believe, but suddenly everything she had ever known to be true was transformed into a gigantic question mark. Could it be true? Could she actually be thinking that it could be true, that her son could rape a girl? She forced images into her mind of Craig at his first communion, Craig at the Honours banquet, Craig handing out cupcakes at the nursing home with his classmates. She forced images into her mind of him as an infant, as a toddler, as he learned to ride his bike. Wave after wave of counter images rushed in: Craig fighting with his father, matching curse words with curse words. Craig plagiarizing a paper in his English class, though she offered to help numerous times. Craig ushering a dark, petite girl out the back door, as Lee Ann arrived home from work, then asking his girlfriend to the prom on the phone that night.

Lee Ann shook herself, sucked in air. She turned and placed her mug on the coffee table next to her pie plate. She folded her hands together in her lap, held her son's gaze once again. She could not ask if he had done it. She could not. It would be a betrayal.

"What is her name?" she asked so quietly he seemed at first not to have heard.

"Deirdre," he said, nodding as if in slow motion, his hands folded together, quiet now, as if mirroring his mother's posture.

They sat this way for some time. Craig's breathing slowed a bit. He looked out into the night, but his eyes were not so desperate as they were minutes earlier, before he had told her he was accused of rape.

Lee Ann tried to sip her Earl Grey, but her hands were shaking too badly. "Tell me what happened, Craig," she managed to say, leaning toward him. "Just tell me."

He told her. The party, the girl, the fireplace, the bellowing crowd. "She was tired, leaning her head on my shoulder. I asked if she would like to lie down. She looked pale. She nodded and then drifted off. I thought ... I don't know, that maybe she fainted." Craig stood, walked to the window, peered out for a time, the moonlight falling on his hair, longish now, below his ears, the way he had worn it in kindergarten. He returned to the fireplace, sat down. He looked at her.

Lee Ann's head pounded. "Go on," she urged.

Craig nodded, continued nodding as he spoke, but he did not look Lee Ann in the eye. He looked left, as if trying to recall every detail, all while nodding. "So, I tried to wake her up, and she seemed to rally, and I helped her upstairs to my room. She sat on my bed. She was talking. I thought she was ... you know ... back to normal. I asked if I could kiss her. I swear to God, I asked if I could kiss her." He stared out the window again. When he returned his mother's gaze, he was no longer nodding, though he said, "She said yes. Yes, she would like me to kiss her."

A cyclone of emotions threatened to crush Lee Ann. For one flashpoint of a second, as she stared at her son, he became his father. She had to look away.

They were quiet for a while now. Craig turned to look at the fire. Lee Ann stared into the fire as well. It burned blue at the bottom, blue like the cornflowers in her tea, Lee Ann thought, and was grateful for that reprieve from this harrowing intensity. They continued to stare until Lee Ann broke the silence.

"What happened then, Craig?"

He pulled his gaze from the fire, looked at her, then lowered his eyes. "She said she wanted to, Mom...."

Daniel's laugh boomed from the hallway. He swooped into the room before either Lee Ann or Craig knew he was there.

Brill had not barked. The truck's diesel had not warned them. He was there, home, *before* midnight. He was drunk. And he had heard.

Lee Ann's shoulders clenched. She tried to stand. "Sit down," Daniel shouted, pointing at her with one bloated forefinger. "Sit down, Mom." She sat.

He plunged down into the overstuffed chair across from both Craig and Lee Ann. "This show is just getting good," he said, his voice too loud. "So Craigy, carry on ... she wanted to, eh?"

Daniel's grin was sloppy and wide. He was going nowhere. He stared at Craig, waiting for him to speak.

"Daniel..." Lee Ann began. "Craig had...."

"Hang tight, there, Lee Ann," he said, emphasizing the syllables of her name. "I want to hear the boy tell his *story.*"

Craig clenched his right hand over his left fist, worked the knuckles of that fist. He was silent, his eyes roving but cast downward. He would not look at his father.

"What's the matter, did I interrupt your girl time? Having tea and chatting it up about university life?" Daniel goaded. Craig shifted his weight, but he remained seated. Lee Ann prayed. Silently, she prayed.

"What the hell, Craig? Did you get some at that fancy school? Now she's cryin' rape? Didn't I warn you over and over?" Daniel sat up now, revved. He leaned forward in the chair, looking unsteady but unstoppable.

"They want it. They don't want it. Like plucking some bloody daisy petals." Daniel's voice was sing-songy. And loud. So loud. Lee Ann's ears hurt. She raised her prayers up another silent notch. Craig remained still. So still that Lee Ann watched him, kept her eyes on him as Daniel ramped up.

"She ratted you out? Hope it was worth it, Craigy. Hope she gave..."

"Daniel," Lee Ann shouted. "Stop. Just stop." She was sitting up straight now, glaring at her husband. "Why don't you just go up to bed?"

He bellowed. So ugly. "He's just like all the rest, Lee Ann," Daniel hooted, pointing at Craig. "*He* – your special boy – the one who is different, not like his old man. Oh, my God, this is too precious."

Lee Ann started to speak. Tears ran down her face. She could not look at Daniel. She turned to Craig. He had not moved an inch. He sat very still, his face grimaced in pain.

"Craig," she said quietly.

He turned to her, and the face she saw was Daniel's. He looked beaten, vulnerable. She leaned toward him. He leaned away, sat up military straight.

Then it happened.

Craig stood. He twisted away from her and faced his father. "Leave Mom out of this. Let's talk. Man to man." If his voice shook when he started to speak, it was one streaming boom by the last "man." He used to do this when he was playing cops and robbers in the backyard with his cousins. He was always the cop, and he always used this very voice: confident, loud, authoritative, even at ten years old. Tonight, it did not fit. There had not been a trace of it when Lee Ann and Craig were alone. Daniel altered their very souls.

Lee Ann stopped crying. She stood. Daniel stood. The parents faced the son. "Go up to bed now, Mom," said Craig, nodding at the stairs to the second floor.

"Craig," she said softly, hoping her voice would jerk him back to the son he had been a half hour earlier. The son who was reaching deeply for some kind of truth he could live with, a truth he could tell her. That son was the one who was special. Daniel was right. She did think Craig was special. She had raised him to be kind, respectful, loving.

But he was Daniel's son too.

Craig walked to her, put his arm to her waist, directed her to the stairs. "Go, Mom," he said.

She did not hug him. She turned, left the room, ascended the stairs to her bedroom, and closed the door tightly behind her.

# 23.

THE MORNING OF HER FINAL presentation in Electrome-chanical Processing of Materials, Marin woke while it was still dark. This was the day she and her team had been preparing for since September. Kinetic parameters leapt through her mind like fluffy sheep over a pasture gate. She got up and put the coffee on to percolate. Outside the kitchen window, the moon was draped in a sheer mist. It looked like a bowl tipped on its side, half of a sphere, fifty-nine percent to be exact, the portion visible from earth. It would take a human 135 days to get to the moon in a car travelling at 113 kilometres an hour.

Marin knew she was a freak, but she recalled some things with an eidetic memory. Her moon project had earned her honours nearly a decade ago, and still, she could speak extemporaneously about the moon. On Christmas Eve every year, her youngest sister Marianne begged her to give a toast of eggnog to the moon and to wax lyrical about it. It was both a family joke and a beloved, if quirky, family ritual by now.

Her holiday break was so close, she could almost touch it. This was the last hurrah. Sybille had called to cancel their dinner date earlier in the week, but they would be going out tomorrow night to celebrate at La Binerie, the sisters' favourite Quebecois restaurant in Mont-Royal. Marin had sworn to Sybille that she would eat all the comfort food she could in celebration, baked beans, tourtiere meat pies, and, for certain, sugar pie. She and Sybille loved the Edmond-Joseph Massicotte illustrations that lined the walls of the tiny bistro. It was a home away from home, and Marin and Sybille had spent many a Sunday afternoon eating breakfast there, one of the few places in town where all-day breakfast was still served. She could taste the nutmeg sprinkled on top of the sugar pie, just the way she liked it, so close was this celebratory meal. Only one day more. Thank God she lived on earth because one day on the moon lasted 708 hours. She was feeling tired and heavy. The coffee would help, and it was spitting its last stuttering drops. She was not sure why she was feeling heavy. She weighed about 120 pounds, which translated to a measly twenty pounds on the moon. She would be the size of Hilaire's dog.

Standing at the kitchen window, staring up at the sky, she recited silently: the surface area of the moon is thirty-eight million square kilometers. The moon was estimated to weigh 81 quintillion tons. Quintillion was one of her favourite words, and one she seldom got to use. Marin poured her first cup of coffee and attempted to banish all moon factoids from her brain. She chuckled, recalling a survey taken just last year that revealed that thirteen percent of those surveyed believed the moon was made of cheese. Science be damned.

She should be focused on her presentation. She should review her notes again, though she had fallen asleep last night doing so for the quintillionth time. She knew her stuff. Geber was the team leader, and she would never let them stand in front of a classroom unprepared. They spoke on the phone last night before Chantal went to bed. She had a set nighttime routine of being in bed by ten p.m., even if she stayed up halfway till dawn, working and reading while under the covers. In a rare moment on the phone, Chantal had asked Marin for some fashion advice. This had never happened. Not that Chantal dressed down. Rather, she dressed like most of the others in practical clothes that allowed for easy movement in the labs and that required minimal attention and adjustments throughout the day. One thing Chantal did not do was wear bright colours, so Marin had been caught off guard last night.

"Marin, I have to ask you what you are wearing for our presentation?"

"Hmm," Marin had said, quickly noting the odds of Chantal asking a question like this rather than a question about shear and torsion were astronomical. "I think I'll wear the periwinkle jacket my sister gave me with a long-sleeved black top and my plaid skirt, the one with the pin that holds the wraparound together. How about you?"

"Well, my grandmother just gave me an early Christmas present, and it's this blazer. She made it for me. Marin, it's, well, frankly, it's splashy. It's this geometric print, all red and blue and pink and green and purple and gold and black with these interconnecting triangles and trapezoids and circles, even hexagons. It's pure crazy, Marin, but I love the thing. It is completely not me, but.... Do you think it will be too much for the presentation?"

"It sounds perfect. You'll look nice in such a medley of colour. Wear it. Absolutely, wear that blazer, Geber. It sounds a little bit like Cyndi Lauper minus the tulle and combat boots."

Geber laughed.

"We'll be the best looking team up there tomorrow," Marin reassured.

Marin thought about that conversation, as she sipped her coffee. In the scheme of things, a bold blazer was no big deal, but in the world of engineering and in the world of Chantal, that prismatic print marked a departure, a step in the direction of confidence. Just when Marin thought Chantal could contain not one more ounce of confidence, here she was busting out and wearing geometry. Go, Geber.

Marin smiled to herself in the kitchen, paging through her notes, listening to the sounds of Trey snoring. By five-thirty tonight, their presentation on Thermodynamic and Transport Properties of Electrolytes – Aqueous and Molten would be done. They would have demonstrated that they had cultivated several problem-solving techniques, could make engineering judgments by eliminating lesser "solutions," and knew full well that engineering was not "crisp," a word their professor's was inordinately fond of. "There are a plurality of reasons and a plurality of ways to solve problems," the professor said. "Engineering is not crisp. There is uncertainty, always uncertainty."

Marin finished her second cup of coffee, ate a bowl of Corn Flakes, and took a shower. After she dressed, she looked in the mirror and thought that though there was uncertainty, she was feeling pretty good in her new black boots and smart ensemble. She was ready to put this semester behind her. She sat on the edge of the bed and brushed Trey's hair back from his face. She leaned over and kissed him lightly on the cheek, whispered, "I love you." He pulled her into him, held her tight.

"I have to go now," she told him.

"Okay," he mumbled, caressing her hair.

"I'll see you tonight," she said, gathering up her bag and opening the front door. She heard him call "I love you" as she closed the apartment door.

# 24.

DEIRDRE WAS ALREADY PACKED for the trip to Montreal for the Solar Conference at CanTech. She had to meet her team and professors at six p.m. in front of the engineering building, but she wanted to make it to her regular meeting with Susan Carson at the Kingston Sexual Assault Centre before that.

"How are you feeling, Deirdre? This has been a long journey, hasn't it? I'm proud of you," Susan said, as Deirdre nestled into the overstuffed purple chair in her office downtown.

Susan was a godsend. Deirdre had been meeting with her weekly since the sit-in. It had been Professor Oliver's suggestion that day she visited Deirdre in her dorm, but Deirdre had declined with a force that surprised both the professor and herself.

"When you're ready," Professor Oliver had kept repeating. Deirdre would not hear her, could not hear any of her friends' questions, could not hear the party mentioned until Jill had shared her story that snowy night at the sit-in. Everything fractured open when Jill had said the name, "Craig."

Deirdre had blamed herself entirely for the rape at first, despite everything she had learned in Feminist Philosophical Thought. After all, she had gone to the party of her own free will, though she had been warned about Commissioner House. She had drunk alcohol there, though she rarely touched alcohol. She had let her friends out of her sight, though they had all

181

pinky sworn before the party to stick together like glue. And she had kissed Craig first.

"Can that mean you were asking to be raped, Deirdre?" Susan had asked at their first meeting.

"No, but if I'd just stayed home or drank Coke instead or stayed with my friends...."

"Deirdre, you were drugged. Sadly, this is becoming more common. They are not legal in Canada, but these drugs called Flunitrazepam, also known as Rohypnol, are on campus, and they are at Commissioner House. What Craig did is a crime. You gave no consent. You were in no mental condition to give consent. This was not sex. It was rape."

"I know. I know," Deirdre had said, sick to death of bearing the weight of that one awful night but unable to shake it until now. It had been a long, dark road, and she was glad she had walked it, but nothing had been easy about it. Even some of the girls in the dorm had asked about that night, what she had been wearing, how much she had had to drink. It was far too easy to blame herself, and Susan had been reminding her of that for about five weeks now.

With the support of Susan and Professor Oliver, to whom she later had told everything, Deirdre had called the police and reported the rape. They were polite when they met her in Susan's office, but it was too late to collect evidence, they pointed out. The fact was, there was little they could do to help. Susan had argued that the police surely had Commissioner House on their radar and that this was not the first sexual assault attributed to that residence. The officers had maintained that they could not comment on that. Deirdre had felt the futility of getting justice like a giant millstone in her solar plexus. They took her information, said they would investigate, filed her formal complaint with Aquitaine University.

Today, still early December, Deirdre was committed to putting that night behind her. She would have one last visit with Susan the next week, and she would stay in touch when she needed to reach out. But she was moving on, getting her life back. That night had certainly changed her, but she was no longer broken. The air was frigid when Deirdre left the office and headed back to campus. She would have just enough time to brush her teeth and gather her things before she had to catch her ride for Montreal. A wet snow pelted her knitted hat, and she walked faster than usual. Typically, she would pop into the bookstores and boutiques along her route to browse, but the weather was wretched, and she had to meet the van for CanTech, so she ran back.

# 25.

THE DOOR TO CLASSROOM 230 busts open. Students in graduate-level mechanical engineering startle, look up. Some skinny guy with a Montreal Equipment cap holds up a gun. Some practical joke. CanTech tradition. End-of-semester shenanigans. He smiles. Then, he is yelling: "Boys on the right, girls on the left."

No one moves. Again he shouts the orders, this time firing the rifle into the ceiling. The student giving a presentation at the front of the room darts to the right, as ordered. The others follow suit, nine women moving warily into the left back corner of the room.

"Men, out. Get out," he wails, pointing the rifle toward the door. No one giggles any longer. Must be a prank, but this is going too far. He is frightening people. "Out!" he roars. The men, all sixty-two of them, move to the door, some rushing, some inching. No one speaks.

They cannot take their eyes from his, the women left alone with the gunman. He moves toward them. *Jesus.* Noelle feels Simone grip her wrist, her fingernails piercing the skin of Noelle's arm. Her breath comes in puffs. *What the hell does this loser want?*

He is speaking, spitting out words: "I am here to fight against feminism. That is why I am here."

The nine of them cram closer together now, grasping at each other's hands and arms. Noelle's heart races. "We are not feminists," she stammers, "just women studying engineering, not feminists."

The gun explodes, ear-splitting. They scream. Noelle slams to the floor, her leg blasting pain, and her temple stinging.

"You're women ... going to be engineers." He is shrieking at them.

*Oh God.* Noelle sees orange balls of light every time the gun fires. Simone falls. Noelle feels warm liquid gushing between them. She fights to stay conscious. Metal smell. Blood in her mouth. Simone's hand slathered in wet warmth. Warm. Wet.

Still, he shouts: "You're all a bunch of feminists! I hate feminists!"

The nine of them lay still. No more shouting. *Is he gone?* Noelle turns her head. Simone's hair is thick with blood. And Andrea's face ... gone. *Gone?* Simone's eyes stare. Smoke in the air. On the walls, floor, ceiling are blood and brain and bone. Her friends.

They hear him. Students in the hallways he is stalking hear him. "I want the women."

He takes the escalator to the ground floor, students skittering out of his way. He winds around the halls and into the cafeteria. Veronique has just found a seat at a long cafeteria table. She removes her coat, drapes it on the back of her chair. She opens the tiny foil packet and pours Greek salad dressing onto her salad. Her husband, Remy, is paying for his meal at the cash register. She places one of the several napkins she has gotten for them at the seat across from hers, for her husband. She is so hungry. Maybe she will take a bite or two before Remy returns. She hates to be rude.

Then, her body slumps back in the seat, blood soaking her winter coat. A bullet in the heart. Two students cower under a tiny table in the very back portion of the cafeteria. They watch her die. Watch him turn their way. No time to run. Surely he cannot see them. Could not see. Tears drench them. Bladders give way. Faces crush into each others' shoulders. *Please God.*

Footsteps. His face. A gun. Blast.

Anything female he shoots.

No one stops him.

People scream. Blood spews everywhere. A bullet grazes Patrice's head. She drops to the floor. Plays dead. Begs her slamming heart to quiet. Feels the slack leg of someone next to her, wetness seeping into her own jeans. Then. He is there. Just above her. She smells the gun, smoke, metal. He slams his boots down. Right there. Nudging between her and the slack leg beside her. Noise ravages her skull, as he shoots the one next to her, again, point blank. Patrice is sure she will die here too.

They hear him, students in the hallways. Stomping back to the third floor. Up the escalator. "I want the women."

When her part of the presentation is finished, Marin sits back in her seat and lets her shoulders and neck relax. Chantal is still in the front of the room summing up the work their group has presented and going over the analysis. She looks even more confident than usual in that smart jacket. Marin lets her arms dangle at her sides, allowing her fingers to loosen and elongate. Her last presentation of the semester is done. She will call Trey after class to check in with him before going out to drinks with her study group. Tomorrow, they will scout out a Christmas tree. Marin loves to put up the tree early, loves to look at the twinkling lights at night when the apartment is still.

Chantal is pointing to the mathematical model on the overhead. George, sitting next to Marin, too close to her, as usual, is taking notes with a dramatic flourish of his mechanical pencil. The overhead projector shines brightly. Marin can see the side of Renee and Stephan's faces in the glow, as they listen to Chantal's summary of their work. The two professors lean against the windowsill. Behind them the dark green curtains are closed. From a crack where the cloth does not meet perfectly, Marin spies snow coming down, pretty white flakes against black sky.

On the other side of Marin sits Don. His very last university class will end in twenty minutes. Exactly twenty minutes. The clock reads five-twenty-five. He smiles over at his girlfriend, Rose. She has another year before she graduates. Tomorrow, they will grab lunch at the new Thai place on Rue Sainte-Catherine, finish Christmas shopping, and then spend the New Year's holiday in Florida.

The door to classroom 311 bursts open. A guy holds up a rifle. It looks so real. Chantal is writing on the board for several more seconds, unaware. Then he is howling. "Men get out!" Don stands, leaves the room with the throng of rushing men. Rose remains. Mark gets up, meets the gunman's gaze, and walks out. His fiancée, Stella, watches him leave. They are to be married a month later.

The men have left the women in the room with the man with the gun.

The man aims and shoots Chantal. Turns. Shoots Rose in the right shoulder. Moves closer. Shoots Mark's fiancée Stella. Dead. *Her head, oh God.* Marin cannot breathe. Fire alarm blaring. Ears shattering. Fireballs. He comes closer. Back of classroom. Explosion. *So close.* Renee crumples to the floor. Her ear and part of her face are torn off. *Oh, God. Why?* He keeps coming and coming. She sees the barrel of the gun. Pain sears. Her arm, her neck. Run. To the door. She is there, almost there. Smoke. Metal. Charcoal. Iron. Run. Fall. Searing pain. Her back. *Oh god.* Heart .... breath....

Genevieve feels a bullet graze her head, as she dives beneath her desk. She sees Renee, who had presented minutes earlier, lying in a pool of blood beside her on the floor. Marin is shot, so many times. She lies still in the back doorway. Genevieve hears Chantal moaning from the front of the room where she has been presenting. The killer moves to the sound, barely audible in the blare of the fire alarm. Genevieve watches as the killer sits down on the stage next to her. Her blazer is wet with blood. He pulls out a knife. Stabs Chantal three times until she is still. Genevieve fights back nausea. He wipes his knife clean. He stands, takes two boxes from his anorak pocket and slaps them onto the professor's desk. He places another box on a chair in front of the class. He shakes his head, like he is talking to himself. She thinks she hears him say "Oh shit." He points the gun to his face and pulls the trigger. His skull explodes. Genevieve heaves and vomits. Sweating and trembling, she gets up and runs for her life.

# 26.

S YBILLE HAZEUR WAS AT WORK when the first bullet hit her sister. At that precise moment, 5:26 p.m., Sybille felt a sharp pain in her head. The numbers 5:26 glowed on the face of the clock even when she closed her eyes. The pain would not retreat, and Sybille felt nervous and edgy. She had a premonition. It was vague at the edges, but it kept thrumming at her right temple, and there was a twinge in her heart, some sort of spasm or cramp. Sybille's history of premonitions was rich, of course, particularly when it came to Marin, and the throbbing in her right temple was always the beginning, but this heart pain was new. She was only thirty-one. Fear of a heart attack she could shrug off, but the premonitions, they were never good.

She begged off work, though it was frenetic, the biomedical researcher's equivalent to tax season. While she was waiting for her car to warm up in the parking garage, Sybille punched the button to her radio, forgetting it was on the fritz again. Damn, she would have to get that fixed next week. Traffic was light. Most folks had gone home already. It snowed steadily. Her mind kept returning to Marin. Her heart felt normal again, but the premonition percussed inside her head still. She made reasoned attempts to mitigate it. Marin was at school, doing her final presentation with her group. They were going out afterward to celebrate. Marin had invited Sybille earlier that week, but she had declined, given that this was the time of year she and her colleagues spent ten hours a day at the office. She simply could not. But she would take Marin out to dinner the next day at La Binerie. She would leave early, though others at the office might look askance. She had not eaten a decent dinner since November. She would celebrate her baby sister's hard work come hell or high water. Marin deserved a break, thought Sybille, so the timing of this upcoming Christmas holiday was perfect.

Sybille pulled into the garage at her apartment just before six p.m. Her sister Natalee was at the door, waiting for her, pulling Sybille inside, her hands moist in Sybille's. She had been crying. Sybille looked at her, but Natalee shook her head, pointed to the television screen. "Something's happened at CanTech, a shooting. Have you heard from Marin?" she asked.

"Not yet," Sybille replied, sloughing off her coat and dropping down next to Natalee on the sofa. On the television, police and ambulances were everywhere, on the scene at CanTech. The camera ping-ponged between the emergency vehicles and the front door of the engineering building. The reporter said there was a shooter inside, possibly two. There must have been victims because of the ambulances. Or were they there just in case? There was no other news. All channels played the same scene at the entrance to CanTech. Natalee and Sybille sat frozen. They could not move away from the television. What the hell had happened there?

That was it, the pain in her head. Sybille had refused to let the connection sink in sooner, and she tried with might to push it away now. She turned away from the television then wrenched her eyes back to the screen. In a blur of motion and flashing media lights, there were people being wheeled out the front doors of the school on stretchers, being placed into ambulances. The sisters searched the screen for Marin, for anyone they knew. Nothing. The reporter was saying the gunman was dead, but police thought there might be a second on the scene. When the names of the hospitals to which the injured were being taken came up on the screen, Sybille called the numbers listed for Jewish General, Royal Victoria, Montreal General. They had no Marin Hazeur there. Sybille's head throbbed, and she had to lean into the sofa after each phone call. She called the telephone lines the university had set up for worried parents and families. There were four lines. Calls were coming in every three seconds, coming from as far away as Florida, an operator told Sybille on one of the dozens of calls she made to those lines. She learned nothing about her sister, yet her heart kept beating. Meanwhile, the revolving lights of emergency vehicles flashed on the television screen.

Sometime around eight p.m., Sybille called Trey. "Have you heard from Marin?"

"No," he said, his voice quavering. "Not exactly ... two people were injured ... I am going to CanTech. My sister is driving me. Come there, Sybille." He faded out, hung up.

"Not exactly." *Not exactly? What does that mean?* Sybille could not think clearly. She called her friend Madeline to take her to the CanTech. She could not drive. She could barely breathe. Natalee was fully fetal, wrapped in a blanket, crying, "You go, Sybille. I'll wait by the phone. I can't go...."

Madeline, still dressed in her pastel nursing smock and white clogs, helped Sybille into the car and appealed, "How do you feel, honey?"

"I have no feelings," said Sybille. But she knew: something had been terminated. "I feel the death of my sister. It's done," she murmured. "It's over." Sybille forced hope, but it would not come.

She and Madeline clung to each other, as they made their way up the slushy steps of the main building at Saint Laurent University. Inside the foyer, a security guard directed them past a horde of reporters and a line of police into a tiered lecture hall. Families huddled inside, about thirty people, waiting for news of their daughter, their sister, their friend.

Sybille and Madeline discovered Trey and his sister near the back of the room. Trey rose when he saw Sybille. Her breath caught in her chest. He was pallid, lifeless. He would not look her in the eye, as if the effort to raise his gaze to hers cost too much. When they hugged, Sybille felt a rush of hopelessness more intense that she had felt in the car. Suddenly, there was movement from the front of the room. A police officer approached a couple who had just arrived. Before they could remove their coats, the officer spoke to them in a muted voice. A boy standing with the couple gave a start, cried aloud. His father pulled him to his chest, and the family held onto each other and sobbed. Another officer walked to the front of the room. "May I have your attention, please. We know this is a long night. We beg your patience." He read the names of two women, and two couples followed him out of the room. "They are going to identify the bodies," said Trey's sister Claudette.

The officer read the names of thirteen people who had been wounded and were being treated at hospitals. Everyone in the room sat up straight, strained to hear their child's name. No one reacted to the list of wounded. When the officer left the room, the families slumped back into their seats, enervated.

Trey took his seat next to his sister, while Sybille and Madeline removed their coats and settled in next to them. At midnight, another officer entered and explained that the police had identified four of the victims, plus a fifth who was the daughter of a firefighter. A man in a black turtleneck and khaki pants stood up and shouted, his arms reaching high into the air, as if calling on the gods to listen. "What do you take us for?" he shouted. "It happened just after five. It's now after midnight. We must get some answers. We can go in and identify them."

"Sir. Please be patient. You must understand that our officers must protect evidence. As you know, our policy calls for bringing parents into the engineering building only after we have confirmed the identity of a student."

The man exhaled and sank back into his seat, holding his

head in his hands. His wife rubbed his shoulders. The air in the room was taut.

Sybille sat next to Trey. They held hands tightly. No one spoke. Madeline asked if anyone wanted her to get coffee from the vending machines. No one wanted coffee. On the hour, it seemed, the police came into the room and called the names of women. The injured, it seemed, were being treated, had been removed. Were all the names remaining to be called those of the dead?

Hopelessness warred with hope inside the families. Sybille's certainty that her sister was gone was a certainty bulwarked by nothingness. She could be wrong. Marin could be wounded, barely breathing, overlooked because officers thought she was dead. She could be alive. She could be saved. Sybille did not want to believe because the crash to reality would be jarring, but how to give up when no officer had spoken her name. *Marin Hazeur.* No one had said that name. She clung to Trey's hand and waited.

She tried to think of other things. One of the officers had said there were psychologists and a priest in 120. Sybille had once taken three courses in Room 120. She had studied there. Police were announcing names of those killed in Room 311, the last room the killer entered. Every time Marin's name was not announced, hope rose. Maybe ... maybe she got out? Maybe she was hiding, not knowing it is over, that the killer shot himself? *Please, God...*

Sybille counted heads. As the oldest sister, she did this often. Natalee was at their apartment awaiting her return. Maman was home with Marianne and her husband. Hilaire was at his home ... at least her father, dead these seven years, could be spared this horror. They were all safe, and she was here in the building with Marin, and very likely Marin was hiding and afraid to come out lest the killer still be loose. Sybille rehearsed that possibility until it took on heft, until she broke from the spell when she thought she heard her name.

"Family of Marin Hazeur?" a tall, skeletal police officer called out in a loud voice, though Trey and Sybille were now alone in the theatre. Madeline and Claudette were still retrieving coffee. All of the other weeping families had left the building to go to the hospital or home to tell their families their beloved children were dead. There was one body left unidentified. Trey and Sybille turned to each other and then to the officer. They grasped each other's hands, rose, and drifted to the front of the room. The clock on the wall said it was nearly four a.m.

As if masking anxiety, the officer spoke in a too loud voice when he told them Marin had been in 311, the last room stormed by the killer. Marin was one of the last ones killed. He was very sorry.

Sybille heard Trey moan, a sound more animal than human. It was a deep sound that swelled to fill the cavernous room. He folded in half, knelt on the ground, rocked himself backward and forward. Deep within the keening, Sybille made out the word "No" as it grew into thousands of "Nos," until she realized, sometime later, that the words were coming from her as well. The word "No" kept her tethered to the sloping floor of the theatre at the university. It was the only thing that seemed real, the sound of that word repeating.

# 27.

JENEAN HAD BEEN AT HOME on Rue Verde when her friend Charlie Genevese, from CN Radio, called at six p.m. the night before

"Have you heard?" he had asked, his voice tight.

Jenean had felt a freezing chill to the bone. Typically lilting, Charlie's voice was ominous. He had bad news.

"It looks like they are shooting women," he had said to her.

A fog had descended. Before Charlie had given her the least of the details, she turned on the television. She had remained there catatonic, in front of the horror playing out, until the dark of early morning.

"All the dead are female," a CNTV "Nightly News" reporter announced from her post in front of CanTech. Anchor Ben Nault had reported that twelve injured students have been taken to hospital. Of the twelve, eight were women and four, men. The killer, who remains unidentified, took aim first at women, and then only at men who interfered. Fourteen were dead. All women.

The gunman had hunted women, targeted them, shouted, "I want the women." *Why? Why?*

One man, a student present during the killings at CanTech, was asked, "So there was no resistance to the killer? The men left without protest?" The student had shaken his head no. Jenean had not been able to move.

Jenean had pulled the pearly blue and yellow afghan her

grandmother had made for her when she was baptized around her shoulders. She had become numb, deadened against what was playing out in front of her on the screen. She should have been writing. She should have been responding to this atrocity, but how could she? Her column would wait. *Mot du Jour* would cope. It had felt like the world was stopping and she had to remain as still as possible for a while.

*

When Clara called, Bart spoke softly into the phone from the kitchen, then peeked in to see if Jenean was awake.

She had never been more awake.

"What time is it?" she asked Bart, who was dressed for work already.

"It's six a.m. You fell asleep on the sofa. I need to leave for work. Will you be okay?"

Jenean nodded.

"Will you speak to Clara, Jenean?" He gestured to the phone. She dislodged her hand from the afghan and reached for the phone. She felt her body moving in slow motion. She was not sure she could speak. There was too much to say. How to say anything at all?

"Jenean." She heard Clara's voice. She was crying. "Jenean...."

"I'm here, Clara. I'm here."

"How can it be? Is it true? Has it really happened? Fourteen women...." She stopped speaking, sobbed into the phone.

Jenean was quiet and crying, willing herself to respond to her dearest friend with some comforting words, but there were no words. They abided, two friends, together in the silence for a time. Finally, Clara blew her nose, whispered, "There is a vigil tonight. I will go. Will you come with me? I don't know what else to do."

Thoughts came at Jenean in staccato: *Outside. Night. Vigil. Women. Dead.* All the dead are women. Shot in cold blood.

It hurt to breathe. She dug as deeply as she could for strength. "I will come with you," she whispered. Had she said it aloud? Had she meant it? "I will come with you," she said again in case Clara did not hear.

"I will pick you up at five," she said, quietly, weakly. "Jenean?"

"Yes?"

"I love you." She was crying again.

Jenean was too. "I love you, too."

Lowering the volume on the television, Jenean pulled the afghan around her tightly. The white mug of tea Bart had made for her before he left was still steaming on the coffee table. Bart had locked the door behind him, something he had never done before. Last night, Bart made pots of tea and answered the phone that rang constantly. He had come into the living room, sat on the other end of the sofa, asked Jenean how she was doing, but he did not attempt to hold her. He did not hold her hand. When he left this morning, he swept her hair from her face and kissed the top of her head.

On the television, there was a constant montage of ambulances and stretchers and IV poles and police lights flashing. When a police commissioner stepped to a podium to speak to the gathered press and public, Jenean turned the volume up again, though she had heard much of it before.

What we know is this: a gunman confronted 60 engineering students during their class inside CanTech here in Montreal. He separated the men from the women and told the men to exit the classroom. He held up a .223-calibre rifle. Before opening fire in the engineering class, he called the women "*une gang de féministes*" and said "*J'haïs les féministes* [I hate feminists]." One person said that they are not feminists, just students taking engineering classes. The gunman didn't listen. He shot the women. The enraged man then launched a shooting rampage that spread to three floors, several classrooms, and the school cafeteria. He is reported to have jumped on top of desks while female students cowered below. He roamed the halls yelling, "I want women."

Jenean stared at the television without really seeing it, her mind free associating examples into a category box, brimming over – Holocaust, Killing Fields. There was no coming back from something like this. It was pure hatred. Hate could pick up a weapon and hack its enemy to death when and where it wanted. How could hate have such power? How had hate come to their island?

She must have dozed because the thud of the newspaper against her front door startled Jenean. A boy on a bicycle maneuvered through hardened rivulets of ice, tossing the *Montreal Messenger* onto neighbourhood porches. His arc was perfect even with the thick woollen mittens he wore. One paper rose two stories and then landed on the porch of Madame Serelle. The next fell with a thud on Jenean's doorstep and a third on the welcome mat of Monsieur and Madame Tremont. Reluctantly, Jenean got up, opened the front door, felt a draft of cold wash over her, and bent for the paper. Closing the door against the winter air, Jenean took the paper to the sofa, wrapped herself once again in the warm blanket, and unfolded the chilled newspaper onto the table.

She was agape for a minute then spun away. When she looked again, it was as she knew it would be: a photo of a woman shot dead in her cafeteria chair, long hair dangling, arms outspread. Behind her a plainclothes policeman, gun in holster, was removing holiday decorations that had been hanging from the ceiling of CanTech's cafeteria. The headline read: "Campus Massacre" in full one-inch print. Beneath the photo, the caption read: "CanTech Victim Slumps in Cafeteria Chair."

Who was this woman? *So young,* her cafeteria tray arranged in front of her on the table. *Her uneaten dinner.* She was unsuspecting, presuming a world where death did not stride into your school to take out your kind. Jenean was heaving before she realized it. *That poor child.* She was a child really. *Why?* The weeping bent her in half, her knees to her chest, her face awash.

Something seized in her. Like a car engine without oil. The machinery stopped, could not re-start. The *Messenger* photo caught her eye again. What of this young woman's family who saw her body on this front page only hours after losing her? Though her face was obscured, her loved ones would know her. Surely such a photo would re-traumatize the families. And yet, that one photo captured the truth: the bestiality of the act of killing women who were simply living their God-given lives.

In the one other photograph laid out on the front page, two women left the university in shock, their faces stricken. Sub-headlines read: "Gunman kills 14 women before killing himself"; "'You are all feminists!' he shouts as he fires"; and, "Killer told men to leave." Jenean could not read the details quickly enough. Horror gripped her through article after article. Words floated into her brain, but would not settle down there. They were dynamic, speeding words that refused orderly filing in her mind. "I want the women," the killer had said, aiming for women. He had killed fourteen women and wounded thirteen other people, nine women and four men. These people were in three different hospitals. The dead had been strewn about on three different floors of CanTech. The scene was "indescribable," said police.

Jenean could not look away. Police were sending the gunman's fingerprints to Ottawa for identification. He had no identification papers on him, but he did leave a three-page handwritten letter in which he blamed women for the failures in his life.

Agonized, Jenean read on. Some sentences stopped her cold. "One student, twenty years old, underwent plastic surgery after having part of her face blown off, reported Dr. Yves Perseaux of the Jewish General Hospital." Jenean stopped, closed the paper, folded it back up. She had read only to page A-2. She picked up her mug, her tea cold by now, and clutched it with both hands. Staring straight ahead at the photo of herself and Bart on the beach in Maine, she tried to calm her burning brain.

Jenean rose from the sofa, turned off the television, and perked up as she heard the radio in the kitchen playing at low volume. She listened and heard Nicole Beaudette, a Montreal writer, tell the CN Radio's *Sunrise* audience, "One reason. One reason alone. Fourteen women are dead for one reason: they are women. Their male classmates are still alive for one reason: they are men."

# 28.

D EIRDRE HAD SLEPT LITTLE. She had ordered an extra large coffee to go when she got to the cafeteria. The dormitory had been so quiet when she had finally gotten back last night from seeing Susan Carson that she thought surely she had missed something. On the door to her room two notes had been taped: one that said the trip to CanTech for the conference was cancelled and one that said, "Call your mom ASAP." In the lounge on her floor, she found all of the girls crowded in front of the television. When Deirdre started to ask what was happening, Rosalie had shushed her, whispered, "There is a guy killing women at CanTech. Sit down, D. This is a nightmare."

Deirdre called her mother, assured her that she was not at CanTech and would call her back after she learned what was going on. Minutes later, in the midst of the blaring television and the anxious girls, Deirdre had heard the phone ring. Roberta was calling everyone from Feminist Philosophical Thought class to make sure they were okay and to invite them to Roberta's to be together to watch the coverage about CanTech. Roberta had told Deirdre that the women who were there already did not feel safe, feared the same thing could happen at Aquitaine, and they wanted to gather as many together as possible.

As Deirdre and Rosalie had grabbed their coats and left immediately for Roberta's, Rosalie filled Deirdre in on what happened at CanTech. It was surreal, and Deirdre had a hard time focusing on what Rosalie was telling her. She felt a trembling in her stomach and her head ached. Roberta's apartment was just around the corner on Quentin Street. Ordinarily, Deirdre had loved visiting this brick house with its steps painted turquoise, its ponderous stone rails, and its noble Japanese maple stretching to the porch. But last night, she had barely noticed it as she and Rosalie had beelined for Roberta's front door. Inside, young women were everywhere, all facing the television set. A tearful Ellen was saying she felt like the killer was yelling at them, at FRRF for their feminist activism. "Maybe he heard about Aquitaine and the No Means No, and he was furious," she kept repeating. "He got the wrong women."

Roberta had put her arm around Ellen's shoulders. "Stop, El. Don't internalize that hatred. Don't do it to yourself. That's what patriarchy wants. Stop it. You did nothing wrong. We did nothing wrong. We should be angry and afraid, not guilty." In one corner of the room a woman Deirdre had not recognized was painting a wooden sign that read "Misogyny Kills." She never spoke, but her brush strokes were fierce and thick with black paint.

Deirdre and Rosalie had found space on the worn carpet, slumped down, and watched the news coverage until two in the morning. They had dragged themselves across the quad and fell into bed, heartbroken and scared shitless. The entire time, Deirdre kept saying, "I was supposed to be there. I should be there now – at the Solar Conference. Oh, my God...." Her head had swum with fear and relief and guilt about the relief. And there had been something else. A quickening, as if all of the work she had done with Susan Carson to put the rape behind her had been erased, as if she were starting over with a mind-numbing dread.

This morning, radios in the Student Centre bellowed, and students in rumpled clothing stared straight ahead, bleary-eyed. Deidre stopped to listen for a few minutes though she had been watching TV almost through the night.

From a TV on the wall, Deirdre heard a male reporter ask several women on a busy Montreal street, "Ladies, let me ask you about your feelings today. Are students afraid on campus?" The first young woman spoke from deep within her hooded woollen coat. Her voice quaked. "I *am* terrified. My roommates are terrified. If this can happen in a university classroom to innocent women ... this is about women ... about violence against women...." She could not continue. The women with her pulled her close, then nodded to the reporter that they agreed with their friend. He moved on to another group of women. This was a media ritual Deirdre had been watching since last night. Three hundred kilometres away from Montreal, she felt fear and nausea. She also felt angry at the reporter for asking such inane questions. A guy shoots women at a university and this jerk wonders if women are afraid? *Idiot.* She wanted to call her mother again to complain, to hear her voice, but she would have to wait until after class.

For the first time in twenty-four hours, something made sense. The Montreal student was right on. Deirdre wondered if she could speak as truthfully if her friends were killed at Aquitaine. This *was* about women. It was not just students who were shot, but women. Why was it so hard to say so? When the television cameras returned to the studio and the discussion of guns, Deidre walked to her classroom. She felt heavy, sad, irked, but the young woman in Montreal who was not afraid to speak what Deirdre presumed was on the minds of many women today buoyed her, gave her courage, clinched an important decision. She would, indeed, go to the vigil tonight in the quad with her roommates. She had not been out much. Rather, she had been keeping a low profile, focusing on homework. But this had to be done, no matter how much of her own fear and shame might still be triggered.

Professor Glennan knew about the CanTech conference, and he knew Deirdre was not supposed to be in class this morning. But fate had intervened, abominable fate. She did not want to be in class, but she had to do something to get away from the news, just for a little while. Only one other student was in the classroom when she arrived. She gave a nod hello and found her favourite seat near the back of the room. From there she could look outside at the sky, a cloud-washed indigo this morning, far too gorgeous for such a gruesome morning after. Deidre slipped her coat, hat, scarf, and mittens into the nook behind her seat, and got herself settled with her notebook, pen, and textbook, then sipped her coffee. Professor Glennan liked to start class on time, so when he entered the room, students were ready to write. She wondered if he would take a moment this morning to acknowledge what happened at CanTech. It was only a few hours away, and it was a fellow engineering program. Surely he would say a word or two.

Students began filing in, removing overcoats, asking if someone had an extra pen. Marta and Gwen, students who lived on the floor beneath hers in Meese, sat next to her. Most of the women on her dormitory floor were engineering majors, and all of them had sat wrapped in sleeping bags in the community lounge last night watching the tiny television that hung in a corner at the ceiling. They were there when Deirdre and Rosalie had returned from Roberta's. There was little noise in the dorm last night, but lights across campus blazed. Once in bed, Deirdre had watched the night pass outside her window until, one by one, the lamps of Aquitaine were extinguished. It was hard to sleep when the tape that kept repeating told you it could have been you.

When Raymond exploded into the classroom, Deirdre turned. If there were such a thing in engineering as a class clown, he was it. Always ready with a joke, always asking Professor Glennan a question that included double entendres. He had a posse of male students who also lived in Commissioner House, and they did everything as a group. They liked to call themselves "boundary pushers," as Raymond often said, citing instances of Volkswagens suspended over rivers and Lady Godiva walks, but it was "good, honest fun," he insisted after every tale of Commissioner bravura, tacking it on like a moral to a story. Deirdre, Marta, and Gwen rolled their eyes whenever Raymond drawled on.

Truth be told, they paid minimal attention to Raymond and the Commissioners until a gang of them burst into the classroom that morning with their hands together, forefingers pointed directly at Deirdre, Marta, Gwen and the three other female students in the room. They pretended to pull triggers, facing the women, and mouthing the words "bang" and "boom." They made no noise but for their heavy boots stomping into the room, drawing all attention to themselves, and then, with exaggerated faces, sucked in their lips and thrust them back out to mimic silent "bbbbbang" sounds.

Then, they bent over with hysteria. Tears streaming from their eyes. They patted each other on the back, made their way to their seats. Professor Glennan entered the room, turned on the overhead projector, and began. "Today, we will examine the...."

Piece by piece, Deirdre placed her belongings into her backpack: notebook, textbook, pencils. She zipped the bag slowly. Then she pulled on her coat and hat. When she mustered the strength, she stood, hoisted her backpack onto her shoulder, shared a long look with Marta and Gwen, and walked out the classroom door back to her dorm room. Had Glennan seen what the boys in the class were doing? His office abutted the classroom. He might have noticed something before entering the room, might have caught a glance of their callous "shooting," their uncouth parody. Either way, once again, no one stopped them. They could do whatever they wanted, and get away with whatever they wanted, even after fourteen female students lay dead three hours away. The sick reality of it drove Deirdre to take refuge in a nap that lasted until suppertime.

# 29.

SYBILLE COULD NOT SLEEP. She lay on the sofa in her mother's house waiting for the others to wake. She had gone over the story so many times that she felt its edges tear and pull. Last night at CanTech, the police had asked Sybille and Trey to follow them upstairs. When they arrived, a uniformed officer had said there was no need to identify Marin. She had already been identified by Thomas.

"Thomas?" Sybille had asked? "Who is this Thomas?" Her hands had been shaking, and so she pushed them back into her coat pockets.

Trey had turned to her, his face swollen and wet. "Sybille, Thomas is my friend. He's in class with Marin. He..." Trey had choked up.

Sybille had waited. The police had waited too, giving them space.

"He called me tonight, early. He saw Marin being.... He told me then...." Here Trey had broken down, and Sybille held him.

He had known then, before she got to the university. Trey had known Marin was dead all along, on the phone even, but he had not ben able to tell her. Had not been able to tell himself. She would not have believed him anyway. She had not wanted to believe him or the police. She had wanted to see her sister. They would not let her, but she had wanted to be with Marin, to talk to her even if Marin could not hear. This nightmare of the night had been never ending. Could it ever, ever end now with Marin gone?

"You knew? You knew, Trey?" she had asked, though he was inconsolable. She had to understand.

"I am sorry. I did not want to believe Thomas. I asked him so many times, 'Could she be alive? Could it be she is still alive?' He said over and over and over, Sybille, how sorry he was, and I could not believe...."

They had clung to each other while the police officers looked on, everyone stricken. When Sybille and Trey had finally been able to stand and move, they walked to the front of the university and said goodbye. Sybille would call her mother once she got home. Trey would come over tomorrow to see the family. For now, he had wanted to be alone.

Sybille could not get Trey's face out of her head, as Madeline had driven her home. She had never seen a human being so broken. She had known she, too, was broken, so her face must look the same. They had been so in love, truly in love. Marin and Trey. Just like her mother and father. Sybille had known she had to call her mother as soon as she got back to her apartment. Natalee had been waiting for her. She had to tell her too. She had thought, *Thank God Papa is already in heaven. Marin is with him. No father or mother should go through this. No sister. No lover. Whoever said God never gives you more than you can handle never lost her sister to a gunman.*

At the apartment, after Madeline had let her off with hugs and tears, Sybille made the sign of the cross, bowed her head, and silently told Marin she loved her. "Please, Papa, take care of her. She should not be there so soon." The night had closed around her, as she ascended the staircase, wishing she were somewhere else. Natalee had been at the door instantly.

Sybille had held Natalee for a long while. "It is over," Sybille told her young sister, stroking her hair. "Marin is gone." The sisters consoled each other as best they could. Settling

Natalee into the sofa with a cup of cocoa, Sybille had dialled her mother's number. Her sister Marianne's husband, Franz, had answered and asked Sybille to wait because there was a knock at the door. Sybille heard it all because Franz was still holding the phone in his hand. The police had just told Mrs. Hazeur and her family how sorry they were. That her daughter had passed. She heard her mother scream, her sister moan. The police handed her mother an envelope that held Marin's driver's license and her necklace. Franz had spoken into the phone only after the police had left. In the background, Sybille heard wailing. On her end of the phone, Sybille and Natalee had wept with them.

"Sybille, it is awful. Can you come? Please come. Your poor mama. Oh my God."

"Natalee and I are on our way, Franz." Sybille hung up, took Natalee's hand, and they left the apartment to go home.

*

The sun was shining through her mother's sheer curtains in the living room. Sybille rested on the same sofa she had tried to sleep on last night while the coffee percolated in the kitchen. Her mother would need a hot mug of coffee this morning. She would take it to her as soon as she could find the strength to stand and breathe and live.

The phone rang. Reporters knocked on their door. This would continue for days. They stayed close and closed. The media were expelled by the family. Immediately. The entire family gathered to be with their mother at Saint-Eustace, all the siblings and their partners and Trey, long part of the family.

Sybille's thoughts were chaotic, twirling. One of the more persistent strands kept repeating: Why had it been so easy to kill those women? People were so anaesthetized, so quick to follow orders. If only one guy had tackled him. If only a professor had.... But these thoughts were less than useless, and they plummeted Sybille into anger that freed her, for brief periods, from the gnawing grief that ate up the household. It would, though, have to be set aside, this anger, if she were to help her mother, her family, so she pushed it down and down.

# 30.

J ENEAN WAS FOLDING LAUNDRY in front of the television when her boss, Florian, called. She wedged the phone into her neck. "Have you seen *Mot du Jour*?" he asked.

"Not yet," she said, stiffening. She had been forcing herself to do something mundane that she could start and complete, holding onto this trite domestic chore as if it could ward off the pain of the turbulent outside world. The smell of fabric-softened laundry grounded her, if but for a moment. She forced herself to focus on Florian. This could not be good. He never called in the morning.

"Brace yourself," he said.

She was braced, no need for a warning. She wondered if she would ever again not be braced against such a malignant world.

"The killer left a third sheet with the two-page suicide letter. It is a list of nineteen names – women's names – women he said he would have killed if time had allowed. Feminists."

"Oh my God, Florian. The police gave that out? How did you get it? Did they..."

Florian cut her off. "Jenean."

"*Oui?*"

"Your name is on the list."

There was a prolonged silence on either end of the phone.

Finally, Florian spoke. "John, you know John, skinny guy with thick glasses, our new police reporter? He got the names, and some of them are printed in today's paper. I'm sorry, Jenean. I was not here last night when the decision was made. This is horrifying. Are you alone? Is Bart there? Do you want me to come over?"

Florian would not stop talking. She wanted to think. She wanted to process this, but she could not while he was chattering. "Florian, please, can you just..."

"Jenean, there is one more thing," he said quietly, speaking slowly now.

"There cannot be one more thing, Florian. There is not one more thing there can possibly *be*. No..."

"The killer had written home phone numbers next to a few of the names. Yours was one of those."

"He had my home phone number?"

"He could have looked it up, Jenean..."

"It's unpublished, Florian."

"Well, he could have..."

"I have to go, Florian. Oh my God. I am going." She hung up the phone and stood catatonic staring at the phone in her hand. Suddenly, she slammed the phone back onto the hook, checked to be sure the back door was locked and went to see if *Mot du Jour* had been delivered yet. It was lying at her front door. The story was on the front page.

### Union Leader and Minister Reported on Killer's List

Arielle Bonaventure, president of the Canadian Unions Trust, former Women's Minister Julianne Moreau, and television personality Marie Steeves are among nineteen women who were listed in a suicide letter by the CanTech killer, police sources said yesterday. Officially, police have refused to reveal the identities of the nineteen prominent women listed in a letter found on the body of the man who shot to death fourteen women on Wednesday evening at the Saint Laurent University.

But unofficial sources have said the women include several

female police officers, a sports journalist, and *Mot du Jour* Sunday columnist Jenean Belisle.

*Mother Mary,* thought Jenean. She was one of the "radical feminists" the police said the killer wrote about. He had met none of them, but he had done his homework. He had phone numbers. That meant he had addresses. *Good God.* Jenean called Florian back at *Mot du Jour.*

"Put me through to John, Florian. I need to know all of those names," she said as soon as Florian picked up.

"He's at his desk. I'll transfer you now," Florian said, and she heard the phone click, then ring.

John told her how sorry he was to have been part of delivering such terrible news. He asked how he could help, and Jenean said she needed the complete list of names. Without hesitation, he gave them to her, pronouncing each carefully and giving her time to write them down. They included the woman who had scored highest in the recent chartered accountant exams; the first woman firefighter in Quebec; the first woman police captain in Quebec; a bank manager; and six female police officers.

Jenean recognized many of the names, knew a few of them personally, but she struggled to find a connection. She had long identified as a feminist. That was no secret. Many people knew she was the founder of *La Vision et La Voix.* She had been outspoken about her politics for as long as she had had politics. But what of these others? The women she knew personally were assuredly not "radical feminists," and the others – first police and firefighter – were women in jobs long held only by men. That a radical feminist does not make.

Exhausted yet wired, Jenean dressed to go into work, though she was supposed to be working from home. She was struck by the way information about the killer and his motivations had leaked out. Police would not release the suicide note. They had summed up its contents, saying the killer resented "feminists" and "radical feminists" and wanted to kill them. But the letter was two pages long. Surely he had said more than that.

And now she knew he had wanted to kill her too. Because she was a radical feminist. Because she was a woman.

Was she really so radical? What was radical about her? The feminist movement had been so intimately connected with her personal and professional life for so long she could not imagine it otherwise, but maybe she could not see herself. Doubt wormed into her. Was it so radical to want equality for women? Were there really people out there who thought women were not equal, should not have equal rights? She knew the answer to this, of course, but everything she had ever thought took on new meaning in light of this assassination of fourteen women.

There were men, she thought, as if conscripting herself to accept it, who hated the idea of women's equality so much that they were willing to kill in cold blood. In Canada. In Montreal, a cultured and urbane city in an independent and feisty province. Her home. This was not Tiananmen Square. This was a province that had come out of the dark and into the light. If Berlin's Wall had just come down, Quebec's walls had been crumbling since the Quiet Revolution some twenty-odd years ago. Such barbarism was foreign to Quebec. It did not make sense. Jenean felt dizzy. She sat on the side of the bed, held her head in her hands, and tried to relax her shoulders. She was alive. The killer was dead. She had to get that letter, had to know what was going on in the man's head before his killing spree. She had a right to see the note. She was, after all, on the hit list. No matter what was in it. She had to understand what was in the mind of this man who wanted to kill her, who could have killed her, who most likely knew where she lived, who could have called her home. Maybe he had. Maybe he had called and hung up. Maybe she had answered a wrong number, and it had been him. She could not remember feeling such terror.

Jenean called Bart at work. His message machine picked up. She really wished he were there. She wanted him to know she was leaving the house and heading to work. If she never got there, she wanted someone to know. She wanted Bart to know.

*

The vigil began at Saint Laurent University on Boulevard Edouard-Montpetit. Each of the five thousand people was given a tapered candle before falling into a ribbon-like procession of flickering light that wound its way up the steep whorl of access road to the engineering school at the top of the mountain. Jenean and Clara listened as a young woman at the table where the candles were being handed out said that there were vigils in each of the ten Canadian provinces, with many dozens in places with universities. This vigil was organized, she said proudly, by a coalition of student and women's groups.

Police outlined a loose perimeter at the top where the engineering school comprised several buildings of pale-yellow brick and expansive windows. CanTech students gathered around a long table where a microphone stood tall. A young male student rifled through index cards, as though to prepare an oral report. News cameras jockeyed for prime positions, as they focused in on the microphone and table. Extension poles hung boom microphones over the heads of those nearest the table.

Jenean and Clara made their way to a bench not far from the main table. They sat, though the evening was raw with cold, and leaned into each other. An older woman with a walker who introduced herself as Rose joined them on the bench. Most of the crowd were women, students making up the greatest numbers, but many were professors and administrative staff.

"How many people do you think are here?" Clara asked, snuggling closer to Jenean.

"Thousands," Jenean nodded her head as if counting the multitudes. "Many thousands. The student giving out candles said they were expecting five thousand."

"It is a good thing ... this vigil. It is something to do," said Clara.

"Something to do," agreed Jenean, before reconsidering. "What is there to do, really?"

"A lot of women here tonight are saying, 'It could have been me,'" said Clara.

"Sure. Women all over Canada are really, really petrified."

The friends looked at each other for a long time, breathed deeply, then returned to face the microphone, which was making preliminary squeaking sounds. Someone was tapping it with a finger, testing its sound and aiming to quiet the crowd. "Good evening," said a young man in a wool cap and grey anorak. "I am Giles Lado, secretary of the CanTech Student Association. I thank you all for coming to this vigil on this saddest of occasions. We are here to remember those who have died – our friends, loved ones, and colleagues." Speaking in French, *Nous sommes ici pour nous souvenir ceux qui sont morts – nos amis, proches et collègues,*" Lado used the male plural French pronoun for "those" or "the ones." Jenean raised her eyebrows, but before she could voice the gendered language implication, there came a shout from a woman in the crowd.

"It is *women* who are dead. Goddamn it. They were fourteen *women*, not *the ones*, not humans, *women*." Vocal support came from several in the crowd. A switch had flipped on. Anger had come loose and was palpable. *It should not be otherwise,* thought Jenean.

A young woman in a white down-filled coat and a broad-brimmed knit hat stepped to the microphone. "We are not here to make distinctions. It's not about male or female. We are here to be together. This gesture is too beautiful to be tarnished by fighting."

The crowd was remarkably quiet after the young woman resumed her place among the organizers, but the tension was thick. Jenean found herself beating back contending forces. She was both savagely grief-stricken and enraged at the brutal

bloodbath that had brought thousands to this frigid moun-
taintop. She was not sure she could find words appropriate to
express such friction. Lado, she believed, was simply young
and insensitive, and believed, perhaps, that by universalizing
the victimization to all students, he was sharing a burden,
bearing a proportion of the load of mourning. He was a fool,
but no mendacious fool. He believed himself.

Another student in a pale green pea-coat came to the microphone and asked the group to join hands. Jenean and Clara rose
to help the elderly woman with whom they had been sharing
a bench. Clara held hands with a male student who looked to
be about twenty-three, the age of many of the women who had
been killed. He wore boiled wool mittens, and Clara's hand
fit into his like a child's. Jenean had the hand of Rose to her
right. A female student on the other side of Rose placed her
embroidered green glove atop Rose's other hand, both hands
resting on the walker.

A tremulous soprano at the microphone began to recite
"Notre Père." The group joined in. Jenean overheard a young
woman next to her whisper quietly to an elderly nun who
fingered silver rosary beads. "I hope the killer comes face to
face with God."

The sister nodded. "I am a true Christian," the woman said.
"I can't understand how this could happen to those women
for no reason."

The nun leaned closer to the young woman and said softly,
"We did not ask to be born women. Why kill us for it?"

When the recitation subsided, a female student in a red-and-
grey plaid pea-coat gripped the microphone tightly with her
leather gloves. She spoke slowly.

"I am Charlotte Severeaux. I am a student at CanTech. I
must speak tonight because I do not know how to accept this
thing that has happened. What has happened here? Why were
our friends killed? Where is the sense to be found in this?"
Charlotte stepped back from the microphone several inches,

composing herself. The women standing next to her stepped in closer. She brushed back the lock of blonde hair that had fallen into her face. When Charlotte returned to the microphone, her eyes were bright with tears. Jenean could see them in the flickering candlelight.

"Please," said Charlotte, "help me to understand why no one helped these girls? Why were they left alone to die? Please...."

It happened so quickly that Jenean could not take it all in at once. In the blink of an eye, Charlotte was escorted from the microphone, and suddenly Giles Lado was speaking. "This is a night for mourning, my friends, mourning our dear fellow students and friends whose lives were lost. It is not, I venture, a time for questioning and accusing. This night, rather, is for mourning in deepest silence. Let us pray: dear God above, let the voices that must be heard be heard by you in the deepest of silences. Let us do you honour here tonight, as we mourn the passing of our classmates."

No one moved for a time. Perhaps twenty seconds. No one touched the microphone. No one proposed a song. Yet, no one seemed to be obeying Lado's exhortation to silent mourning either. Something had opened up. Some crack in the cosmic egg had splintered. The candle flames blew, slanting windward. The stars were as bright as they had ever been over a Montreal sky, and the sky was dark, the deepest navy.

Then Rose stood taller, inched her walker straight across the circle. No one spoke. When she arrived at the microphone, just now deserted by the righteous Master of Ceremonies, she indicated that the microphone was too high for her to speak into. The student closest lowered it for her. Rose stared out at the crowd, took its circuitry in, looked people in the eye. She reached into her purse, which hung from a hook on her walker, and unearthed a folded piece of paper. She opened it, pressed out its folds carefully, and read from it, her voice quavering but not without punch: "I am an old woman. This may be all you see now, but I was a mechanical engineer in a large and bustling city for more than thirty years. I know what life was like for these young women, these fourteen. It was not easy for them in their classrooms, and it was horrific the terror they endured at the end, in those selfsame classrooms. Unfathomable and yet perfectly and completely the completion of the equation. When a train filled with animosity and resentment travelling at X speed intersects with a train filled with guns and acrimony travelling at Y speed, on what scale do we measure the impact? What happened yesterday at CanTech has been chugging toward us for some time. That train has arrived. Its passengers have disembarked. They are among us. Sadly, this is not the end. Please, whatever gods are listening to our gathering here tonight, please, intervene to save your daughters."

Rose folded her paper, returned it to her purse. She leaned into her walker, slowly made her way back to her place in the circle, beside Jenean. She was trembling. Jenean wove her arm through Rose's and leaned her head gently against the fuzzy wool of Rose's hand-knitted cap. Someone had spoken the very words that would have been in her soul had the formulation of words been possible.

Where there had been a profound silence as Rose spoke, a quiet born of respect for age perhaps, there was a shuffling and a clearing of throats now. Something had risen into the concentric vigil circles, a breath, an energy, an agency. A young woman tapped the microphone, began speaking.

"I am Violet Cochey. My cousin was killed yesterday at Can Tech. I loved her. So much. And I feel so sad, but I also feel angry and what Rose said...."

From the depths of the crowd came a murmuring, barely noticeable. It might have passed for a breezy oak tree were it not continuous and disruptive.

Violet continued, despite the noise and movement behind her. "What Rose said makes so much sense. We are in danger here...."

"Enough!" was heard from immediately behind Violet. The crowd began parting, as Giles Lado made his way to the front. He lurched toward the microphone, grabbing it from the hands of the speaker. "This is simply enough," he shouted, glaring at Violet. "This is neither the time nor the place. This is a vigil, a time of mourning, a time of silence. We will resume the vigil, as we intended it, in silence. That is how it was planned; that is how it will go." With that, Lado made a show of turning the microphone off, yanking on its cord, unplugging it from its source. He wrapped the long cord around the microphone and placed the nested thing onto the ground, in front of the stand.

"Yeah, brother," a male voice shouted from the edge of the crowd.

"Way to take control," barked another.

From the darkness came shouts, female voices. "Hold on just a minute," one said. "Hold up."

A groundswell of women moved through the crowd, from the very back of the circles. Two women at the front of the group moved forward to the centre of the circle. A trail of women followed and formed a queue behind them. Television cameras moved through the crowds from several angles to get closer. Microphone booms lowered over heads.

One of the women bent to retrieve the unplugged microphone on her entry into the circle. She unwound the cord and handed the plug to the woman next to her. Suddenly, the tapping on the microphone was loud and clear.

"I am Lyla Laramie, from the Women's Coalition. I am deeply sad today. We are all sad today. Our spirits are slain ... but our voices are not. This is, indeed, as Giles said, a moment for mourning and quiet, but it does not have to be a moment for silencing voices that cry out in pain. Voices that yearn to be heard. Our fears became real last night. This is a time to come together, to stand together, to think together. To make what sense we can of this assassination...."

"Shut up," a man's voice shouted from the darkest corner of the crowd. "Shut up, bitch. Go home. This is not about you." Jenean leaned forward. Clara clutched her hand.

"It is about me," Lyla rejoined. "It is about all of us here who are female. What happened at CanTech last night is what has been happening to individual women for years. It is about violence against women."

A rush of movement sparked in the crowd. Four male students burst through the masses and into the circle. The TV booms reached far into the circle like giraffe necks. Lyla held onto the microphone with both gloved hands, while one of the men tried to pry it from her.

Jenean and Clara looked around the perimeter for the police officers who had seemed ubiquitous only a short time earlier.

"Say what you must," she said to the men, "but this microphone, on this night, is for the voices of women who need to speak."

"What the hell are you talking about? You don't think men were victims too? Men were shot. Men were hurt. They are mourning too. You do not have a monopoly on this tragedy. You...."

"Where were the men when the killer shot fourteen women in cold blood?" she shouted into the microphone. "Where were the professors, the male students? Why did no one stop him?"

Shouts of "Yeah, yeah" resounded throughout the crowd. "Where were they?" became a short-lived chant, until one young man went face to face with Lyla, shouting into the microphone in her hands.

"How dare you? How dare you hijack a vigil, a time for silence, with your shrill bitching? Men are sobbing and in anguish all over Quebec, all over Canada, and you blame them for this?"

"I am simply asking the question. No one is blaming."

"Men are victims here too. Let us not forget. They had to witness the horror. They tried to help."

"Witnessing horror is not the same as being *murdered*. They left defenseless women in a classroom with a man with a gun."

The police came then, shoving TV cameras aside and lining up around the contentious parties. Jenean could not hear what was said, but suddenly Giles Lado was at the microphone again, calling for a closing prayer, which he read slowly, enunciating each word. The vigil was over.

"We need a warm café, coffee, and a serious debrief," Jenean told Clara. Clara nodded, and the two made their way back down the hill, arm in arm, shivering.

# 31.

LATER THAT NIGHT, Deirdre lay in her dorm-room bed and watched the evening news program. CNTV Anchor Catherine Zahn was asking her guests these questions about the CanTech murders:

> News columnists have said this is an act against women. Such a heinous crime undeniably reduces our humanity. But, I wonder, doesn't it reduce it further when some people contend it was just an act against one group. Isn't this cold-blooded killing a crime against all human beings? I'm puzzled hearing so many women all day long saying that this horror has happened because our culture, our country, allows violence against women to go unpunished. What I see is shock and anger from Canadians. No one is allowing such violence. Isn't violence the enemy here?

Thunderstruck, Deidre turned off the TV and watched an electric moon slip behind a cloud. Zahn was one of the most trusted female journalists in Canada. Where was the permission? Everywhere. No one knew this more than Deirdre after only one semester of university. Her rape report was as good as useless. Her rapist was a free man. How could Zahn be so clueless?

Maybe, Deirdre thought, she should pray. Her heart was

broken, and she wanted to honour those young women, but she simply could not go to the vigil, though she had committed to going earlier in the day. She begged off, saying she had cramps. The same heaviness she experienced when she spent her first night at Aquitaine had returned. She felt deeply homesick, but she knew going home would not help. She needed to be by herself, to write in her journal, to think about what had happened at CanTech. She could not get those dead students out of her head. They were just like her and Lea and Rosalie and Roberta. They were only a few years older than she. Why CanTech and not Aquitaine? Deirdre had been driving herself mad for days with this question, and she needed to find a quiet place inside if she were going to find any peace.

When the girls had left for the vigil, their faces peeking out of furry hoods, their necks wrapped multiple times in knitted scarves, Deidre had taken a shower and put on her warmest flannel pajamas. Her mother had bought her these last Christmas and wrote on the card: "For those coldest of nights when all you want to do is crawl into bed with lemon tea and your journal." *How well my mother knows me,* Deirdre had thought, as she set her mug on the edge of her desk and pulled her quilt up onto her lap.

Now, Deirdre turned on the radio to 950 AM CN Radio Montreal, a talk show she listened to when she could not sleep. The hosts, Roger and Pete, discussed the issues of the day with listeners who called in. Too often, the program was boring, with callers complaining about Quebecoise who refused to speak French. Tonight was different.

"What are you saying, Jean?" the host was challenging a caller on the line as Deirdre got the radio tuned. "Are you actually saying that the killer was justified in what he did at CanTech? Seriously, man?"

"No. No, I am not saying that, Roger. You are not listening to me." The caller sounded aggravated. She sipped her tea and listened for clarification that made sense. There was no way someone would call a public radio station and say this was justified.

"Okay, Jean. We are all ears. Talk to us, brother," said Roger, attempting to appease the distressed caller.

After an audible sigh, Jean continued. "Okay, man, what I am saying, and let me be crystal clear here: I am not alone in this. I am calling you from a bar in Laval, and there are at least a dozen guys here, respectable, hard-working, family men, who agree with me." Deirdre heard hooting from the background, which she took to be Jean's barroom supporters. "So, what I am saying is that the killer was a victim too. You can't forget that. He had no father, well for all intents and purposes, he had no father. He was rejected from the army and CanTech. How the hell was he supposed to grow up learning to be a man?"

Deidre wrapped the quilt more tightly around herself. She resisted the urge to turn the radio off. This was ludicrous, but she had to hear it. Maybe it was a joke, like that "War of the Worlds" thing her dad was always going on about. Maybe she had tuned into the middle of some weird pretend drama.

"Jean, Jean," Roger was imploring, trying to get the caller to listen to him. Jean was on a roll. He was not stopping.

"Did you hear that psychiatrist on television this morning, Roger? This kid, this killer, was the victim of a merciless society. The society he was talking about is our society, right here in Montreal. The problem? You want to know what the problem is, Roger? You want to know: that kid with the Mini-14 called it – feminists. Feminists and their unrelenting agenda for world domination. We are in the age of the feminist. The triumphant feminist, my friend. And do you know what that means for you and me and Petey boy sitting next to you? Do you know what it means for all the guys here who've worked hard all day to bring home a paycheque so their wives can spend it? It means, Roger, that feminists have been given an inch, and now they want a mile. Look at it. It is right there in front of you. You need look no further than your own house, I suspect."

Roger managed to interject while Jean took a rare breath. "So, do you think he had the right idea? Just kill those feminists? The final solution? Is this what you are advocating, there, Jean?" Roger was riled, Deirdre could tell, and so was she. Why did they give air time to lunatics?

Jean shot back with a vengeance. "The time has come, Roger. The time has come for men to demand respect and recognition for the massive number of things they have done and will continue to do for mankind. It is not that he did the right thing. Killing is not the right thing, but the poor kid was at wit's end. Maybe, subconsciously, he knew the time had come. You know what I mean, Roger? We're all coming to this point. Men need to free themselves from the chains women have got them tied up in. Vaginocrats! Fundamentalists!"

"Jean. You cannot be serious with these terms."

"You bet I'm serious. More serious than you can know. What that boy did to those girls at the university may not have been right. Nope. A man's gotta keep his cool, but you have to admit, Roger, man to man, what he did was something every one of us has fantasized about."

"I am going to have to cut you off, Jean..." Roger's voice was quavering.

"Face the facts, Roger, old boy. I speak the truth. This feminist shit...."

Suddenly, the radio went silent. Deirdre realized she had been holding her breath. She was shaking beneath the quilt, and her tea was nearly cold in her mug. Through the window, she watched the flickering of hundreds of candles coming from the yard outside where the vigil was being held. The candles were so bright against the dark night that Deidre could not draw her eyes away. She should have gone with them. She should be there now. The radio conversation was haunting. She wished she had a friend there who had heard it too because it could not have been real. None of this seemed real.

"Okay, folks, welcome back to CN Radio Montreal 950 on

your AM dial. Our lines are open, and the night is heating up. We are discussing the massacre of fourteen women at the Can-Tech here in Montreal on Wednesday night, and we have just finished speaking to Jean who offered some very provocative thoughts on the killer and the plight of men. Our board has lit up; we have several callers in the queue, so let's turn now to Brian from Pembroke."

"Hey, Roger. How's it going? That last caller is just plain nuts. It is really quite simple. People who do what that guy did are mentally ill. They are victims, it is true, but victims only in that they are not responsible for their violence. They are sick, and we, as civilized people, need to be compassionate, not hateful. That's all, Roger. Thanks."

Deirdre relaxed a bit, but she could not focus on her journal or the vigil any more. She was drawn back to the radio show.

"Thanks there, Brian. Short and sweet. Brian says the guy was nuts, and we need to be nice about it. What say you, caller? Let's see, we have Leo on the line. Leo?"

"Hey, Roger. I happen to be a friend of the killer's high-school chemistry teacher. He tells me that the guy did not hate girls. He had a girl lab partner, and he ended up doing all the work because she was a simpleton. My friend says he was nice to her."

*What does that have to do with anything?* Deirdre wondered. This radio show was getting more bizarre by the minute. She envisioned sharing this insane conversation with her Feminist Philosophical Thought class. Deirdre opened her journal to take notes.

"Roger, it's George. What else could one expect, really? The fact of the matter is that feminism has, once again, brought on violence. It does not happen only in the States. It is happening here. Feminists provoke the wrath of men. *They* are to blame for this atrocity. They make mountains out of mole hills, urge us to believe that men commit more violence than women, when statistics show us that women commit just as much, if not more, violence than men do. How about this for a revolutionary idea: what if some feminists – call me crazy – just loved the gunman, before he became 'the gunman'? What if some feminists had treated the gunman nicely? Do you think we might be having this conversation on this frigid night if that had happened?"

"George, we have a professor on the line who wants to speak to you," said Roger. "Welcome, Virginia, to the show."

"Thanks, Roger. Listening tonight, and reading the *Montreal Messenger* and other papers this week, I am becoming concerned that the killer is receiving more sympathy from callers and writers than the fourteen dead women and the injured victims. What is happening to Montreal, Roger? And George, you're falling victim to masculinist propaganda. Men's violence against women is disproportionately greater...."

"Here we go again, Roger. The feminists dominate the airwaves and scream their statistics and lies...."

"Whoa, there George. I hear no one screaming, and if memory serves me correctly, Virginia is the first female caller we've had tonight. I'm going to ask you to let her finish, please, George."

"Thanks, Roger. The fact is that every week, women are murdered in Canada by those who are enraged because 'their' women want to determine the course of their own lives. There are men out there, and we have heard from far too many of them on this show tonight, who downplay domestic violence. They refuse to believe reliable data and proclaim that violence of women against men is equal – even greater – than men's violence against women. That is simply not so; the data are clear. Yet, men persist in these claims, believing that any recognition of rights for women means a concomitant reduction of rights for men. It is not a zero-sum game, Roger."

Deirdre breathed deeply and rested her head back on her pillow for the first time since turning on the radio. This woman made sense. Deirdre had jotted down many of Virginia's words in her journal. She wanted to remember her words, so she could share them with her class, but it was more than this. Virginia's voice was so calm yet so somber. She was nothing like the students in her class. She was more like Professor Oliver, but even calmer than that.

How, Deirdre wondered, could this woman listen to such tripe and remain unflustered? This radio show got under Deirdre's skin, penetrated her very core. She felt murderous, furious, wanting to lash out at these male callers. She wanted to rage against them with what Professor Oliver called "*ad hominem*" attacks, attacks on them as people, rather than on their asserted positions. She could not help it. They were such jerks. How could anyone side with a cold-blooded murderer? How could anyone hate so much?

Deirdre sat up straight in her bed, her eyes wide open. She hated Craig that much. That was the truth. There it was, plain as day. The simple fact of it stunned Deirdre. Was she like them, these callers? But Craig had raped her. She had a reason to hate. The CanTech killer had not known these women.

Roger was speaking with another woman named Lina on the line, and Deirdre caught only part of what she said, so preoccupied was she with her own emotions.

"...Shown us how easy it is to commit acts of violence and cruelty when the victim is depersonalized," said the woman.

"So, Lina, can you explain to us exactly what you mean by 'depersonalized?' What are you saying here?" Roger queried.

"When you think about a group of people as a group rather than as individual people, it is easier to demonize them, to think of them not as single human beings but as a block to be rid of. This is how the Nazis got their troops to commit the horrors they committed in Germany. Hitler convinced many Germans that Jews, for example, were a blight on the world, that they were threatening the health of Germany, that exterminating them was doing the work of nationalism. It is a dangerous path to take...."

George interrupted. He was still on the line. Deirdre was

dismayed, wishing him long gone.

"Lady, are you for real? Comparing a guy who kills only fourteen people to Hitler? See what I mean, Roger? This looney you've got on the line is one of them, and it sounds to me like she's got you in her snare. Beware, buddy. They are legion." The sound of George being disconnected was like an overblown click.

Deirdre reminded herself to breathe again, as Roger apologized to Lina and to the listening audience for being out of time and needing to sign off for the night. Deirdre turned off the radio, and slumped down into her bed, pulling the sheets and quilt up under her chin. She did not want to hate, not if hate could turn people into beasts. But how to stop? What were you supposed to do when the person who hurt you did not care, did not apologize, did not change? Deirdre tossed with these demons and the murmurs of her friends remembering the dead outside her dormitory window.

# 32.

S HE PUT ON HER NIGHTGOWN in the bathroom and brushed her teeth. Jenean looked at herself in the mirror and hardly recognized the face there. Her skin was pale, her eyes swollen and red. She looked tiny in her Lanz nightgown, vulnerable and heartbroken. This was a calibre of sadness she had never known.

At the vigil, Jenean had never seen so many distraught people. They held each other and wept and prayed and pleaded for answers. Jenean closed her eyes and held tightly to the sink, steadying herself. She needed to sleep, but she doubted she could. She needed to put the horror out of her mind for an hour or two.

Bart was asleep when she pulled back the blankets and got in next to him. Staring out of the window, Jenean saw one bright star, brighter than the others, and she concentrated on it, hoping this simple focus would bring some peace. She kept rewinding something Clara had told her earlier that night. When she had first heard the news, Clara was inconsolable. Her husband Frank had tried to hold her, but Clara needed to be alone and she spent several hours in her room. Frank had come in with chicken soup because he had not known what else to do, but he needed to do something. She had simply cried even harder. Then, he climbed into the bed beside her, pulled up the covers, stroked her hair, and held her for three hours. For three hours he had not uttered a word, just held her while she cried and screamed and despaired.

"Didn't he have to go to work, Clara?" Jenean had asked her, trying to imagine Bart in the same scenario.

"He called in, said he would not be there, that he had to be with me," she had said, looking at Jenean, both of them wondering at this simple act of healing.

Beside her, Bart slept soundly. Jenean could not help but be jealous. Frank was a gem. In their circle of close friends, the women had long ago voted Frank "Number-One-Sensitive Husband." They had even toasted him when he took Clara for her birthday to the Musee D'Art Contemporary to see the Judy Chicago's *The Dinner Party* exhibit and to attend a lecture and discussion about transgressive feminist art. They were the last to leave the discussion because Frank had asked so many questions about Judy Chicago and her work.

"Did he really care, Clara, or was he kissing up, you know, to get some birthday action later on?" Suzanne had asked, their friend who could be counted on to pull a crude question out of her hat at any given moment.

"No kissing up, I'm afraid. He's the real deal. Has his own subscription to *Ms. Magazine*, I tell you. He reads it at night in bed, and he always wants to talk about the 'Back Page' section where women write personal essays. He loves the thing."

Jenean rolled onto her side and faced Bart. He was sprawled on his back, arms over his head like a dog basking in the sunshine. Jenean had read that people who sleep on their backs with their bodies fully open had no cares. Feared no attack in the night. Had a sense of confidence, were able to fully relax into sleep. For one second, she hated Bart's body. Even if he could sleep, how could he sleep so intensely? With no qualms? How fucking unfair was this?

She needed him now, yet she could not make herself go to him, put her arms around him or her head on his chest. She fantasized that Bart woke up, asked how she was, listened to her talk about the vigil and the "hit list" and the fact that a cold-blooded killer had longed to kill her. To kill her with a gun. She had told Bart, of course. He had been perfectly quiet for a long time. Then he had said, "That guy was nuts. A freak show, Jenean. You can't let this get to you, baby. He's dead. It's over." It had not helped. He had not held her. He had patted her on the back and run out the door to take Gertrude for her walk, leaving Jenean and her rabid mind alone.

Her brain looped, replaying the same questions, the same stark realities. She could be dead now – should be dead now – instead of fourteen young women the killer did not even know. How had she gotten here? How had he found her? Had he read her column? Had he read *La Vision et La Voix*? She doubted that. *La Vision et La Voix* had nothing like the readership *Mot du Jour* did. But the killer was French, shouting, "*J'haïs les féministes!*" Maybe he had read her columns.

She turned again to look at the star shimmering in the black sky. She could not halt her flummoxed brain. Someone had wanted to kill her. After Florian had called this morning to tell her this news, she had immediately called Arielle Bonaventure who was also named by the killer. Arielle's husband had been frantic, she had said, not wanting her to leave the house and talking about hiring a security service. He feared a copycat would act on the killer's list.

That thought had never entered Jenean's mind, but once Arielle had spoken it, she could not erase it. Arielle had reminded her that the celebration of the fifty-year anniversary of women's right to vote in Quebec was in the planning. Arielle and many others were to be honoured as "godmothers" of the event. "These young girls were killed, Jenean," she had said on the phone, "because he did not have access to us. We were the symbols."

Jenean struggled to fit all of the chaotic pieces together. It all kept coming at her like a driving rain, flooding her senses. She grew so chilled that she had to move more deeply under the covers. How surreal to be singled out. A man who did not know you wanted to kill you. He wrote your name on a list. Your phone number. He was so close. He had a gun, a semi-automatic rifle, and he had killed other women because he could not get to you. Was Arielle right?

It had never happened before anywhere in the world, such a large-scale explicit crime against women, such a rampage of hate. Jenean tossed. She could not sleep. Bart was silent beside her, his chest barely moving. She had been a fool. A total fool. She had been convinced that society had been as accepting of this great revolution called feminism as her friends were. Sure, there were a few chauvinist men, there always were, but on the whole, she would have wagered her soul that feminism was solidly rooted in her country. That it was here to stay.

But men were threatened. Why hadn't she thought they would be? How could she not have foreseen this? Every revolution comes with a price tag. She knew this. Had not the French Revolution and South Africa taught her anything? Somehow, she had lost sight, caught up in the passion of making equity happen.

Jenean shoved her pillows against the headboard and sat up. She could not sleep and was tired of working at it. Why fight it? The one thought she did not want to come shimmied its way in then. Men and women were supposed to love each other. Feminism got in the way of that – somehow. We were supposed to be partners, to share life. What was it about equality that enraged so many men? Could men and women be equal *and* in love?

Clara and Frank seemed to be doing it. What about her and Bart? One snapshot of the two of them in this moment would indicate otherwise. Bart was on his side now, one leg hanging off the edge of the bed, one arm stretched fully onto her side, spraddled over her knees. His body was loose and heavy, its muscles limp. Her body, on the contrary, was taut with anxiety. Her jaw was galvanized steel, her neck and shoulder muscles adhered into a solid mass. Bart's mind was free, untethered from any quotidian troubles or massacres or guilt. Jenean bore it all. There they were, life partners in the bed they shared: one done in by the events of December 6, and one far, far away, unavailable. Uncaring? Jenean gazed again at the star hanging in the dark like a lantern. She did not want to feel it, but she let it inch in anyway, the chasm. The deepening rift that yawped between her and Bart

# 33.

"FOR CRYING OUT LOUD," groused Daniel from the kitchen table. Lee Ann stayed still in her chair by the living room window.

"Do you hear me, Lee Ann? Have you read the paper? Now this gunman is the symbol for all men. We're all bad. Can you hear me, Lee Ann?"

"I hear you, Daniel," Lee Ann called, wishing he would finish the paper and go outside to the garage like he usually did on Saturday mornings.

He was on a roll. "The killings at the university in Montreal have provoked a crisis, this guy says, some professor...."

Lee Ann hears Daniel push his chair away from the table, hears the newspaper shuffling in the air, as he walks with it wide open into where she is sitting. He stands in the doorway staring at her with the paper in front of him, holding it as if it reeks.

"Sure, there's a crisis." Daniel sat now on the sofa facing Lee Ann. He read again from the paper, "'There are forty-four shelters for battered women and their children across Quebec.' Yeah, and you know who's paying for that? This professor says, 'At least half of all women who stay longer than a week in a shelter never return to live with the batterer.' Never return to their husbands. Can you believe this?"

Lee Ann remained silent. This was the absolute time to stay as quiet as possible. She had read the pamphlets about how to de-escalate a potential fight, but more important, she knew from experience where Daniel could end up when he read about December 6. He had been fuming since the first reports that suggested the men at the school might have stepped in and stopped the killer. "Why should they risk their lives? The guy had a freakin' semi-automatic?" He was shouting, and pacing.

He stopped suddenly and turned to face her. "You do realize, Lee Ann, what the problem here is. Radical feminists who hate men. I'm not kidding. I'm all for equality, as much as the next guy, but how the hell much more equality can there be? Look at that school in Montreal. Overrun with women. If that's not equality ... Jesus Christ."

Daniel stalked out of the room, into the kitchen, where Lee Ann could hear him pouring cereal into a bowl. Her body was taut. She wanted to go upstairs to her room to call her friend Joan. She could not bear to hear another word from Daniel, but she was afraid to leave. If he returned to the living room and she was not there, he would think she did not want to listen to him. She had been down this road before.

He returned almost immediately, holding a huge bowl of Froot Loops. "All right. Let me just say this because I need to get on with my day here, can't sit around yakking about this BS CanTech stuff with you all day. The bottom line is there is a natural order to the world, and when you mess with it...."

Lee Ann shifted her position in her seat slightly, and Daniel glared at her. "Is there a problem, Lee Ann? Somewhere you need to go? Am I boring you?"

"You are not boring me, Daniel. My foot fell asleep, and I was...."

"All this about safe houses ... what happened to marriage? If people stayed married there would be no need for any of this. Life is hard. Marriage is hard. You have to work at it. One little fight, and these women run off to the courts and cry abuse. "

Daniel stopped talking. He ate his cereal, looked at Lee Ann.

He waited. She waited. When she could stand it no longer, she said, "What would you like me to say, Daniel?"

He laughed. Then he rolled his eyes and shook his head. He finished his cereal and stood up. He walked to Lee Ann and stood towering over her. His pupils were huge. The hand holding the cereal bowl trembled. With the other he pointed at her, almost touching her nose.

"Say this, Lee Ann. The kid who shot up CanTech was a nut. This was a crazy thing, not some symbol for feminists to use to rag on men. Men are not the bad guys here. But ... if men keep getting pushed ... it could happen again."

Daniel left the room, then the house. She heard the truck start and back out of the driveway. He would be at the bar for the remainder of the day. This was a blessing, at least for the next several hours. Lee Ann willed herself out of the chair and upstairs to the bathroom. She was shaking so visibly that she decided to take a long, hot shower to calm down. She needed to think.

Lee Ann was heartsick at what happened to those poor engineering students. She thought about them when she woke in the morning and when she went to bed at night. At all other times, she thought about her son. Since that visit home in November, Craig had called, as was their arrangement, every Sunday at six p.m. Theirs were conversations that never dipped below the quotidian. *How was school? Was he eating well? What are you reading? How are your church friends doing, Mom?*

Beneath the surface, Lee Ann ruminated about that last visit home, the way Craig had escorted her to the stairs, the loud and intense male voices she heard below, into the night. In her room, she had thought about the letter she got from the Concerned Women at Aquitaine. She had thought about the girl, Deirdre, and how she had said her son had raped her. She was nauseated by all of it. He was her charming and handsome boy, and Lee Ann had wanted to believe him with all her heart, but what she wanted to believe no longer mattered. Craig was his father's son too. Their voices had risen to her room as one, their rage twinned.

On that night, with Daniel and Craig arguing downstairs, the thought first came to her: she would pull Craig out of Aquitaine. She would move him to a community college, one where he would get away from that fraternity mentality for a while. She knew Daniel would fight her on it. But the more days that passed, the more certain Lee Ann became. Now, with the Montreal massacre a brutal shock, she nearly lost her courage. She kept praying for the strength to save herself and her son. Maybe it was too late. He was in university, no longer a child, but she had to try.

Lee Ann confirmed her plans. She would withdraw Craig from school. She would leave Daniel. She and Craig would move to her mother's house an hour away. He could commute to the community college there, and, perhaps, in a few years, he could go back to university, when he was more mature. Such rage as that which consumed the killer had started somewhere, certainly with a violent father and maybe with a mother who could not stand up to him.

Lee Ann was convicted, catalyzed, and alarmed by what a twenty-five-year-old Montreal killer did, terrified that her son too could be a danger, as that letter from the Aquitaine women had said. It all seemed so clear, a path without weeds or obstacles, whenever she sat in that office with Dr. Rasmussen, the spiritual counsellor her friend Joan had recommended. At home, her courage retreated like a turtle into its shell, but with Dr. Rasmussen, she had learned to articulate her fears, her hopes for a future without an abusive husband. Since November, she had begun mourning the loss of the dream she had held onto, the dream that her love could heal the little boy inside her husband, the little boy whose spirit had been broken by his cruel and philandering father. She knew he had been hurt since then, as everyone had, by girlfriends, by his mother's slow and painful death, by job losses, each loss resurrecting that primitive loss and hardening it over with yet another toughened shell. She had cared deeply, but she would let Daniel go. He was beyond her fixing. She loved him. She simply could no longer live with him.

Seeing Craig that night usher her to the stairs in such a loving *and* condescending manner, just like his father, had punched her worldview in the nose. The bruise it left caused such unbearable soul-wrenching reality to arise that Lee Ann had called Joan the next day to tell her about her decision. Twice a week she continued to see Dr. Rasmussen. Her prayer chain had her back. She was finally able to breathe. She would tell Craig when he came home for Christmas. She would convince him that her plan was best for all of them. He would have to see reason.

Of course, she was not at all sure he would. Craig had changed, or the way she saw him had changed. He was always a boy who took the humour route, joked about adversity, assured her that her worry was misplaced. He was confident but never cocky with her. When he was angry, it was a microburst. Then it was gone. He had changed, however, and Lee Ann saw it now.

She had seen so much now in such a short time.

Dr. Rasmussen said she had been ready to see it for some time, and that watching Craig transform into Daniel had finally snapped her eyes wide open. Lee Ann had to agree. While the massacre of those fourteen women terrified her, it also emboldened her. She would leave her husband. She would save herself and her child. What she had witnessed this week gave her no doubt that she had to escape.

These past few nights, Lee Ann had heard Daniel listening to the radio call-in shows late at night in the kitchen while she sat up late reading. He had talked back to the radio as if in direct dialogue with it. The things Lee Ann had heard from the callers would have been shocking if she had not heard Daniel spew the same ideas over and over. Still, some of the men, like the killer, were so young. One in particular had kept her up for an entire night.

"Hey," he had said to the host, "I'm Will. This guy, who killed those girls at CanTech? I think we are missing the point. This rebel decided to fight back. The rest of us – we just talk about it, but he *did* it. Single-handedly. He spared the men, told them to clear out. He only killed feminists. Here's a question all men out there should answer: how many of you mentally pulled that trigger that night?"

Lee Ann had not believed her ears. Then she had heard Daniel guffaw. This caller had sounded eighteen tops. He was still young, but Daniel. For all of his bluster and rage, could he really pull that trigger, mentally or in reality?

She had heard another voice, another caller then. "For the feminists and Women's Studies programs and for our precious universities, the time of reckoning has come. You need to learn when too much is too much. Maybe now the feminists will cease and desist."

Lee Ann had not heard what the host was saying in-between callers. There had been two of them, two men, and they seemed to be asking questions, probing for more information about the thinking behind the hateful comments.

When she had finally heard a female voice, Lee Ann sat up and leaned closer to the doorway. The woman was a professor from Xavier College, Lee Ann had thought she heard her say. She had only heard bits of what the woman said because Daniel had been *harrumphing* throughout the entire call.

"The women of Canada saw their sisters mowed down by a small man with a big gun. Gender roles are changing. I would argue they are changing for the better, but not everyone sees it this way. Men are threatened. Brute strength is no longer the guarantor of superiority. Alas, as we saw on December 6, the brute power of a semi-automatic rifle trumped."

The caller had continued. "We know some things, however: women are less violent than men, physically, biologically, traditionally. They think about organizing a culture along peaceful lines. I suggest that their contributions should be applauded, welcomed, rather than resented and assassinated."

With that, Daniel had turned off the radio and mumbled his way up the stairs to bed. He had not even said goodnight. He probably had not seen her sitting there. Quietly, she had stood up and turned out all of the lights left on in the kitchen and dining room. She had then returned to her chair and turned the reading light off as well. For the remainder of that night, an afghan pulled over her shoulders, Lee Ann had sat up. the dog at her feet.

Now, by the light of day, with Daniel out of the house, Lee Ann sat up straight. She knew she must leave. She also knew that the most dangerous time for a woman was when she was leaving her husband. This was the very time when most abused women were killed. She could not leave now with Daniel so crazed about the murders at CanTech. She could not imagine him actually killing her. Then again, she could not have imagined her loving Daniel becoming this alter ego who lived with her now. She felt groundless. Afraid.

Just maybe her leaving would put him over the edge. So what? She *was* already over the edge. And she was almost out the door. No matter what.

# 34.

FILED WITH *MOT DU JOUR* December 9, 1989:

**HEARTBREAK BY JENEAN BELISLE**

Heartbreak stymies my pen.

Those young women at CanTech, the fullness of life and love and career ahead of them, earnestly pursuing a path that would allow them to solve problems, to better humanity – lost.

Meticulously slaughtered when a twenty-five-year-old man took it upon himself to play some sort of brute god. The irony – our media's breathless amassing of the details of the killer's biography indicate he was, above all, notably unremarkable.

Quebec is not used to such American barbarism. Even Americans do not kill women *en masse*. Yet, this massacre was home grown, born of a hatred of women our media is reluctant to name. Surely this was a crime against "humanity," one public personality claims, shoving gender off the table and neutralizing the facts: one man killed fourteen women, deliberately, with premeditation. He left a suicide note that explained he hated "feminists." Witnesses heard him say the same. Yet, we fear the truth.

It is called misogyny. Feminists know the word well. All women know the feeling: that of contempt, condescension, and cruelty. Misogyny is the ideological ballast that supports rape, stoning, female genital mutilation, honour killings, domestic abuse, and murder.

To call what happened at CanTech unfathomable madness is, in itself, madness. These were calculated actions. The killer stalked, hunted, and killed his prey. His lucidity is terrifying. His message clear: this is a warning to those women who live their lives as if they had the freedoms of men – death is the price tag.

Were what happened at CanTech not enough, to add violence to violence, there are those who sidestep the massacre itself to insist that the real problem is the angry and traumatized reaction of the targeted group: feminists. The oppressor blames the oppressed.

How will we ever heal the families and friends who loved these young women? How will we ever heal such a wound to our society's soul? Surely, as one feminist has proclaimed, this is the most blatant misogyny Quebec has ever known. And just as surely, we have a long way to go. Our men must evolve beyond their hostility to half the human race. They must get right sized. They must stand up to their brethren who take arms against their sisters. Our women must remain undaunted by such virulent and bloody tantrums. But for a while, while the excruciating pain rocks our very being to the core, we must abide, not in silence, but in solidarity, one woman with another.

Protean and prolonged reflection is required after an event like this: the mass execution of women because they are women. Pray that will come when the minds and hearts of Canadians find a shred of solace.

# 35.

D EIRDRE NEEDED A WALK even if it were freezing cold outside. She needed to be alone to think. So much had happened in the last few days. Deirdre decided to take the route along King Street, by the shore of the St. Lawrence River, the route that went past the park, hospital, and old stone tower, heading downtown.

Lea had called last night to tell her about what happened at the University of Ontario vigil at the statue of the Crucified Woman. Deirdre thought about the call as she walked. Lea was obsessed by this sculpture. She told Deirdre something new about it nearly every time they talked, and Lea had sent Polaroids of the statue.

Almuth Lütkenhaus-Lackey was the artist. She had given the statue as a gift to the university, and it sat on the university grounds surrounded by silver birches, junipers, and scarlet sage in warm weather. The statue itself was a bronzed, elongated female figure, about seven feet tall, secured onto a four-foot concrete base. Deirdre could see from the photos that there was no cross. There were no nails or puncture wounds, but her arms were outstretched, and there was suffering in the woman's face. She was quite the controversial figure, and Deirdre assumed this was a large part of the appeal for Lea.

Because it was Saturday, Deirdre had time to stroll. Today, she would rather take a left at the park and cut over onto Sydenham Street with its little homes reminiscent of cottages she had seen in a coffee-table book about Martha's Vineyard, but older and almost all brick. Today she needed the comfort of their coziness. Even the Hochelaga Inn looked like an old friend, solid and steady, built in 1879 and haunted. As she gazed up at the inn's highest peak, the widow's watch, Deirdre recalled that a ghostly nine-year-old boy with blond hair had been overheard crying by a guest at the inn. This had been followed by a woman singing a lullaby – a dead mother singing to a dead son, the guest had surmised. Suddenly, Deirdre was gripped with a grief that rocked her. She sat down on the stone steps of the inn and rested her head against the railing. All those mothers mourning for their daughters killed at CanTech, mothers who had sung to their baby girls lullabies like the Hochelaga Inn's ghost mother. Deirdre let the tears come, grateful for the early hour that allowed her to be alone in this moment.

When she felt ready, Deirdre continued onto Earl Street, one of her favourites. She gazed up at the quaint dormers high atop the third floors and wondered who slept there. Who lived behind the windows and doors grated in filigreed wrought iron? Who tended the pristine gardens in summer with their tiny wicket fences? She passed the one-storey LaSalle cottage built in 1865 and sitting primly between two brick buildings near the corner of Earl and Wellington. She made her way back to King Street to her familiar haunt, Morrison's. Though the restaurant opened in 1921, it had soundly settled into a 1950s décor with a stainless steel milk dispenser and lighted display case featuring slices of homemade pie in cellophane wrap. The overhead fan never stopped. Deirdre took a booth across from the counter. She felt a bit of normal return when she placed her palms in the centre of the Formica tabletop, spied the tiny boxes of Raisin Bran, Froot Loops, and Rice Krispies arranged neatly next to the pie case.

No potted palm trees in brass containers. No brick walls or recessed lighting. Just plain old beige walls and the best rice pudding in Ontario. Because Deirdre embarked on the twenty-minute walk from Aquitaine to Morrison's every weekend and several days during the week, she knew that behind her, above the cash register, perched a framed photo of the long-dead original owner in a bowler hat and wool coat and the Mrs. in a puffy coat that looked her Sunday best. The waitress called her "Honey," something Deirdre otherwise deplored, but at Morrison's, she felt like she was at home, like her aunts and grandma were there, calling her "Honey."

While waiting for her coffee and pudding, Deirdre thought again about Lea's phone call. It was frigid and perfectly dark on the night of the U. of Ontario vigil, Lea had said. There was this famous poet who was there to speak at the event. Lea had forgotten her name. She had been walking with Lea's group of friends, and she was telling them how distressed she had been upon hearing about the shooting. As they had passed by one of the fraternity houses, three male students leaned out of the top floor windows and bellowed: "We love nubile chicks! Yowwwww!"

The poet, a woman in her forties, had turned on her heels and slipped on the ice. "Shut up. Shut up. Shut up," she had screamed at the men, trying to get up, her arms flailing. Her face had boiled with blood. Lea and the other women had grabbed her, and together they slid along behind the group of protestors. One guy with a ponytail and a fatigue jacket walking behind them had said, "Some people are idiots." He had tried to be supportive.

"The woman just lost it, D. This massacre is getting to people," Lea had said. "It's getting to me, for sure. How are you doing, Deirdre?" Lea knew about the rape, of course. Deirdre had called her after the Sit-In at Principal Plumber's office, when she finally could admit to herself what had happened. Lea had cried very hard then, and the friends wept softly together on the phone until they could speak again. They had vowed to talk every night, even if it only for one minute. Sometimes it was for hours. Deirdre had shared her heart with Lea. The massacre at Montreal had set her back. She was supposed to be there that night, at CanTech, at the opening dinner for the conference. It had all been cancelled, of course, and Deirdre was safe, but she found herself anxious all the time, especially at night. The combined violence of the rape and the massacre all seemed too much. She stayed in her dorm room whenever possible. She slept poorly. Talking to Lea had helped, and she promised Lea to tell her parents about the rape when she went home for Christmas.

"I'll ask Mrs. Plumbere to watch over you when I say my prayers tonight, D," Lea had said when they last spoke, and Deirdre felt a brief rush of relief wash over her.

She could not get the Montreal numbers out of her head. They invaded her dreams every night. In that first classroom, sixty-two men had left the room. Nine women remained. He shot them all. He shot twenty-three women in all and four men who got in his way. Fourteen women dead. The worst detail of all crept back in somewhere around three a.m. Something Lea had told her on the phone. At a university in B.C., in the library this week, someone had written on the wall: "Montreal Score: Them – 0, Us – 14."

This one phrase hammered at her peace. Though she had watched victims being wheeled out of CanTech on stretchers, though she had had imaginary guns pulled on her in her own classroom, though she had been drugged and raped, Deirdre found this unconscionable graffiti – this representation of pure evil as a game score – absolutely unhinging.

When her pudding and coffee arrived, Deirdre opened the *Montreal Messenger* and read Sean Ortiz's thoughts on the massacre.

I am humbled this week because I am a man who did not know what he did not know. I figured I had the skinny on bad guys. I knew they lived in the states, clustered in New York, L.A., and the mean streets of Chicago. They carried assault rifles, shot at regular folk with a kind of barbaric whimsy, and strode off into the night with impunity.

I could not have been more wrong. The bad guys live here too. In Canada, in our cosmopolitan Montreal.

And I was woefully naïve about something else: how real is women's fear of men. Sure, I had observed it, women holding their purses close to their bodies in big cities; women carrying their car keys aimed in front of them like a weapon; some refusing to enter an elevator unless another woman boards as well. I saw these things, but I never saw them in the way I cannot help but see them now – as part of a wide, wide spectrum of violence against women. Now that a man barely in his twenties assassinated fourteen of our most promising engineering students – all of them women – I cannot look away.

Everything changed when that man fired that first round into Noelle, a CanTech student, because she was female. Naiveté is a luxury item we no longer stock in Canada. It is time to assess, to garner a place on the psychiatrist's couch of life, and to look carefully and compassionately at what we have wrought.

Am I blaming men for this, for the actions of one man? No. And yes. For days I've read about the CanTech massacre as an isolated act, the vengeance of a disturbed man. I've read about this being a crime against humanity, not against women in particular. I've read about how so many, among them politicians and university administrators, simply cannot understand why the killer did what he did. While all the time, police have been in possession of a suicide note that purportedly declares that the killer killed because he hated feminists. All the time, we have known that he shouted that in the classrooms as he gunned down our daughters.

This is not a time for confusion. The sun is shining brightly on a very ugly truth: one half of us is hated, deeply and venomously, because of our sex. We are insulted by sexist jokes, pornographic photographs, chilled work environments, and open hostility. And now we – that half of us – are murdered in our own classrooms. Because we are women.

I am not confused about my pronouns. No, no. I am he, but today I am we. I stand with these women, with the fourteen killed, with the several injured, with the nineteen targeted but left to live – in fear and confusion. I want to be part of the healing, if healing is possible.

This was not a random act of violence. It was not an isolated act. It did not take place on U.S. soil. It is unthinking and unconscionable to believe so. This was misogyny, pure and simple and brutal. Women have known it for years, and they've tried to tell us – with their words and with their actions, with their purses held tight, with their keys poised, with their hesitancy at elevator doors.

Let us listen to them, so we might save their lives and our humanity.

Deirdre let her breath out, grabbed at her napkin, dabbed her eyes. Morrison's began to fill up with students and the six ancient men who claimed the booth in the corner every morning. She stuffed the column in her bag. She would photocopy it to send to Lea, maybe write to this dear Sean Ortiz.

# 36.

THE POLICE HAD STILL not released the killer's suicide note. Jenean was furious. This was a huge ethical breach. If they could leak the names on the killer's hit list to the press but not the letter that explained the motive behind the murders, something was wrong. When she had gone to the police station, they had refused to give her the letter, though her name was on the list. Citing "security reasons" and fear of a copycat crime, they said it was dangerous to publicize what this "crazy man" had in his mind.

Jenean had to know exactly that – what he had in his mind. She would fight for that letter. The police administrator had listened as Jenean told him she would pursue a hearing for access of information using *Mot du Jour's* attorneys. Still, he had not budged.

It was to be a day of moral dilemmas and hair-pulling frustration. Before she had even gotten out of her pajamas, Jenean read John Ward's column in the *Montreal Messenger* on the media. Readers had been outraged at the front-page photo on Thursday's early edition, Ward wrote, the one of the dead student in the CanTech cafeteria, the very one that still haunted Jenean.

On the night of the massacre, Ward wrote, the photographer persuaded a few male students to boost him to the sill of one of the windows of the CanTech cafeteria. Through a six-inch sliver of window, he shot more than a dozen frames of the murdered woman in her cafeteria chair. Editors at the *Messenger* had been intent on using a photograph of an ambulance crew carrying a stretcher until the film arrived. They changed their minds. One of the cafeteria pictures in colour was slotted onto the front page – it covered almost the entire page. The photographer had gotten the only shots in the cafeteria. No other Montreal paper had such a photo.

The fallout was rough. The paper had received hundreds of phone calls from angry readers. What if her parents recognized her, they had shouted. Imagine how they would feel? Jenean was not insensitive to this. She could well imagine that seeing one's child on that cover would be wounding. More wounding than her actual loss, however? More wounding than the atrocity of one brazen man killing women because he could? No, Jenean would have stood staunchly by that editorial decision to print the photo, to put it on the front page. Canada had to see, *really see,* what misogyny looked like at its most malevolent. It looked like this. Yet, who could bear to look at this poor unsuspecting woman in her cafeteria chair whose life had been vibrant moments before it was stolen.

*What have we come to?* Jenean wondered, as she closed the paper without reading further than page A-4. Images and phrases from the newspaper she had just closed whirled about in her brain. She recalled the photo of Noelle taken from her hospital bed. This was the young woman who had dared to speak back to the killer. "We are only women studying engineering. We are only women in engineering who want to live a normal life." She had told him they were not necessarily feminists and did not have anything against men. The killer had not been interested. He had shot, and a bullet grazed her temple, and she had undergone surgery for bullet wounds in her leg.

Who could blame that student for claiming they were not feminists with a semi-automatic rifle pointed in her face? No one. Yet these young engineering students were clearly benefitting from the arduous work of feminists who had come before them. And still, they had died as feminists. The boundaries blurred again and again, and Jenean felt overloaded with ambiguity. Even national boundaries were bleary. In interview after interview, people were calling this an American crime. One quote stuck with Jenean: "We thought this kind of thing happened in places like New York and California, not in kinder, gentler Canada ... not in Montreal, not in our town, which most of us like to think is the finest place to live in the country." Another said, "Not even in the worst murder rampage in the most savage corner of America were the victims selected because they were members of one sex."

Try as she might, Jenean could not get the news stories out of her head. One paper reported that on the late-night hot line shows since the CanTech shootings there were threats phoned in to the offices of women's organizations. There was absolutely no reason, one person interviewed said, "That what happened on Dec. 6 shouldn't happen again. I wonder if women in this town will ever look at the men in the streets in the same way again." *How true,* Jenean thought. *Hard to say.* She knew this for sure: but for hello and goodbye, she had not talked to Bart and he had not talked to her since the massacres

The arrow that stuck in the bull's eye of Jenean's heart was the statement made in one of the last articles she read by Professor Paula Jenkins of U. of Ontario. "The chilling thing about the CanTech massacre of women is that it was not a senseless slaughter ... ghastly as it is. It makes sense in a society that condones hatred and fear of women.... It's all part of a continuum of fear and anger and hatred of women gaining power in our society." There was no denying what Paula Jenkins had said. Jenean had said it herself in her last column. Seeing it there, in black and white, in another woman's words, confirmed her thinking in a way that was at once heartening and sickening. If this were true, that the killings were part of a continuum of hatred of women, where had feminism gone wrong? How could their tireless work on behalf of *one half of the world's population* have ended so bloodily?

She made herself a bowl of oatmeal with walnuts and turned on the television. Last night the owners of the store from which the killer had bought the gun talked about how polite he was, how all of his paperwork was in order, how he knew what he wanted. Nothing in his demeanor warranted undue attention. Just another assault-weapon purchase. Today, more talk of guns and bullets, more defensiveness. It was not the gun's fault, not the gun maker's fault, not the seller's fault. Jenean had to look away after five minutes but not before ballistics experts pointed to diagrams about trajectories and held .223 bullets in their hands, allowing cameras to zoom in. Jenean stared at the bullet. It was about two inches long and had a tiny copper tip. Two experts from the Canadian military explained that the cartridge was made up of a copper-jacketed bullet the size of the tip of a ballpoint pen encased in a brass case. They held up both pieces for viewer clarity.

Jenean washed her bowl in the kitchen and stood at the window for a long time, pondering the snow-covered ground outside her window, the barest of tree branches arching toward the clouded sky. When she returned from the kitchen, the camera had moved to a fat man with a goatee wearing camouflage gear and holding a Sturm-Ruger Mini-14, just like the murder weapon.

"Welcome, Colonel Jacques LaFramboise," said the young news anchor. "Thank you for being here with us this morning to help us understand a bit about the murder weapon used to kill fourteen at CanTech on Wednesday and to wound another nine."

"Thank you, Anton," the Colonel said, moving only his lips and staring straight ahead.

"What our experts were just telling us is that for each shot, the trigger has to be pulled, all of the mechanics just described happen very, very quickly, and then the gun is ready to be shot again. Is this so?"

"Yes," said the Colonel. "Since this is not a fully automatic weapon, the trigger must be pulled for each shot. Each shot is a fresh load."

*A fresh load,* Jenean thought. *Like laundry, everyday clean clothes, floating in the springtime breeze. A fresh load. Good God.*

A representative from Sturm, Ruger & Company was speaking. "We produce high-quality firearms for the commercial sporting market. Ruger offers consumers more than seventy products with hundreds of variations. That is to say, twenty-five product lines."

"And one of your weapons, the Mini-14, was responsible for the deaths of fourteen students on Wednesday..." began Anton.

"Hold on. Let's be crystal clear here, Anton. Our weapon was not responsible for anything. One lunatic from Montreal killed those people...."

"Indeed," said Anton. "I stand corrected, sir, but allow me to ask...."

It was all too predictable.

What about the dead women? Who were they? Where did they live? What did they do and say and wear and think? She watched their photographs float by on the screen, every half hour, but she wanted to know their stories. Her heart broke for fourteen women she did not know. Who could tell her about them? Jenean went to the window in her living room that looked out onto a field of white snow. A slick of hard ice covered the softer white beneath. Behind the clouds, the sun attempted to shine through but could only provide a muted glow. The world outside that window was albino, pure white but for twiggy trees and distant paved roads. It was whitewashed like Tom Sawyer's fence. Alabaster and tumescent like Moby Dick.

The literary allusions kept coming, hard and fast, and Jenean knew what that meant. She was emotionally overloaded. It had been that way since university. When times got tough, when she had written as much as was humanly possible into her diary, when she had talked her issues through with countless girlfriends, when she had nowhere else to go with her emotions, she read fiction. Not just a novel or a short story, but dozens of novels and short stories. Jenean read fiction like her father drank single-malt scotch: constantly and with a high-mindedness. Henry Belisle drank only the best single malt from Waterford crystal tumblers. He took considerable umbrage at the fact that the Sainte Magdalene distillery, built, famously, on the site of a twelfth-century hospital built by the Knights Templar to treat lepers and later replaced by the Sainte Magdalene convent, closed due to overproduction in 1983. This forced Henry to carry on with his second-favourite, Laphroaig, which he drank in the den, a room lined with books and antique curios. He did this every day, from the minute he got home from work as a commercial banker to the minute he fell asleep in his plump leather chair. His pattern never varied. Jenean's did not either.

She had read all the way through Balzac's *La Comédie Humaine* when Mathéo left to take a teaching job in Mankato, Minnesota. She and he had both known he was never coming back, and that she was never going there. But they had not spoken it aloud. They had carried on as if he were going to a conference. He had left some clothes in the bureau, left the framed photograph of his parents' wedding day on his dresser. He had not disconnected the cable service, which was in his name alone. But they had both known. To deal with the knowing, Jenean had read all ninety volumes of Balzac's fiction including V.S. Pritchett's biography of Balzac. There she had learned that the rotund Frenchman ate a small meal at five or six in the evening, slept until midnight, then rose and wrote through the night, consuming bottomless cups of black coffee. He was known to work fifteen hours at a time. Once, famously, he claimed to have worked for forty-eight hours, resting for only three hours in-between.

Jenean jolted from her reverie at the window when she heard the news anchor ask, "The question to ask, then, is who is the real victim in this tragedy?" She sank into the sofa. What was this? Three men sat at a horseshoe-shaped desk. All were dressed in suits. No more camouflage. No more guns. According to the titles ascribed them, one was a psychiatrist and the other was a homicide expert and professor from Toronto. They were discussing the gunman, as they had been discussing the killer constantly since reporters had excavated the tawdry details of his life.

"What we know is that the twenty-five-year-old gunman was abused by his father," said the psychiatrist. "Children of abuse, unless they receive some form of clinical therapy, all too often become abusers themselves. This young man's father was an immigrant from North Africa and a wartime survivor who allegedly beat his wife and children. If they sang too loud – the killer had one sibling – or if they left their toys out, the father might become enraged. The father's respect for women was nil. Men, he believed, were innately superior. That was made manifestly clear in his household, and one can surmise it is what led to the divorce of the killer's parents."

The professor jumped in: "Indeed, the mother took the children and left the father when the boy was just seven. Seven." Looking down to check his notes, the professor repeated the word "seven" yet again, adjusting his burgundy-striped tie, and looking concerned.

"Yes," said Anton. "So the mother took them when they were still so young. Can the father's violence still have a profound influence given that the children lived apart from their father for most of their lives?"

"Ahhh, Anton," interrupted the psychiatrist, "those formative years, those years of imprinting, children are most vulnerable...."

*Are you kidding me,* thought Jenean. *Now the guy who killed fourteen women is the victim?* Frustrated, she scuffled into the kitchen to make coffee but decided against it. The television was too rife with guns and ammo. She would take a long walk in the cold with Gertrude, shake off the frustration, and think about fourteen women who would no longer take a walk.

# 37.

I N THE HAZEUR HOUSEHOLD, no one watched the television reporting. No one read a newspaper. Sybille's family existed, simply existed, in the days after Marin's murder. Father Brunton was there every day. Madame Hazeur and he were long-time friends.

"You must decide what you will do, Estelle. How shall we honour our Marin?" he asked, as the family sat in the living room of their mother's home early in the morning. Natalee held her mother's hand, while Hilaire and Sybille gazed out the window at the sky white with looming snow.

"The university is offering a public wake today, but some of the families will hold their own private vigils. Then there is the funeral at Sainte-Mère...." Father Brunton offered up these thoughts, expecting no immediate answers. When Estelle spoke, everyone in the room turned. She had said so little in the days since her daughter's death. She looked so frail. All of them had feared this grievous loss of her daughter would crush her. This time, when she spoke, it was without tears. Perhaps she had no more tears to cry in that moment.

"We will go to the university today. We will see Marin. We will be with the families of the other girls. It is the right thing," she said, looking at each of them briefly before lowering her eyes to the rosary beads in her hands. They were Marin's beads, the ones she received on her First Communion from their grandmother. Estelle had been clinging to them since

Thursday morning. Sybille could not imagine where she had found them after all these years.

Sybille thought to make another pot of coffee when her mother cleared her throat. She had not said all she had to say.

"Please, Father, we will hold two funerals, as we discussed the other day. We will be at Sainte-Mère on Monday with the other families. Then we will be in the parish church, with our friends and family. Thank you for being so kind as to arrange this, we are so grateful to...." Estelle drifted then, let her words linger in the air. She looked down, fingering the rosary beads with one hand, running the tip of thumb of her other hand over the crucifix, over and over the corpse of Christ.

The last four days had seemed both preternaturally long and numbingly identical. There had been more coffee and flowers and baked goods. There had been talking. Phone calls from family in France, friends in the U.S., neighbours. Mostly, they had all sat quiet, crying together in the living room. Trey had been there every day, silent in an overstuffed chair near the window, holding a needlepoint pillow to his chest, and accepting only black coffee.

Now, family members got up to get ready to go to the public wake at the university, leaving Sybille and Trey alone in the living room. He leaned forward in his chair. Sybille looked at him, and her heart sank. He was shattered. She reached out and placed her hand on his forearm.

He looked up at her, held her gaze.

"Sybille. If the person you were looking for all of your life came to you, and she was beautiful and you loved your life together and you were best friends, and then, then she was gone, and she cannot be, cannot be ... retrieved. How, then, Sybille, can my life be retrieved?" His eyes begged her to answer, to tell him how to go on. She did not know how to go on. She had no answers. She held out her hand to Trey. He took it and held her hand in both of his. For a long time they sat this way, all healing words out of reach. When

Marianne came into the room and said they were ready to go to the university, Trey let go of Sybille's hand, and they both stood. *He is dying of a broken heart,* Sybille thought. Marin had opened the world for both of them, and they were in it alone now.

Sybille held her mother's elbow, as her brother Hilaire dropped them off at the front of the main building of the Saint Laurent University in the Pavilion. It was made of the same yellow brick as CanTech. At 10:00 a.m., the sky reflected nothing. Grey clouds hung over Montreal, blotting out sunlight. They made their way up the wide granite steps and entered through the enormous centre doors. The school had arranged for this private viewing, a two-hour period, for the families and classmates of the victims at the Chapel of Repose, under the tower of the university's main building. The foyer was elegant with marble floors, thick brown marble pillars, and polished woodwork. Chandeliers with concentric circular features hung low and blushed a golden light.

In anticipation of a massive crowd, administrators closed all parking lots to the public and made an appeal for visitors to take public transportation, arranging for extra Metro trains to the university station. Dignitaries, including the Prime Minister, would arrive to pay their respects and would be ushered through the university's pavilion after the families' private viewing. Citizens would be directed through a side entrance from which they would move, ever so slowly, down the long corridors, past walls bearing condolences from all over the world. There were letters from mothers, sympathy cards from organizations, and artwork from women and children. Crayoned drawings of doves and angels and daisies blanketed the walls. Oil and watercolour paintings hung from brass nails. There was an announcement that fourteen memorial trees were to be planted in Jerusalem. So many messages of sadness and understanding and hope that they could not be read in their entirety by the passersby.

This morning, however, was a time for the families only. The crowds would come later.

The coffins of all but five of the slain women were displayed along the perimeter of the hall. The other families were holding private vigils. For the families present in the Grand Hall, this was a moment of cruel reckoning. They moved about slowly, greeting each other sombrely, often without words but with the grasping of hands and the embracing of shoulders, each group seeking out and finding the wooden box that held their loved one.

Sybille guided her mother slowly to Marin's casket. Her siblings followed. Trey came last. Marin lay there, so still. She wore her favourite dress, the one she had worn to Trey's sister's wedding. It was deep turquoise velvet with a dropped rolled neckline and cap sleeves. Sybille remembered that a delicate underslip of turquoise sateen fell an inch or so below the velvet hem, giving the dress a look Sybille and Marin liked to call *diaphane,* a word the sisters had used as often as possible. They had purchased *diaphane* curtains for their first apartment. They had noticed their beloved father's hair was becoming *diaphane* in the year before he died. These memories distracted Sybille from the actuality of what she saw there, what her poor mother saw there.

Sybille's mother kissed Marin on the cheek, rested her head against Marin's. Her tears fell onto Marin's hair, yet she remained perfectly quiet, the grieving mother. The others stood alongside Marin on the other side of the casket. All gazed into her face, all held their shattered emotions together.

Though her friend Madeline had attempted comfort by offering that Marin had died quickly, suddenly, without knowing pain, Sybille now knew differently. *My little sister looks like an old woman*, she said to herself. All of the nine women looked this way. The pearl-white coffins, each with rose trim and three gold handles on the sides, surrounded and suffused with bouquets of fragrant flowers – roses, daisies, carnations, tiger lilies – contrasted too sharply. The dead could not be prettied up. Sybille took her time, examined each of their faces. It was all the same face. These nine died in fear and pain. Sybille saw it there and could never forget. At least the caskets would be closed by the time the public arrived to pass by. A pearl white box, a carnation, a day lily, masked a gruesome reality.

Sybille was the first to break away. She wanted to greet all of the families, to pay her respects to Marin's classmates before the public was allowed in. The first in line of coffins was that of Stella. A white teddy bear sat beside a basket of roses with a crucifix perched among the blossoms. Sybille learned that Stella had lived in a small apartment in Montreal. She had had a job interview scheduled for December 7. She had been engaged to Mark who stood by her casket and kept repeating, "She was shot in the last class she would ever take before graduation. The last class ever...."

Chantal, the only victim to be stabbed to death, came next. Sybille had met Chantal once when she came to celebrate Marin's birthday a year ago. Her nickname was Geber. Marin had spoken about her just Tuesday, told Sybille that she and Renee and Stephan and Chantal were the last team to present in their Materials class. Sybille had read that Chantal was presenting when the killer entered the classroom and began firing. Marin and Renee and Stephan had already done their part of the presentation and were seated again.

Sybille held the hand of Chantal's father, a firefighter who was on duty the night of the massacre and part of the emergency response, only to learn his beloved Chantal was among the victims. That classroom tableau, his child, would never be exorcised from his memory, but he bore up well today under the strain, telling Sybille how sorry he was, how highly Chantal had spoken of her teammates, and of Marin in particular. "The ever bubbly Marin," he said.

Chantal's boyfriend stood next to her casket with his arm

draped around the far end, as if around her, holding her photo in his hands.

"She is beautiful. Chantal is beautiful," Sybille said to him and then could say no more.

Sybille stepped outside and into the hallway for a drink of water after kissing Chantal's father on both cheeks. She needed to breathe, to regroup. This was a wretched business to grieve publically, to witness your own grief mirrored back to you nine times over. Were she alone, she would have abandoned the entire thing, gone home, and stayed there. But her mother and family were there. Marin was there. She would take a lesson from the stalwart firefighter who found his daughter dead, an unimaginable horror. As she was returning to the hall, Sybille passed a group of women holding plastic cups of water. "It's not just women's problem," said one woman who pulled the collar of her red plaid coat closer to her throat. "It's men's problem – they're the ones with the problem." The others nodded but remained quiet. Sybille passed them and entered the great hall again.

The coffin of Veronique was next to Chantal's. Veronique, a first-year student, had been eating dinner in the cafeteria, waiting for her husband to join her, when she was shot. He had been in the cafeteria line to pay for his meal when the chaos broke out. When police had finally allowed him back inside to find his wife, she was dead. The husband told his story over and over to anyone who came upon his wife's white casket. He clung to the story of his wife's last minutes as if to a buoy. Sybille listened, hugged him, moved on.

Renee had been about to graduate. Her father stood at his daughter's side motionless, expressionless, though Sybille noted tears falling slowly down his cheeks. She touched his arm gently. Simone's casket was the simplest. One pink rose lay atop, and an elderly woman with white braids coiled around her head in soft loops rested her hand on the rose's stem. She looked up as Sybille approached. Their eyes met briefly, and Sybille touched her hand. "She was only twenty-two," the woman said so quietly, Sybille almost could not hear. "We had her for twenty-two years. I wanted so many more."

"I know. I, too, wanted more. I am so sorry." The woman's gaze lowered, and Sybille stepped away.

Next to Marin was Andrea, who had been in her final year of mechanical engineering and planning to do her Master's degree immediately after. She had several job offers but was leaning toward accepting the one from a company based near Ottawa. Henriette's father sat in a chair by her casket. Sybille spoke quietly to him. He looked at her, but Sybille was not sure he saw her. He spoke only once, saying, "She was killed in her school. Shot. Shot. My child. For what?"

Before she made her way to the last, Sybille watched as a group of young women dropped little bouquets of carnations in front of the coffin. It belonged to Gabrielle. At her coffin tarried the editor of the *Montreal Messenger*. Gabrielle used to give swimming lessons to their daughter. She had been a second-year student in mechanical engineering. In a gush of words, her mother told Sybille that Gabrielle had sung in a professional choir and loved to play racquetball and swim. "She was that rare thing: smart, strong, sweet, kind," the weeping mother said. "At the university, I identified her body. My husband is dead these seven years. It was the two of us, Gabrielle and I, who did everything together. I kissed her goodbye. They let me stay with her for a bit. I held her. She was so cold, so beautiful. She was my life." When Sybille put her hand on the mother's shoulder to say goodbye, she took Sybille's and held it tight. The look on that mother's face pummeled Sybille's soul, and she was forced to nod and walk away.

Ten thousand Quebec residents and visitors lined up outside the Saint Laurent University chapel to view the caskets of the murdered women. Steaming breath rose in the sub-zero air. For eight hours, mourners passed by the caskets of the women killed four days earlier. A light snow was falling at eight p.m.

when viewers were told that no more visitors would be allowed. A field of flowers sprouted on the steps to the building. Someone had placed a handmade card in the snow nearby. It read: "My mother still has her daughter. I grieve for the fourteen who do not."

Sybille knelt to read the card, as she was escorting her mother out of the building. She nodded and the tears came again. She looked up, through the tallest of overhanging lamps near the entrance to the building. Slow flakes fell, one at a time, glistening in the streaming light, coming and coming, incrementally, and blanketing Montreal's grief.

# 38.

VERY EARLY ON THE MORNING of the state funeral for nine of the fourteen women, Jenean heard the phone ringing while she was in the shower. She did not rush. Whoever it was would call back if it were important. She let the hot water wash over her, as she imagined what the scene would be like at Sainte-Mère. The Prime Minister would be there and tons of politicians. Cameras, microphones. The curious, the mourning, the families, the dead women. Sainte-Mère was enormous, but would it hold all those who longed to be there? She heard the phone ring again just as she stepped out of the shower. This time she wrapped a towel around her and went to the kitchen to answer it.

"Hello," she said.

"Hello. Is this Jenean Belisle, the writer?" a man's voice asked in English.

"*Oui*," she said, wary. Who called a writer so early in the morning and at home?

"Well, Jenean Belisle, if you want to interview the CanTech murderer after his death, interview me," he said. Jenean started.

"Who is this? This is not funny," she said, louder than she intended.

"I am serious. If you want to understand why he did it, shot those women, interview me. I will tell you. I would do it too."

"How did you get my home number?" she asked.

"I called the paper, *Mot du Jour*. They gave it to me. I said

266

I had an important story for you," he said.

Jenean's mind was racing. "Why me? Why tell this story to me?" she asked, attempting to assess the threat this man posed over the phone.

"You are a writer. You were on the infamous hit list. I imagine you, more than others, want to understand how he thinks," he said, impatient now.

Before she could stop herself, Jenean said, "Okay. Where shall I meet you?

"This morning at eight a.m. La Belle Café at 300 Maisonneuve. Do you know it?"

"I do," she said. "I will be there." She hung up when she heard the line click off on his end.

*What am I doing?* she thought. *Am I crazy? I need to be at that funeral by ten-thirty. This can take no more than an hour. Is this guy dangerous? Of course he is; he said he would do the same as the killer. But he won't do anything in a café, in public?*

Bottom line, she had to know. She was desperate to know the mind of the man who had said he wanted to kill her, who had killed fourteen women in cold blood and wished he had time to kill more. She left a message on Clara's machine telling her what she was doing, when she would be in touch, what to do if she were not in touch. She left Clara both Florian's number at *Mot du Jour* and Bart's work number. She dressed, quickly applied makeup, unearthed her black pumps, and left the house with her tape recorder and a new notebook in hand.

He would not give his name. He had ordered coffee for them both before she got there, and the waitress had arrived with a mug of ink-black coffee just as Jenean removed her coat and sat across from him in the crowded café on the busy Maisonneuve. She took out her recorder. He agreed to have his voice recorded, so long as his name was not revealed, and he was not revealing it. Jenean opened her notebook, sipped some coffee, and looked the man in the eye.

He was about fifty years old with dark hair, heavily greyed. There was scant balding at his pate, which she noticed when she entered the café, before he rose to greet her. Gentlemanly, she thought. He was nothing special, but certainly no schlub. Ordinary, really. Unsophisticated. He wore blue jeans and a long-sleeved blue top of some heavy cotton fabric. He was a working-class man who had an air of the old fashioned about him. From time to time, he stretched out his legs and winced quietly, as though hard labour had left him with arthritis.

What he had said on the phone was seared into her brain: "If you want to interview the CanTech murderer, interview me." He looked at her. They remained this way for a full minute before he began. Once he started, there was little stopping. Jenean took notes and listened. This was his show.

"I understand the feelings that man had in that engineering school. I have them. I hate feminists too. They have ruined my life too." He paused, watching her as she took down his words.

She looked up from her notes, nodded for him to continue. The café was chock full of customers, but none paid them any attention. He stretched his legs, pulled up his sleeves to his elbows, crossed his arms in front of him and continued.

"My ex was a feminist. A bitch. She wanted it all. Thought she deserved it all. I was an idiot. I gave her everything, but it wasn't enough, never fucking enough. I told her we should have a joint checking account. After all, we're living together in a nice apartment. We both have jobs. I had asked her to marry me that Christmas, and she said she loved me and that we would definitely get married but that we should wait until she was finished school. She was a history major at Saint Laurent. So, I said we should get a joint account, start saving to buy a house."

He stopped speaking, clamped his lips together and shook his head from side to side a half-dozen times. Suddenly, he blew air out from his closed lips, letting off steam. He uncrossed his arms, dropped them to his sides, then re-crossed them in front of his abdomen.

"'No,' she said. She fucking said 'no'. Joint accounts were not the way modern couples did things. Women needed their own money, needed to maintain their independence even if they were in relationships. She actually said this shit, probably quoting from one of her feminist history books. Jesus, she pissed me off."

Again, he shook his head side to side and gritted his teeth. Jenean waited, refrained from taking a sip of coffee lest he get more distracted than he was. She nodded to encourage him. This seemed to work.

"Anyway ... she had complete control – of everything. We had sex when *she* wanted to have sex. If she wasn't in the mood, tough luck, Charlie. My needs did not matter. At all. She went out with her friends when she wanted. When she was home, she was always studying or writing papers. Forget it if you think she cooked one stupid-ass meal a week."

He uncrossed his arms and leaned forward, looking intently at Jenean. He spoke rapidly and his breathing matched. He was ramping up, getting louder.

"One night, don't I come home late from work, and there she is, her highness, sitting on the couch with three friends, two of them guys. One of them is sitting in my chair. They all look happy, say hello to me, happy to meet me. They offer leftover pizza and beer. There must have been fifteen empty bottles on the coffee table and one lousy piece of pepperoni left in a damned greasy box."

"One of the guys leans forward, rubs Ruth's – that was her name, Ruth." Jenean notices that he spits this last "Ruth" out like something toxic. He continues, "This guy rubs Ruth's back, says she is the best, that he loves studying with her, but he has to go. The others have to go too. They all hug and laugh and make these 'in' jokes and look at me with this look, you know that look that says, why-the-hell-is-she-with-a-loser-like-you, and then they all leave. This is the last straw. I snap. 'What the hell is this?' I ask Ruth. 'This mess? These people? Is this how it is going to be all the time now. Guys in my house, touching you all over, *loving* to *study* with you so much? What do you take me for, Ruth?'"

"She looks at me, this cold look. 'I am in college,' she says. 'These are my friends. We were studying. We might study again. In fact, we will study again whenever we want. You will have to either get used to it or leave,' and she turned to walk out of the room."

He was breathing so quickly now that he had to take a break. He rolled his head and shoulders, stretched his legs, and released his fingers, which had been cramped into fists. Jenean put down her pen, and she picked up her mug. They both needed a recess. When he had calmed and was able to speak again, he resumed.

"I grabbed her by the arm, pulled her back into the room. Made her face me. 'What the fuck do you think you are doing, Ruth Eleanor Jameson?' I used her full name. I was pissed. 'This is my house too. A little fucking consideration is what you owe me. Do you hear?'

"She pulled away. I held on tighter. 'Let me go,' she demanded. 'You are a loser, a jerk, and we are done,' she said. 'We are so totally done.'"

He picked up his coffee and drank a gulp, finished the mug, and waved to the waitress for a refill.

"She left that night. But she wrote me a letter. In it, she wrote out a list of feminist books she thought I should read, so that I would not fuck up my next relationship like I did this one. She said I had to learn that women are now equal to men. That they can have separate and full lives and still be in love. That the world had changed since the days of dinner on the table at five and joint accounts."

"She thinks I am an idiot. When really, what I am is pissed off. At her and at her books and at all the people who think like her. What, please tell me, was wrong with the way it was? She makes it sound like a wife making dinner for her family is slavery. Like sharing money is primeval. What the fuck has happened to the world? When did women get so equal that they need to crush men's balls in order to be free? This is wrong. This is what makes men like me, men like that gunman, do what they do."

He slammed his hand down on the table, shaking it. Jenean jumped. Her coffee sloshed onto her notebook. "That is your fucking story," he said. "Have a happy funeral." He stood, slapped a five-dollar bill onto the table, and walked out of the café into the freezing December.

Only after giving him enough time to get far away, did Jenean turn her tape recorder off, stash her notebook into her bag, pull on her coat, and leave as well. She was trembling. Her head was pounding. She had just enough time to get to Sainte-Mère, but all she wanted to do was go home and cry. This was no crazy lunatic madman. This was a guy you passed on the street who looked like any other man who harboured in his heart a hatred of women so deep that it was poisoning him. How many more of him were there?

# 39.

S YBILLE SAT AT THE KITCHEN TABLE with her mother early in the morning. They would bury Marin today. They spoke little at first. Sybille was deep in thought, reviewing all that had been said and seen at the wake yesterday. The framed photos of the young women had hung on walls of the study area. All of the thousands of letters and telegrams, even faxes, had been stapled to coloured paper on the walls. There had been cards, poems, banners, even children's colourings and some paintings. Montreal artist Charlene Pereault, who used to work at CanTech, had done an enormous painting of the fourteen women with doves and flowers in the foreground, set against a deep indigo, a work resplendent with compassion and heartache. The messages and sympathies had covered every square centimetre from floor to ceiling. Shared grief from around the world. One student, Hanna, had arranged it all, requested the photos from the families.

Hanna had been at CanTech on the night of the shooting, and she had told Sybille, "I was in the student study room. We were just down the hall from the cafeteria. Someone came in and told us there was a guy with a gun. We shut the door, turned out the lights, and stayed completely quiet. We heard gun shots. It sounded like planks of wood falling on the floor. We did not move, stayed there forty minutes before the police came and escorted us out."

"Did you see anything on your way out?" Sybille had asked.
"Nothing. Only later on TV. One does not believe it at first.
I did not want to believe it. On the news later that night, I
learned all that had happened."

Sybille had been touched by the young woman's story and
her diligence in arranging the photo and letter memorial for
her sister and the others. Sybille told her mother what Hanna
had said about the care she took in arranging the CanTech
memorial. Madame Hazeur said she would send the "lovely
girl" a thank-you note when she felt up to it.

When her mother left to get ready for the funeral, she and
Trey sat together in the living room. Sybille picked up a well-
worn book – *Out of Solitude* by Henri J. M. Nouwen – that
sat on an end table by her mother's novenas and rosary beads.
Her mother had had this book since her father died years ago.
Sybille had never opened it, but she did now, turning to a page
that held a bookmark with the Sacred Heart of Jesus on it. She
read the passage underlined in red ink:

> The friend who can be silent with us in a moment of
> despair or confusion, who can stay with us in an hour of
> grief and bereavement, who can tolerate not knowing,
> not curing, not healing and face with us the reality of
> our powerlessness, that is the friend who cares.

Sybille read it again. Then she touched Trey lightly on the
forearm. "Trey, listen to this." She read the passage to him.
He nodded and closed his eyes.

Sybille wondered who her mother's friend was. Was it God?
Jesus? Who was her own friend? Certainly, Madeline had been
a constant since that awful night at the university, calling and
bringing over lasagna and muffins. Otherwise, she supposed the
person she had spent the most time with in the last four days
was Trey. Almost always silent together, sometimes he spoke
and she listened. Sometimes, it worked the other way around.

One day her head ached so desperately that she remained in the twin bed upstairs in her mother's home until suppertime. One day Trey had lashed out in such anger that he rushed out the door and walked for three hours. "I didn't want anyone to see me that way," he had explained when he returned later that night. "I cannot make sense of it, Sybille," he had said when they were alone again after the others had gone to bed. "If I can't make sense of it, how can I survive?"

"Would that I knew, Trey," she had responded, taking his hand. "There is no sense. This is just hell. The only hope is that nothing lasts forever, so this cannot last forever."

"I want to believe that," he had said, removing his hand from hers, standing up and putting on his coat. "I need to go home now. I know I can't sleep, but I need to be alone. I need to be in our bedroom. I dread it, Sybille, but I need to be where she was ... with her books and her sweaters ... those new sneakers she just got...." Trey had given her a quick hug and left by the front door. He had not returned until the next morning.

Sybille had not known Marin had gotten new sneakers. They had not talked on Wednesday, just on Tuesday. She did not know about the sneakers, but they made her weep now. She held onto her mother's book, sat upright in the chair that was once her father's favourite, and she wept for those new sneakers.

# 40.

FIRST THING MONDAY MORNING, Deirdre read about the public wake over rice pudding at Morrison's. It was heartbreaking, but it was the impromptu interviews that staff writer Shalene Rogers did with young women outside the school that caused Deirdre to stop eating. A nineteen-year-old student in Montreal told Shalene that what happened on Wednesday had changed her life forever.

"I cannot imagine going back into my school. Even though the shooting did not happen there, I am afraid. I am a girl, and classrooms are not safe for us."

Shalene asked her whether this was going to change how she felt about men.

"It already has," she said. "My boyfriend pushed me around just once, but I stayed with him. When this happened – this massacre, I said that if he ever so much as touched me again, I would leave. He said that if I was going to go all rabid bitch on him just because some other guy played hardball with some engineers, he was leaving anyway, and he left. And that is damned good."

A woman named Wanda Westering told Shalene that she was attending her book club at a church near Laval when a priest referred to her as a *"fille."*

"I'm twenty-nine years old, " she said. "I'm a woman."

"Maybe they should send you up to Saint Laurent University," the priest had said. "That will toughen you up."

Deirdre put the paper down. It seemed to her that the murders at CanTech had unleashed all of this pent-up hatred for women. Had it been hidden in plain sight all along? Had she looked it square in the face before the massacre and somehow not recognized it? Not recognized it in Craig? Even as bad as the No Means No campaign was, she had not experienced the boys with the nasty signs as hateful; they were more like immature jerks. Deirdre chalked that up to boys being immature and idiotic at first. But these past few days with the all ranting men on the radio and the kinds of comments she read every day in the paper, revealed a new reality.

She had not known these things before coming to university. The story Mrs. Longre had told her about her experience in engineering school now had a whole new context. The things Ellen and Roberta said made more sense. The rape should have solidified it for Deirdre, but she worked overtime not to turn her rage at Craig into rage at all men. She thought of her father and uncles and the boys in her classes, especially Ben and Whit. Still, the kinds of comments that kept coming in the wake of CanTech put Deirdre on edge, made her confused. She did not want to be afraid of all men. She folded the paper, put it into her bag, and felt more on guard than ever, as she began the walk back to campus.

# 41.

SOME THOUGHT THIS "INVITATION ONLY" state funeral in bad taste until they witnessed the throngs of people lining Rue Sainte-Mère and expanding out, sometimes five people deep at the corner of St. Suplice Street, and filling Place d'Armes Square across the street. Women were weeping, holding the hands of children bundled against the unfathomable -20 degrees Celsius. Cameras flashed, and media vans formed a cohort near the front entrance, leaving only the walkways clear. There were three thousand people at the funeral, nine hundred of these were relatives or close friends, and five hundred were CanTech students wearing white armbands and scarves as a sign of mourning. Nine of the fourteen young women killed at CanTech would share this funeral. The other five would have private funerals.

Sainte-Mère Basilica, the neo-gothic immensity, was hushed with snow and glittering entry lights when Jenean arrived to join fifty other reporters and photographers from Canada and many other countries in the second-floor balcony. Six CNTV cameramen were filming from the ground floor. In a hall downstairs from Sacré-Coeur Chapel, another two hundred reporters would watch the funeral Mass on a giant screen. The Mass would be broadcast live over loudspeakers in Place d'Armes on CNTV English and French networks. Five thousand people gathered there, one of the reporters told Jenean, as she pulled off her wool coat. Otherwise, everyone in the balcony was perfectly quiet.

Jenean was still shaken from her interview with the Can-Tech-killer clone, an interview that took nearly two hours. She needed to calm herself. She picked up a pamphlet lying on one of the seats. Completed in 1829, she read, Sainte-Mère Basilica is considered a masterpiece of the Gothic Revival style and is its most distinctive example in North America. The Irish-American architect, a Protestant from New York, was said to be so proud of his work that he converted to Catholicism so he could be buried in the church's crypt. Quebec personalities had their funerals held in this basilica, hockey's greats, former prime ministers. Sainte-Mère had been designated a site of national historical significance by the Historical Sites and Monuments Board of Canada, a place that welcomed hundreds of thousands of visitors a year, from all over the world. "Guests find peace, harmony and serenity," its literature boasted.

Jenean put the pamphlet back where she found it. Where might anyone find peace, harmony, or serenity ever again, she wondered? She closed her eyes for a few seconds. She had not slept well since the murders and felt depleted. Today's early morning interview brought her strain to an entirely new level. That Bart had not thought it important to attend the ceremony with her also contributed to her feelings of profound loss. Perhaps this ceremony would bring some measure of relief. She was just overwhelmed enough to hope for anything.

When the organ groaned and swelled, Jenean closed her eyes against the coming surge of emotion. *Pachelbel Canon in D* got to her every time, calling forth many sadnesses tucked deep inside. She recalled this music played at weddings as well, but it always struck a melancholic chord with her, and today, it felt like the perfect piece.

Jenean's mind drifted back to her Music Appreciation class in university. *Pachelbel's Canon in D* had been her professor's favourite musical text. She could hear his British accent as he explained how *Pachelbel's Canon* was like voices "conversing" above a drone-like effect that represented the endless progression of life, how it went on and on. It was both mathematical and beautiful, and it took Jenean momentarily away to safer times, when she was in university, hopeful and fearless.

When she opened her eyes, the cerulean and gold of the sanctuary shimmered. Incense wafted and mixed with the scent of the perfumed and after-shaved mourners, all scrubbed clean to bury their dead. The VIPs entered first and were seated, among them the Prime Minister, Premier, Mayor, Parti Quebecois leader, Education Minister, and Governor General. Jenean had read that the mourning families were to drive to a city parking lot at Victoria Pier this morning. From there, three city buses were bringing them to Sainte-Mère starting at 10:00 a.m.

For days, students at CanTech had helped organize the mailing of letters to all women engineers in Quebec, inviting them to attend the funeral in large numbers to serve as role models and leaders and to wear the symbolic white scarf to mark solidarity with the slain engineering students. The Quebec Order of Engineers joined in the effort and declared the day a provincial day of mourning. Jenean watched as they walked in pairs down the center aisle. There were two hundred and fifty women engineers and a host of female engineering students wearing white scarves around their arms. The Baroque music rose and fell away. Two violinists moved their bows across the strings, evoking the human melancholy that filled the basilica. Male engineering colleagues followed the infantry of engineering women. All told, they numbered so many they had to split off and fill the pews on either side of the main sanctuary.

For a moment, she felt faint, her every emotion on high alert. She took three deep breaths, recalling the words of her yoga teacher: "For all troubles, just breathe."

When the engineers were seated, the organ stopped for a moment. Everyone girded themselves against the coming funeral party. It was really too much, a house of God filled to the brim to bury its innocents. *None of us should be here,*

Jenean thought. We should be at work, at play, at school. *What had allowed this cleft in the cosmos? What human hatred so fomented that it took up arms against women?*

For one brief moment, Jenean felt a swelling despair so profound she could not breathe. She took her seat, leaned forward, pressed her head into her hands and prayed. To whom? To what? To anything that could hear a broken woman begging for mercy. In her mind's eye, she saw her heart obliterated into a powder so fine it looked like sand. *We could not have known,* she told herself. *We could never have foreseen that our work for equality would come to this. Those bullets were intended for us, the real feminists who wrote and protested, who spoke their minds, who thought our hard-won freedom would come without a cost. We should have known, but how could we know that such hate lived among us?*

Jenean felt the congregation rise to its feet even before she opened her eyes and raised her head. The organ wailed, *Baroque Funeral March in C,* the same song they played at her mother's funeral five years ago.

The families came then, one by one. Young women in coffins, followed by their mothers and fathers and lovers and beloved girlfriends and nieces and nephews, their grandmas. Everyone wept. The reporters, cameramen. Mothers' gloved hands held firm to their daughters' coffins, as if pushing a stroller, walking their girls around the block for the last time. Fathers held their other children by the shoulders. When a sister could no longer stand upright, behind her sister's coffin, her brother supported her. The procession of tormented families, the smoldering incense, the lament of the organ made for an unbearable sadness. When the music stopped, when the funeral procession was complete and all were seated in a uniform hush, the sound of grief was everywhere, in the pews, in the balcony, from the side aisles.

From their perch, Jenean and the reporters watched. Nine caskets, draped in white, filled the centre aisle of the basilica.

No one could look away. The terrible beauty of the tableau. A desperate need for understanding and healing strained at the enormous stained glass windows, at the statuary looming above, at the wooden basilica doors, being closed now by the funeral director in a charcoal suit.

Cardinal Paschal brought his palms together and bowed deeply to the congregation. He spoke then, calling on God to welcome His children home to His kingdom, invoking the Catholic deity to show mercy to the grieving families.

His words began to blur for Jenean, as the altar came into focus. She saw it then: a sea of men, the highest-ranking Roman Catholic priesthood, draped in white, filling the grand altar, an entirely male magistrate.

Jenean took it all in.

The men in white.

The women's coffins in white.

The men outnumbering the women three to one.

The men alive.

The women dead.

Sainte-Mère had separated the boys from the girls. Just as the gunman had.

Jenean leaned against the back of the pew, her breathing ragged. She was sweating, and she felt as if she might throw up. She leaned forward, keeping her head low. She did not want to look at that altar again. Was she the only one for whom the gendered symbolism was tantamount to heresy? She looked around at her tearful colleagues, looked below at the families and the snow-white coffins. She put her head between her knees and tried to pull herself together.

Suddenly, Jenean felt the congregation rising to its feet. She must have missed part of the Mass because Cardinal Paschal was rising to give the eulogy. Jenean removed her white wool blazer, and fanned herself with another pamphlet, still lightheaded.

"The moment has come to pray. Before doing so, I ask all

of you to observe a deep and total silence. The tragedy we are living through calls for silence." After a time, the Cardinal began again. "This horrible event has thrown us into dismay. At any age, death is a tragedy. Fourteen young students were brutally taken from us in the strength and beauty of their youth ... in a few minutes, all it took was the desperate and abhorrent act of another young person to destroy so many dreams, so much promise.

"We carry the cross of Jesus Christ today. Our hearts ache. We may even ask 'Why?' But we know not why. What we know is that our Lord Jesus Christ welcomed our beloved daughters into his Kingdom sooner than we, with our human understanding, would want. His is almighty timing. CanTech mourns. Canada mourns. Our great loss is incomprehensible. Yet, need we comprehend? Or need we simply reach out to the offered hand of Almighty God? Let His soothing grace ease our souls. Our daughters are in a far, far better place, a Kingdom beyond imagining. They suffer no more. His ways are inscrutable, but His mercies are for the multitudes." Cardinal Paschal brought his palms together and bowed deeply to the congregation. He resumed his seat at the pinnacle of the host of seated white men.

From the front of the basilica, a young man began to sing Schubert's "Ave Maria."

Jenean watched the men on the altar shift in their places, so too the mourners. Some raised their eyes to see grandeur and hauteur compete in the ornate ceiling. The azure aisles were buffed to a glaze. Everywhere was polished mahogany. All of the opulent materials colluding to bring the mortal eye up to the jutting spires of the altar, the ceiling's arch open, painted in placid hues. Looming thirty feet above the main sanctuary, were imposing statues: St. John the younger. St. Peter. Evangelists John, Matthew, Luke. Moses. Aaron. Abraham and Isaac. Melchizedek. Jesus.

*No female god lives here,* Jenean thought.

Highest of all is Jesus on the cross. Dying Jesus is flanked on the left by his mother Mary, on the right by his beloved apostle John, and at his feet by Magdalene. They are so still. Theirs is mourning carved into wood, inert, an ending of a life that would bring about an unforeseen and enormous beginning.

The rush of rising people snapped the mourners to attention. The song had ended. A priest came to the altar and spoke into the microphone. "Dearly beloved, let us pray." Students were shuffling in their seats, readying to carry the coffins, each coffin to be followed by family and friends to limousines and city buses that would take them to different cemeteries for private burials.

*Surely, it could not be over,* thought Jenean, though her watch indicated nearly two hours had passed. She could not reconcile it. She had heard nothing about the murdered women. Did she even hear the word "woman" mentioned once? She needed closure, comfort, hope. If she needed it, surely the families were also desperate for something. She closed her eyes against the vertigo that had plagued her throughout the funeral and dropped back into the pew, fighting her dizzying brain for consciousness.

What was that? A clicking of high heels? A woman in a blue suit with a white scarf around her neck rose from the side pews that ensconced the engineering contingent. She walked slowly, deliberately toward the altar. The priest, arms wide open, stopped. The woman kept coming. The priest dropped his arms. He looked at her. Everyone looked at her. The organ remained silent. The only sound in the entire arching basilica was of those heels, and their beat was steady, unwavering. The woman walked to the front of the basilica, turned to face the families in the rows on the left side of the church. Like the priest before her, she drew her palms together in front of her chest, and she bowed to them. She held their gaze for a time, but still, not a sound could be heard. She nodded to the mourners, then proceeded to the centre aisle of the bascilica.

She turned to face the thousands of mourners gathered there, and it seemed she was about to speak, but again, she drew her palms together and bowed slowly, gracefully to the white-robed caskets. She remained bowed for a long time, the time it took a stunned Jenean to count out fourteen beats. The woman repeated her pattern. She nodded to the caskets slowly then moved to the right pews and bowed to those families. This blue-suited woman engineer moved with the grace of flowing water. When she had acknowledged the families of the dead and the dead women themselves, she turned, faced the altar with its robed men, and bowed deeply.

The priest who had been offering a final prayer two minutes earlier, stared at the woman. She stared at him. Jenean craned her neck to see. The entire congregation craned as well. This was unlike any other Catholic Mass any of the Catholics gathered here had witnessed.

The woman walked up the burgundy carpeted steps onto the altar. Jenean took in a deep breath. *What is she doing? Oh my God.* She walked around the altar, ascending the three steps to the mahogany-and-gilt podium. She adjusted the microphone slightly, and she looked out over the crowd. She stood several feet above the priests, and she appeared but a tiny vision, until she spoke.

"Good morning, ladies and gentlemen." Her voice was like homespun cotton, soft but sturdy. "I wish you peace. I am Teresa Simard, an alumna of CanTech. I am a mechanical engineer with the firm Maurois and Simard. I am here today because, like you, my heart is broken."

The basilica was filled to capacity that morning. There was not one empty seat. Yet, there was not a sound, not a shuffle of feet, not a cough. The priest who had been praying took his seat again.

"I know it is unusual for a woman to come to the altar in this great church to offer her thoughts in her own words, particularly when Cardinal Paschal was preparing us for concluding this funeral ceremony. But I must. Today is not a day for silence. These beautiful young women were not killed in vain. That must not be our truth."

The coughing and the fidgeting began in earnest now. The priests themselves moved about beneath their spacious robes. They whispered to each other, looked desperately to the archbishop on high. Suddenly, the sound of heels, again. A woman in a grey suit, white scarf, walked toward the altar, bowed as she came to the altar proper, walked up the burgundy steps, and stood beside the podium, alongside the speaker. She did not speak, did not move. The mourners stared.

"This has been a lovely funeral, saturated in historical ceremony," Teresa continued. "I hope dearly that it has provided comfort to some of you, particularly to the families of these beloved dead. But, I, for one, remain uncomforted. I have known *no* peace since I learned of the shootings. I will know no peace until I can hear about the vibrant and loving lives of Marin, Chantal, Stella, Renee, Henriette, Noemi, Gabrielle, Veronique, Simone, Andrea, Bernadette, Blanche, Julie, and Deline.

An "Amen!" came from a remote section of the basilica, and it was joined by several more, a few from the back, several from the balconies. The body of mourners, however, remained alert and silent.

"With all due respect, fathers," Teresa said, turning now to the priests on the altar for the first time, "time had not been allotted to speak of these women's lives, of their dreams, of their humanity, and of our deepest love for them. That time, fathers, is now."

The clapping began in the balconies, a few hands at first, tentative, but then dozens of hands, hundreds of hands. Even some of the reporters clapped. Some congregants sat stock still, Jenean observed, clearly uncomfortable, but the white-scarved engineers were clapping continuously, and they were not alone. Some two dozen women from the engineering contingent then rose and walked the same path carved out by Teresa. They took up positions on either side of the altar, some nearing Teresa on the podium, some standing across the vast expanse of altar on the other side.

A burly bishop stood then. He walked to the archbishop and whispered. The archbishop nodded, and the bishop walked to the podium and whispered to Teresa. She turned to hear him. When she responded, she spoke into the microphone rather than to him directly, so all could hear. "Bishop Bronceville has asked me to step away from the microphone and to allow his priests to conclude the funeral Mass. I have declined his request. Thank you, Most Reverend Bishop."

The bishop walked briskly around the altar and out of sight. The priests' eyes followed his path until he vanished. They squirmed a bit, but returned their gaze to the woman with the microphone.

"Please hear me out, here, my dearest families and mourners. Let us honour these women. In *this* most holy place, whose reign is held by our most Blessed Mother. Come forward, one and all, in your own time, and honour the dead, speak your truth, renounce the hatred of women that brings us here. I offer you – your voices."

The engineering women's applause was extended. The balconies were with them. Jenean clapped, and she continued to clap after others' raised eyebrows warned her to stop. "Sacrilegious," a reporter in the pew behind her hissed.

"Oh, Monsieur, I beg to differ. It is time, beautiful, righteous time," Jenean said.

Police boots have a decidedly clunkier sound than heels, so when the police entered the vestibule and made their way down the centre aisle, taking up posts at every ten pews and forming a phalanx, all speaking from the podium ceased. The Montreal officers did not move toward the altar. They simply stood at attention, arms crossed in front of their chests. The priests, Jenean observed, glanced at the officers with longing.

She could imagine their thinking – get these wretched women off the altar, haul their sorry asses into a jail cell and spare us all their incessant diatribes.

But the brotherhoods were not connecting today. The priests remained hostage on the altar; the police stood still. The women kept coming, one by one, sometimes two by two, to the altar, forming a queue. When Chantal's grandmother rose to approach the altar with her cane, one of the white-scarved women met her at the bottom of the stairs and held out her arm. The elderly woman took the arm, walked the stairs slowly, and ascended the podium after kissing Teresa on the cheek.

"Good morning, everyone. I am Chantal's *mémère*. In the moment she was born, Chantal was a beautiful girl. The day before she died, Chantal came to visit me. I gave her an early Christmas present – a lovely blazer with so many colours and shapes. I made it just for her. I knew she had an important presentation and that she was nervous. Her mother told me she had been working on it every night, had practiced in front of the bathroom mirror. I wanted to lighten her load. 'Mémère,' she said, 'I will wear this for my presentation. It makes my eyes sparkle, don't you think, Mem? Just like yours.'"

Chantal's grandmother took a white handkerchief from her pocket and wiped her eyes. She stood quiet for a time. Then, she spoke slowly and softly. "I loved her so, my precious Chantal, as I know you loved your daughters and grand-daughters. Pray that whatever world can allow such horror will pass away swiftly, and that a world made of civility and love appears. We can abide no more of this...." Chantal's *mémère* stopped here. The engineer helped her again, returning her to her seat. The basilica was perfectly silent but for weeping, deep and utter.

*If no female God lives here,* thought Jenean, a lump pushing at her throat, raising her eyes once again to the dead and deified males, *female humans are vying for the position.*

A small man came to the podium and looked out at the people. He looked to be about thirty, Jenean thought. "I am Remy," he said. I am from Belarus, studying engineering at CanTech." He tucked his chin into his chest and remained still for a moment. "I found my wife's body in the cafeteria hours after the shooting. A bullet finished everything that had value in my life." The poor man stood there weeping, everyone weeping with him.

"We came to the cafeteria every Wednesday evening to spend a little time before I studied all night long. We loved Canada. It promised us a new beginning. We hoped to have a child here...."

Jenean could not imagine how this young widower could go on, but he seemed to need to tell his story.

"There was free wine in the cafeteria that night because it was the end of term. There were shiny decorations. My wife Veronique was so hungry. She paid for her food while I was waiting for mine in the line. Then suddenly people running, closing the door to the room I was in. I lay on the floor inside the kitchen with the others. I could not understand what was happening. We heard gunshots then. After a time, the police arrived and made us leave building. I did not know there had been a big shooting until I reached one of the offices and saw police everywhere."

Again, Remy sobbed, leaning heavily into the podium. "I was in a horrible state for a couple of hours. The police would not let me in. In the middle of the night, I finally got inside. I found Veronique in the cafeteria. She was still a little bit warm

"I felt safe in Canada. Veronique felt safe in Canada. But there she is in that white casket there." He pointed to the queue of caskets, then dropped his hand to his side, nodded to the congregation and took his seat once again.

Suddenly, Jenean jolted. The organ had been droning, the families had processed out of the building. She shook off her nesting malaise and nausea, and wondered at what she had just heard, wondered if she had heard anything at all, or if she had fantasized a funeral in which fourteen young women had lives that mattered, had stories that could be told, rather than the insistent, strangulation of a cardinal's admonishing silence.

# 42.

FROM THE FAR END of the corridor, Deirdre could feel the charged energy of the classroom. She came early to class because she needed to be with the others, to hear what her classmates and Professor Oliver had to say about the Montreal shootings, though this was their first class since December 6. She had been in contact with the FRRF members almost every day since the shootings, everyone gathering at Roberta's in the evenings. Today, she had made enough copies of the moving columns from the *Montreal Messenger* for everyone in the class, but she had them tucked away in her backpack. She would bring them out if the right moment presented itself.

Inside, Roberta and Ellen, Ben and Whit, sat huddled near the windows. Ben was bent over in his seat, his hands holding the sides of his head, fingers threaded through his dark hair. Whit was sitting up straight, hands and forearms on his desk, perfectly parallel. Roberta and Ellen were volleying for speaking rights, talking over each other.

"No one stopped the guy," shouted Roberta, as Deirdre entered. "Tell me why that is? Not one guy had the balls to try…"

"I don't know, Roberta," Ben barked, looking up and leaning forward in his chair toward her. "I wish to God I knew why no one stopped him." Whit leaned back in his seat and sighed. Roberta turned to him. "What, Whit? What do you have to say about this?"

Whit looked off to the door, saw Deirdre come in and take her seat. He turned to her and gestured her over. She took off her coat, hung it on the back of her chair, and came to join the group.

"We're talking about what happened in Montreal on Wednesday night," Whit said, to bring Deirdre up to speed. "Why none of the guys tried to intervene to save the women."

"Mmm," said Deirdre. "I have asked myself that a million times."

Ellen said, "They let fourteen women die. They had nearly half an hour to step in, to tackle the guy, and no one, no one did anything. How many people were in that building?"

"Twenty-five hundred," said Roberta, looking at Deirdre.

Deirdre said nothing. She had given the scenario so much thought in the week since the killings, but now that she was in the middle of a heated conversation about it, she could not come up with one intelligent thing to say. It was all so fraught. She folded her hands together on her desk and stared back at Ellen and Roberta.

"Maybe in situations like that, people are just frozen in fear. They aren't in their right minds. Not all men are trained to act like some hero at every moment. They froze, those guys..." Ben stammered.

"Maybe," said Roberta, her tone less hostile than it was a moment ago. "I read that some administrators hid behind their office desks. Totally terrified, I suppose."

"How can it not occur to you to help? Seriously?" asked Ellen.

"How do you *know* what you'd do in a situation so sudden? Can you really know until it happens?" asked Ben, clearly shaken.

"Is it really about courage?" asked Whit. "I have to admit, I would have thought, before this, that I would have jumped the guy, punched his lights out. I would have sworn to it, but I listened to some of the guys from CanTech on TV and the radio, and they were scared shitless. They were confused. They thought they were going to be robbed. I'm not so sure how brave I'd be."

They heard footsteps entering the room and turned to see Sarah walking over to the group. "Stop the insanity. This is not some Hollywood screen set. This is real life. What if some guy with a rifle came in here right now? Even after what happened in that engineering school, would we know better what to do now?"

Letting out an audible sigh, Ben said, "I don't know what the fuck to think. I'm so tired of thinking about it."

"But we have to think about it," said Roberta. "Look, Ben, and even you nit-Whit. I'm not saying you have to represent all men here, to justify why they did nothing to save those women. But that is the question out there. All of Canada is asking it, for Christ's sake."

Ellen said, "The men left without protest. The killer tells them to get out, and they obey. There were, what, sixty or so of them, and they all obeyed like schoolchildren?"

"I don't know what to say to that, Ellen," said Whit. By now, almost all of the other students had come in and were sitting in their seats. Deirdre felt the tension in the room. She wished Professor Oliver would get there and take charge. She understood Roberta's frustration. On the other hand, she felt sorry for Ben and Whit, the only guys in the class, made to speak for men, as if that were fair.

Professor Oliver entered the room without notice. When she cleared her throat, the entire class turned around. She spoke quietly and with a gravitas that surely struck every person in the room. "'Fourteen women are dead for one reason: they are women. Their male classmates are still alive for one reason: they are men.' That's what writer Nicole Beaudette said on CN Radio's *Sunrise* last week."

She walked behind her desk, removed her coat and gloves, and came around to face the class. "This has been a hellish week. We have much to discuss. I am heartbroken. 'And zero

at the bone,' as Emily Dickinson wrote. I am sure you are too."
Deirdre thought she saw the professor's eyes grow watery. Her
own tears were threatening to wash down her cheeks.

"But we have work to do. The media is giving no voice to
a feminist perspective. Ironic, given that the killer was quite
clear in his motivation: he hated feminists." Professor Oliver
stopped here to compose herself. In a choked voice, she continued. "We cannot ... cannot let anti-feminism define ... this
event. We need to help shape the meaning of December 6."

That was when Ellen started to cry, all of her fury melting.
She wept openly, as Deirdre had seen her do at Roberta's when
they all sat around the TV that first night. The room became
silent, and for a long time it remained silent.

"It felt like he was aiming at us," Ellen said in a voice flush
with pain. "The killer."

"Why do you say that?" asked the professor.

Ellen wiped her face with her sleeve and sat up straight. "He
got the wrong women. We are the feminists he was after. We
called the boys out on their sexist posters. We sent the letters
to their mothers. We burned their nurse effigies. It feels like this
is our fault. He killed those women who did nothing wrong.
We scared the shit out of the rich boys here, and this happens.
How can this not be our fault?"

Deirdre found herself baffled. The whole thing was so horrifying, but how could these women think they were responsible?
Does spray-painting STOP RAPE in Kingston at 5:00 a.m. on
sidewalks really *cause* the mass murder of women in Montreal?
Is there a connection?

The professor stood at the front of the room facing them for
a full minute. Her palms were flat against her desk. She looked
tired and sadder than Deirdre had ever seen a human being.
The students slumped in their seats and wiped their faces. No
one moved, but Deirdre felt the collective grief she knew she
would be able to fully share only with this class. If there were
ever a place in which any of the Montreal horror could make

sense, this classroom and these people were it.

"Our hearts are broken," the professor said, allowing herself to cry as she spoke. "And we are hearing that the students at CanTech were killed because of feminism. And we feel guilty. We feel responsible. As if our actions, our standing up to the sexism on this campus, caused this killing on another. As if we pushed too hard against injustice and brought upon ourselves – and innocent others – this deadly backlash."

She stopped here and looked at everyone, making eye contact with each student. Her face softened, and her mouth turned upward ever so slightly, as if it might someday smile again.

"We are afraid. Rightfully so. Maybe we feel shame, as if those bullets were meant for us, meant for those of you who call yourselves Fucking Radical Rogue Feminists."

She brought her desk chair around from behind the desk then. She placed it in the front of the room, very close to the students seated there. She lowered her voice, and her tears came again.

"I am here to tell you – this one thing I know for sure. Feminism never killed anyone. Feminism never killed anyone." The professor spoke slowly, taking care with every word, making sure every student took her message in. "Those are the words of historian Micheline Dumont, and I want you to write them down, memorize them, breathe them in."

"Though your emotions are all over the place right now, you are not to blame. We are not to blame. It is our obligation as human beings in a civil world to speak up about social injustice. Backlash is inevitable. But this ... this brutality ... it is repugnant. And we are right to feel everything we feel. Still – and I cannot say it enough – we are not to blame. We must let that go, when we are able to. It fuels a dangerous thinking. If feminism – the belief that women are inherently equal to men – is to blame, the killer and those like him are justified in their bloody actions to keep one group of people subservient to another. That is not the kind of world we want to live in."

Deirdre noticed that Ellen's crying had stopped. Everyone was listening to Professor Oliver.

"Maybe if we do some work, we can think more clearly about this. It will be hard, and you won't feel like taking notes, but let's try."

Though they all moved sluggishly, everyone dug out a notebook and pen.

"Let me give you some facts and some ideas I jotted down while reading and listening to the late-night call-in shows on the radio," said the professor, holding several sheets of paper in her hand.

"Write them down, and we'll analyze them afterward. What happened on December 6 has rocked our world, and we will need to talk about this historical moment for the rest of the semester. We're in the midst of a life-changing horror. It is our work as scholars to grapple with it, just as it is our work as people to mourn it. So, for now, just take down what I tell you in your notes. Okay, so here goes:

"'We are the only species where the male kills the female,' says historian Florence Montreynaud.

"The feminist movement is the only movement that never took arms to kill.

"Journalist Jenean Belisle maintains, 'The gunman could have killed women in a nursing school. He could have killed far more women there. But he chose an engineering school. Why?'

"Has feminism gone too far? The open-line phone callers say 'Yes' – that the killer is justified because feminists went too far, disenfranchised men, took their jobs, etc.

"Some people, like CN Radio *Sunrise* host Herman Francoeur, say that this is a time for mourning rather than opinion. Is feminist analysis opinion?

"And finally, Catherine Zahn says, 'Surely this is a crime against humanity, not women.'"

Deirdre started at this last one. She had heard this comment when Zahn first said it last week, and it had gnawed at her since then. Zahn was a respected journalist, a television personality. How could she be so clueless? She might not have wondered at it so much before this class, but now that the semester was nearing its end, she could not help but see it as some kind of denial of reality. What motivated someone to deny what was in front of her? The guy had killed women, had said he intended to kill women, said he wanted to kill even more women. What about this entire drama was *not* about women?

Even as the professor was speaking, Deirdre was keenly aware of how dramatically the world had shifted. She felt different at the end of this semester, not the person she was when she came to Aquitaine and even more changed from her old self than she could have imagined. What happened at CanTech had burrowed into her heart. She did not know any of those students, but she could not help but think of them every day since December 6. How easily it could have been her. What was the difference really? She was studying engineering. She was supposed to be at CanTech that night. There were an awful lot of guys on her own campus who made it clear she was unwelcome. There were guys who took the entire massacre as a joke, like Raymond in her calculus class. *It could happen here,* Deirdre thought. It would not surprise her if it did happen here. It would not even surprise her if it happened in the very town she grew up in. It could happen anywhere. The men she heard on the call-in shows – she had heard these sorts of comments from some of her neighbours, from the man who worked at the gas station, from the boys' gym teacher. She had always sloughed them off as callow jerks. But for some, the full humanity of others cost too much. They had to kill in order that the freedom of others did not take away from their own.

She thought of Mr. Marche then, of how he was so passionate about social justice and issues like apartheid, free speech, religious freedom. Until now, she had never compared FRRF with Mr. Marche. All they wanted, those women who called themselves FRRF , a nasty label given them by a drunken student, was respect for human dignity. They wanted to be heard when they said "No." They wanted civility. FRRF wanted what everyone wanted: to live life fully.

Deirdre shook herself. It was all coming together too clearly. She did not want to look at it, not for one more minute. Just as she was ready to get up and go to the restroom to splash herself with cold water, she heard the professor's voice. "Our job is to shine the light of feminist analysis on this and not to look away." Deirdre blanched. Denial was not an option in this class, no matter how ugly the truth.

# 43.

A S SHE WAITED AT THE RESTAURANT on Rue Peel for Bart, Jenean was thinking about the news reporter who had said she was at her most iconic when she recently appeared as a guest on a panel on *Sunrise*. "She is taking what some would consider a bold stand, refusing to let fear keep her cloistered," the host said. Cloistered. Jenean let the phrase swirl around her brain, mingling with the crisp sauvignon blanc she had ordered. She had not thought of staying private, of hiding. Maybe that was a mistake. Even the police were worried about copycats.

Jenean would not live her life that way. She was alarmed. That was a fact. Hell, all Canadian women were frightened out of their wits now. But that was what terrorists like the CanTech killer wanted – to force women to change their behaviour, to leave the public playgrounds of education and jobs and money to the boys, in effect, to remain in the kitchen, pregnant and barefoot.

She was not playing that game.

Jenean thought of it this way: she was simply telling the truth when she appeared on radio or television. The murders at CanTech were "an odious backlash against feminist activism." She speculated, out loud, "I don't see it ending here."

The host pushed back at her feminist analysis by saying, "Yes, but is this the time for such analysis? Might it be time for somber reflection and silence?"

Jenean ignored him and stayed on task. "If not now, when? Someone has to make plain the disregarded reality that feminists have garnered a measure of success in recent history and that this very success wears like water torture on the skulls of the most ardent patriarchs." This was a systemic problem, not a story about one twenty-something madman who couldn't get a date.

She was insistent, as she began appearing on air and television regularly after the massacre, that the future must incorporate a strategic plan for healing relations between the sexes. Men are defensive now, after the killings. They are trenchant in their fear and anger. They need time. Women need time to trust again. Sometimes she felt like she was channelling other feminists who were offering the same messages.

Suddenly, there was a bluster of cold air and snowflakes, and Bart plopped down in the seat across from her. "Sorry, honey, couldn't get away any sooner."

Jenean managed a smile.

"I just got here myself."

"Quiet tonight, eh?"

"Yes. The whole town is quiet. In mourning. Even Etienne's," Jenean said, examining the near empty restaurant through the clarity of her oversized glass.

Bart ordered a Sleeman's and slipped out of his coat. He reached for her hands, held them both in his. "How are you? Are you doing all right?"

"No."

"I'm sorry. You know I am sorry about the girls ... the Can-Tech ... this whole thing is such a freak..."

"Bart," she said, louder than she had planned. "What are you going to order for dinner?"

Bart looked at her, held her gaze for a time. He let her hands go and looked at the menu just as the waitress arrived table side.

"I'll have the shrimp and scallops," Jenean said.

"I'll have the tartare," Bart said, looking at Jenean. "Okay with you, Jenean?"

Jenean stayed the course. Bart knew that the idea of eating raw meat made Jenean nauseated, but she had no fight in her for this. She looked him in the eye and nodded.

When Jenean's meal was delivered, and when another glass of wine had been poured, the waitress set a plate of bibb lettuce topped with a plump burger of raw meat on a nearby table. Atop the meat was perched a half shell of raw egg. The owner of Etienne's appeared to render his creation. Tartare was the restaurant's signature meal. People came from all of the provinces and even from the States to try this tartare and to witness the extravagant display of making it tableside. Dressed in a grey pinstriped suit, the owner greeted Bart and Jenean with a *"Bon soir,"* then poured the egg into a bowl. Tabasco, olive oil, mustard, Worcestershire sauce, tiny diced onions and dried parsley were added to the bowl. He then took the salt shaker, holding it near level to his ear and spewing salt into the bowl, letting it glide off the open palm he had turned upside down and over the bowl. *Like a waterfall*, Jenean thought. He then took a fork and gently mixed the ingredients. He lifted the soppy raw meat with the fork and placed it in the bowl. He chopped the meat with the fork, crumbling it into the wet mixture, saturating the beef with the sauce, until the bowl held a porridge of creamy meat. This he pressed onto the bibb lettuce, rendering a round, near flat patty. He topped it off with the remainder of dried parsley and placed the meal in front of Bart.

"Our applause," said Bart to the owner, clapping loudly and looking at Jenean. She was not clapping. The owner nodded and walked away. A waitress appeared to deliver Jenean's meal and to clear away the owner's ceremonial utensils and bottles. Bart took a long gulp of his Sleeman's, rolled up his shirt sleeves, and rubbed his palms together dramatically. *Henry VIII readying his overblown self for yet another orgy of food*, Jenean thought, looking away, staring out the window at the falling snow.

"This is extraordinary, Jenean. Here, try some.... Mmm...."
Bart held a forkful of the tartare in front of her mouth. She
shook her head with minimal movement but clearly indicated
"No."

"Oh, honey, you don't know what you are missing. This is the
way to eat meat. Everyone should have tartare once in his life."

"Bart," she said, "Stop."

"What? What did I do?" he asked, thrusting a forkful of
meat into his mouth.

"Just stop with the meat," she said, gazing again outside
onto Rue Peel, watching the snow fall beneath the streetlamps.

They were quiet for a while, Bart fully involved with his meal,
Jenean gazing at him, taking in his hair, his face, his still-crisp
shirt and tie, his half-consumed raw meat. She sighed and took
a sip of her wine and watched the snow pitter onto Rue Peel.

# 44.

WHEN SHE HAD LIVED at home, Deirdre rarely glanced at the three newspapers her father read religiously after dinner, the *World and Post*, the *Kingston Eagle*, and the *Montreal Messenger*. But since December 6, she read every newspaper she could, even those from the U.S. that Rosalie got in the mail every day, and brought down the hall to Deirdre when she was done. Deirdre held fast to her early morning routine of walking to Morrison's and reading at the coffee shop. Deirdre and Rosalie talked incessantly about the murders. Their friends were sick of it, tired of the gloom and doom talk, but Deirdre and Rosalie could not get enough. They were both obsessed, afraid not to be vigilant, even after a week. They worried it could happen again here at Aquitaine.

Today, Deirdre learned that eighteen hundred students at CanTech had returned to school to take end-of-semester exams one week after the murders. The exams had been delayed because of the massacre. Most of the students wrote their papers despite the university allowing them to write an "X" on an exam paper if they were still under too much stress because of the killings. The newspaper said that news photographers were not allowed into the exam rooms.

Deirdre had to shout down the hall for Rosalie when she read this. "Rosy, come here.".

"Busy, Deirdre. What is it?" Rosalie shouted back. Their

rooms were across the hall from each other, though Rosalie's was down two doors.

From the hallway, one of their friends declaimed, "There is more news about CanTech. Extra! Extra! Read all about how the killer liked mashed potatoes with gravy. Big news!" Deirdre heard snickering from the open doors along the hallway and found it insulting and insensitive.

"Very funny," Rosalie retorted, coming down the hall and bounding into Deirdre's room. "What's up? I have a lot to do, so lay it on me." Rosalie stood in the doorway, one hand above her head resting on the door jamb. Her wet hair was wrapped in a turbaned towel, and she wore a pink bathrobe and flip-flops.

"Why would photographers want to be in the exam rooms with CanTech students while they take their exams? How in the world is this news?" Deirdre held up the tiny *Messenger* article as if to demonstrate her confusion.

"For the same reason they want to be everywhere. Look at that photo on the front page the day after the massacre. The body of a woman in the cafeteria. What is more outrageous than that? Seriously."

"That was heinous. But in this very next paragraph they talk about how more than half of the school's support staff showed up for sessions with the psychologists as well as many of the school's researchers, professors and students. They need help, not photos," said Deirdre.

"I thought for sure you called me down here to tell me about that guy at U. Ontario. Did you read that yet?" Rosalie asked, coming over to sit beside Deirdre on her bed. "Here," she said, pointing to a brief article one the second page.

Deirdre read aloud, "The University of Ontario has ordered one of its male employees to take an indefinite leave of absence after he was charged for bringing an unloaded handgun to work. The man also commented on how pleased he was about the massacre last Wednesday of fourteen women at CanTech."

"Disgusting," Deirdre said, thrusting the newspaper away from her.

"Yep. And some administrator goes on to say they are worried about the safety of employees, particularly the women. No shit, Sherlock. This guy had an arsenal when they arrested him. Not just a handgun, but a rifle and another handgun and ammunition," reported Rosalie as if she had memorized the article.

"How old was he? What was his job?"

"Fifty years old. He worked for the custodial staff. The gun permit allows him to carry the weapons only from his home to the shooting range. Idiot," Rosalie concluded.

When its lower edges flapped in a sudden breeze, both Deirdre and Rosalie glanced up at the new poster Deirdre had purchased yesterday in the campus bookstore. It read: "What sane person could live in this world and not be crazy? By Ursula K. LeGuin."

They looked at each other, shrugged, and raised their eyebrows.

"We are in the grip of this thing, D," declared Rosalie.

"We are. I don't know about you, but I can't help it. It's as if I want to know every detail, so I won't be caught off guard. Sorta like nothing bad can come at me if I'm watching all the doors and windows," said Deirdre.

Rosalie sighed and let her shoulders slump. "Yup," was all she said.

Deirdre picked up the paper again. "Tell me, Rosy, that there is nothing else in here that will make me crazy."

Rosalie patted her friend's back but did not speak. Deirdre turned away from the paper and looked into her friend's face. "What? Are you serious? Rosa...."

"Just read it. The students will be all over it in class on Tuesday anyway. Better to be prepared. Just read the next two articles, and call me when you're done. I'll make us some herbal tea after I dry my hair." With that, Rosalie walked out of the room, pulling the towel from her head and running her fingers through her long black hair.

Deirdre bunched her pillows up against her headboard and read on. At U. of Ontario, six male students had lit firecrackers under the women's dormitory windows. They were on probation and will be fined, said a U. of Ontario dean. The women were petrified, believing they heard gunshots. The Dean of Women said it "shows a stupendous insensitivity to the fears justly felt by women students at this university and universities across the country."

*Does it not end?* thought Deirdre. She knew how those women felt. She felt furious and a bit insane when the guys in her class had come in pretending to shoot the females in the class on the day after the massacre, but at least she had known they were not real guns. Just asshole guys. These women at U. of Ontario must have been so freaked out, thinking there was a war being waged against university women. Unbelievable. She would have to ask Lea about this when they next spoke.

Deirdre closed her eyes for several seconds, contemplating the difference between insensitivity and stupidity. Before she closed the paper up, exhausted, she turned to a cartoon on the editorial page. Illustrated there were the backs of a father and a young daughter walking hand in hand down a snowy tree-lined lane. They were looking at each other, as the daughter asked: "What's up, Dad? You seem particularly attentive this week."

Deirdre let the paper drop to the floor, and she stared straight ahead. Tears trickled out. She would talk to Rosalie later, and they would all talk in Professor Oliver's class. For right now, she needed to be quiet before she called her father just to talk.

# 45.

ONLY BECAUSE HANNA, a student who survived the massacre, promised there would be no press did Sybille agree to go to the buffet put on by CanTech. Hanna wanted to bring the families of the victims together in one place, so they could talk, so they could meet the friends their daughters had made at CanTech.

Most everyone was coming, Hanna told Sybille, except for Veronique's family who lived too far away. The last thing Sybille felt like doing was socializing. Her mother could not go. Her siblings were ambivalent about the event. They appreciated the gesture, but they were not sure they could bear to be in the company of so many grieving families again. The state funeral had nearly done everyone in, and then there was the private funeral that followed.

The plain truth was that Sybille was running on empty. She had been taking care of her mother and sisters and Trey and Marin's girlfriends and she felt depleted. At night, she lay in her bed and the tears came. Her best friend was gone. She was giving all day long to ease the agony of her family. Who was there for her? She felt bereft of resources by the end of each day. She could only lie there and let the days' events glide through her mind.

Hilaire felt guilty. Maybe if he had not supported Marin so much, had not helped her with math and encouraged her she would be here today. Alive. Had he pushed her? Sybille soothed him. Of course it was not Hilaire's fault. It was the fault of a sick young man who hated women. And he picked a random group in an engineering school. If he could not have it – entry into CanTech – no female would. Twisted thinking. Marin happened to be there. Freewheeling, spontaneous, adorable Marin had been there. The kind of girl who would catch your attention. She looked best in blue, the kind that could most closely be called periwinkle. She had known this. For her presentation, she had worn the periwinkle jacket with enormous shoulder pads that Sybille had given her for her birthday. Beneath it, she had worn a long-sleeved jersey and a black plaid skirt. As always, Marin had a small crucifix on a gold chain around her neck. Sybille had watched her mother fondle that necklace every night since Marin's death. She held it in her hands all mixed in with her rosary beads. When the police had delivered it, along with Marin's driver's license, the finality of the horror descended. There was no exit. That crucifix marked the moment their family died a million tiny deaths. There in her mother's hands, the necklace represented the last thing to touch Marin, when her family could not touch her. If there were a lifeline to her daughter, this was it. Sybille's heart broke every time she saw it. She held her tears in abeyance until she fell into bed, and there she embraced a grief that stunned her silent.

As she entered CanTech for the banquet, she put her arm around Natalee then turned to embrace Marianne as well. She had convinced her sisters to come with her, and now she had to support them through this. "We can do this," she whispered. "This is what Marin would have wanted. We'll meet her friends and professors." The sisters nodded and wiped away tears. They took the staircase in order to buy time to compose themselves. At the sixth floor, the scent of flowers wafted into the stairway when the sisters opened the door. Immediately in front of them was the spacious study room with its enormous bay windows. There were flowers everywhere, sent by the Montreal Botanical Gardens, she learned later. Photos of Marin and the others were hung on the wall to the right, in the most prominent of positions. Elsewhere about the room, everywhere in fact, hung cards and letters and drawings, Sybille knew that these had been here when she had come for the public wake, but she could not pay attention to them then. Today, there were more, hundreds more.

There were cards from all over the world.

School officials were there. Parents and families. Students. There were no speeches. It was all very informal. The Dean of CanTech made introductions, but they were spared any more platitudes and sorrowful dirges. They had done all of that. There were no sad words left unsaid. This was a soiree, Hanna had promised when she called Sybille at home, for the families to be together for the first time since December 6. It would be emotional, Hanna knew, but maybe, on some level, it might bring peace. Or closure. Sybille was grateful. There was no doubt that this was generosity the likes of which she had not expected. It was just that it came so soon. Her own family was still so fragile. Surely the others were too.

What happened in that room amazed Sybille. She watched the parents of Chantal hug their daughter's girlfriends. Each had a dozen stories to tell them. They had answers for all of the grieving parents' questions. *Where was she sitting in the classroom? Can you show me? Where did she study? What did she eat for lunch most days?* Sybille watched as the students led the couple, holding hands like parents and small children – to give them a tour of their daughters's favourite places. They showed them where she worked on the yearbook staff. Sybille overheard one mother tell the girls that she could still feel her daughter's energy all around her.

The event was a blur. Sybille and her sisters met Marin's classmates and professors. They held tight to George and Stephan, who said they loved Marin best of all. They listened as each told stories about Marin's sense of humour, her brilliance with numbers and formulas, her clumsiness in the lab that never became exactly dangerous. Those stories brought Marin back to them for an hour or two, and their hearts were lightened. They returned home to share with their mother all of the tales, and they laughed for the first time since December 6. It was short-lived, a tiny measure of forgetfulness to break up the expanse of pain that loomed ahead. Sybille was thankful, no matter the agony of remembering. Any ounce of relief from the continuous mourning was welcome.

# 46.

## DEIRDRE ~ JANUARY 1990

S TEPPING OUTSIDE, DEIRDRE FELT a shift. The heaviness she had carried around with her all night adjusted itself to the light of day. As she walked out of the dormitory, into the open air, Deirdre knew she would not meet university students at this early morning hour, some of whom had gone to bed only hours before. She would be alone for a while in the wind and sunshine of a new morning.

Spring semester classes would start tomorrow, and last night had seen students reuniting and celebrating after a month-long winter break. The bracing air stung her cheeks, and she pulled her parka closer around her neck and face, tugged her mittens more snugly onto her hands. As she crossed the street, she took a deep breath of river air. The beach and grassy areas were deserted, and no one sat on the benches along the walkway save for the old woman Deirdre saw there every morning she walked along the beach to Morrison's last semester.

An entire semester had passed, her first in university, and Deirdre was on the eve of her second semester. She had grown up. The girl from Renfrew had been drop-kicked into a real world that brought danger and fear and heightened consciousness. If she could endure a semester like the fall of 1989, she could do anything. Amongst the hardest parts was telling her parents about the rape at Christmas time. She had waited until the day after Christmas, when her sister was out sledding and she was alone with her parents by the fireplace.

She had rehearsed what she would say, how she would say it, with Lea several times. But she had still been afraid they would be angry or blame her. This did not seem likely, but still, she had learned enough in Feminist Philosophical Thought to know people often blamed the victim in rape cases. When she finally blurted it out, the entire story, her parents had sat her between them on the sofa and hugged her. Deirdre had never seen her father cry, and this melted her heart.

"Are you okay, D? Are you sure you're okay? I am so sorry. My girl. I am so sorry," he had kept repeating. Deirdre's mother had patted his shoulder, her arm around both Deirdre and her husband. She, too, wept, but her voice had remained calm.

"You are so brave, Deirdre. You did all the right things," her mother had said, composing strands of Deirdre's hair into slim, neat braids. "Let's get you to Dr. Song for a checkup just to be sure you're all right. But I'm so proud of how you handled this, and all on your own. I wish so much I could have been there. My heart is broken, but you are healing, really healing ... such a wise young woman is my daughter." They sat there, all three, for a long time. Deirdre had been thankful her father did not fly into a rage at Craig, as she had feared. She had had enough of male rage, what with the semester of hateful signs and massacres.

On Christmas Eve, Deirdre had discovered the library copy of *The Satanic Verses* under her bed. Camille had forgotten to return it. That one book, a work of fiction, had spawned such wrath. More male rage. Was it everywhere? Could you ever see it coming, or was it always knee jerk? After the massacre in Montreal, Deirdre had wanted to break it down, to deconstruct it. If she could get at the "science" of it, she could be prepared and protected. By the holiday break, she had spent herself and given up. How could she make judgments about things she did not know? Rushdie's book warns us about "absolutism of the pure," as Mr. Marche had pointed out. Wasn't that what the killer wanted – a purely male world, power concentrated in men's hands? Was this his personal *fatwa*? Deirdre had closed down her racing brain the way Susan had taught her, with three deep breaths to slow her heart rate.

Deirdre now recalled again the scene at the fireplace with her parents. She breathed in contentment and felt she could put the rape, maybe even all of the horror of last semester, behind her with this new year. She had a glimmer of hope. The hyper-analysis of last semester's hell could be put on hold. She had the tools to do so now.

The woman on the bench wore a wool coat of purple plaid, and Deirdre imagined her mother calling it Tartan. Her mother could not help herself when it came to indulging talk about fabrics and textures. It was her way since her days as a fashion design student at Concordia. She was a consummate toucher, nuzzling laces and silks in department stores and even petting gabardine dinner coats at summer weddings and gnarled leather jackets at October beer fests.

Deirdre shook these thoughts of her mother off and drew her attention back to the woman in purple plaid. She had two dogs with her – one was a shaggy white terrier mix and the other an ancient mutt with bad hips and a protruding mass on his front leg. Deirdre could feel the dog's anguish, as he tried to get up to garner the treat the woman was drawing from her coat pocket.

"Good morning," Deirdre dared, though she had never spoken to the woman before. She stopped in front of the bench to see if the she might respond.

"Hiya, dearie," she said, the faintest of accents that could have been Irish.

"How are your friends doing today in this chilly air?" Deidre asked, nodding at the two dogs.

"Oh, my dear, how kind you are to ask. Tory here, my little bumpkin, loves the cold. She was designed for it by the good Lord. And Raskins, he's such a sad old goat, the rheumatism you know – but we need our constitutional, so to the beach we come, wind or snow or rain...." She trailed off, petting Tory and smiling wanly at Deidre.

"Good air is the key to healthy living, my mother always says," said Deidre.

"The woman stopped petting the terrier. She stared out at the water for such a long time that Deirdre wondered if she had heard her. Still, Deirdre waited, rubbing her mittened hands together and breathing out clouds of warmth.

The woman pulled the collar of her coat up around her neck, tucked her plastic bag of dog treats back into her pocket, and looked at Deirdre. For some moments, they contemplated each other. The waves lapped onto the shore, and a distant metal buoy clanged.

"Good air, my dearest girl, is the only hope against the banality of the world," said the woman, who sat up straight now, leaning away from the bench, and reciting her words as if long-ago prepared. "If we are to be human and experience wholeness of soul," she paused and looked out at the waves, then looked at Deirdre for some time and resumed her recitation, "we get outside of our houses, and we breathe."

The woman gathered her collar about her again, reached for another treat for Tory, who had taken the opportunity to sprinkle a nearby maple while her mistress was speaking. The distinct smell of peanut butter made Deirdre think of Mrs. Plumbere. The woman looked up only once again. She smiled at Deirdre and held her gaze, and said, "Even when you do not feel it, my dear, you are whole. We are all whole. *Guid cheerio the nou.*"

Deirdre whispered a quiet, "Thank you, Ma'am." into the frigid air, took a deep breath, and made her way along the path.

# 47.

A CLOUDY MASS WASHED the black sky. The bright, round moon glowed through, illuminating the emaciated stick arms of the tallest trees. It was dead quiet but for the crunching of frozen grass beneath Craig's running shoes. He strode rapidly toward the beach. No one was about. It was a Wednesday, so the crashes and gongs of weekend parties were both past and future. Craig crossed the road, headed straight to the shore. There, he sat and stared at the moon. No trees to mar the night sky from the beach, just pure light against darkness.

He had come here to think, to calm his raging brain. He had wanted to be an engineer since he had taken apart his mother's food processor when he was six, and when his father threatened to whip his hide, he immediately put it back together, then handed it to his mother. He had a way with mechanics. He knew how systems worked, how to understand them, how to fix them.

Now he had been withdrawn from Aquitaine, from his dream, by his mother. His life might well be ruined because some chick could not shut her mouth. It was not as if he were a complete asshole like Jack and Kevin. They were bonafide idiots. He was not. Women wanted equality? Well, damn, so did he. Equal treatment – and now he was enrolled in some two-year sissy-assed place for losers who could not make it at university, all because Deirdre Sevier woke up in the morning, looked in the mirror, and realized she was a skank like every other girl who partied at Commissioner. Why in the hell was that his fault? It was *just* sex. Get over it. For goddamn sure it will happen again sometime in her life, so just deal.

Yanking the wool watch cap off his head, Craig raked his fingers through his hair. He glared at the moon, his heart clanging in his chest. He had tied his sneakers so tightly in his hurry to leave the residence hall that they hurt. He was not supposed to be there, of course. The Aquitaine campus was no longer his home. He had stayed with Kevin for two nights, slipping into the closet when the don came by.

He had to move now, had to walk. Craig jumped to his feet and stomped along the beach. He ran then at a clip, the wind picking up and assaulting his face. It felt good, "bracing," his mother would have said.

His mother. Damn. Stupid, naïve, Lee Ann loved him. Huh, loved that guy she thought was him. What she really loved was the idea that her son was not like his father. So she came up with this master moronic plan to save Craig's soul from becoming black like Daddy's. She pulled him out of school. Moved him out of his house. Moved them both in with his eighty-year-old grandmother. Fucking ruined his life.

His father. Egocentric. Drunk. Craig hated him with a passion. If Jack and Kevin were assholes, his father was the alpha and the omega asshole. Primo. Number One. *Ph.D. of assholes. And his mother loved him. She must. She stayed with him until now. Way to wait, Lee Ann, after twenty-two years.* Christ, she stayed with the jerk when he smacked Craig for snapping the kickstand off his new bike. An accident, and the old man swatted him, like he was in a barroom skirmish. His mom? Where was she? In her room saying a rosary? Making him hot cocoa for when Beating Hour With Daddy was over? *Where the fuck were you, Mom?*

Craig was bolting now, chest heaving, head down. He had run all the way past the Kingston Sexual Assault Centre. When he finally bent in half, unable to catch a breath, he looked up to see that he had run all the way through town, on the sidewalks, past the cafés and the park and the luxury boats, but he recalled nothing save the raw hatred he felt for his parents. For miles, he had been fuelled by crude hate.

As he worked to stabilize his breath and to ward off the nausea that came in waves, Craig felt an urge to cry. For a sliver of a moment, the tears came, his throat swelled, and he heaved. He allowed the image of his mother to linger in his consciousness for a moment, and he knew the most excruciating heartbreak. He loved her. He hated her. She would be judged by her beloved God for her good-for-nothing maternal instincts that failed to protect him from that beast of a man she had married. It was too late now to try to fix her son. She did not believe this, but Craig knew it to be true. He was who he was. Even his douche of a father knew who he was. Only his mother held out hope he could be a good man someday – whatever the hell idea she had of what a "good" man would look like. His mother was too trusting, simple. *Just like Deirdre*, he thought.

The moment passed.

The tears dried. His throat opened. His mother vanished. Deirdre remained. And, yes, she was just like his mother. Did not know what the hell she wanted. Could not protect herself worth a shit. She comes to Commissioner, a place where men are men and who make no bones about it, and she leaves with a vengeance. *Rape, rape, rape.* If he had a nickel for every time he had heard that cursed word. *Is there really such a thing as rape, Deirdre? Really? Date fucking rape. Spare me. Then how the hell did you get into my dorm-room bed? Did I throw you over my shoulder cave-man style and haul you upstairs? I think not. You walked up those stairs all by yourself. You sat on my bed. You leaned onto my chest, and you never, ever said "No."*

Craig groaned then. Furious. The insanity of it all. Girls like Deirdre were a problem. His problem. The university had gone loony. Good God, all of Canada had gone loony. Shooting girls at an engineering school – yeah, he got it. Sick bastard, but geez, on some level, it had to feel good. Even if for one minute. Craig did not know the whole story, but he knew the feeling that went along with a monster need to shut women the fuck up.

Craig strode back to campus, as the horizon flushed pinks and golds. He would get some sleep, prepare for the Commissioner mixer tonight. He would mix. Oh hell, he would mix. Maybe then he would pay Deirdre a call. Invite himself to her residence hall. At midnight. For a chat. Just Deirdre and Craig. *Set things straight. Fix the problem.* The Dean wanted that, ordered that, had he not? Had he not told Craig to fix the problem? Pretty, little Deirdre could be convinced to re-examine her conscience, recant her accusation. Then maybe she would tell the university and the police and whoever else cared, like his mother, that he was not a rapist and should be reinstated with all due honours and respect to the engineering program at Aquitaine University. But he knew none of that would happen. *Shit no.* His parents were getting a divorce. He was no longer a student at Aquitaine. Deirdre Sevier was sitting pretty in her dorm room. *Screw it. Forget Deirdre Sevier.* There were more fish where that one came from. No one, no one was going to take his life away from him.

# 48.

IN NOVEMBER, ALMOST A YEAR later, when the plain brown envelope arrived on her desk at work, Jenean studied it. The work address had been typed on a Remington typewriter. There was a Montreal postmark but no return address. Though she had seen enough quirky mail in her day, the calculated anonymity of this envelope was unsettling. She opened it carefully, took out its contents, then stopped breathing for several seconds. No way was this happening. Inside was a photocopy of the killer's hit list (with her name on it) *and* the suicide letter – the very materials she and the *Mot du Jour* attorneys had been trying to obtain since the massacre, nearly a year ago. The police had held firm: it was dangerous to divulge what this "crazy" man had in his mind. But someone understood. Someone had sent a copy to her, someone who wished to remain anonymous, someone who agreed the letter should be public. Slowly, her breath uneven, she read the murderer's suicide note word for word:

> This is war. I have decided to put an end to feminists who have ruined my life. Over and over again. They suck up every male opportunity. Impotent Canadian politicians roll over when they shriek about their rights – that they deserve more. *They* deserve? No. The time has come to exterminate them. Thousands of millions if I could. I will be called demented. I am not. Look at

the facts. Study history. Women have built their suc-
cesses on the backs of men. I, for one, will not bend
over. Feminists hold the reins with their overweening
entitlement. Someone has to stop it.

Women have not learned from the wisdom of men.
They butcher what men have created. Striking the death
blow to these termagant feminists is sweet – is mine.
*Ardeant in ignibus inferni.*

See supplementary page: radical feminists who
would be roiling in the depths of *ignem et sulphur* were
it within my power to make it so. Almost executed
today.

Jenean read the letter again. Then again. She put it down on
her desk. She picked it up again. Her mind was reeling. She
read it in all its screeching clarity. He was making a political
statement. He knew others would try to twist it, so he clarified
in a letter. He was doing this for political reasons, because he
hated feminists.

The Latin made clear to the reader the killer's in-your-face
erudition, lest someone call him a dumb yokel. "The jackass,"
Jenean said aloud. Jenean worked at the phrase, translating
with whatever leftover skills she had retained from high school.
*"Ardeant in ignibus inferni"* meant "may they burn in the fires
of hell." He had finished the letter knowing his next move
was inevitable – to kill as many women as possible and then
himself. Then he had added the hit list. Jenean looked at her
name there, among the others. He had written her name on
a list. If he had planned better, he might have killed her too.
She shuddered, pushed the letter away from her, covered her
face with her open palms.

But all the shit about women – where had he been getting
these ideas, this hate? Shrews? Termagants? The guy had been
nuts. But the problem was, the guy had *not* been nuts. He was
perfectly, intelligibly clear in the letter. He had intended to kill

women. He had left a letter explaining exactly why. Then he had killed women. Evil, horrible, unforgivable -- but not crazy. *And that,* thought Jenean, *is the most awful thing of all.*

That last page, the list of women who were "almost executed today." Her name, her phone number printed next to it. Someone had wanted to kill her. Not just an angry moment. This guy had put it in writing. And because he had not had enough time, she survived to read this letter and list. Where else in this society did people make lists of women they wanted to kill?

Jenean folded up the letter, put it back into the brown envelope, packed it into her briefcase and went home. At home, she did the only thing that made sense. She locked the door, gave Gertrude a treat, got out the lavender bath salts, and ran the water into the tub as hot as it could get. She needed to think clearly, something she had not done since December 6. She needed to feel human again, to take that plunge into vulnerability, into raw feeling. Risky business given her woman's body and radical feminist mind.

Slipping into the scented water, steamy mist rising around her, Jenean pulled her journal from the table and read what she had written late last night.

*The December 6 assassinations have shattered my world. That is a truth I will live with forever. My illusions – they have imploded. I have to accept that I was part of what fueled a killer's anger, tormenting as this is. He must have been reading my columns. He was sending a message to women who spoke out. Some people seem not to be able to hear, but I hear. I hear that twenty-five-year-old man's message loud and clear: the price for being a woman who steps out of conservative gender roles is death. I think I will never really get over the Montreal Massacre. It has done me in somehow. It was a crime against women. It had never happened before anywhere in the world – not*

*in this way. And to make it worse, my name was on a*
*list, so in a way, I was sort of responsible.*

Jenean closed the journal and returned it to the table. Now that she had seen the letter and hit list, she felt everything she had written last night tenfold. Feminism had taught her to quest after the truth. Then the truth landed on her desk in a plain brown envelope, harsh and recalcitrant. There was no way to un-know this killer's savage truth.

Plunging beneath the water, Jenean resurfaced with a new awareness. Suddenly, the war of the sexes made sense. She had never seen it so clearly before. There was a huge chasm between men and women. Everyone was defensive. Just last December, for the first time ever, the editors would not publish her column in *Mot du Jour*. They had said it was anti-male. She had written down everything the guy in the coffee shop had said that morning before the state funeral, how he was furious with his feminist girlfriend and all feminists. She had embellished nothing. But they had refused to publish it. They had not wanted to know that this massacre had to do with men and women and feminism. It was mindfucking, like the tower of Babel, like being in war.

And the war had come home to roost. Bart had moved out in February after she had asked him to. He had said he was more than happy to. He could not take it anymore, her moods, her inability to move on. Sure, her name had been on that damned list, but *she* was not dead. She had to look on the bright side once in a while. Jenean dipped beneath the water again, washed Bart out of her head.

One of the illusions that had died for her in December 1989 was that the feminist movement brought to Canada the greatest revolution of centuries. Women had worked tirelessly to bring about the National Action Committee for the Equality of Women, bringing together three hundred feminist groups from all over Canada who insisted upon improving opportunities and equality for women. Jenean was proud of this movement and of her province. Quebec had become the modern, progressive province populated by a "miracle people." They had left the bad behind, taken up the good. What had once been a priest-ridden province whose babies were born to girls as young as ten years old, was transformed in the Quiet Revolution. Overnight it happened.

In short order, the country as a whole had adopted universal health care, abolished capital punishment, and Quebec was rendered free of the yoke of France. The Prime Minister had liberalized divorce laws, ended restrictions on homosexuality and access to abortion. He had passed the law requiring bilingual labelling on commercial products and another that emphasized the equality of all "cultural and ethnic groups" in Canada. Canada had been in the midst of a revival and Quebec had led the pack.

Then the assassination of fourteen of its young female engineers weeks before Christmas. And illusions died.

*This was our loss of innocence,* she thought. No one had seen this coming. It changed our view of our province. The founding myth of Quebec, of Quebecoise fighting to resist Anglo invaders, of being victims of history, was invoked. We could not be culpable. This must be someone else's fault.

That one of our own killed many of our own must be denied.

To keep our sanity, to maintain our belief in our province, in our very stability, we must deny this. And so the trenchant refutation began. What one man did left men and women divided, in full-out acrimony. Those who could not look away saw that the CanTech murders were iconic, and the outrage was instant and vicious. Jenean could not stop the loop in her brain, the questions haranguing her. Would she live this massacre out in her head every day of her life?

Perhaps there would be no healing. It was not even the crime itself that weighed so heavily any more on her and on other women across the globe; it was the aftermath, the backlash that continued to flog, reopening unhealed wounds. And it was the fact that violence against women was not over, had not ended with a hateful shootout at an engineering university. Those deaths had not been enough to atone for the crime of being a woman.

That night, Jenean called one of the other women on the hit list to confirm her thinking that the letter should be made public. The two agreed. It was a hateful piece of business, and she wanted to do the right thing. Later that night, Jenean turned the letter over to *Mot du Jour*. In its entirety, the letter was published on the front page the next day.

The battle ensued. In lavendered waters each week, Jenean Belisle endured.

# 49.

MARIN'S MURDER WAS STILL a throbbing pang in the heart of her family when the Coroner's Report arrived by mail at Madame Hazeur's home, one and a half years later. Everyone, including Trey, was gathered for Sunday afternoon dinner, a ritual the family had been observing every week since December 6, 1989. They needed to be together. They spoke a common language, a phonetics that alternately ached and raged and surrendered. Their individual grief, if not identical, was certainly unbearable in similar ways.

They had all felt the constant need to be reassured that Marin's death was quick and painless, that her suffering was minimal. For six full months, every Sunday, they had fixated on what Marin must have felt, what she might have been thinking, as the killer entered the room and shot her friends. Everyone had taken a turn imagining, and the imagining grew into narratives that were increasingly fatted with grace: Marin had not seen the gunman. She was alive, then she was dead. She never knew her friends had been killed, that she, herself, had been shot. Our worries, they had told themselves, after a half year had passed, were for naught. Marin had not suffered.

Sybille had known otherwise. She had known, for one thing, that all of these buffering stories did not erase the pathos that presented itself to everyone there when Marin's birthday fell on a Sunday that first year. They had a cake, ice cream, her favourite mimosas. She would have been thirty. She and Trey would have been married, Trey had repeated over and over. They might have been parents someday. It was one of the worst days since the funeral, Marin's thirtieth birthday. Yet most of them still had their faith in a Catholic God, in society, in civility, in the legal system. Sybille had known otherwise. She had looked unwaveringly into her sister's casket, into Marin's face. She had known, beyond any doubt she begged to arise, that her sister had suffered terror and anguish and excruciating pain. But she had never spoken about this certainty to anyone. What would be the sense? Her mother and brother and sisters and Trey had to go on with life, and if believing Marin died instantly and painlessly allowed them to sleep at night, so be it.

Sybille had known otherwise. What kind of God lets young women be hunted and assassinated at the hands of some loser with a gun? In what world was this fair? Compassionate? Understandable? Sybille had suffered mostly in silence. Her family relied on her. She was the captain of this grief ship. Sybille was the oldest. She and Marin had been the closest siblings, yet she had to get a grip, to keep things balanced.

She had trouble focusing on her work. She was inordinately impatient with the trivia that preoccupied her co-workers. One had sciatica and could no longer work out seven days a week at the gym. Another had a teenage son who smoked marijuana in his room at night. Another's aunt had left her estate to the Church and not the family who cared for her throughout her years-long cancer treatments.

*Who gives a shit?* thought Sybille. *Are you kidding me? These are not real problems.* She had never voiced her exasperation, but it was perturbation of the deepest degree. In the ladies room, she had sobbed out her fury and frustration at God, at her insipid co-workers, at the revolting gunman. She had railed at the media who kept her sister's violent death in front of her family all this time, milking it, exposing it, embellishing it. For what? To what end? On Marin's most recent birthday, Sybille had baked her favourite German Chocolate cake, bought the vanilla bean ice cream Marin so loved, and she even found her sister a birthday card, the funny kind they always bought each other.

When she had not been able to sleep the night before Marin's birthday, while a slip of a moon shone one single spaghetti ray into her window, she had written out the card:

*Dearest Marin,*

*If I could come to you now, I would. Maman needs me. They all need me. Trey is so brave; you would be proud. I am not brave. They think I am. They think I am steady as a rock, their rock. It is not so. I miss you beyond what I ever thought possible. You were – you are – my twin. Please be at peace somewhere, so this will all make sense someday. I think of you every day. It is not every minute like it was in the beginning. Forgive me for this. I am not forgetting. I can never forget you, but I am trying to have a life, whatever that means. I thought that was impossible on the night at CanTech when they told me you were dead. May no other sister ever have to live through such a ghastly moment. But I have lived through that moment and so many more. Your wake. Your funeral. Your beloved husband (let's face it – that is what he was) breaking his heart every day. He cannot get over you. None of us can get over you being gone. Yet, on my best days, and I do have a few, I know you are not gone. You are with us. You are us. I love you so much. I live for the day I will see you again.*

*All my love, your twin, Sybille.*

Sybille had sealed the card and put it away in her drawer, the one where she kept Marin's new sneakers. The one where she kept the cards she had written for Marin's thirtieth birthday, for

Christmas, for Easter. She had kept the memorial card Father Brunton had made up for the Saint-Eustace funeral. She had kept Marin's barrettes and bracelets.

On this particular Sunday, Sybille announced that the Coroner's Report had finally arrived and was on the kitchen counter. No one made a move to the kitchen to retrieve the report. No one spoke about it. Not a word.

They ate quietly, there in her mother's house, as they did every Sunday, enjoying an early afternoon brunch. After, they played cards, but mostly they watched television or sat together in the living room, barely speaking. In the presence of this long-awaited official report, they were silent. They would all read it, eventually, on one of the following Sundays.

Sybille and Natalee were the first to read it and the only two to speak about it out loud, to each other and only to each other. The Coroner's Report came in two parts; Part I gave the autopsy details regarding how each woman died. Both Sybille and Natalee read that part last. Part II gave details about the incident itself and the emergency response. Until Sybille read that report, all fifty-eight pages of it, she thought she knew everything about the massacre that had killed her sister. This was not true. The Coroner's Report was a play-by-play. Every detail accounted for.

Sybille did not know that in that first classroom the killer shot the women he had lined up from the left to the right, firing about thirty times. She had not thought about his methodology. In the corridor outside that room, he shot at students standing at the photocopier. Backtracking, he went to Room 220 and shot into the door lock three times but was unsuccessful at getting in.

In the hallway again, he shot at a female student who was getting off the escalator. He hit her, but she got up and ran. He then fired on a person hiding behind a table in the foyer, but missed.

Roughly one hundred people were present when the killer

reached the cafeteria. He immediately shot dead a woman near the kitchen then two others. The killer made his way from the cafeteria to the second floor then walked up a non-functioning escalator to the third floor. There, he shot three students in the hallway before entering Room 311, Marin's room, at 5:25 p.m. "Five-twenty-five p.m.," Sybille said out loud. Calculated. By 5:25, the killer had been shooting people in the building for fifteen minutes, since 5:10 – the time he entered the classroom where he killed six women. Thirteen minutes before the killer got to Marin's room. By the time the killer got to 311, there were a dozen police vehicles and even more officers on the scene along with the first of several ambulances. All of these people were there several minutes before the killer entered Marin's classroom. Sybille had been inside CanTech many times. She imagined, over and over again, how those officers might have run to Room 311, and saved her sister. The report claimed, however, that the police were securing the perimeter, evacuating the crowd, and assisting injured people who were able to get out of the building. Sybille read this again, and she understood that from the time the police arrived at the scene at 5:22 p.m. until they finally entered the building at 5:36 p.m., after receiving word from inside that the killer had committed suicide, they had been standing outside waiting for the command to enter for fourteen minutes. Fourteen minutes of nothing, no stopping one man with one gun. Why had they not gone in with guns drawn to neutralize the killer? There had been time. There had been time. Three full minutes from the time police had got there to the time the killer had entered Marin's classroom. There had been time to save Marin.

At 5:36 p.m., the police got word from some student or professor inside the school about the killer's suicide. Police then entered the building. Too late. Too, too late.

Once inside room 311, Sybille read, he shot Chantal who was at the front of the room. Two women who ran for the door, were shot and killed. He shot at students crouched under desks, hitting four and killing one. After replacing his magazine, he stood on a desk at the back of the classroom, jumped down, returned to the the front, and shot in all directions. Then he removed his jacket, placed it around the barrel of his gun, and shot himself in the head. That was 5:28 or 5:29 p.m. The killing spree lasted nineteen or twenty minutes.

Ultimately, Sybille read, it was concluded, "that none of the victims who died could have been saved by medical treatment." Their injuries were immediately fatal, and even if emergency medical services had responded more rapidly, they would not have survived. The only question, according to the report, to be answered was this: "Would each and every one of the victims who died have been shot if the police had been able to enter the building sooner to neutralize the attacker?" – exactly Sybille's question, precisely the question of every mother and father and sister.

The report determines that "it was not possible to answer that question in the affirmative" for certain.

In Sybille's mind it was possible to answer the question in the affirmative with utmost certainty. Marin could have been saved if the police had been allowed by whoever had been in command to enter and neutralize the gunman. But they had not. They had been securing the perimeter while inside a man was gunning down her sister. The rage she felt when Marin died and that she felt on and off over the last year and a half returned full force. Who the hell could you trust if not the police to make brave moves, to save lives? What good were they?

Sybille breathed deeply, calmed her brain, talked to herself. It was over. All of it was over. There was no going back. This rage was hurting her, hurting Sybille herself. She had suffered for over a year now with headaches and back pain. She did not want to go back to that dark place. She had to let it go. The police had done their best in an utter chaotic hell of a situation. They had been at the funeral. Many had come all the way to Sainte-Eustache to attend Marin's private funeral. They had told Sybille and her family repeatedly how sorry they were. Bearing a grudge would do no one any good. Marin was not coming back, no matter what had gone down on December 6, 1989.

Sybille made coffee and allowed herself plenty of cream and sugar to get through the autopsy portion of the Coroner's Report. She determined to read the report in its entirety in one sitting. She wanted this onerous task behind her, and she was not sure anyone else in the family would actually read it. It was too hard. It was too painful for her too, but it had to be witnessed. Someone in the family had to know what happened to Marin in her last minutes. Marin could not be alone in that school all over again. Sybille began Part I.

There was the Clinical Summary and General Findings that described Marin as a twenty-nine-year-old Caucasian woman whose health was unremarkable before December 6, 1989. She had no scarring, no congested organs. The Pertinent Gross and Microscopic Findings were difficult to read, explaining in detail the damage done to Marin's internal organs by the bullets. The findings supported a classic, acute trauma associated with the incursion of gunshot wounds. The Conclusion was one dense paragraph long. Just one. One paragraph caused Sybille to drop into the kitchen chair.

The twenty-nine-year-old victim suffered three gunshot wounds: one to the arm, one to the neck, and a third directly to the heart. This last shot was the fatal shot. The cause of death was massive bleeding in the lungs and cardiac muscle. Despite suffering internal trauma that would most certainly have precipitated imminent heart failure, the victim appeared to have run to the door of classroom 311 in order to save her life. The victim's body was discovered lying half way inside the classroom and halfway outside the classroom, with her head lying in the corridor just outside Room 311. The final gunshot wound to the heart led to the victim's immediate death.

Sybille wept as she had never wept. Her entire body shook with grief and with joy. Joy. Her little sister had stood up – after having been shot twice –- she stood up and ran. To get out of there. To get back home to her family. He shot her in the heart when she ran. She stood up to him and his big gun. "No," she said. "My life is too important to hand over to the likes of you. I will get out. I will be free." She ran. She did not give in, did not take orders from some white Montreal punk. That was the Marin Hazeur Sybille knew.

That autopsy report changed everything for Sybille. But she wondered, would it change everything for the others, the grieving mothers and sisters and fathers? The fact was, they – all fourteen – wanted out. They all chose life but had it wrested from them. This small thing – the belief that Marin was, somehow, a superhero in the midst of murderous chaos – comforted her, and for right or for wrong Sybille held onto what she could.

"She refused to die, to wait and see," Sybille told Natalee when they spoke about the report that afternoon.

"Yes," said Natalee. The sisters were laughing and crying at once, holding the report between them.

"I'm so proud of her," said Sybille. "Good God, it is all so horrifying. But damn, our sister was tenacious. She died for her dream, but it was *not* her will to die. She nearly made it out..."

"No, Sybille, she did make it out. She was out that door when he fired that final shot. She was coming home to us, and he killed her. She ran. She ran...." The sisters knew the running was futile; it changed nothing in the real world. Yet, somehow, it mattered – as much as anything connected to this atrocity could matter.

Sybille went to bed that night and knew she would sleep. For the first time since that frigid and loathsome night in 1989, just weeks before Christmas, Sybille could catch a full and deep breath. She could relax her shoulders into her pillow. She spoke to Marin, as she did every night. This time was different. She knew so much more.

"You were so brave, Marin. I am so proud of you. I know you are okay now because you were never a victim. Until your last breath, you fought. The fire in you was fierce. It was alive and daring and brilliant until the very end. You were out that door, Marin. I cannot tell you how much this means to me, that you valued life so fully. I love you. I will see you again, my sister, but for now, I will sleep, and I will try to live. It is a crazy, maddening world, but it is what I have, and I will live it – as you did – until it is taken from me. Sleep well, my Marin, *Auf Wiedersehen*."

# 50.

"**Y**OU ARE SO FREAKIN' BEAUTIFUL," he whispered into her ear. She could barely hear him with the music pounding from gigantic speakers.

"I am?" she asked, placing her palm squarely in the centre of his chest and pulling back to look at him. He was tanned. His dark hair was thick and fell in waves around his face. His eyes – God, they were stunning.

He took her chin in his hands and said, "Like you don't know that, Tina. I'm sure I'm like the millionth guy to tell you this, but geez." He brushed her hair from her cheek, and kissed her gently on the lips, as if afraid he might be too forward. "I am going to get us another drink," he said. "Wait here for me, okay? Please? Don't move."

"Okay," she said, leaning into the corner of the sofa, laughing a bit at his chivalry. Maybe all the nice guys had not been killed off in the Middle Ages.

When he returned with two red plastic cups, he held them in front of him and gestured to the hallway. "Hey, will you come with me for a minute? I want to show you something."

Tina stood and followed him into the hall and up a set of stairs. Inside a dark room at the top of the stairs, he handed her one of the cups and said, "Shall we drink up?"

She waited for him to turn on the light, but he did not. Instead, he made a performance of gulping down his drink one long pull and wiping his mouth with the cuff of his blue-striped button-down shirt before placing the cup on a tall dresser. He put his hand alongside Tina's jaw, an enormous hand. "Your turn, baby," he said, whispering again into her ear, then kissing her forehead.

Tina drank as much as she could, then paused. He was looking at her steadily. He took her hand in the two of his and said, "Go on, Tina, finish that bad boy up, so I can kiss your beautiful face. Will you let me do that?" He kissed her fingertips one at a time.

She drank. She was charmed. He took the empty cup.

"Good girl. Come here," he said, gently pulling her to him. "I need to hug you."

Tina smiled and nodded. He walked her over to the edge of a twin bed, which she made out as her eyes adjusted to the darkness. He sat her down next to him. She felt so tired. He was so handsome. He put his arm around her to hug her. A door slammed somewhere far away. It was so dark. She was so tired. He was on top of her. Holding her down. She tried to speak, to sit up. In her ear, she heard, "Shhh ... you're so beautiful. Trust me."

# Afterword

These are the fourteen women whose lives this book hopes to honour:

Geneviève Bergeron
Hélène Colgan
Nathalie Croteau
Barbara Daigneault
Anne-Marie Edward
Maud Haviernick
Barbara Klucznik-Widajewicz
Maryse Laganière
Maryse Leclair
Anne-Marie Lemay
Sonia Pelletier
Michèle Richard
Annie St-Arneault
Annie Turcotte.

At a coffee break during the 2009 International Colloquium on the Montreal Massacre, exchanging niceties with other attendees at the University of Quebec at Montreal, I told one man that I was in the process of writing a book, wanting to tell the story of the women killed at École Polytechnique on December 6, 1989, and the excruciating aftermath of that tragedy for their loved ones.

"What story do they have?" he quipped. "They were just victims."

Just victims. That phrase stung. His implication: the story that mattered was that of the killer, the one who took action as opposed to those acted upon.

"I see it differently," I said, walking away with a determination to bear witness to those fourteen daughters and wives and friends who died.

In the days and months after the massacre, the media sated itself on a surfeit of details about the killer. No trivial facts extracted from his family, friends, acquaintances, or neighbours were too small. Psychiatrists populated television talk shows to analyze his dysfunctional childhood and doleful young adult life. This seemingly unquenchable thirst for details about men who kill women is banal. It has all been rehashed. Men who kill women are legion. We already know all we need to understand these men – and none of it helps to prevent the next killing.

And so, I read and researched and – most important of all – I asked people to talk to me. The sister of one of the Polytechnique victims walked the streets of Montreal with me, in winter and in summer, during some mornings and sometimes late at night, sharing her story. Women who survived the shooting shared their experiences with me over long telephone calls. Over coffee or lunch, some who found themselves altogether too close to death that December did the same. I listened deeply. I am grateful for their trust and have held their stories in my heart, recognizing their vulnerability in this sharing, cognizant that not all "read" the Montreal Massacre in the same way they do, in the same way I do.

Generously, several of the women who were at the center of the Queen's University No Means No campaign in the months before the Montreal Massacre shared their vivid memories and their copious documentation of the events with me. I saw as linked the two historic events, the Montreal Massacre and the No Means No campaign, along a spectrum of violence against women.

The decision to write this story as fiction was belabored and arduous. In fact, the book's generic form alternated several times – from fiction to nonfiction and back – before author Slavenka Drakulić's philosophy laid claim to my pen. Drakulić, the Croatian author of *S: A Novel About the Balkans*, told NPR that she spent hours interviewing victims of the Serbian rape camps in the Bosnian war of the 1990s, intending to chronicle their experience of atrocity in nonfiction form. Ultimately, Drakulić chose to write a novel, "fiction with the terrible authority of truth," as Michael Ignatieff calls it, in order to get at the emotional truth of what happened in those "Women's Rooms." She wanted to put a human face on the estimated 25,000 to 60,000 Muslim and Croatian women raped during this war.

Drakulić's interview shifted my project with finality into fictional mode. Like my esteemed mentor, I wanted to explore the subjectivity, the interiority, of my characters. I wanted to be able to imagine into the places where poet Marie Howe says "the real story is inarticulate."

The instant I had learned of this massacre, I longed to know who these women were, what their experience was like, what their families felt, how they coped. They were someone's daughters, girlfriends, sisters. They went to school one day to learn to be engineers – a field that still badly needs women – and they never came home. My own daughters were readying for college at the time I learned of this massacre. How might I feel if a man walked into their classrooms and killed them because they were women, spared my young son because he was a boy?

As a scholar of literature and women's studies, I know about misogyny in the same way I know about racism and homophobia. They are the dirty "facts" of life. The more I researched this book, however, the more I was stymied by its depths and breadths.

The task of writing a book about hate and murder and grief is soul pummeling. People made the difference. Befriending the sister of a student killed at Polytechnique honed my understanding and tempered my judgment. We formed a bond that surpassed the boundaries of a novel, and I am blessed to call her a friend. The support of others whose stories have inspired this book has steadied me during the darkest hours. The work and wisdom of the brilliant scholars who presented and attended the 2009 International Colloquium on the Montreal Massacre have given me fortitude. The book you hold in your hands is a work of fiction inspired by two real-life events. The characters are fictional. The world they inhabit is, still, all too real.

As American writer Walter Mosley might say: this is the story that clawed its way out from my core.

# Acknowledgements

I owe no fewer than 1,000 thanks to so many people:

Luciana Ricciutelli, for her sustaining confidence and whip-smart editing.

Margaret Atwood for her poem, "A Red Shirt," that inspired this novel's title. That poem is from *Selected Poems 1966-1984*, by Margaret Atwood, Oxford University Press © 1990. Used with permission by the author.

The Whiting Foundation and Franklin Pierce University for generous research and travel grants.

Those in Montreal who allowed me to listen and learn: Sylvie Haviernick, Francine Pelletier, Nathalie Provost, and Heidi Rathjen. Across languages, Melissa Blais, author of *J'aïs Les Féministes,* and I found a twinned passion for understanding people who hate people like us, and the generous and patient translating of Francis Dupuis-Déri enabled a communication that was enriched by his own commitment to comprehending the incomprehensible. I cherish their comradeship. Those from Queen's University for their generous sharing and copious documentation: Penelope Hutchison, Kelly Jordan, and Christine Overall.

Librarians and archivists, Melissa Stearns, Meredith Martin, Jill Wixom, and Becca Cahill of Franklin Pierce University; Lisa Tuominen of the *Ottawa Citizen*, and the generous folks at Library and Archives Canada in Ottawa and the Bibliothèque et Archives nationales du Quebec.

*Ms. Magazine's* Eleanor Smeal, Michele Kort, Jessica Stites and the *Ms.* Feminist Scholars of 2010 who championed this project from the start.

Engineers from Tyco, Renee Duval and Robin Perkins, who talked to me about the ins and outs of the engineering profession; special thanks to Bruno Lenart of Tyco for arranging those interviews. Dr. Ana Muriel, Associate Professor of Mechanical and Industrial Engineering at the University of Massachusetts, Amherst, who graciously allowed me to sit in on her graduate course in Logistics and her undergraduate course in Production Planning and Control. Dr. Lorna J. Gibson, Professor of Mechanical Engineering at MIT, who opened the door to a world of engineering MOOCs. University of Massachusetts student, Briana Tomboulian, who taught me all about life as a young woman in engineering school.

Early and gut-honest readers who engaged enthusiastically with the messy and fraught process of giving feedback: Caitlin Reck, Allie Reck Catlin, Bridget Tucker, and Danielle LeBlanc. Stellar readers and teachers – and sublime girlfriends – Melanie Gallo, Jo Ferrell, and Joan Hathaway – women I counted on for that delicate balance of love and candor. Special thanks to dear Cathy Nicastro for abiding with me in this process and being ever willing to read just one more draft.

My Franklin Pierce University colleagues who have offered enthusiasm and advice: Provost Kim Mooney, Deans Kerry McKeever, Jed Donelan, and Karen Brown, former Provost

Suzanne Buckley, my English department colleagues Gerald Burns, Sarah Dangelantonio, Joan Dion, and James Maybury, and many, many others, none more so than Mary C. Kelly. Alumni from my Fiction III class who read one nascent chapter and offered much-appreciated advice: Caitlin Carroll, Sara de la Vergne, Erin Deuso, Cameron Parchment, Amanda Paul, Jeff Payne. Students in "Intentional Venom: Making Meaning of School Shootings" seminars who believed that this book might shed some light, do some good, in particular Tim Armstrong and Katelyn Donga for partnering with me in a conference presentation on school shootings. Evan Jay Williams, alum, who offered his musical wisdom regarding Pachelbel's *Canon in D*.

My parents, Mary Lou and Ralph Decker, who always indulged my love of books and believed in quirky me; Glen and Maribeth Decker, the brother and sister who are rock solid; my children, Caitlin, Allie, and Kellan Reck, for bringing me to life in newer and better ways every day.

Women who routinely love and nurture me – and who get me – my bookgroup, the best women in central Massachusetts; Sooz, with whom Friday breakfasts sustain a life-giving friendship; my baby sister, Juliann, without whose cherished daily phone calls and resilient spirit I would be a lesser human.

And, of course, John Hobson Sharp, beloved, kind, and patient, he who has lived this book with me. I owe him many more than a thousand thanks.

I am indebted to so many writers and journalists whose work has inspired and ballasted this novel. Particular and heartfelt thanks to:

Adrienne Burk. *Speaking for a Long Time: Public Space and Social Memory in Vancouver.* 2010.

Dale Bauer and Susan Jaret McKinstry's *Feminism, Bakhtin, and the Dialogic*, whose introduction introduced me to the Montreal Massacre.

Melissa Blais. "Masculinism and the Massacre at the Ecole Polytechnique de Montreal." *Rain and Thunder.* 2009.

Melissa Blais and Francis Dupuis-Déri. "Masculinism and the Antifeminist Countermovement." *Social Movement Studies.* 2012.

Maureen Bradley. *Reframing the Montreal Massacre.* 1995.

Diana Bronson on CBC's *Morningside* radio show who said: "Fourteen women are dead for one reason: they are women. Their male classmates are still alive for one reason: they are men," which inspired a moment in Chapter 27.

Alison Dickie. "The Art of Intimidation: Sexism and Destiny at Queen's." *This Magazine.* 1990.

Peter Eglin and Stephen Hester. *The Montreal Massacre: A Story of Membership Categorization Analysis.* 2003.

Barbara Frum, whose interview on *The Journal* on Dec. 7, 1989, with Susan Hyde, June Callwood, and Michael Kauffman, inspired a pivotal moment in Chapter 31.

Irene F. Goodman, et al. "Final Report of the Women's Experiences in College Engineering (WECE)." National Science Foundation and Alfred P. Sloan Foundation Grants. 2002.

Debbie Wise Harris. "Keeping Women in Our Places: Violence at Canadian Universities." *Canadian Woman Studies/les cahiers de la femme.* 1991.

Sybil E. Hatch. *Changing Our World: True Stories of Women Engineers.* 2006.

Lee Lakeman's article, "Women, Violence and the Montreal Massacre," in *This Magazine,* March 1990, inspired sections of Chapters 27 and 43. I am deeply grateful for her insights.

Susan C. Lyon. *Women in Engineering: Tell Me What You Need to Succeed,* a dissertation. University of Massachusetts, Amherst. 2009.

Don MacPherson's *Montreal Gazette* column of December 9, 1989, "Massacre Reveals the Stark Face of Fear," inspired the fictional column in Chapter 35.

Louise Malette and Marie Chalouh's *The Montreal Massacre,* 1991, an out-of-print book I treasure.

Judith S. McIlwee and J. Gregg Robinson's *Women in Engineering: Gender, Power, and Workplace Culture.* 1992.

Christine Overall. "A Tale of Two Classes" from *A Feminist I: Reflections from Academia.* 1998.

Francine Pelletier, whose column in *La Presse* on December 9, 1989, "They Shoot Horses, Don't They," prompted the fictional column in Chapter 34.

Julianne Pidduck. "Feminist Rhetoric of Violence Against Women and the Production of Everyday Fear." *Problématique.* 1995.

Sandra Pyke. "Sexual Harassment and Sexual Intimacy in Learning Environments." *Canadian Psychology.* 1996.

Judy Rebick's "Reaction and Resistance: The Backlash" in *Ten*

*Thousand Roses: The Making of a Feminist Revolution.* 2005.

Donna Riley and Gina-Louise Sciarra. "'You're all a bunch of fucking feminists:' Addressing the perceived conflict between gender and professional identities using the Montreal Massacre." ASEE/IEEE Frontiers in Education Conference, 2006.

Sharon Rosenberg. "Neither Forgotten nor Fully Remembered: Tracing an Ambivalent Public Memory on the 10th Anniversary of the Montreal Massacre." *Feminist Theory.* 2003.

Sharon Rosenberg. "Beyond the Logic of Emblamization: Remembering and Learning from the Montreal Massacre. *Educational Theory.* 2000.

Jack Todd's *Montreal Gazette* column of December 11, 1989, "Anger Mixes with Sorrow for the Slain," inspired Chapter 37.

Robert Walker's *Montreal Gazette* column of December 9, 1989, "Readers Outraged Over Front-Page Photograph of Murdered Student," informed Chapter 36.

Photo: Rich Berube

Donna Decker is Professor of English and co-founder of the Women in Leadership Program at Franklin Pierce University in Rindge, NH, USA. Formerly a newspaper columnist and reporter, Decker is a *Ms. Magazine* Feminist Scholar who writes and blogs for the magazine, spotlighting the dangers that lurk in failing to startle. The university seminar she created, "Intentional Venom: Making Meaning of School Shootings," grew out of her research on the Polytechnique murders. Born in Pittsfield, Massachusetts, she is the mother of three and now lives in Ashburnham, Massachusetts.